BAL AF/SAGA 11/22. AF.

BAIN

(Condition noted — TP Bal 11/23)

w/d

This book should be returned/renewed by the
latest date shown above. Overdue items incur
charges which prevent self-service renewals.
Please contact the library.

Wandsworth Libraries
24 hour Renewal Hotline
01159 293388
www.wandsworth.gov.uk

Wandsworth

D1491997

THE WOMEN OF FISHER'S WHARF

TRACY BAINES

B

Boldwood

First published in Great Britain in 2022 by Boldwood Books Ltd.

Copyright © Tracy Baines, 2022

Cover Design by Colin Thomas

Cover Photography: Colin Thomas

A CIP catalogue record for this book is

Paperback ISBN 978-1-80426-523-9

Large Print ISBN 978-1-80426-522-2

Hardback ISBN 978-1-80426-521-5

Ebook ISBN 978-1-80426-524-6

Kindle ISBN 978-1-80426-525-3

Audio CD ISBN 978-1-80426-516-1

MP3 CD ISBN 978-1-80426-517-8

Digital audio download ISBN 978-1-80426-520-8

Boldwood Books Ltd
23 Bowerdean Street
London SW6 3TN
www.boldwoodbooks.com

To Gylettie Emma Meadows
A promise made. A promise kept.
And to my mum
For everything

1

GREAT GRIMSBY, MONDAY 29 APRIL, 1912

They didn't have much, but they had each other, and that was enough for Letty Hardy. It had to be, for everything else she loved had been left behind in Lowestoft: her family, their farm, the wide green fields broken by hedgerows, the sprawling trees, the brook that ran by the lane to the village. She longed for them now, her heart already heavy with doubt at what she had done.

It had been a shock when they had finally arrived at Mariners Row. She'd not expected a palace but had expected more than this. The shabby two-up, two-down dwelling was one of eight – four houses on either side of a narrow cobbled yard, their front doors facing each other. At the back they each had an outhouse, a coal hole and a scrappy bit of yard. There was an alley between the second and third houses, the walls blackened by soot from the numerous trains that ran along the railway line a few yards away. A long high wall that divided them from the stables of Dawson's haulage yard closed off the other end. Below it stood the shared pump – the only source of fresh water.

Letty tried not to dwell on it as she plumped the feather pillows and ran her hand over the patchwork coverlet, keeping her gaze from the filthy walls of the room, away from the broken window that Alec had patched with a piece wood taken from a fruit crate that held her small pieces of china. The delicate tea service was a wedding gift from her godmother and she'd placed it on the pine chest at the bottom of the bed, a small thing of beauty in the chilled, damp room.

Had it been only one week that she, four days shy of her twentieth birthday, had walked down the aisle of the village church to stand beside Alec? Her mother had urged her to wait, but Letty hadn't wanted to, longing to be with Alec, in his arms, in his bed.

'So soon after his brother's death?' her mother had questioned when she'd given her the news of Alec's marriage proposal. They'd courted only eight short months and for most of that time Alec was at sea. His absences filled Letty with a sense of urgency – that so much had to be packed into the time he was ashore.

There had been plenty of time to reflect on her mother's gentle warnings as they had travelled by train to Grimsby that fresh April morning. Instead of the excitement and anticipation that had carried her through the preparations for their departure, Letty had felt a leaden fear gather in the pit of her stomach as the distance between Lowestoft and their destination grew, and now here she was, and that heaviness remained.

The bed made, Alec laid on it and patted the place beside him. Letty pointed to his boots and he adjusted his legs so that his feet hovered over the bare floorboards. Only then did she come beside him. He lifted his arm, draping it over her shoulder and pulled her close. Through the open window, they heard coarse shouting, a loud thwack of old hand against young flesh, a child bawling.

'Welcome to your new home, Mrs Hardy.'

She laughed, they both did, and it was like the cork coming out of a bottle.

'Our new home,' she corrected. There was time yet to improve it.

'No regrets?' he asked.

She shook her head in answer, fearing her voice might betray her, glad he couldn't see her face. A swell of sadness rose up inside her and she pushed away thoughts of the lonely hours that lay ahead. She'd had little time to learn what being a fisherman's wife entailed, her time spent on goodbyes and preparing to travel north to the thriving fishing port of Grimsby on the south bank of the River Humber. Alec had fished out of Lowestoft, as had his father, and his father before him, making a fair living but not a good one. Sail had given way to steam and Alec had his eye on the future. He had come to Grimsby for the deep-sea fishing, for trips that would take him way for weeks at a time, in fair winds and foul. How would she live here without him?

He placed his hand under her chin, tilted her face to his, kissed her. His full lips were warm and hard on her mouth and when she closed her eyes, the shabbiness of their surroundings faded.

'Are you done up there?' came a voice from downstairs and he let her go, sitting up to call out to his mother.

'Just finished.' He kissed her again, briefly this time, and got up from the bed, pulled her to her feet. 'Come on, lass. We'll get a crust to eat, then go out and get some air.'

She followed him down the narrow staircase, through the small front room and into the kitchen, where her mother-in-law, Dorcas, was standing by the table, slicing bread. Her work-roughened hands moved quickly, and her grey eyes briefly flashed at Letty, indicating her disapproval. She was a woman bleached of colour, her long grey hair plaited and wound about her head, dressed in the black of protracted mourning. The loss of her husband, Will, nine years ago, and more recently of her seventeen-year-old son, Robbie, had robbed her of so much and the only source of light and colour in her life she gained from Alec. He was fourteen when his father was killed in a freak accident at sea and he'd stepped up to become the man of the family. His father's half-share of the fishing smack, the *Stella Maris*, had been passed to his sons on his death, and the brothers had learned to handle a ship under the guidance of their Uncle Eric, owner of the remaining share. When Robbie had been washed overboard nine months ago, Dorcas had sunk into deep depression and Alec had convinced her that a fresh start would be the healing she needed. Letty had not known her long enough to disagree. Uncle Eric, father of daughters and no sons, was all for selling up and using his share of the sale to buy into a smokehouse. A buyer had been found for the *Stella Maris* and Alec had left the sale in his uncle's capable hands, on the understanding that Alec's share of the profit would be sent on to them in Grimsby. It had all happened so fast and Letty had been swept along by Alec's vision of their bright future.

Today, excusing her mother-in-law's sourness for tiredness, Letty made for the shelf where she'd placed the preserves her mother had given them from her own stores. She took down a jar of honey, removed the cork stopper and passed it to Dorcas, who snatched it from her.

'We'll need more than honey to sweeten this mucky hole.' She banged the jar on the table, making Letty startle.

'Now, Mother,' Alec soothed. 'I wasn't to know, was I?'

Dorcas softened slightly. 'It's not you, lad. I wasn't blaming you.' She stared down at the bread, shook her head. 'To think I left my dear cottage for this. My friends, my...'

Alec picked up the bread she'd scraped with honey and took a bite, chewing hungrily, sucking at the honey that clung to his fingers. 'Now, I wasn't going to leave you behind, was I?' He put his arm about her shoulder. 'Rooms in Grimsby are like gold dust, let alone finding a place of our own. We've been lucky.'

'Lucky, my eye!' Dorcas hacked another slice from the loaf.

Letty took up a pan of water and set it to boil on the range and busied herself gathering the brown teapot and mugs from the shelf, pulled a chair away from the table and sat down to eat.

'You can look for something better once I'm away at sea.' Alec rubbed at his chin, smiled at Letty. She returned it, her comfort brief.

Dorcas put down the knife. 'Oh, we can, can we? And how will we pay for that? There'll be nothing in the tin for a while. And I've yet to find braiding work.'

Alec took another slice of bread. 'We can take a bit from the money we get from the sale of the *Stella Maris* when Uncle Eric sends it on.'

Dorcas's response was venomous. 'That money is not for frittering. It's to be invested. In a ship. Your father's legacy.' She stuck out her chin. 'And Robbie's.'

Alec was suddenly subdued and the look of sadness exchanged between mother and son excluded Letty. Their loss was not hers.

Dorcas put the stopper back on the jar of honey and, wiping her hands on her apron, took a slice for herself and sat down in the chair opposite Letty. 'It would be what your father wanted.'

Alec agreed and they continued their small repast in silence.

When they were done, the two women cleared away the plates. Letty wrapped the bread in a damp cloth and placed it in the crock, Alec slipping from one side to another as they moved about the cramped space. As Letty came close, he took hold of her hand. 'We should go out, get our bearings.'

'Eh, that would be grand,' Dorcas said. 'You can show us the *Black Prince*.'

Alec stood away from the sink while Letty shook the crumbs from the damp cloth into the earthenware sink. He shifted uneasily.

'I was thinking me and Letty. Just so we can spend a little time together before I sail. Is that all right with you, Mother?' He bent forward and kissed her head as he had kissed Letty's only moments ago and she looked away. She mustn't be afraid of the love he had for his mother, or hers for him, for didn't she love her own parents as much? And yet there was something about Dorcas's manner that made her feel an intruder, like she had come between them – and that hadn't been her intention at all.

Letty quietly took her jacket and hat, and as she fastened it, Alec came over and placed his hand on her back, guiding her towards the door. As he made to open it, Letty caught the bitter expression on Dorcas's face and quickly stepped outside.

By the water pump, a gaggle of kids were playing in a tin bath that had become a ship, a broom for a mast and a scrap of old sheet for a sail. Their feet were bare, their shabby clothing too big or too small. A toddler squatted by a dirty puddle and ran her fingers through it. Letty knew she belonged to Sally Penny who lived at number six, in the house opposite the yard to theirs. Her husband was away at sea and she had five children, but that was all she knew of her neighbours, Sally the only one to make herself known. She gripped Alec's arm. 'Perhaps we should ask your mother.'

'She'll be fine,' he reassured her, striding out of the yard. 'She's had the pleasure of me company for twenty-three years.' He took her hand. 'I want you all to meself. It's only right.' He pulled her forward and she pressed her hand to her hat as they stepped out onto King Edward Street and down towards the docks, the Italianate dock tower rising above the town like a beacon.

They hurried across the railway lines and down Fish Dock Road, weaving through the men and women that were going about their work. He pointed out the yard where he'd stood earlier that morning, hoping to get a ship, his elation that he'd secured a position – even if it was less than he was qualified for. 'It's a start, Let, and that's all I need.' She nodded, breathless, as his pace quickened the closer they came to the water.

On the quayside, she marvelled at the trawlers crammed tightly in the dock, watched as men leaped from one to the other. Seagulls soared high above them, screeching and calling. It was a world away from the farm, from the port of Lowestoft that was still mainly filled with wood and sail and mast. Sail ships jostled for position here, but they were far outnumbered by those of steam, bows to the dock wall, their funnels belching fumes of black smoke that drifted on the late-afternoon air.

Alec marched ahead, sidestepping the men that stacked crates and baskets, then stopped abruptly and threw out his hand to introduce the *Black Prince*. The ship was high in the water, a ladder secured against its bow.

'She's a fine ship, isn't she?' Letty smiled, nodded. 'Third hand; for now,' he said proudly. 'I'll get mate soon enough, then I'll sit for my skipper's ticket. My certificate of proficiency,' he explained for her benefit. There were so many things she didn't know – the hierarchy of crew for one – but did it matter that she was of the land and he of the sea? If they loved each other...?

They stood quietly, watching men run nimbly up and down ladders, boxes under their arms, bags across their backs.

Alec stood taller, tilted his chin, his jaw set. 'One day it will be my trawlers going out to sea. A fleet.'

She didn't doubt him. He was so full of life and vigour that at times she felt she could almost touch the energy that emanated from him. Alec was different from the boys she knew in the village, her brother's friends, the lads who worked summers at the farm and, if she was truthful, it felt a little dangerous being with him.

He led her toward the lock gates, where the ships readied themselves to leave, while out in the estuary more waited to enter. He pointed to the left. 'Across the water, that's Hull. And out there,' he pointed to the right, 'is the North Sea and the way to the fish. There are fortunes to be made and I don't see why we shouldn't have our share.' She must have looked doubtful, for, noticing, he said, 'We'll be all right, Let.'

Would they? He was going away, and this time further than he'd ever been, to the frozen waters off the coasts of Russia and Iceland, for three weeks, maybe more. She would be alone with Dorcas and the thought made her shiver. 'Your mother thinks I won't take to this life.'

He looked down at her. 'She's worried for you. It's a different life to what you've known.'

Letty got the feeling that she would never suit Dorcas's notions of what a good wife was. 'It's a different life for us all, isn't it?' she answered.

He put his arm about her, and they watched the lock gates push back and the boats prepare to leave.

Plumes of black smoke drifted about them and it caught at her throat and made her eyes smart. She took out her handkerchief to dab at her eyes and he mistook them for tears.

'Hey, don't cry. I know Mother can be sharp but she's grieving. She's angry at the world, not you; angry at the sea that took her men.'

Letty wanted to weep then, for the dread of losing Alec stirred again in her stomach. The great *Titanic* had been lost in the days before their wedding, turning the conversation from joy to one of shock. Fear had taken hold then; for if a great unsinkable liner, pride of the White Star Line, could be swallowed by the deep, what chance did a small crew have in a trawler?

Alec's voice was gentle. 'It's hard for her. We've got each other.'

She gave him a reassuring smile, wanting to force her dark thoughts away, and he took her hand; they turned their backs to the sea and headed back the way they had come.

On Pollitt Street, Alec stopped to admire the terrace of three-storey houses.

'Railway built them years ago to attract captains and trawler owners.' He gazed at the top windows, twisted to check the view they would have of the docks, grinned at her, his blue eyes twinkling. 'By, they attract me, what do you say?'

Letty stared at them, imagining the rooms, the space inside.

'Fine they are, but not for me.' She didn't mind where they were for now; as Alec had said, it was a starting place. She tucked herself close, held on to his arm. 'One day I want a house with a bit of land so I can have my hens and pigs and we can have our own little piece of Lowestoft again.'

'But look how much room there is, Let. We could fit ten of what we've got now in that one. You couldn't get closer to the docks. I'd make sure you had help. A maid or two.'

She laughed and he became serious.

He looked again at the houses, the large solid front door. 'I'd be home, off the ship with a hop and a skip.'

She nodded, trying to ignore the unease that stirred within her. Was what they wanted so far apart? They'd moved here for a better future, but they'd not discussed the finer details, only that they wanted to be together – and she wanted more than anything to bear his child, to have part of him always. Always.

Suddenly she knew that that was what Dorcas saw when she looked at him, her son. A part of all she had lost. Letty smiled then, loving him, and he lifted her off her feet and swung her round and she held on to her hat for fear it would blow away.

'You'll have your land, our Letty, just as I'll have my ship, for I'll perhaps spend more time on that than at home.'

She tensed at this last remark and he put her down gently. She took hold of his hand, gripping it more tightly than she'd done before.

He faced her, people passing them by, looked into her eyes and she saw her love reflected in his. He touched her face, and she tilted her cheek to his hand. 'You shall have your heart's desire, my darling.'

She placed her hand upon his, took it from her face and kissed his palm, his skin rough and scarred from years at sea. 'I already have it.'

It was the truth, but would it be enough?

2

Letty and Alec stopped to buy fish and chips to take home and found Dorcas in the kitchen, her sleeves rolled up to her elbows. She brushed a strand of hair from her face with the back of her hand, so that they saw the scrubbing brush she held. A patch had been scrubbed clean on one wall, large enough to look like Dorcas had used much effort, Letty thought wryly.

Alec put the parcel of food on the table, took off his cap and stuck it on the chair post. 'What ya doing, Mother? I thought you and Letty was going to do that when I'm gone.'

'I couldn't sit idle.' She sighed with irritation. 'I won't be able to sleep in this filthy pit.'

Letty slipped off her coat and hat and hung them up on the pegs behind the kitchen door. She did the same with Alec's when he handed it over and turned back to her mother-in-law.

'We'll soon get it shipshape,' she said, brightly.

'What would you know about shipshape?' Dorcas sneered.

Letty felt herself shrink.

Alec stepped in to soften his mother's raw edges. 'Now, Mam. Let's eat, shall we?' He pulled out a chair and made her sit down, did the same for

Letty, giving her shoulder a gentle squeeze to reassure her. It was Dorcas's grief, wasn't it? It wasn't her fault.

Dorcas took her place, her jaw set as she unwrapped the parcel.

Alec pushed fish Letty's way, but she'd lost her appetite.

* * *

After they'd eaten, Letty cleared the paper and wiped down the table, while Dorcas picked up her knitting and went to sit in the small front room with Alec. Letty joined them shortly after. That day, they'd managed to scrub the floors upstairs and down so the rugs could be laid, but the walls were bare of pictures, and what they had were stacked on the sideboard. On the mantel above the empty grate were framed photographs of Alec's father, Will, his brother, Robbie, another of the whole family staring sombrely into the camera and one of Will and Dorcas's wedding. Tucked behind them was one of Alec and Letty's own wedding. Had Alec noticed? If he did, he didn't say. There was no room for Letty's family photos which had been left, by Dorcas, in a small pile on the stairs.

There were two fireside chairs, so Alec fetched a bentwood from the kitchen, set it beside him and drew Letty in. He talked of his ship.

'I'd liked to have seen it,' Dorcas said, peering over her knitting at Letty.

'There'll be time tomorrow.'

Dorcas dropped her knitting onto her lap, stilled her needles. 'I'll not see you off on sailing day, lad. What's come over you.' She looked pointedly at Letty, who felt her cheeks burn and she looked up to the photos on the mantel, anything to avoid Dorcas's accusing stare.

Alec shrugged. 'It's just a steam trawler when all's said and done.'

'Aye.' She resumed her knitting, the needles clicking faster than the clock. 'It's hardly the *Stella Maris*.' Her voice took on a wistful tone and she gazed into the middle distance. 'Now, she was a beautiful boat.'

'She was, Mother. The best sailing smack in the harbour.' They exchanged smiles. His voice was gentle, but when he spoke again, there was a firmness to his tone. 'But she belongs to yesterday, and we've got to be looking forward.'

Dorcas turned her attention to the photographs and stared at them for a long time. Letty thought she saw a tear drop onto her mother-in-law's cheek and her heart tensed with compassion. To have lost her husband and her son so tragically didn't bear thinking about – and Letty didn't want to think about it, for her biggest fear was that she would lose Alec to the sea. She shivered.

Alec reached out and clasped Letty's hand. It comforted. Dorcas went on with her knitting and the steady click of her needles caused Letty to close her eyes once or twice. She got to her feet.

'I'll fill the jugs and be to bed.'

Alec stretched his arms above his head. 'Aye, it's been a long day. I'll be up soon enough. I'll sit awhile, just me and Mother.'

Letty nodded. Dorcas's silence spoke volumes.

She fetched the plain porcelain water jugs from upstairs, went out into the courtyard to fill them at the pump and took them with her as she went to bed, leaving one in Dorcas's room, taking the other to their own at the front of the house. Releasing her long brown hair from its pins, she brushed it through, got into her nightdress and into their bed, taking Alec's pillow and placing it on top of her own.

As she settled, voices of mother and son rose up through the floorboards and Dorcas's voice became sharper. 'The lass has no idea. She can't braid – and she needs to earn her keep. It'll slow me down to teach her and set her filling needles.'

It set Letty's teeth on edge. She had no intention of spending her days braiding fishing nets and had told Alec as much, hoping he would tell his mother. It was clear that he hadn't. Was that down to timing – or fear? Truth be told, Letty was a little afraid of her too, but when all was said and done, she was a farmer's daughter and a market trader. If she could sell cabbages and cauliflowers, she could sell anything – and what's more, she intended to. Alec wasn't the only one with ambition.

She listened as Dorcas prattled on. 'She's going to pine for you. Moon about the place.'

Alec was dismissive. 'Letty's not like that, Mother. She's a strong lass.'

The click of the needles again, then Dorcas, louder this time – was it on purpose? 'Strong in the arm mebee, but it's the heart that matters.'

'She loves me. That's all I need to know.'

Letty's heart swelled with love for him.

Dorcas cut back. 'Now, she does. But can she wait? Will she be steadfast when you're away? When she's afraid? Who will she turn to? Not me. I can tell you that!'

Alec lowered his voice and Letty leaned towards the open door. 'She's not flighty, Mother.'

'It's not about being flighty, it's about being lonely. There'll be plenty of other men about.'

He laughed, his voice louder, confident. 'Now why would she look anywhere else when she's got a catch like me.'

Dorcas tutted. 'Don't you be so cocksure, my lad.'

'Well, she left her family behind. That's how much she loves me. I don't doubt it, and I never will.'

Letty felt close to tears at his defence of her. He knew what it had taken her to leave with him, how much it hurt her.

She was aware that Alec had stood up and was walking about the room. 'She's got her own mind and that's what I love about her.' He sighed, loudly. 'We're married. That's an end to it.'

His mother huffed. ''Twould be better you'd married Becky Drew. She was the lass for you. Or any of them other lasses that fawned over you.'

'But Letty's the lass I wanted.'

'Aye, but not the lass you needed. That lass upstairs knows nowt of the ways.'

'She'll learn. She's a clever lass.'

'Clever catching you.' She paused. 'Poor, lovely Becky. What a beauty that girl was. You broke her heart.'

Alec did not respond.

Dorcas said no more – but she had said enough.

Letty heard Alec say he was coming upstairs to bed and she replaced his pillow, ready for him to take his place beside her. The thought of being alone with Dorcas for the next three weeks chilled her. In her haste to be with Alec, she'd only thought of being with him. It was with cold resignation that she realised she had married his mother too.

3

Alec sailed the following day and Letty and Dorcas spent the remainder of the week erasing the grime left by the previous occupants of No. 3, Mariners Row, along with the vermin that had taken full advantage of the neglect. Evicting them had no doubt been more challenging than the poor family who had been unable to afford the rent.

That Friday morning, Letty gave the front window a final wipe and went into the kitchen.

Dorcas indicated the fresh bowl of water in the sink with a nod of her head and Letty plunged her hands into it, enjoying the warmth as it travelled up her arms before reaching for the soap, then drying her hands on the scrap of cloth that hung by a nail on the back door. She opened it to let in some fresh air and leaned against the frame.

'A good end to the week,' she said, trying to thaw Dorcas's frostiness. Her endeavours so far had come to nought – Dorcas was resolute in her irritation of her son's choice of wife, but Letty was stubborn too. It was only a matter of time, and they had plenty of that.

Letty peered out into the yard. A bird flew against the window, startling her and Dorcas shrieked.

'Shut the door. It's bad luck to have a bird in the house.'

Letty bit the inside of her cheek. Superstitions had come thick and fast from the day Letty began walking out with Alec. She hadn't been able to see him off at the docks; she couldn't wash on the day he sailed lest he be washed overboard... There seemed to be an endless number that Dorcas used to build a wall against misfortune.

Letty closed the door.

'The sisal for the nets will be delivered from Hawkin's first thing Monday,' Dorcas said with no preamble. 'I've asked for more needles. You'll need your own. You can learn to fill them. When you're good enough, I'll teach you to braid. See what we can make of you,' she said pointedly, as if Letty was a piece of cloth that needed mending. Well, Letty would decide what she made of herself. It was Dorcas's insistence that she learn to braid nets as the other women did, but Letty was determined to get something else, and she knew from her visit to the docks with Alec that there was plenty of opportunity. Braiding would keep the wolf from the door, but it was poorly paid piecework, and why spend time learning when she could make more elsewhere? Not that she would give her reason to Dorcas. She would find work first; then tell her.

Letty changed the subject. 'Shall we leave for Hammonds early, to collect Alec's pay? We can take a look about the town?'

Dorcas shook her head. 'The yard needs a good swilling.'

Letty persevered. 'Sally said there's a fine hardware shop on Freeman Street and we can get our vegetables from the market on the way back. It will be as well to get to know the place better.' She leaned into the small square of mirror that hung above the table and tidied her hair, removed her apron and rolled down her sleeves.

'I've already said. I won't go down the docks until my boy can take me. I'll wait.'

Dorcas had always collected the men's pay. As Alec's wife, it was now Letty's duty but... She thought of Alec and altered her tone. 'It's a glorious day.'

Dorcas shot her a look and Letty knew it wasn't worth pursuing. Perhaps two stubborn women in one house was a recipe for disaster.

Dorcas picked up a pail. 'You can get what we need from the market by yerself.'

* * *

In the courtyard, a neighbour was taking in her washing, and over by the long wall, two boys were playing with an old tyre. The older kids would already have left for the fish dock races as they were called, when the women and children went to stand in line for their man's weekly allotment, a sub payment from the trawler companies in advance of wages while the men were at sea.

Letty pulled the door closed behind her. Four-year-old Alfie was sitting on the step next door, his chin resting on his scabby knees. 'All right, Alfie?' she asked kindly.

He looked up. 'Yes, ta, missus.'

She smiled. He was a sweet child, with his sandy hair and freckles, his serious blue eyes. That he was on the doorstep meant only one thing and she heard the sound of laughter and the creak of bedsprings drift out from the open window above the door. Anita was entertaining.

From the other side of the yard, Sally Penny called out to her, pulling her door shut and hurrying across. 'Off for your man's pay?' She linked her arm through Letty's and leaned into her. 'Your ma-in-law not coming?'

Letty shook her head.

Sally tilted her chin in reply, turned her attention to Alfie. 'You'll get chilblains sitting on that cold step,' she said, cheerfully. 'Why don't you go over to play with the lads.'

Alfie shook his head. 'Mam told me to stay on the step and not move or she'd tan my backside.'

'I know someone else who wants their backside tanning,' she said under her breath.

The door of No. 2 opened and a pinched-faced woman came out and shook a tea towel, looked Letty up and down.

'All right, Bet?' Sally asked.

The woman huffed and shut the door.

Sally shrugged, steered Letty out of the courtyard by her elbow. 'Bet Chapman. She's a nasty old sod, but she'll back down if you stand up to her. Her kiddies are all grown.' She sneered. 'Can't say a good word about any of 'em, but there you go. It takes all sorts.'

Letty asked about Anita.

'Poor lass, she's had her share of heartache.' Sally shook her head. 'A pitiful life for one so young, but she loves that little lad. What she does, she does for him.'

They crossed over the long railway bridge and made their way to Freeman Street, Sally pointing out various shops as they walked in the direction of the docks. A lad stood on the street corner calling out, a sheaf of newspapers over his arm, his fingers and face dirty with print. Letty read the headlines on the boards propped by the lamp post: *Trawler wrecked off Norwegian coast. Twelve feared lost.*

Sally gave it a cursory glance. 'Did you say you're with Hammonds?'

'Yes. Are they a good company?'

'Not bad. My Bob's with Erikson's, been with them a good few years. Your man'll get to know what's what, by and by.'

The roads around the docks were busy with people and traffic, carts and bicycles, wagons and trucks. Trains clattered past them, taking fish one way, coal another.

Presently, Sally pointed to a building across the road. 'That's Hammonds, up them stairs there.'

Letty saw the lettered sign above the door frame.

'Thanks, Sally.'

The older woman smiled. 'Ta-ra, ducky.' Letty watched her bustle over the road, calling out and acknowledging others as she went before she was swallowed within the mass of humanity.

Letty got into line and waited as the queue crawled forward and up the stairs to the first-floor office. The man in front of her was dressed in his suit, shiny at the elbows, his hair a mass of unruly curls escaping from beneath his tweed cap. His cheeks were ruddy and he looked a jovial sort as he leaned against the wall. People tucked themselves into the sides as those already paid made their way down the cramped stairs. Behind her, a woman soothed a troublesome baby, and Letty turned and offered a smile. The baby gurgled; people chattered. A boy of about nine skipped down-stairs, thrusting the brown envelope deep into his pocket and keeping his hand there.

The queue moved forward. It was hot and stuffy with so many people crammed in such a small place and Letty wished she hadn't worn her jacket, for there was not room to remove it. She'd wanted to make a good first impression, for Alec's sake as well as her own. If she was to be noticed, it would be for all the right reasons. She dabbed at her neck with her handkerchief, looked along the high windows at the top of the stairs to check if any were open. They weren't.

The queue moved again, and she was glad to find herself in the small office, where the bald-headed cashier sat behind a dark wood counter, an open ledger before him. A large tin drawer to the side contained the pay packets, towers of silver and copper coins beside it. A younger man sat next to him, cross-checking the money that was handed over.

The cashier spoke to the man in front of Letty.

'Name?'

'As if you don't know it, Perkins.' He sounded tired, surly.

The man behind the desk asked again, seemingly taking pleasure from irritating him. 'Name?'

'Stevens, Walter. Name of ship, *Golden Harvest*.'

Perkins ran a slow finger down the columns. The man brought his shoulders back. The air tingled with tension. Perkins turned a page, smirked, pushed his glasses onto his shiny bald head. 'Ah, yes.' He reached across to the coins. 'Not the golden harvest you expected.' He smiled at his joke. 'A princely sixpence.' He picked up a coin, but before he could hand it over, Walter Stevens reached across and took hold of Perkins's shirt, dragging him over the counter. The man's glasses went awry and there was a gasp and commotion on the stairs as people crushed forward to see what was going on. Sweat was beading on Perkins's forehead, his face growing puce, the younger man trying to pull him back.

The fisherman raised his fist. 'I'll teach you to smirk at me, ya bastard. Three weeks at sea for sixpence, and you sat on your arse while I'm 'auling nets day and night.'

Letty stepped forward and grabbed hold of him, feeling the strained muscles of his arm. 'Don't,' she said quietly into his ear. 'Don't give him the satisfaction.' Her heart was hammering in her chest. What if he turned his anger on her? There was little room; if he lashed out, she would get hurt.

The baby began to cry and the mother jiggled it up and down to soothe it.

The man let his arm drop, and Letty felt the tension ebb from him. He turned to her and nodded, then gave his attention to the mother. 'Sorry, missus, if I upset the babby.'

The woman shook her head. 'It's all right, Walter. Better trip next time. Eh?'

'Aye,' he said.

Behind the counter, Perkins was adjusting his shirt.

Walter snatched the silver sixpenny piece and pushed it into the baby's hand, forcing himself through the silent crowd and down the stairs.

Perkins regained his composure as Letty stepped forward, her cheeks burning with anger. He'd taken satisfaction in humiliating Walter Stevens. Would he do that to Alec? Humiliate him? She could feel the sweat trickling down her back, her forehead.

Perkins cleared his throat. 'I beg your pardon, miss.' Letty waited while he rearranged his shirt, moved the ledger so that it was square on to him. 'Name?'

'Hardy,' Letty said. '*Black Prince*.'

The man quickly ran his finger down the columns and found the name. The speed in which he did so made her stomach turn. 'Alec Hardy?'

She nodded.

Perkins counted her money, smiled. It sickened her. 'I do apologise for the outburst.'

She leaned forward. 'Perhaps he has a right to be angry,' she said, irritated by the injustice. 'Did you consider that? He's been away from his family for weeks, worked day and night in heavy seas, risked his life, and that's his reward. Perhaps you too would be aggrieved?'

He sat up sharply then and she noticed his ears redden. Big ears they were too.

The young lad at his side bit his lip to suppress his amusement.

She caught his eye and mellowed a little, turned her attention back to Perkins and added sweetly, 'In the same circumstances, of course.' She could hear the murmurings of those behind her. She hadn't wanted to cause a scene, but she couldn't help herself.

Perkins handed over the money without another word and she purposely made a show of checking it was correct. From the corner of her eye, she could see him bristle with indignation and it gave her a small frisson of satisfaction. That man wouldn't last three minutes on board a trawler, she was sure of that. She placed the money inside her bag and turned to leave.

The woman with the child touched her shoulder. 'Here, lass, catch up with Walter and give him his sixpence. Happen he'll regret his generosity in an hour or two when he fancies a pint.' She pressed the coin into Letty's hand and whispered, 'Good for you, putting that 'oick in his place.'

Letty didn't look back; perhaps she too would regret her actions in an hour or two. She hurried down the stairs and out onto the pavement, waited for a moment while her eyes adjusted to the light. Standing on her toes, she peered out above the people who spilled past her, left and right, across the road, decided to turn towards the town, weaving through the crowd, searching for Walter Stevens.

It didn't take long to find him, his curly hair, the bagginess of his suit. He was talking to another man, who handed him a cigarette and struck a match. He leaned in to take the light, drew on his cigarette, puffed out the smoke. Letty waited. He looked at her and frowned, then recognition dawned. He put the cigarette to the side of his mouth, held up his hands. 'I owe you an apology, missus.'

Letty stopped him. 'You owe me nothing. I'd have done the same myself if he'd smirked at me like that.'

The older man turned to talk to a boy who had pulled at his sleeve, and Letty discreetly pressed the coin into Walter's hand.

'I was told to return it to you.'

He looked down at the sixpence and she saw the disappointment sweep across his weather-beaten face.

'Thanks, lass. Too quick to lose my temper. Doubt I'll ever learn, but that sarky...' He smiled. 'Thanks,' he said again.

He walked off and she felt dread drag at her stomach. Sixpence. How could he bear it? It could happen to Alec. The skipper and mate were share fishermen. They took a basic wage and a share of the profits – if there were any to be had. It could be famine or feast and Letty knew that if a ship missed the best market prices, the men could land in debt to the owners. The enormity of their situation bore down on her and she couldn't move. Carts clattered past, trains rattled in the distance, and ship's hooters screamed out from the dock basin. Suddenly she was overwhelmed by the noise of it all, the smell. She longed to be back with her family, to smell the clean fresh air of the countryside, to run through the fields and shelter under the outstretched branches of the oaks and beech trees. Could they make a success of it here? It was all well and good talking it over with Alec – when he was with her, she was strong.

She pulled herself taller. Self-pity would never do.

'He's not a bad 'un, our Walter.' She turned to see the woman with the baby. 'Trying to get hisself back together again.'

Letty reached out and touched the child's hand, shook it gently up and down and cooed to it. 'I gave him the coin.'

'Aye, I saw you. I knew you would.'

The woman moved the child into her other arm and held out her hand. 'Ivy Major. My hubby's on the *Black Prince* as well. Engineer.'

Letty took the woman's hand and introduced herself.

They began to walk back towards the town, men stepping off the pavement and into the road to let them pass. Children were still leaning against the wall, waiting for their fathers and brothers, women waiting for husbands and sons. Letty longed for Alec to be home. What if he came back to sixpence – or worse? The incident at the office had rattled her.

'Is the *Black Prince* a good ship, Ivy?'

The older woman smiled kindly at her. 'Fair enough. Len has no complaints. He's been with Hammonds a while.' She stopped, pressed her hand to Letty's arm. 'They're all much of a muchness. It's down to the skipper in the end. A bad skipper makes a bad ship, no matter who he's with.' The baby pulled at her hat and she released its fingers, smiled at Letty. 'Best not to fret, lass. Your man'll do all right on the *Prince*. Sam Harris is a fine skipper and he does well. Looks after his crew as well as his ship. He'll not be out of pocket. What is he, deckie?'

'Third hand, but he already has his mate's ticket.' Alec had been glad to get any work when they arrived, knowing he could work his way up once they got settled. And he could read and write – which was an asset, for many a good fisherman had been cast aside once certification became necessary as proof of competence. 'He's going to put in for his skipper's ticket when he can.'

Ivy nodded approvingly. 'Good for him. A young man as wants to get on. I'll have a word with Len when they land. He'll see him right. But Hammonds is a good firm. He could've done worse,' she added, giving Letty another reassuring smile.

Letty returned it but it didn't make her feel any less worried. What good was the best skipper and the best boat if the weather was bad, if the fish were not to be found. She could see why the women took to braiding, but it wasn't for her.

They stopped as the crossing gates were pushed across in front of them and waited for the train to pass, its many wagons taking fish all over the country, faster and further. As the last one disappeared down the line and the gates swung open, the two women crossed to safety and parted, Letty's thoughts tumbling. She'd put her faith in Alec, but what control did he have over the might of the sea and the vagaries of the market? Dorcas's misgivings had been well founded. Maybe Alec would've have been better marrying a girl who knew the ways of fishing families, but he had married her and she would prove Dorcas wrong.

4

Sally was right about the market. Letty had filled her string bags with potatoes, carrots, onions and a cabbage, and at a good price. From the butcher, she'd bought an oxtail and beef bones. She was tired and her arms ached, but she was pleased with her efforts – not only for the food but the information she'd gathered. Walter Stevens's predicament had frightened her to begin with, but now she was fired up to succeed. She had to do what she could while Alec was at sea; their success as a family depended upon it.

The courtyard was quiet when she returned, the washing taken in; smells of cooking drifted from open windows and doors and mingled with the smell of horse dung from the stables. She was surprised to see Alfie still on the doorstep.

'Surely you haven't been there the whole afternoon, Alfie?'

Before he could answer, the door opened and a tall man with red hair forced his way past the boy.

'And what's it to do with you?' he snarled, squaring up to her. 'One thing I can't abide it's interfering women.'

Anita appeared, laid her hand to her son's shoulder. 'Away inside now, Alfie.'

The boy did as he was told.

Anita folded her arms, leaned against the door frame. Letty saw Dorcas twitch at the curtain.

'Don't be so miserable, Baxter.'

He didn't comment and Letty wasn't sure she wanted him to. His hair made him distinctive, his manner more so. Did he have the temper to go with that fiery hair of his? He pulled on his cap, glaring at Letty and then turned to Anita.

'Look after yourself, Neet. And the lad.' He pressed something into her hand, turned on his heel and swaggered out into the street.

Letty adjusted the bags, the handles cutting into her fingers. 'I didn't mean to cause you any trouble.'

Anita laughed. 'You haven't. Take no notice of 'im. His bark's worse than his bite. Like most blokes.' She nodded at Letty's bags. 'You found everything all right then?'

Letty put down a bag and opened the door to No. 3. 'Enough to be going on with.'

Alfie called out and Anita went inside.

Letty set her bags down on the kitchen table and began unpacking her bounty. Dorcas took the butcher's parcel from her and unwrapped it, dropping the bones into a pan of water she had set on the stove earlier. Letty took Alec's pay from her purse and brought down two of the three tins from the shelf above the range. One for the rent, another for food and coal, and one for savings. One of them would be empty for a while yet. She felt awkward dealing with the money. It was something else she'd taken away from Dorcas, but there was nothing she could do about it. She pushed the lids down on the tins and put them back.

'You should have come with me. You would have enjoyed it.' Letty could sense that Dorcas was agitated as the older woman moved about the kitchen, putting the vegetables in a basket on the shelves that ran top to bottom of one wall. She rummaged around in a drawer and took out a small knife.

'It's not right. Living next door to that hussy and hearing all those goings-on.' Dorcas wiggled the knife towards the party wall. 'And that little lad. Sat on that step the whole time you were gone.'

Letty removed her jacket and hat and hung them up, taking her time so she didn't have to look at Dorcas's miserable face.

Dorcas began peeling the potatoes. The smell of boiling beef bones filled the air and the windows soon clouded with steam. Letty was about to open the door but, remembering the bird, thought better of it. She put on her apron,

'I quite like, Anita. I've found her nice enough. She's on her own. Doing what she can to look after her boy. And if what she can is, well...' She paused, searching for words that wouldn't inflame. 'What would we do if we found ourselves in the same position?'

'Not that!' Dorcas spat. 'Never... I wouldn't.' She bristled, attacking the potatoes with vigour. But who knew what lengths a woman would go to, to protect her child? Anita must love the boy with every breath in her body to go so far. The workhouse was full of children whose entrance into the world had been beyond their mother's care, abandoned on the highways and byways, left on doorsteps in the hope that someone would take care of them. They were the lucky ones – if you could call it lucky. 'Sinful it is. Sinful!'

'Are ya there?' Anita called out.

Dorcas froze.

Letty turned to go to the door, but the young woman was already in the room. Had she heard? She carried a parcel wrapped in newspaper and held it out to Dorcas.

'Baxter brung me some fish. Me an' our Alfie can't eat it. There's too much. It'll do for your tea.' She was gabbling. It gave her away. She'd heard right enough.

Letty scowled at Dorcas, who made no attempt to take the fish from her.

Anita offered it again. 'It'll only go to waste.'

Letty stepped forward. 'That's so kind of you.' She took the parcel and unwrapped it. Four pieces of best haddock and a fillet of plaice. 'Why, Anita, this is wonderful.' She could barely contain her irritation with Dorcas and eating in silence one more day was more than she could stand. 'You and Alfie must stay for your tea? The broth will keep and we've plenty of potatoes. It will take only a minute to peel a couple more.'

Anita glanced at Dorcas, her cheeks reddening. 'Oh, I di'n't bring it for that.'

'We know you didn't, but it would be mean-spirited on our part if we didn't offer to share it.' Letty was barely able to contain her contempt of her mother-in-law, hoping her words had galvanised Dorcas to apologise for her behaviour. Yet it was Anita who was gracious.

'That's right kind of you both.' She glanced about the kitchen, taking in the two chairs. 'Shall I nip back and get a chair, and a stool for Alfie?'

Letty took the large plate from the shelf and laid the fish on it. 'That would be perfect.'

Anita's delight was obvious and Letty was glad she had made someone happy, for try as she might, she didn't have that effect on Dorcas.

When Anita left, Dorcas slapped her drying cloth down on the table and exploded.

'How dare you invite that woman into my household.'

Letty bit back her words, then corrected her. '*Our* household,' she said firmly. It was *her* home. Hers and Alec's. If there was a pecking order, surely Dorcas was at the bottom of it. Letty sensed a need to stand her ground. If she kept making excuses for Dorcas's behaviour, it would be a life of misery. She wouldn't have it. 'Anita's been generous – and welcoming.' How she longed to add 'which is more than you have been'. She took down the jar of flour and sprinkled some over the fish, concentrating on what she was doing to avoid looking at Dorcas. 'We know nothing of her. Nothing at all. Only that she's kind and generous. And she loves her boy. As you love yours.' Dorcas sucked in her breath, but Letty wouldn't be interrupted. 'It's not a comparison in any other way, but a mother's love speaks volumes.' Letty calmed a little, let her shoulders drop. 'And a mother's sorrow too.' She paused, having felt she had gone too far.

Anita returned, calling loudly this time before she stepped over the threshold, carrying a chair and a stool, gently chiding Alfie to walk a little faster. She placed the stool by the wall and sat Alfie on it, brushed at his knees and pinched his cheeks. 'Can I help?'

Letty waited for Dorcas to speak.

'No, Letty has it in hand.'

There was an uncomfortable silence as Dorcas busied herself putting the potatoes on to boil. Letty wrapped the peelings in the newspaper from the fish and placed it in a pail outside the back door. She wrung out a cloth and handed it to Anita, who wiped down the table. Alfie was silent, watching the women, looking intermittently to his mother, who smiled encouragingly, reassuring him with slight movements of her head.

Anita put the cloth in the sink. 'You've made the house lovely, haven't they, Alfie? Don't it look nice?'

The boy nodded. He sat on his hands, his legs swinging. He was a scrap of a thing.

'The state of the place before you came. Mucky devils they were.'

Letty could well imagine.

She spoke to Alfie. 'Would you like a drink, Alfie?'

He looked to his mother.

'Speak up. The lady asked if you wanted a drink.'

He nodded.

'Milk or water?'

'Water, please.'

Letty smiled. 'What lovely manners you have, young man.' She poured him a cup from the jug on the side.

He reached out, holding it in both hands. 'Thank you, missus.'

Anita beamed at him, tugged at his shorts. 'He's such a good boy.'

'He's a credit to you, Anita.' Because he was.

'We do our best.'

Dorcas wordlessly placed a little scrap of bread and jam in front of the boy. 'Tea'll be a while yet.'

Alfie looked at his mother, who nodded and only then did he take the bread from Dorcas's outstretched hand. Letty relaxed. It would be all right. The boy's presence would make sure of that.

Letty and Anita chatted, while Dorcas concentrated on the cooking, disapproval oozing from her turned back. Letty ignored it as best she could, took out the knives and forks and placed them on the table. Anita reached across to help.

'Have you settled in all right?'

'More or less – everything I need for now anyway,' Letty replied. 'Sally walked with me to the offices, pointed out the places to go to – and ones to avoid.'

Anita laughed. 'What she don't know i'n't worth knowing.'

Letty nodded. 'I rather gathered that.' She fried the fish in a little butter while Dorcas dealt with the potatoes and when it was ready, plates were passed over and filled, and they settled down to eat. Somehow the food tasted better with four of them around the table. It was a little of her old life, the way her mother kept a home – always room for one more; food could be stretched, and people made welcome.

Afterwards, when everything was cleaned and cleared away, Anita picked up the chair and the stool.

'I can't tell you how lovely it was to be in company,' she said. There was a gentleness about her, and Letty could only wonder as to what had brought her to her present circumstances. 'What do you say, Alfie.'

'Thank you, missus.' The boy yawned and she nudged him with her elbow towards the door.

'Come on, my lad. We've your letters to do yet before you go to your bed.' She tried to catch Dorcas's attention. 'Thank you, Mrs Hardy.'

Dorcas replied with a nod of her head and Letty wanted to shake her.

She took the stool from Anita. 'Let me take that.'

Anita released it and the two of them left the house, Alfie leading the way. The boy opened his front door and Anita hurried forward, setting down her chair and taking the stool from Letty, putting it at the oak table at the back of the room.

Letty was taken aback by how well cared for the house was. What had she expected? Red walls and velvet curtains? She was disappointed with herself and wondered how many other people judged Anita wrongly. The wallpaper was faded and peeling from the walls and torn in places, but Letty could well imagine that it had looked lovely once. A neat but battered armchair was set in front of the fire, a small carved wooden chair with a cushion set beside it. In front of them was laid a small peg rug made from scraps of old material. It was easy to imagine the pair of them sitting there of an evening.

Letty beamed. 'It's so cosy.'

Alfie went over to a small shelf by the fireplace and picked up a slate
and a piece of chalk.

'Good boy.' Anita quickly drew the letter B. 'Practise that one, Alfie. B.
B. Bumble bee.' She turned her attention to Letty. 'I like it. I don't have
much, but I love what I have.'

Letty smiled. Hadn't she felt the same the day they arrived at Mariners
Row?

Anita took a lamp from the table and adjusted the wick. Letty caught
sight of a framed photograph next to it, a young man in sailor's uniform.
Anita picked it up and passed it to her. The man was dark-haired and
square-jawed, with laughing eyes in spite of his serious expression.

'My Danny,' Anita explained. 'Lost at sea, he was.'

Letty swallowed down her own fear.

'I'm sorry. It must be hard.'

'It is. Harder than I ever thought.'

Letty handed back the photo and Anita returned it to the table, traced
her husband's face with her finger.

'Those...' she leaned close to Letty and lowered her voice, all the time
watching her boy, '...stuck-up buggers at the poor relief. They want to see
you grovel. They wanted to take Alfie and stick him in the children's home.
I wasn't having it. I told them to stick their money where the sun don't
shine.' She gave a small laugh. 'That di'n't do me no favours.' She shook
her head, obviously remembering, and when she spoke again, her voice
trembled with old fury. 'I'd lost the man I loved, and they wanted to take
my boy.' She pressed her lips together. 'Danny was in the orphanage. I
won't let Alfie have the same life his father had.'

Letty moved to the small painting that hung over the hearth. A view of
fields and a river running below, trees beyond it and the sun rising through
the mists. She turned back to Anita.

'Surprised?' She smiled wryly.

Letty felt her cheeks burn.

'It's all right, you know. Most people think I'm a poor ignorant girl who
knows no better. But I'm more than that. We all are.'

Anita checked Alfie's work, ruffled his hair. She returned to the lamp
and lit it with a match. The room took on a rosy hue from the pink shade.

Letty made towards the door.

'Thanks for the fish, Anita.' She held on to the doorknob, not wanting to leave, overcome by the feeling that she was going back to something less.

Anita walked towards her. 'I hope I haven't made things awkward for you. It was right kind of you, to ask me in.'

Letty's irritation at Dorcas's harshness flared again.

'It was kind of you to share your fish.'

She called goodbye to Alfie, who lifted his head and said quietly, 'Bye, missus.'

Anita opened the door. 'I hope we can be friends, as well as neighbours.'

Letty stopped on the threshold. 'Of course we can.' Dorcas might disapprove, but who Letty chose to befriend was her business.

Outside, dusk was falling and Letty stood in the courtyard for a moment listening to the horses shifting in the stables on the other side of the wall, a raised voice, a dog barking. There had been no time to be still these past few days. Alec was doing his best, somewhere out on the vast oceans of the north, and she hoped with all her heart that he was being watched over, by God, by his father, his brother. The first stars were visible, faint above her as they would be with Alec. She missed him.

Back in the house, Dorcas had lit the lamp and was knitting seaboot socks using thick obb wool. The click of her needles didn't miss a beat as Letty entered the house.

'Anita has it very nice next door,' Letty remarked.

Dorcas concentrated on her knitting, lifting her arms to free the yarn.

'Don't you get cosy with her. Bet Chapman t'other side of us has already marked my card about the likes of Anita while you were out.' So, it hadn't taken long for that hatchet-faced woman to spread her poison. 'I know you don't care what people think, but you will if they're thinking the wrong thing.'

Letty bristled. 'There's nothing *to* think.'

Dorcas looked up, shaking her head, her disdain clear. 'Not at the moment, perhaps. But people like to talk.'

'For sharing a bit of fish.'

Dorcas pursed her lips. 'Aye. Then it'll be more than that you're sharing.'

'Dear God!' Letty gasped.

Dorcas rested her knitting in her lap. 'I know you think I'm a miserable old woman, but I'm right, you see if I'm not.' She stared across into the empty grate. 'When people have nothing better to do, they'll find something to talk about it. Don't let it be you.' Dorcas checked her stitches. 'Have you thought what she's doing here. Who's paying for it all? Well, we perhaps know a little of that. But the child sitting on that doorstep. It's not right. Doesn't matter how she comes round here offering us to share her...' She sniffed. 'Payment. You'd no right to accept that fish. Or make me share it. It makes me retch to think on it.'

Letty felt a sudden rage rise in her throat. To think they would be together, day after day, braiding. Braiding! There was no way on God's earth Letty would sit with her, with her cruel comments and her inhospitable air. Before Monday came around, before the twine for the nets was delivered, Letty would have found work elsewhere. She would make sure of it.

5

It was fresh the following morning, the wind blowing sharp off the estuary as Letty strode onto Fish Dock Road in search of employment. She needed egg money. The thought made her smile, bringing with it memories of running the market stall with her mother, selling produce from the farm. Her mother's egg money was used to clothe them, and for little extras. Egg money would keep them going if Alec came home to sixpence.

She stopped outside Wiltshire's on the corner of Hutton Road. The wall to the side of it was painted with what they had to offer: groceries and provisions, merchant oils and paraffin, twist and tobacco. She peered in the windows, saw someone moving about and hurriedly tapped on the glass of the door. A smartly dressed man walked forward and she waited while he unlocked it.

'We're not open.' He considered her for a moment.

'I'm looking for work.'

'The early bird, eh?' he smiled. 'I admire you for your get-up-and-go, lass, but I don't have need for more staff. I have sons enough for that.' He studied her. 'Come inside. I can perhaps save you some shoe leather.' He stood back to let her pass.

The shop was lit by electric lamps, but only the one behind the counter was on. The shelves were stacked with tins and boxes of all

manner of things, from shaving soap and razors to paraffin lamps and
lanterns. Everything neat and orderly and it induced a sense of calm.

'Wait here while I get the wife.' He disappeared through a door at the
side marked *Private*.

While he was gone, Letty looked about the shop, admiring the abun-
dance and variety of the stock. Practical and indulgent side by side. She
heard footsteps, a lighter step, and when she looked up saw a neat woman,
her dark hair piled high upon her head.

'Edward said you're looking for work?' The woman's eyes flicked
quickly over Letty, assessing her. Letty stood taller. The woman nodded
her head in subtle approval. 'I do know of something. Can you be persua-
sive?' She studied Letty's face. A smile played about her lips. 'Yes, I do
believe you can.'

It was Letty's turn to smile. 'It didn't take you long to get my measure.'

'All part and parcel of the business.' She took a deep breath. 'Parkers,
the ship's outfitters on Henderson Street, Norah and Percy. It's Percy you'll
need to charm.' She paused. 'Norah could do with the help. I've been
trying to convince her for months, but that curmudgeonly...' She stopped
herself from saying more as her husband returned. 'You look spirited
enough.' Her eyes sparkled with mischief. 'It's all a bit... chaotic. You'll see
for yourself. A drop of young blood and youthful energy is just what they
need.' She walked to the door and indicated to Letty to follow. Out on the
pavement, she turned towards the dock tower, gestured with her hand.
'Down this road, turn right after a small side street. Halfway down you'll
find Parkers.' She turned back to Letty. 'Tell Norah that Alice sent you.'

'I will.' Letty put out her hand and the woman shook it firmly. 'Thank
you.'

Alice stood back onto the tiled entrance of Wiltshire's. 'Come back and
let me know how you've got on.'

Henderson Street was closer to the fish dock and pontoons, and
halfway down, just as Alice had indicated, was Parkers. It was a single-
fronted shop with a door to the right-hand side, less than half the size of
Wiltshire's, but from the window, it appeared it had just as much stock –
and if the window was an indication of the inside, it would indeed be
chaos. There was jumble of ropes and packets of soap, tin bowls stacked

untidily on tin plates. Oilskins and boots hung along the backboard and obscured the interior. It was as if everything Parkers had to offer had been squeezed into the one small space.

A bell tinkled over the door as Letty opened it and stepped inside, her boots clicking on the wooden floorboards. A man with a few strands of white hair about his ears was sipping tea from a metal mug and leaning on the counter reading a newspaper, his spectacles sliding down his nose. She was almost in front of him before he looked up and scowled at her.

'Yer a bit early?' His voice was gruff, abrupt, and for a moment she faltered.

She mustn't give up at the first hurdle. She wanted a job.

'The door wasn't locked.' She twisted a little and pointed towards it. 'I thought—'

'Well, you know what thought did.' He stood more upright, placed his hands on the counter. 'What will you be wanting?'

'I'm looking for work.'

He shook his head, was about to speak and she boldly stepped closer. 'Alice at Wiltshire's sent me.'

He sneered, making clear his opinion of Alice.

Letty glanced at the cascading jumble about them. 'She said you'd been talking of getting someone in to help you and your good wife. And, well, I'd like to think I'm that person.'

He rubbed his hand around his chin, furrowed his brow. 'Alice is wrong, Miss...?'

'It's Mrs, Mrs Hardy. Letty.' She held out her hand and he hesitated, then took hold of it, unsure. 'I'll do anything, Mr Parker. I'm not afraid of hard work.'

A small thin woman appeared from the darkness behind the counter clutching a sheaf of what looked like invoices and began to berate him. 'Oh, Percy. I've found all these stuffed in the drawer. How will we get things straight if we don't keep on top of it all? I've told you time and time again. I...' He began to look a little uncomfortable and his wife started a little when she saw Letty. 'Oh. I do apologise.'

'No need. Please, I'm here to help.' The woman was bemused. 'Alice sent me.' Letty threw back her shoulders and tried to act with authority. 'She said you'd spoken of taking on help.'

The woman sighed, pressed the papers to her thin chest. 'All the time. All the time.' The poor woman was weary; it was obvious to everyone except perhaps her husband, drowning among the papers as well as their stock.

Alice had said to be bold. Letty whipped off her gloves, put them into her handbag and placed it on the counter. 'I can see quite plainly that you do need some help. I can stay for the day.' She sensed Percy bristling beside her. She ignored him, focusing her attention on his wife. 'No charge. And you'll see that I can prove my worth. I'm certain I can make life a little easier for you both.'

Norah's eyes twinkled with amusement. She looked to her husband, sucked on her lip, looked at Letty, then back to Percy. She paused, moved, hesitated, then nudged her husband out of the way and lifted the counter.

'That's a kindly offer, lass. And one I'd like to take you up on.'

Percy grumbled, but Letty sensed Norah was grabbing on to the metaphorical life belt Letty had offered.

Norah twisted and said firmly, 'It won't cost 'owt, Percy, the lass has offered her services for free.'

'Aye, but there's no such thing as free. Never is.'

Norah shook her head and muttered, 'God give me strength.' She glanced down at the floor and bent to retrieve a piece of paper, black with footprint, turned it over: an invoice. She shook her head in despair.

It galvanised Letty, who slipped off her hat and coat, wondered for a moment where to put them.

Norah dropped the papers she'd been holding on top of Percy's newspaper. He huffed and puffed with indignation but didn't say any more. Looking at his wife, he probably thought better of it. He was a great lumbering thing and moved slowly, whereas she was brisk, like a squirrel. Norah held out her hands. 'Let me take them. I'll put them through the back way.' She gave Letty a grateful smile and Letty knew she couldn't leave now, even if she wanted to. One day wouldn't hurt and even if they didn't take her on, she would perhaps be able to spread a little kindness. It always came back some other way.

Norah bustled away into the darkness of the doorway beyond.

Percy eyed Letty suspiciously. 'No pay?'

'None.'

He leaned back on the counter, watching her, screwing up his mouth as he did so. It was the look her older brothers gave her when they threw down a challenge they were sure she wouldn't master. She hadn't failed then, and she wasn't going to fail now.

Rolling up her sleeves, she stepped into the middle of the shop, slowly taking it all in. It would keep anyone busy for weeks, but she was damned if she couldn't make her mark today. She put her hands to her hips, tutted and turned to face Percy, who tilted his chin and peered at her over the wire rim of his glasses.

She took a deep breath. 'The problem is, Mr Parker, you have carrots with your onions and eggs with your cauliflowers.'

He stood back from the counter, his thick grey eyebrows rising up his head. 'Now, you stop right there. Norah!' He became all of a fluster, his cheeks beginning to redden. 'If you think for one moment... for one ruddy moment. Norah!' He lifted the flap of the counter. 'Don't you touch anything in my shop, babbling on about eggs, and cabbages.' He went back behind the counter and shouted through the open doorway. 'Norah! Get ya sen out here, the lass has lost hold of her senses. Norah!'

His wife came rushing through. 'What in heaven's name is the matter?'

'I'm not having her touch a thing. Not. One. Thing.' Percy stabbed at the counter with his finger. 'A young lass interfering, telling me I don't know what I'm doing. I shuda known, saying she'll work for nowt. Who works for nowt?'

Norah rested her hand on his arm and stopped him, looked to Letty. 'What on earth have you said?'

Letty was mortified. 'Perhaps I didn't explain myself properly. What I was trying to say was that you need more order – a system.'

Percy jumped in before Norah could answer. 'System. I've got a system. I can put my hand on anything in the dark if I need it.'

Letty held her ground. 'Yes, but can anyone else?'

Percy spluttered. Norah became agitated at her husband's outburst.

Was she a little afraid too? It was hard to tell. He'd said she was interfering. It was what that man, Baxter, had said, at Anita's yesterday.

Letty came close to the counter, her voice soft but firm. 'Mr Parker, I don't want to interfere, really I don't. I want to help.' She turned about her, opening her hands. 'You have such a beautiful little shop and you're not showing it off to its best.'

He calmed a little. 'Nowt pretty about trawler gear.' He ran his hand over his head, making what hair he had stick up in tufts. 'I tell you, Norah. You've given a madwoman free rein in our shop. Our shop!'

Norah rubbed at her husband's arm. 'She's right though, Percy. It is a lovely little shop. It always has been. It's just got out of hand.' She turned to Letty. 'I think we're too far gone now, dear, for you to be of any help.' She seemed so resigned, when earlier she'd been so enthused. But Letty was not going to give up.

'Please. I know I can help. I used to work on the market selling our farm's produce with my mother and sisters. I was explaining to Percy that things seem... chaotic.' Norah nodded, sighed. 'And what I said, in my clumsy way, was that things are in a muddle, that you have, so to speak, carrots with onions and eggs with cauliflower.' She picked up a rope and a metal bowl.

Norah gave her husband a nudge with her elbow. 'You daft beggar. I know what the lass means. It's a jumble and she's going to sort it out.' She turned to Percy, folded her arms, a strength to her again. 'Well, I'm happy to let her have a go. I don't have the energy – and neither do you.'

He grumbled, but Letty could tell Norah was beginning to warm to her.

'Just for today, Percy.' She winked at Letty.

Letty looked to Percy for his agreement.

He inhaled long and hard, then gave a slight nod.

Norah pressed her hand on the counter and moved the newspaper in front of him. 'Read your paper. I'll make a brew.'

Percy growled like an old dog and pulled the paper towards him, glaring at Letty before looking down at it.

Grumpy old devil. She was giving her time for free. It would be easy to take umbrage and leave, but she would never quit once challenged, even if it was a challenge she'd set for herself. And yet she knew it wasn't down to her stubbornness. There was something about the shop that felt cosy and embracing, although why that was with someone as grumpy as Percy Parker in charge was a conundrum.

Letty walked about the shop floor, assessing the stock. It was a mishmash of clothing and equipment with no logic to it at all. It made her head spin. She went outside and looked again at the window display, compared it to the shop next door: *Gilbert Crowe – Tobacconist and Newsagent*. It was immaculate. Plenty of people were passing by on their way to the pontoons, but no one stopped to look in Parkers. Why would they? Quite possibly, it hadn't changed for years. There was nothing at all to tempt them to stop. The glass was filthy and thick grime gathered along the sill.

Letty crossed to the other side of the street and inspected every detail. The black paint on the woodwork was chipped and peeling, but the signwritten name of *Percy Parker – Ship's Outfitters* over the window was unmarked, though the gold was dulled by dirt. Letty was going to make that gold glister. The thought invigorated her and she marched back into the shop ready to start digging.

Percy looked up from his paper. 'Thought you'd given up and left us.'

'I'm not that easily defeated, Mr Parker.' She rubbed her hands and made her way to the left-hand side of the shop, along the wall of which ran floor-to-ceiling shelves of various sizes, and in various degrees of disarray. She began to empty them, stacking them in piles, Percy pretending not to notice but clearly watching her surreptitiously. 'Carrots with carrots, onions with onions,' she teased.

He harrumphed, the paper crackling as he gave the page a sharp turn, making a great play of smoothing it out with the flat of his hand.

'Do you have a duster, and some polish?'

He shrugged.

'I thought you could put your hand on anything.' She couldn't stop herself from grinning. 'In the dark?'

He stood away from the counter and took a deep breath, clearly about to bark his answer, when Norah appeared carrying a small tray with three mugs of steaming hot tea. She peered over the counter to the piles arranged on the floor.

'By, lass, you've cracked on and no mistake.' She put the tray on top of

Percy's newspaper and handed him a mug. 'I put plenty of sugar in. Thought you'd need it for the shock.' She slipped past Percy and came around the counter clasping her mug, handed one to Letty. 'Well, it looks better already. Doesn't it, Percy?'

He looked down into his tea, grunted.

'I was asking Mr Parker where he kept the duster and some polish, but he...' Letty turned to him and he glared at her.

Norah laughed. 'No good asking him. Oh, he knows where the rope and tin mugs are, and he'll find you a nail or a needle. But cleaning stuff,' she wafted her hand, 'forget it.' She took a swig from her mug. 'Drink your tea, and I'll get you something.'

A short, thickset man came limping into the shop and studied her before moving to the counter, casting his eye over the shop floor. 'Eh up, Percy. Di'n't know no hurricanes was forecast t'day.'

'More like an ill wind.' He slurped his tea loudly.

Norah glowered at him.

The two men began discussing that afternoon's football match, who would play for the Mariners, and if Tommy Edwards had recovered from his dodgy ankle.

Norah pulled out a small stool and sat down with her tea. 'You're a brave lass.'

Letty frowned. 'Brave?'

'Aye.' She held her mug with two hands, rested it in her lap. 'Emptying that wall for one, and not backing down on Percy for another. Alice is quite right; I've been trying to persuade him for months to get some help.' She sipped at her tea. She was a lot older than Dorcas, more her grandmother's age. 'It's the expense.'

Hardly anyone had come into the shop since she'd been there, and Letty realised with a pang of sadness that they wouldn't be able to afford staff, no matter how badly they needed it. She couldn't afford to work for nothing. Today she would do her best and start looking for work again on Monday, and yet... she liked it here, among the jumble, a mountain she could definitely climb and conquer, and there was something about Norah, even Percy, that she'd warmed to. She drank her tea.

'We're caught between the devil and the deep blue sea.' Norah went quiet. Letty could hear the men murmuring behind them.

'You have a lot of stock.'

Norah nodded, seeming to break from her daydream. 'We do. Most of it we've had years. The lockout did for us and we never really recovered.'

'Lockout?'

'The fishermen went on strike – 1901 the bad one was. Terrible. It lasted weeks. The docks were packed tight with trawlers. Idle. Families were starving. If it hadn't been for the mission and the like, it would have been far worse.' She sipped again, paused, considering. 'We'd just borrowed a lot of money from the bank.' She put her hand out to take Letty's empty mug. 'Never really got back on our feet after that, just managed to tick along.'

Letty understood the hardship they must have faced. The papers had been full of details of the miners' strike earlier that year. It had ended only a month ago, the miners having held out since February. The repercussions had been felt across the country and Alec had had cause to question his decision to come to Grimsby. Trawlers couldn't steam without coal. Happily, it had been resolved before their wedding, but it had been a tense few weeks until the government intervened and passed the minimum wage act for miners.

Norah got up, the mugs held in one hand. 'You said you were Mrs, Letty.'

'I am. My husband's at sea. We arrived last week. He got a ship straight away.' Did she sound as lonely as she felt?

Norah pressed her hand. It was cold, her skin papery. 'Thanks for what you're doing, lass. I'll talk him around. Lord knows we need the help, but he's stubborn. It means he'll have to admit to himself that he can't cope any more.'

'Don't you have children to help?'

'No, we were never blessed in that way. The shop is everything we have, and each other of course.' Norah glanced across to Percy, who was now holding forth about the Kaiser and his ships, then turned to Letty, raised her eyebrows. 'I'll get you that duster.'

She came back with a tin of lavender polish, a rag, a bucket of warm water and a damp cloth and handed them over, then went back towards the counter.

'Are you going be in here yarning all day, Dennis? How's the missus?'

'Why d'ya think he's in here, woman,' Percy said, quick as a flash.

Norah laughed. 'What have you done this time?'

Letty left them to talk and moved the ladder to the first shelf, walked to the top with the bucket and cloth and gave everything a good wipe, working her way down and along until they were all done. By the time she'd finished the last, the first was dry and she began again, this time with polish. It was hard work, reaching deep into the shelves, up and down the ladder, sometimes catching snatches of conversation, at other times deep in thought.

She finished the last shelf and stood back to admire her work, then turned her attention to the piles of clothing. She called out to Percy. 'How do you organise your shelves, Mr Parker?'

'They wuz all right as they wuz.'

'But they weren't,' she insisted. 'The customers can't see what you have to offer.'

Dennis knocked on the counter with his knuckles. 'I'll leave you to it.'

Percy said goodbye with the lift of his chin. Dennis winked at her as he left.

'You should've left it as it wuz,' Percy said.

Letty put her hands on her hips. 'Perhaps I should. Perhaps I should have walked on by and gone somewhere I might be appreciated.'

He shrugged. 'Don't you get uppity with me.'

At the sound of raised voices, Norah hurried into the shop. She glanced quickly to Letty.

'Norah, are you happy for me to arrange the clothing as I think will be best for *both* of you?'

'I am.' She sniffed the air. 'By, it smells lovely and clean.'

The delight on her face was reward enough for Letty. She would carry on for Norah's sake. If it made her happy for one day, her time was worth it.

6

When all the items were returned to the shelves, Letty stood back to admire them, feeling Percy's eyes burn into her back. She twisted quickly and he flicked his attention to the paper, pretending he hadn't given her a thought. Letty set to work moving the rails, ordering the boots so that they sat in a regiment on top of the boxes. She would have liked to have a go at the window, but it couldn't be done in a day.

Norah's face was a picture when she returned with yet another brew for Percy, who had barely moved the entire time. She nudged Percy, pushing him aside and made her way to Letty, her face alight with pleasure. 'It looks terrific, it really does.' She made Percy come out from behind the counter – which he did with a lot of fuss and bluster, and stood beside his wife.

'Doesn't it look wonderful?' A sharp elbow to the ribs prompted him to answer.

'Aye, I s'pose it does. But it wuz all right before she started. Nowt wrong with it.'

Norah slapped his arm. 'You old devil. The lass has worked a damn miracle.'

He ambled back to the safety of the counter. 'Dare say she has. But no one's going to take a blind bit o' notice. Not our customers anyhows.'

'New customers will like to see it looking just so, Mr Parker,' Letty said, trying to instil a little enthusiasm.

'New customers. Hah! Ain't been none of them for a while.'

Letty followed him. 'But there will be, Mr Parker. If you give me a chance.'

He leaned on the counter. 'What makes you an expert on sailing gear. Bet you've never been on a ship in your life.'

'I haven't. But I can sell.'

'Aye, so you said. Cabbages an' eggs, weren't it? Well, we don't sells 'em.' He took a scrap of paper and pencil, licked the end of it and began writing a list, turning his back on her. She couldn't hide her annoyance.

'How ungrateful. Why I...'

He raised his head. 'Why shud I be grateful? I di'n't ask you, did I?' He went back to his scribbling.

Norah glared at her husband, who looked away and went into what Letty thought was a store cupboard. 'He is grateful, we both are.' Norah pressed her arm. 'It's late. You've had a long day. Let me get your hat and coat.'

Letty waited in the empty shop and Norah returned with her things. Norah went behind the till. The bell rang as the drawer opened. Percy dashed back in. It was the fastest he'd moved all day.

'What ya doing, woman?'

'Paying Letty.'

'Lass said she was doing it for nowt.'

Letty agreed, holding his gaze. 'That's very kind of you, Norah, but your husband is quite correct. I offered.'

Percy nodded with satisfaction. It hadn't cost him at all. Not yet.

Norah continued to take coins from the till, the sound of metal being scraped against the wooden drawers, the coins clinking in her hand.

'I know I could bring more customers in if you give me a chance. Plenty of people pass by—'

'Pass by,' Percy interrupted. 'One thing we agree on. Look, lass, let me be straight with ya. I'll admit you've made it look tidier.' Oh, a small victory. Norah's eyes looked like they would pop from her head – it couldn't happen very often. 'Though I doubt I'll be able to find a ruddy thing now. But...' There was always a *but*. 'It won't bring folks in. And we can't afford to pay anyone else.'

Seizing the opportunity, Letty jumped in. 'But I can do that, Mr Parker—'

He held up a hand to stop her. 'Me and the missus have enough to keep us going and that's all I can ask for.' His tone had changed, and she saw the gentleness in his brown eyes as he tried to dissuade her. It wasn't his fault, was it? He hadn't led her on; but she wanted to help them. It would be easier to turn around and look elsewhere, but something tugged at her heart. She liked them.

'Take me on trial. A few weeks. A month. I'll earn more than my pay in profits, I promise you.'

He hesitated. The two women watched him, Norah's hand holding the coins. He opened his mouth, closed it again, turned to his wife. Norah tilted her head to one side, waiting. He harrumphed.

'You women'll be the death of me.'

Letty wanted to hug him, it felt such a triumph. The two women exchanged smiles. Letty turned to Percy. 'I'll make sure you're not out of pocket, Mr Parker.'

'I do believe you will, Letty Hardy.' He put out his hand and she took it. 'Monday. Eight o'clock sharp, mind. Bah, must be going daft in my old age.'

Norah gave him a gentle slap and reached up and kissed him lightly on the cheek.

'Ah, be off with ya, woman. Folk round here'll think I'm soft in the head.'

Letty grinned. 'I'll be here at eight. Just you make sure that door's open.'

He rubbed a hand over his head. No doubt he was still wondering how the women had got the better of him.

Norah pushed past him and walked with Letty to the door. She tried to give Letty the money, but she refused.

'You're a force to be reckoned with and no mistake, lass. Thank you.'

'It's Alice Wiltshire you need to thank. It was she who sent me your way. She wanted me to go back and tell her how I got on.'

Norah, nodded, thoughtful. 'She's a good woman. Tell her thank you until I can tell her myself.' She opened the door and the slow sounds of the day drifted in. It had started to rain and small drops washed away the dirt of the pavement.

'I'll see you Monday.'

'I'll look forward to it.' Norah beamed.

At the end of the street, Letty looked back. Norah was still there, watching her and she smiled and waved. Letty returned it. Monday couldn't come soon enough.

Alice was turning the sign on the door of Wiltshire's when Letty arrived to thank her. She smiled broadly, opening the door wide to let Letty enter. 'I can tell by your face you were successful.' In the shop, three young men she assumed to be Alice's sons were about their businesses, sweeping and polishing ready for Monday opening. Letty felt a surge of excitement at what the coming week would bring.

'It took me all day to persuade, Percy. I've a month's trial. Norah said to give you her thanks.'

Alice reached out and pressed her arm. 'Oh, well done, young woman. I'm sure they won't regret it.'

'I'll do my very best to make sure they don't.'

7

What started as a shower gathered momentum and became a downpour. Rain seeped through Letty's coat but didn't dilute her spirits as she bent her head against it and hurried home, her mind swimming with ways to help the Parkers. It was good to have something to think about, other than torment herself with imaginings of whether Alec was safe or not. She paid for her distraction with a soaking. A bear of a man driving a coal wagon called out a warning, but by the time she looked up, it was too late. Dirty water splashed against her skirt and boots. He called his apology over his shoulder as she brushed away what she could of the filth. It was an annoyance, but her own fault. Still, it would dry; Dorcas would have the fire going. Letty was suddenly hungry, thinking of the beef broth that should have been yesterday's meal.

The courtyard of Mariners Row was empty of people and washing, and in the grey light, it appeared drab and dismal. Small lights could be seen in some windows, the soft amber reflections spotting the cobbled yard in patches here and there. Alfie was at his window, tracing raindrops on the glass with his fingertips. He saw her and gave a small wave. She waved back and went to her own door and opened it.

The house was cold and dark, the fire unlit. Letty felt a twinge of disappointment wash over her, followed by a flicker of relief. Dorcas was out.

She peeled off her hat and coat, shaking them on the doorstep, before closing the door, glad to have the house to herself. She lit the lamp, leaving the curtains open so that it would be the first thing Dorcas saw on her return. A warm welcome. Slipping her coat over her arm and her damp hat, floppy with rain, in her hand, Letty went into the kitchen.

She jumped out of her skin when she saw Dorcas motionless on the chair, the finished socks upon the table, her needles and the remaining wool beside them.

'Goodness, Dorcas. You startled me, sitting here in the darkness.' Letty draped her coat over the back of her chair. The range was almost out. 'You'll catch your death sitting in the cold like this.'

'It's warm enough,' Dorcas answered.

Letty opened the grate and raked the embers, added a small shovel of coal. Her heart was hammering against her chest.

'I didn't know where you were.' Dorcas's voice was flat. Had she sat there all day?

Letty shut the range door and replaced the shovel. She wiped her hands on a cloth, moved the pan of broth onto the hotplate. 'I didn't intend to be out all day.' She lit the lamp on the table and turned the wick to brighten their surroundings. Dorcas was grey-faced. Letty's nervousness switched to concern. 'I thought you'd have had the broth on? Have you eaten?'

Dorcas shrugged. 'Didn't want it to boil away. Didn't know when you were coming back.'

It would have been kinder to have called upstairs before she left, and looking at Dorcas now, Letty felt bad. She softened her voice, anticipating the challenge that would come. 'I went to find work.'

Dorcas raised her eyebrows, suddenly animated. 'Work? You have work with *me*. Filling needles.' She eyed Letty suspiciously. 'The twine arrives Monday.'

Letty turned her back. 'I know it does...' She hesitated, knowing her news would not go down well, stirred the broth. 'I've got work in a chandlery. Parkers. I'm better suited for it. I could never be as fast as you at the needles...'

'We all have to start somewhere,' Dorcas snapped, getting to her feet.

'You'd have been doing this as a child not a woman, had you lived the life I had.' She folded her arms. 'You'll have to go back and tell 'em you can't do it.'

Letty thought of Norah. How lovely it had been to spend time in her company; she'd even warmed to Percy. She knew she could win him over in time – but Dorcas would always be set against her, wouldn't she? She was not of fishing stock and there was nothing she could do about it. Letty twisted to face her.

'It will take months, perhaps years, for me to learn to braid quickly. I'd earn so little.' She would be paid from Dorcas's own earnings, that was the way it was – but it wasn't the way it was going to be, not if Letty had her way.

Dorcas was dismissive. 'You have t' be quick at the needles afore I can teach you t' braid. The faster you are, the more you'll be paid. Same as me.' She sat down again in her chair and Letty held her tongue, too tired to argue.

The room was beginning to thaw and she gave the pot a stir, dropped in the cold potatoes left from yesterday. They would both feel better with nourishment. She made tea and pushed a mug in front of Dorcas, adjusted her own chair in front of the stove to dry her coat. Steam rose from it and the windows started to cloud with condensation. The lid began to rattle on the pot and Letty moved it to the side. She unwrapped the rest of the bread from the cloth and cut two slices, put them on a plate and placed them on the table. Dorcas made no attempt to move, so Letty got the bowls and utensils and dished up the broth. They began to eat in silence, save for the rain as it pattered hard against the windows. It was dark now. The day had gone, and Letty felt her happiness had gone with it.

'I thought I could fill the needles in the evenings, so that they're ready for you the next day.'

Dorcas huffed. 'Do you know how many needles I get through in a day?' She pierced Letty with her gaze, knowing she couldn't answer.

'We could get more needles. I could fill as many as you needed. I wouldn't need payment.'

Dorcas stiffened.

Letty hadn't meant to offend her, but it seemed she couldn't do right for doing wrong. 'Can't we work it out between us? It would be more money to the house. To our savings...'

'What about Alec?'

'Alec?'

'What will you do on landing day, and when he's home?'

Letty paused, drank more broth from her spoon, her hand trembling slightly. She hadn't broached the subject with the Parkers, had only thought of filling the long days when he was away, days she didn't want to spend with Dorcas. There was no guarantee that Alec would land on her day off, or that they would have the Sunday together. Time ashore could be forty-eight hours, a little more, perhaps less. Dorcas was staring at her.

'We'll work something out.' She tried to sound casual, tore at her bread.

'Is that Alec and yourself who'll work these things out? Or you and the Parkers?' She gave a sarcastic laugh. 'Can't say they'll like that. Alec won't like that.'

Letty chewed on her bread. Alec would support her. They were a couple. They had plans. 'Alec will understand. We're working for a better future. For all of us.' She looked up. 'I feel I'm better suited to selling.'

'Selling!' Dorcas sneered, looked as if she was about to make a barbed remark, opened her mouth, closed it, got to her feet. 'You can't work in a shop!' she snapped. 'You need to be here. For Alec. What if he has a bad trip, comes back to debt? It always falls on the women. Us! You'll have to keep the house running.'

'And I will.' Letty paused. 'I'll just do it in a different way to you.'

Dorcas snorted. 'And you'll take your babies with you, will you? To this *shop*?'

'There are no babies. Not yet. And babies never stopped my mother working.'

'Nor me, madam. Nor me!' Dorcas spat. 'I kept my boys on braiding. Fed and clothed. Might not been of the quality you're used to, but I kept my boys, yes I did.'

Letty twisted her hands in her lap, stilled them before she spoke again. 'And you kept them well, Dorcas, kept them close.' It sounded patronising, but she hadn't meant it to be.

Dorcas gripped the sink and Letty saw her knuckles whiten.

She tried to calm things between them. 'Life's changing so fast. One day we'll have water inside the house, that we don't have to pump; a bathroom, things we never dreamed of.' She understood Dorcas's fear, she was fearful herself. Dorcas had already lost so much, she was still grieving that loss, and Letty knew she had to be strong or else they would stay in this misery forever.

She saw Dorcas's shoulders sag and after a while she came back to her chair, picking up the socks she had pushed to one side, touching the wool, the needles. She did not say anything more. Letty cleared the bowls, took a damp cloth and wiped the table. Dorcas moved the socks and wool to her lap.

'We should go out tomorrow, together,' Letty said, trying to mend things between them. 'You would see for yourself how things are different here.' She dropped the cloth in the sink.

'What do you know?' Dorcas spat at her. 'Selling! You'll be selling yourself next, like that hussy next door.'

For two pins, Letty would have struck her, instead she balled her fists, keeping them stiffly at her side.

'This isn't about me, or Anita. It's about you. How long do you think you can go on like this? You can't hide away for ever. What will Alec think when he comes back and sees you like a... ghost?'

Dorcas sprang to her feet. Letty stood firm.

'How dare you.' Dorcas's eyes flashed. 'You know nothing of my life! Pah! I warned my boy. The very idea of working when he comes home!' She sank back into the chair, shook her head. Her voice was almost a whisper when she said, 'He needs you.' She bent forward and picked up the socks from where they had fallen on the floor, placed them on the table, stared at them with such sadness.

'He needs you too,' Letty said gently, 'but I can't spend the rest of my life just... waiting.'

Dorcas stared at her. 'You're his wife. That's what you do.'

'I want a better life, don't you? It's what we came here for.'

Dorcas shrugged. It stoked the flame of Letty's exasperation.

'I'm not going to sit and fade away. If you want to, fine.' She picked up a cup from the shelf by the sink, her hands trembling. 'We need sugar.' She marched out of the house and into the yard, stepping around the puddles, letting the cold air cool her temper. It was spotting with rain now and she leaned against the wall for a while to calm herself before going over to knock on Sally's door. Light and warmth flooded over her when little Dora opened the door.

Sally was sitting by the range, darning the elbow of a sweater, the open door exposing the glowing coals of a small fire. Her two younger boys were at her feet, poring over a tattered copy of *Puck* and Evie sat with her hands apart wrapped in a skein a wool. Sally beckoned Letty inside and Dora closed the door behind her, returning to sit winding the wool as Evie moved her hands in a swaying movement to assist her.

'Can you spare a cup of sugar?' Letty asked.

Sally threaded the needle into the sweater and put it to one side. 'Sit yourself down, lass. Dora, leave that. Get Mrs Hardy some sugar.' She moved the kettle to the hotplate of the range. 'Will you have a drop of tea with us now?'

'I don't want to disturb you...' But she did; she longed to melt into the warmth of a family again, any family, instead of going back to the cold house. No fire could ever warm it while Dorcas was there.

Evie got up from the chair, her hands still apart with the wool, and knelt on the rag rug on the floor.

Letty picked up the wool. 'Can I?'

Evie nodded and Letty began winding, glad to be part of something familiar.

Dora set the cup of sugar on the mantel and sat on the arm of her mother's chair.

'How's it all coming along?' Sally asked.

Letty wasn't sure what the older woman meant, but perhaps that had been her intention. 'The house is in order. And today I got work. Parkers. On the docks.'

'Oh, aye. Norah and Percy? No doubt they'll be glad of your help. They should've got someone long since, but some folk seems to leave things till they're gone past saving.'

The kettle whistled and she nudged Dora with her elbow. The girl got up and fetched a teapot, handed it to her mother, who proceeded to make a brew.

'I thought I might have seen your mother-in-law about. I knocked but no answer. She wasn't with Bet Chapman.' Dora handed Letty a jam jar filled with tea and Sally took her own and placed it on the mantel shelf.

'She hasn't been out since we arrived.'

'And you're worried?'

'She lost her son a few months back.' Letty told her of Robbie's accident, that Dorcas had lost her husband and brought the children up alone. 'We clash. She doesn't want me working outside the house. She expects me to braid, like her.'

'She'll be afraid for you. Like as not, her old man came back in debt as well as in profit. Aye, and the profit might be nothing to speak off.'

Letty thought of Walter Stevens.

'Many a woman has kept the wolf from the door by braiding. If the wolf comes knocking, it's a short walk to the workhouse.' Sally drank a little of her tea. 'Poor woman. She has nothing of her past that's of comfort. 'Tis a good job she has you.'

Letty shook her head. 'I don't think she feels that way.'

Sally nodded sagely. 'Oh, she does, lass. From what I've seen of her, which isn't much, mind, but from the few glimpses, she has a kindly face underneath all that sorrow.' She stared into the fire. 'Bad times don't last forever – same as good times. We all gets our fair share. We hopes.'

That was all Letty wanted, her fair share. Sally had seen something in her that perhaps Dorcas hadn't. She stayed a while longer enjoying the company until guilt made her move. She got to her feet.

'Tell your ma-in-law she's welcome any time. Being as you'll be at work, like.'

Letty smiled, ruefully. 'I'll try.' She went to the door.

'Letty.' Sally was holding out a cup. 'Your sugar.'

Letty reached out to take it from her and Sally put her hand on hers as she handed it over.

'A little extra sweetness goes a long way.'

Letty nodded, knowing Sally wasn't talking about the sugar.

It was quiet in the courtyard. In the distance, Letty could hear a pair of cats fighting and someone yelled, 'Give it a rest.' A wobbly moon was reflected in a puddle disturbed by raindrops and she stepped over it as she went to the door. The lamp was still alight in the window. Was sweetness all that it took?

Back in her own house, Letty put the sugar into the jar she knew was not empty, wiped the cup and put it away. She heard the creak of floorboards above as Dorcas got into her bed and sighed softly, wondering how to make herself sweet. Her mother would laugh at the very idea, for Letty had never been the sweetest of her children.

She went back into the room and sat to catch the last of the mean fire, raked over the glowing coals to stir the heat. If Dorcas were her mother, it would be easier. She must learn to think of her as if she was. Letty closed her eyes and tried to conjure the farmhouse so dear to her, so far away. Safe. Was Alec safe? Was he warm? She felt foolish. Dorcas was right, but it didn't make it any more palatable. She had no idea of what being married to a fisherman was all about.

Letty took her notepaper and pencil from the sideboard and began a letter home. Mother would want to know of how she was faring and Letty would tell her of the Parkers. Of Dorcas she would say little. Her mother would read what she could into that.

Later, upstairs in her bed, she moved her hand over the space where Alec should be. She took his pillow and curled into it, trying to imagine that it was him, craving his warmth, his strong arms about her. They'd had so little time together. Could she endure as well as learn? She had to make certain that she did.

8

By Saturday, the *Black Prince* had been steaming north for five days and there had been a steady rhythm to the ship and the work upon it as they headed for distant waters. It would take another five to get home. They would be perhaps ten days or more on the fish. Three weeks away. It had given Alec plenty of time to think over the last few weeks, their move to Grimsby, his marriage to Letty. His mother's words niggled at him. Would Letty be constant as he thought she would? It hadn't crossed his mind before, for the lass was as much in love with him as he was with her – or was he mistaken? It would be better when they were on the fish for he knew full well too much thinking could drive a man insane.

The rota for the watch had been set as they steamed out of the Humber and into the North Sea and Alec had quickly made himself familiar with the ship and crew. Now he leaned against the rail and watched the smoke pour forth from the funnel, not reliant on the wind as the *Stella Maris* had been. The crew numbered twelve. The old man, as they called the skipper, second in command was the mate, and Alec third hand. There were two engineers, a coal trimmer and cook, the rest being deckhands, the youngest of which, Ben, was the skipper's lad. This was his first trip as deckie-learner, although, like most other boys, it wouldn't have been his first time at sea. Many of the lads accompanied their fathers on the shorter summer trips when the seas were calmer. He'd done the same with his father. A pleasure trip it was called – although, for some, the swell of the sea was anything but and many took to their bunk for the duration.

Deckhand Puggy Marsden pocketed his knife and came beside Alec, and the two of them looked out onto the rolling waves. A Grimsby man born and bred, he'd been on the steam trawlers for the last six of his twenty-seven years, working first the northern waters and then to the White Sea fishing grounds off the coast of Russia, where the cod and other bottom feeding fish were more plentiful. Alec had never sailed this far before and it was noticeably colder as they passed the Norwegian coast, the mountains and the fjords, marvels such as he had never seen before. He pulled his cap down over his ears. Puggy pointed to the snow on the mountains, how far it coated the lower landscape.

'Hard winters ahead of us?' Alec asked, gathering every scrap of information that would help in the future. When he was skipper himself, he intended to head for the distant waters – for that was where the top money was.

'You ain't seen the like. When the ice comes, you know about it. You'll have to get yer axe out then.'

Alec had heard the stories, of how the water froze as the waves washed over the deck, icing the masts and ropes, making the ships top-heavy so quickly that they rolled over, the crew lost. The risks were high, but the rewards were too.

Puggy slapped him on the back. 'That's to come. You'll not face that this time.' He rested a hand on his shoulder. 'Make the most of these next few hours for we'll be on the fish soon enough.'

His words ignited a flicker of excitement as Alec followed Puggy down the ladder into the belly of the ship. The hunt was almost upon them.

They made their way forward to the living quarters, where another deckhand, Mouse, was seated at the mess table, reading an old copy of the *Grimsby Telegraph*. He was a thin whip of a man, not at all like Puggy, who was thickset and almost square. And he had nothing of Puggy's joviality, for Alec found him sullen and morose.

Ben, the skipper's lad, was sketching, his hands steady as he shaded the bow of the *Black Prince*. To the foreground, in a separate sketch, there was no mistaking the face of his father, his flat cap pushed back on his forehead, his neckerchief knotted just so. He looked up as Puggy and Alec came in and moved further along the bench that surrounded the table on three sides, then carried on sketching.

Puggy shuffled his way next to Mouse at the table and Alec slipped around the other side. Ben's hand slowed and he closed his sketchbook and put it underneath him. He was a big lad for fourteen and Alec couldn't work out if his shyness was because his father was skipper or his natural disposition. Perhaps he was as wary of the men as they were of him. Would what they say be spouted back to the old man?

They heard Tosh Webster pound down the steps before they saw him, his boots heavy on the ladder. He gave them a gap-toothed grin. 'I'm ready for me grub. Hope Cookie comes up with something better than last night.'

'Don't let him hear you say that, he'll spit in it,' Mouse said, nose stuck in his paper.

'Tastes like he already did.' Tosh slid onto the bench next to Alec, his big hands holding the ridge of the table.

Cookie called out, 'I heard that, you bugger.'

Tosh nudged Alec. 'He's one of the best is Cookie. That's why we stay on this ship, nowt to do with Skipper or the money.' They were used to Tosh's sense of humour and no one took offence, least of all Ben.

Cookie came in with a large plate of bread and placed it on the table. 'Pan o'shackles tonight, lads. Skipper's smelled the fish. Make the most of it.'

Mouse folded his paper and stowed it behind him.

Cookie returned with bowls of stew and they pushed it around the table until everyone was served.

'Which ships should I avoid then?' Alec asked. 'Or should I say, which cooks?'

Puggy tore at his bread. 'Don't go near Branstons if ya can help it. Difficult bastards they are.'

'Aye,' Tosh agreed. 'They'll take a couple o' coppers off ya for a lost rivet. No bugger likes 'em.' He chewed again, his cheeks pouched. 'They gets newcomers who know no different.' He nudged Alec and the stew dropped from his spoon and splashed his tunic. He wiped it away, licked his fingers.

'Waste not want not.' The pair of them grinned at each other.

'You wus lucky getting with us. A lucky break for you, but not for Badger.'

Alec smiled at the daft joke. His place here was a stroke of good fortune – for him if not for the man he replaced. The skipper's nephew, the third hand, had broken his leg and Alec had appeared at an opportune time.

'Evans is best, I'd say. But Hammonds is a good enough firm.'

'As long as ya avoid Pip Bramley,' Mouse added. The other men grumbled their agreement.

'His lad's not much better,' said Tosh.

Alec soaked his bread in the gravy and pushed it into his mouth.

'He used to be all right, until his missus left him, did old Pip,' Puggy chipped in. 'He weren't that bad.'

'He were,' Tosh argued. 'He's allus been a bad 'un.'

'Mebee, mebee not. He was worse when his missus went off with that butcher. Wot were his name?' Mouse looked up to the ceiling for the answer.

'Simmons,' Tosh said. 'Got butchers down Wellington Street. Went in for a sausage and got more than she bargained for.'

Three of them laughed but not Mouse. 'Happen if our missus went off we'd be bastards too.'

'Ruddy hell, Mouse,' Puggy said. 'Yer knows how to put a man's mind to rest when he's away from home, don't ya.'

Alec didn't comment. Mouse had only said what they all worried about when they laid in their bunks at night. He listened to the men talk, but his mind was elsewhere, back in the dingy house they'd arrived at only days ago, his mother's words coming to him again. Had Letty really understood the life that lay before her? If she was perturbed, she hadn't shown it. She'd already mapped out what they would do and when, and now he couldn't stop the smile from coming to his lips. She was a strong lass, she would look after his mother. In time, God willing, his mother would regain the spirit she had lost when Robbie died. He closed his eyes, saw Robbie fall into the water, sucked beneath the waves, and snapped his eyes open again.

Puggy pushed his empty bowl away from him, sat back and folded his arms. Mouse picked up his paper, shook the page and turned it. The headline told of German naval developments. Tosh poked at the paper. Mouse grunted.

'They reckons it'll be war soon enough. Out o' date that newspaper, Mouse, we might already be fighting the Kaiser.'

'How the hell would we know out 'ere,' Puggy said.

'We'd know soon enough. Them buggers and their submarines might be underneath us right now.'

'Not out here, Tosh,' Ben said, his worry evident.

'Out here. Everywhere. They's putting a diesel engine in submarines. Our navy'll be doin' the same. They've been trialling trawlers as minesweepers. 'S' only a matter of time. We won't be catching fish then.'

'I'll be on the fish no matter what,' Puggy said. 'They won't need us.'

'That's as mebee. None of us knows. 'S'lright them ruddy papers writing stuff, but when it comes down to it, it'll be us beggars dodging the bosh.'

Ben sat upright. 'I'll go in the army.'

The men turned their attention to him.

Tosh was surprised. 'Has the old man heard ya say that?'

'No.' His cheeks were flushed, but his chin jutted out in defiance.

'Yer but a bairn anyway,' Puggy said good-naturedly. 'It'll all be over afore you get yer uniform on, lad.'

Cookie came in with mugs of tea and passed them around. Puggy slurped loudly. Tosh slapped his stomach and belched. 'Better out than in.'

Ben scratched at the table with his nail. His hands were not yet calloused by months at sea, the skin not hardened and scarred by the hauling and mending of nets. His cheeks still held the residue of unwanted attention, but he was trapped at the table until the men moved. Alec nudged Tosh, who got up, as did Alec, and the boy freed himself. Would he go to sit with his father in the aft mess? Alec hadn't seen him go there yet.

* * *

Up on the deck, it was still daylight, though it was already late in the evening. Alec took in a breath of the cold sharp air and made his way over to the business end of the boat. The skipper was up on the wheelhouse veranda, his hands moving along the rail as he observed the waves, the horizon, assessed the clouds. He could see the change in the way the man held himself, the tension of his body. Alec knew it too, for his father had taught him well.

Puggy and Tosh checked the ropes slow and steady, for now they were full-bellied and sluggish. The lad went up on the bridge to his father and they stood side by side and a shaft of envy seared though Alec's chest and he had to look away, down to the deck, not the skies that would remind him of his father, nor the sea that would remind him of Robbie. He checked the winch and the trawl and went to the rail. In the far distance, he could make out a trawler heading south, back to the docks. He half wished he were heading home too, back to Letty, and yet the build-up of excitement as they neared the fishing grounds was palpable. They all knew it. Even if the other men were not aware of how best to find the fish, they knew they were near.

The skipper called down to them. Tosh stuck his fag in the corner of his mouth and went towards the trawl doors. Ben joined them on deck and Alec watched him closely. The lad wasn't for the fishing – his hands were for other things, his mind and his passion left on his bunk with his pencil and sketchbook.

Alec steadied his position at the winch. The chain began to clatter as the great trawl doors opened and the men paid the net out as they moved along. The engines slowed. The sky and the sea were almost the same colour, the horizon indiscernible. They would have a few hours now before the nets started to fill – and then the real work would begin.

9

On Sunday morning, Letty moved silently about the house while Dorcas slept. Before going to bed, she'd soaked some oats in water and now she put them on the range and gave them a stir. Sleep had come, and with it dreams of Alec. It had not been a week since they'd walked along the docks together, finding their way in this new world, this new life.

She warmed some water and took a jug to Dorcas in her room, knocked on the door and went in without waiting for an answer. Her mother-in-law was awake, and she looked blankly at Letty. 'I thought you'd like a wash this morning. Before we go out.'

Dorcas stirred, pulled herself up on her elbows. 'Out?'

Letty poured water into the plain porcelain bowl, knowing Dorcas wouldn't want to waste the warmth of it. She handed Dorcas a towel.

'I thought we'd go to the Bethel Mission Hall.' Alice Wiltshire had told her of its whereabouts when she'd gone to update her on the outcome of her visit to Parkers. The Bethel was the fisherman's chapel and non-denominational. Letty would have gone to St Andrews, the Church of England, on Freeman Street, but there were bridges to be built. 'I was thinking you'd prefer the chapel to the church. It's a fair walk, but the weather is fine.' She stood by the door, tapped it. 'Breakfast's ready.' She smiled, glanced towards the water. 'It's lovely and hot.' She closed the door behind her and stood by it, waiting for sounds that Dorcas had moved. When she heard the covers being pulled back and Dorcas's faint grumbling, she went back to the kitchen.

When Dorcas came downstairs, the porridge was on the table and a hot drink placed in front of her. 'I don't know what all this is in aid of.' She eyed Letty suspiciously.

Letty pushed a jar of her mother's honey across the table. 'A little spoonful of Lowestoft.'

Dorcas stared at it for a moment, then pulled it towards her, dribbled a spoon of the golden liquid into her bowl and stirred it in. Letty sipped at her tea. Dorcas began to eat.

'Good to have the house straight,' Letty ventured. It wasn't perfect, but they had made the most of it, and they must do the same with their relationship. For Alec's sake as well as her own.

Dorcas didn't answer.

Letty pressed on. 'I thought if we left early, we could look in the shop windows on the way.'

'I'll not come.' Letty frowned, and seeing her, Dorcas added, 'It was good of you to think of the Bethel, but I haven't been to the chapel since...' Her voice trailed off and she stared at her bowl, pushed it away. Letty picked it up along with her own and took it to the sink.

'All the more reason. We can say a prayer for Alec, for all the fishermen, that they keep safe.'

Dorcas gave a small laugh. 'God didn't keep Will safe, nor my Robbie. Prayers are no use.'

Letty stared out of the window. 'We have to hope they do, for everyone we love deserves our prayers.' She turned back to Dorcas. 'Those we love. And those we have lost.'

Dorcas pulled the chipped teacup towards her. 'What do you know of loss?'

Letty stared down into the whiteness of the sink. All the honey in the world would not make Dorcas sweet enough. She felt a sudden surge of anger for Alec. He'd left her to the dirt and disappointment, and worse, he'd left her to deal with his mother. 'I'd rather put my faith in God than in superstition,' she said quietly. She would go alone, and while she was there, she'd ask the Lord for patience, for Dorcas was surely trying her to the very ends of it.

She untied her apron, took down her coat and hat and put them on, fiercely fastening the buttons. She wouldn't argue, but she would go to church, as she had done every Sunday of her life.

As she went to the front door, she heard footsteps.

Dorcas came beside her, stabbing a pin into her hat. 'I want to see for myself how the Bethel is.'

Letty didn't comment, simply opened the door and stepped outside. The courtyard was quiet and she was surprised by the sun, so dingy was the house inside. The windows in the houses opposite were pushed high and nets billowed and sank back and forth.

Letty waited while Dorcas fastened the door and the two of them made their way to chapel. They walked over the railway bridge in silence and headed to Freeman Street. Letty began commenting on the shops and displays, Dorcas only responding with a nod. At Riby Square, her mother-in-law gave a quick glance towards the dock area but nothing more and fell into step beside Letty as they walked the length of Cleethorpe Road – Letty chatting animatedly, Dorcas still mute. They came to a junction at Park Street and crossed over into the neighbouring town of Cleethorpes and Letty suggested they might one day pay a trip to the seaside. Still Dorcas did not respond. Letty directed Dorcas to turn left onto Tiverton Street and they walked along the row of terraced houses to the mission building on the corner. Letty waited at the entrance to let others pass. Dorcas hesitated. Would she go in after all?

A man stood on the step, looked up and down the street for latecomers and, seeing there were none, beckoned them in. Letty stepped forward, turned to Dorcas, waited again and Dorcas, with a heavy sigh, followed. The door was closed behind them.

They made their way to the end of an empty pew. In front of them, a woman in a fine hat twisted and smiled at them. Letty looked up at the arched window that faced out onto the sea, the morning light spilling down upon the congregation through the plain leaded glass. It was a simple building, free of adornment, the paraffin lamps on chains at inter-vals above their heads. It was far removed from the village church back home, with its familiar square tower and stained-glass windows that cast rainbows on those attending.

A hush descended as the port missioner stepped up onto the low platform, cleared his throat, and said, 'Welcome.'

Hearing that simple word, Letty felt her shoulders relax. It was what she needed to hear – that she was, at last, welcome.

As he began to speak, Letty's thoughts drifted. The last time she'd been in church had been her wedding day, holding on to her father's strong arm as he had walked her down the aisle. She felt a faint shiver of irritation at the memory, that Dorcas had not shared their happiness that day. Her mother had put Dorcas's sourness down to grief. 'She has lost one son to the sea, Letty, and now she has lost her other to you. Be kind to her in her sorrow.'

They stood to sing 'Eternal Father' and when they sang the last note, he waited for them to take their seats and settle again before making an announcement. 'As many of you know, I'll be moving at the end of this month.' There was a small murmur, nodding of heads. 'Therefore, I'd like to introduce you to the man who will take my place.' He smiled down at someone on the front row that Letty could not see. Many of the congregation leaned from side to side in effort to get a glimpse of the newcomer. 'Some of you may already have made his acquaintance. He has come to us from Scarborough where he has been working with our brethren at the mission there. Mr Colin Wilson.'

The port missioner stepped away from the lectern, and a man got up from the front row. People craned to get their first glimpse of someone who would be both welcomed and feared.

He wore the familiar navy uniform, the brass buttons catching the light. His white cap was pressed under his arm and he withdrew it and placed it on the lectern. He was tall and dark-haired with a thin, open face. What struck Letty most was that, even from this distance, he looked kind. She supposed that you wouldn't do the job if you weren't kind, for the burdens of the port missioner were many; that she did know. Part of his job would be to comfort those whose men had been lost at sea. He would be the bearer of bad news, the man that women would fear walking towards their door. He would be there to lend a hand, for kind words and solace only went so far, but the material and financial help he offered would save them from the workhouse. Letty had seen missioners in Lowestoft, taking children to the orphanage. It wasn't a job everyone could do. She thought of Alfie, of boys and girls like him, whose families couldn't manage. Had the missioner visited Dorcas and offered to take her boys when her husband died? Was that why she was loath to come?

A hush fell among the congregation as he stood before them and smiled out to them.

'I hope in time to get to know all of you gathered today, and to be of service. My door is always open.' He spoke of how he had come to be here, of the work that lay ahead. He offered up a small prayer, the organ began wheezing once more and the congregation rose to its feet for another hymn. Letty joined in. Dorcas did not sing, she did not join in the prayer, and Letty regretted that she had made her come. Perhaps it had been the wrong thing to do. There was no one to ask.

When the service was over, they waited while the port missioners, old and new, filed past. They were followed by Alice Wiltshire and a younger woman Letty took to be her daughter. More women followed, wives of influential men of the area, Letty surmised. As they passed, Letty felt a tap on her shoulder and turned to discover a rotund woman with two small children, a babe in her arms.

'I thought it was you, Mrs Hardy.' She gave a nod across to Dorcas and spoke to Letty.

Letty couldn't remember the woman's name, but the child she recalled immediately from the offices on Friday. She took the babe's hand and jiggled it up and down. The baby gave a slobbery grin.

'Ivy Major,' the woman offered.

Letty flushed, embarrassed. 'Of course, forgive me.' She moved back a little. 'Dorcas, this is Ivy Major, her husband's the chief engineer on the *Black Prince*.'

'He's with my son?' Dorcas seemed to perk up.

Ivy chattered on, all the time jiggling the child in her arms. It was a bonny child, and it had its mother's nature.

'It's grand to see you here. Come and say hello to a few people. Be nice for them to get to know you, and you them.'

They walked towards the entrance and waited as people stopped to speak to the port missioner. Behind him, his successor was listening intently to a couple of stiff-backed men in good suits, their gold watch chains stretched across generous, well-fed bellies. Through the open door, Letty saw people in clusters on the doorstep and on the pavement. They followed Ivy outside to where a group of women stood in the sunshine, the breeze blowing in off the sea, the rich smell of coal drifting across from the railway line on the other side of the wall.

Ivy made a great fuss of Dorcas and Letty stood back, relieved. Alice Wiltshire caught her eye. She spoke gently to her companions and indicated that she was going over to Letty's direction.

'Hello again, my dear.' Her smile was warm, and she glanced across to Dorcas, smiled again and nodded. From the corner of her eye, Letty saw her mother-in-law stiffen. 'I had to come over. What a change in Norah. The woman looked years younger.' Her green eyes twinkled with kindness. 'I knew you had spirit.'

Dorcas came over to them.

'Is this your mother? What a girl she is.' Alice held out her hand.

'Mother-in-law,' Dorcas corrected, taking it.

'My apologies,' Alice said, still smiling graciously in spite of Dorcas's rudeness. She flashed a quick glance to Letty, her eyes indicating her sympathy.

They were rescued from further awkwardness when Ivy turned and took Dorcas by the elbow. 'Come talk to Betty Nuttall. She's from Lowestoft. You'll have things in common.' Ivy's cheery face was aglow. 'Excuse me, ladies. If you don't mind?'

Alice gave a polite shake of her head and Letty's shoulders dropped with relief as Dorcas was led away. When she was safely out of earshot, Alice leaned towards Letty. 'Looks like you're in need of a little respite.' She looked about the crowd, from right to left, searching, then beckoned Letty back inside the chapel.

Grateful, Letty followed her.

'Let me introduce you to Ruth.'

The young blonde-haired woman Letty had noticed earlier turned, tilted her head to one side. When she saw Alice, her face brightened, and she excused herself from the conversation with the port missioner and came to them.

Alice introduced them. 'Ruth, this is Letty Hardy. She's moved here with her husband this past week. He's on the *Black Prince*.'

Ruth's small hand had a strong grip and Letty liked her immediately. Her features were delicate, yet Letty had a sense her constitution was not. 'A Hammond ship.' Letty's face must have shown her surprise. 'I know all the ships, it's the only conversation at home.'

Alice turned to Letty. 'Ruth's father owns Excel Trawlers.'

Ruth gave a small grimace. 'All my father and brothers talk about is what trawler is where.'

Her name was called and one of the stiff-backed men beckoned her over.

'Nice to meet you, Letty.' Ruth returned to the small group interrogating the new the port missioner.

'That's her father, Richard Evans, next to her. A good man. A big supporter of the work of the mission.' Letty saw the way Ruth's father looked at her, his pride clear. 'Her mother, my younger sister, died when she was a child,' Alice told her as Ruth was absorbed into the conversation. 'She's very involved with the mission. You must come along to one of our meetings. It would be good for you. And for your husband. It pays to get in with the right people.'

'I thought she was your daughter.'

Alice sighed. 'Alas, I have only sons. Love them as I do. But it would be so nice to have female company at home.' She dipped her head. 'Although not all female company is a blessing, is it?'

Letty bit back a smile at Alice's perceptiveness.

Alice lifted a hand to her husband hovering by the open door. 'Time to leave.' She turned to Letty. 'Once you've settled, got your bearings, come to the mission at Riby Square. We meet on Friday afternoons. We're always looking for more good women to join us.'

Dorcas was waiting for her in the street. They watched as Alice was helped up into the carriage along with another couple, then her husband took his place beside her.

'Friends in high places,' Dorcas said as the carriage moved off.

'Not friends, Dorcas, just people we've met. You *and* I. And Ivy was nice, wasn't she? What about Betty Nuttall?'

'Nice enough, but you should keep with your own kind. Doesn't do to mix with your betters.'

Letty stopped. 'Betters?'

'Aye, you know what I mean. You don't want to go getting yourself involved with trawler owners.'

'One day Alec will be a trawler owner. That's what we came here for. Better that we rise up to meet the challenge than hide away, don't you think?' She quickened her step, hoping the pace would dilute her sudden irritation. Dorcas lagged behind, but Letty didn't care, and the gap between them widened as they headed home.

10

The twine arrived before seven on Monday morning. Letty had been up at five to do the washing, depriving Dorcas of any objection to her working at Parkers. She heard the wagon pull into the yard, a man shout his arrival. Doors were opened and Letty followed Dorcas outside.

The man jumped down from the wagon and began dragging the heavy sacks from the back of it. A lad who had been sitting on them passed them down, pushing forward the ones from the rear as it got taken by the women. Of the eight houses, six took in the braiding twine. Anita's door was shut, the curtains closed.

The man heaved the sack towards Dorcas and explained the procedure for collection. 'I comes by of a Friday morning to collect ya finished nets. Yer goes to the office on the wharf Saturday morning fer yer pay.'

Dorcas nodded.

Letty took one corner, Dorcas the other, and they dragged the sack into the house between them. Dorcas took out a bale and set it by her chair in the kitchen. A pole was fixed along the wall and she pulled out her basket of wooden needles and sat down. Letty got ready to leave.

'Is there anything you'd like me to do before I go?'

Dorcas raised an eyebrow, turned away from her, bent over and picked up one of the needles that bore her burned-on initials. There were twenty in all, long flat pieces of wood about six inches long and two inches wide, pointed at one end, with a half-moon carved out at the other. The middle of the upper half was carved out, leaving one tooth like a comb. Dorcas pulled off a length of twine and cut it with her knife, held one end at the half-moon end and began wrapping it up and down around the tooth, her hands moving quickly until no more twine could go through the gap. Letty watched as she quickly cast on a row of stitches, the pole like a huge knitting needle. Dorcas leaned down and picked up a wooden block and set it against the twine, using it as a spacer for the mesh of what would become the fishing net – or part of it. She was quick. She would be quicker if there was someone else to fill the needles. Letty was sick with guilt.

'I'll call in at the net loft and get more needles. The more I can fill in the evening for you, the better. It will be of help.'

'It would help if you were here filling them while I work,' she said bitterly. 'I'm paid for the work I produce, not for my hours.'

There was a rap on the back door and Bet Chapman walked into the kitchen, sneered at Letty. She turned to Dorcas. 'It's going to be fine all day,' she said. 'I'll be doing my braiding out back if you want to join me.'

Dorcas bent down and took up another needle. 'Aye, I will. 'Twill be good to have company.'

'I've plenty of tea. Len brought a bit back from his shift on the docks. There's a lovely slice of Dundee cake to go with it.'

'That'll be grand,' Dorcas replied.

Letty looked down at her feet. Odd that Dorcas should enjoy sharing things of dubious origin and yet had caused such a ruction about eating Anita's fish. Sally had put her right about Bet from the beginning – and her husband. Len had a reputation for miraculously coming by certain luxuries now and again.

Bet turned her attention to Letty. 'You're not staying?'

'I have work at Parker's,' Letty replied, picking up her basket.

The woman pushed her lips forward in disapproval. 'So I heard.'

'She'll not be missed,' Dorcas snapped. 'It'll slow me down, teaching her. I'll get my rail and needles and I'll be about with you.'

Bet gave Letty another once-over.

'My lass'll fill for yer,' she threw over her shoulder as she left.

* * *

The door of the shop was unlocked, the sign to Closed. Norah was polishing the counter and looked up, smiling when she saw Letty. At least someone was pleased to see her.

'I don't think I've looked forward to a Monday morning for years. Percy had a bad night and I've told him to stay through the back. Not that he'll listen.' She lifted her eyes to the heavens. Letty removed her hat and coat and Norah placed them on hooks by the side of a door behind the counter. She opened it a little and peered round. 'Lass is here.' There was a mumble that Letty couldn't quite hear, and Norah said, 'I'll show her what's what, then I'll make you a brew.' She closed the door and turned her attention to Letty. 'Now, where were we.'

She showed Letty how to work the till, how to fill in the ledger, where the brown paper was stored, pointed out the balls of string under the counter and a myriad of other things she might be in need of.

'Now, did you want to ask me anything?' Norah tilted her head to one side and Letty was reminded of her mother. It gave her reason to smile.

'What would you like me to do today?'

Norah stepped onto the shop floor, looked about her. 'If you can make a start on organising anything else in the shop as you did on Saturday, well, that would be grand.'

Letty rolled up her sleeves. 'And Percy won't mind?'

Norah shook her head. 'I'll deal with Percy if you can deal with the mess.' She slipped back behind the counter and into their private quarters, closing the door behind her.

Letty assessed her surroundings. She had to make sure she was worth what they were paying her, but sorting wasn't enough; she needed to get more customers through the door. She'd watched people pass by on Saturday. There were plenty of them yet very few stopped. But she had to start somewhere, so she opened the cupboards underneath the window display and dragged everything out.

* * *

The few customers that called in that morning were surprised to find her working there.

When there was a lull, Norah disappeared and came back with a mug of tea and a sandwich. 'There, that'll keep you going for a while.'

Letty was grateful. 'I wasn't expecting anything.'

Norah flapped a hand. 'I was making one for Percy and myself, a bit more takes no doing. Leave that and eat.' Norah put the plate in front of her and placed her hand on her arm. How long since she had been touched at all. A wave of longing swept over her and tears welled, teetering on the edge of her lashes, and she blinked them away. 'Oh, lass, have I upset you?'

Letty swallowed her sadness away.

'No, not at all. The very opposite.' She gathered herself. How silly to be brought to tears. 'Such a lot has happened this last week. I'm missing my husband and it all seems strange, this place, this life.'

Norah moved a small step stool across with her foot and nodded for Letty to sit down. She indicated that she should eat. Letty obediently took a bite from the sandwich. She told Norah of their arrival, and Alec going the next day.

'And Dorcas...'

Norah waited.

'Alec's mother,' Letty explained. 'I can't do right for doing wrong.'

'Early days, Letty. I suppose with her losses she feels the need to hang on to the old ways. Sometimes that's all we have left.'

The bell over the door rang out and a man came in and walked slowly towards them, looked about the shop, his eyes taking in the changes.

'Now then, Walter.' Norah placed one hand on her hip.

He frowned. 'Not selling up, are you, Norah? Percy's all right, in't he?' He stared at Letty, pushed his cap further up his head and rubbed at his chin.

Letty got to her feet. 'Hamond's office on Friday. I was behind you in the queue.'

He smiled then, his eyes creasing. 'Aye, that's it. You returned me sixpence.' His hand went to his pocket, pulled out the empty lining. 'Didn't last long.'

'Never does, Walter.' Norah lifted the counter. 'You'll find Percy through the back. He'll be glad to see you.' She stepped back to let him pass, and he removed his cap and pushed it into his empty pocket.

'I'm away on the late tide. Thought I might get a jar with him before we sail.'

'Go through and get yourself a cuppa. There'll be one in the pot.'

Walter placed his large hand on the oak counter. 'Working here, are ya, lass?'

'For the time being,' she said.

He nodded approvingly, looked to Norah. 'Good to have the company, eh, Norah, and a pretty face too.' He winked at Letty.

They heard him hail Percy, and Percy call out in reply. Walter closed the door behind him.

'You've already met Walter then.' Norah said, urging Letty to finish her tea.

Letty explained about the kerfuffle at Hammonds. 'Perkins took pleasure from it.'

'He would. Sits there smug, counting out money he hasn't risked life and limb for.'

Letty didn't want to think of the risks. She changed the subject. 'Are Walter and Percy old friends?' She sipped at her tea. The dust from the cupboard had caught in her throat and made her thirsty.

'Walter's father was a friend of Percy's. He's known him since he was a lad. I think he gets a lot of comfort from that.'

'Doesn't he have family of his own?'

Norah grew solemn. 'He did. He was the happiest lad around here, always a smile on his face.'

Letty agreed. 'He seems that sort; kindly.'

'He is. Give anyone his last penny.'

'Yes, he did.' Letty told her of the child and Ivy.

'Well, that's because Ivy knows Walter of old. Those who do look out for him.'

'What happened to his family?' Letty got up, ready to get back to work.

Norah gave a sad shake of her head. 'Walter was on the fleets. He could be away weeks at a time, or months. One ship does all the fishing, then passes it over to others to bring back to market. Dangerous work, but he earned well. He had a bonny wife and family. Four kiddies: a girl and three boys.' Her eyes became glassy. 'His wife took ill and died. The kiddies were taken to the orphanage. When he came back, there was another family in his house and he'd no idea where the kiddies where.'

Letty sank back on the stool. 'Poor man. Did he find his children?'

'Not that I know of. He was out of it for a long time, with the drink. Friends rallied round, got him on ships. He stays at the mission when he's ashore. They collect his allotment on a Friday for him, as they do for the other men who have no family. He works and he drinks, and in between he probably remembers – so he works some more, and when he can't work, he drinks to forget.'

Letty felt a lump swell in her throat.

'He comes here regular for Percy. When he's flush, anyone can have his money and when he isn't, folk are glad to help him out.'

Letty got up and began folding a jumble of vests, conscious she should be working not chatting. 'I met Alice Wiltshire at the Bethel yesterday. She was talking about the fundraiser for the mission. They're trying to get a new building.' She placed the neat pile of vests into a cubbyhole. 'I suppose there's a lot of call for it.'

Norah nodded. 'More than ever.' She picked up the empty plate and mugs. 'She's a good woman, Alice. I bless the day she sent you my way.'

'Aren't you in competition?'

'What, Parkers compete with Wiltshire's?' Norah laughed. 'We couldn't if we tried. A lot of the firms use them, and they've been able to grow. They have sons to help them do that. There's just me and Percy here. As long as we can get by, and so far,' she rapped her knuckles on the counter, 'we've managed to do that.' She looked down at her hand, at the gold band on her finger worn thin with years. 'We should've taken someone on before.' She looked about her. 'Perhaps it wouldn't have got in such a mess.'

* * *

The two of them worked steadily all afternoon and Letty began to hum to herself as she moved around the shelves, bringing order to chaos. Among the jumble, she found a box of braiding needles. She placed it on the counter and Norah peered in.

'Well, where on earth did they come from?' She took out a couple and held them. 'They must've been here years. I shouldn't think even Percy knew we had them.'

Letty knew she could put them to good use. 'Can I take them as part of my pay?'

'Course you can, lass. Sort out what you need.'

'I don't really know what I need. I'm simply trying to meet Dorcas half-way. She was against me working here. Said I should be learning to braid so that when babies come along... If they do come along.' Letty was awkward, she should have chosen her words better. How hard it must be to have hopes that were never fulfilled.

Norah touched her hand. 'Go on. You were saying?'

'That I could work on, bring in money, but the thought of sitting day after day with her criticising and picking...' She closed her eyes to the thoughts, opened them again. 'I know very little of her life, but I do know how hard it is. And I don't want it.'

'There's nothing wrong with wanting something different.'

Letty glanced down at the needles, running her fingers over the smooth dark wood, touching the tip of the tooth that ran from the middle. 'If only Dorcas thought like that.'

Norah pressed her shoulder. 'She'll come round. Just you wait and see.'

* * *

When Letty left, Norah locked the door behind her and pulled the blind down over the glass. She looked about the shop, taking in the orderly shelves, breathing in the smell of lavender polish. The girl had worked wonders.

Percy came ambling towards her. He looked tired, but at least he'd been able to rest. After Walter had left, he'd nodded off in the chair. The nap had done him good for there was colour to his complexion.

'Can I come into me own ruddy shop now, Norah Parker?'

'You can if you don't grumble.' She walked towards him and waited in the centre of the shop for him to join her. He draped his arm around her shoulder and kissed her cheek. She took his hand and rubbed it. 'That lass has worked like a Trojan today and we're not the only ones to notice. Word's got about and people are popping in to see what's going on. Folk I've not seen for donkey's years.'

'She's moved me ruddy pots and pans.'

She nudged him in the ribs. 'Thank the Lord for that.'

It had been difficult persuading him to keep out of the way and let the lass crack on, but, oh, it had been worth it.

Norah turned the lights off and followed him through to the back room. Percy sat down in his easy chair and picked up the newspaper.

'Walter said word's going about that we've come into money. All the goings-on in the shop, like.' He gave a little laugh, shook the pages as he opened them, his arms outstretched.

Norah kissed his forehead and gave him a gentle tap on the shoulder. 'We have, love. The lass is a little pot of gold.'

* * *

Dorcas had left her finished net by the front door so that when Letty opened it, it was the first thing she saw. She had to step over it to get into the house and she pushed at it with her foot, then bent down and tucked the stray rope to one side. *Well, she didn't have to be that obvious*, Letty thought. The floor was sprinkled with small fibres and some floated in the air from the draught as she walked through to the kitchen. The back door was open, and Dorcas was in the yard, bringing in the washing from the line that stretched from the house to the privy. Letty went out and picked up the basket as Dorcas dropped the last peg on top of the clothing. 'I saw the net,' she said. 'I still can't believe how fast you work.'

Dorcas was not flattered, not that Letty thought for a minute she would be, but it was something to say.

'Years of practise. Years. Nothing clever about it.' She looked at her hands, picked at the skin. They were red with dried blood and pink with blisters, the skin broken and weeping. 'Doesn't take long for them to soften when you're not doing the work.' She rubbed her palm with the fingers of her other hand. 'They'll soon harden.' She led the way to the house.

Letty put down the washing, removed her hat and coat. When she turned, Dorcas was filling the kettle. She placed it on the hotplate. Letty took the washing into the other room and picked up an apron, tying it about her. 'I bought a ham hock on the way back. Save a lot of fuss on our first day at work.'

Dorcas sniffed. 'Fair enough.' There were no questions about the shop and Letty forced herself to be cheerful. Dorcas would thaw eventually.

When all was cleared away, Letty brought the needles from her bag and offered them out to Dorcas. Dorcas nodded towards the basket by the twine in the room.

'I'll start filling them, shall I?'

'Might as well. Although I'll soon get through them.' Dorcas pulled the basket toward her chair and sat down.

Letty picked up the twine, keeping the loose bit of thread in place with her thumb, pushing the twine through the hole in the middle and around the tooth. She got quicker as she went along but nothing of the speed of the older woman. When all the needles were filled, Letty took the basket and put it alongside the net.

'I know that won't keep you going for long, not at your pace, but every little helps.' She brushed her hands down her dress, the fibres stinging her hands, and wondered how on earth women did this day after day. She went to the kitchen and brought out the jar of petroleum jelly, rubbed it on her hands and passed it to Dorcas.

'Bet's granddaughter filled for both of us. It helps while the weather's fine, though what I'm to do when the weather turns, I don't know. I suppose I'll have to find someone. That'll be money going out of the household.'

Letty wouldn't be drawn. If she gave in now, there would be no way back.

'I'm bringing in more from the shop.'

Dorcas picked up her knitting and began to cast on with navy wool. 'Not if you're getting paid in needles, you're not.'

Letty put the lid on the jelly. She glanced at the nets laid against the wall, the sack of twine beside them. 'Would you like me to store the finished nets in the outhouse?'

'They can stay where they are. I'll have to drag 'em back of a Friday ready for collection. *More* work for me.'

Letty couldn't be bothered to reply. In the kitchen, she placed the jar on the sill. A line of blackbirds stared at her accusingly from the roof of the outhouse. The nets would be far better stored in there, but that wouldn't suit Dorcas. She sighed, Dorcas would not bend, but then neither would she.

11

They were out of bed at first light. Alec had slept the full six hours, but it was not enough. It never was. The lamps were lit and they struggled to their feet in the cramped space, rolling with the sway of the ship, squinting in the harsh light, and trudged bleary-eyed up the ladder and back on the deck they had left barely hours before. Alec emerged into the dim light, the spray washing over the deck as it dropped in and out of the swell. It would be eighteen hours on and six off now that they were in the fishing grounds and Alec was beginning to feel every one of them on his body.

The Old Man was in the wheelhouse, his pipe clamped in his teeth, his flat cap pushed back and he leaned out of the window and signalled to Puggy and Tosh, who were making their way to the trawl doors. Replies were nothing more than hand signals and nods, for the wind snatched the words away.

Alec, head down, began to operate the winch. There was a great clatter as the steel lines groaned into action and began to wind their way around the capstan as the net was hauled up through the trawl doors. The ship sliced through the waves, the bow high and then low into the water, surf crashing over the sides.

Puggy made a winding motion with his hand and the net appeared, tails and heads poking from every angle, the silver skins writhing and glinting in the early-morning light. Alec and Puggy were at the cod end now, the net suspended high above them. Ben stood ready, watching, waiting, his father looking down on him from the bridge. His eyes darted quickly back and forth. Alec remembered doing the same with his own father, seeking his approval and yet not wanting to be seen to be doing so. He reached forward, untying the cod end, and the net parted, fish cascading down onto the deck, tossing and wriggling, their mouths gaping, gills flapping. Alec drew the net away, retying the cod end, and with a shout and a wave of his arm, the winch raised the net. They set to, pushing it over the side, and turned back to deal with the fish.

Mouse and Tosh stood amid the catch, Ben too, all hands plunged among the fish. Alec stood with legs shoulder-width apart and bent down, took hold of a large cod, drew his knife along its belly. One swift slash and the guts were out and thrown over his shoulder. The livers were set aside; they would be rendered to oil and sold. For hours, they bent and stood, expertly gutting and tossing the fish into baskets which Ben hauled and sent down to the fish pounds.

The swell lifted them up and slapped them down as they worked, knives in hands, their legs rigid as they kept themselves upright, the ice-cold waves drenching them. The work was dirty and monotonous, their bare hands cold and they were glad when Cookie came on deck with tin mugs steaming with tea. Alec leaned against the wall of the funnel and sipped, the thick strong brew burning his throat as it went down. Puggy came beside him.

'Good haul so far?'

'Reckon Skipper has best part of four hundred kits already.' A kit being ten stone of fish, the skipper would be pleased.

Puggy supped from the tin mug, nodded. 'He has a nose for the fish, not all of 'em 'ave.'

Alec agreed. Some things couldn't be taught. It wasn't only the clouds and the depth of the water, the set of the wind or the clarity of the stars, nor was it the hours or the years afloat, it was something more, something intangible.

Puggy opened a packet of fags, passed him one and they turned their back on the wind and huddled together, cupping their hands. Puggy struck a match and they leaned closer to draw on their cigarettes then, fags alight, they turned back to work with it clamped in their teeth.

The net was hauled again and they prepared themselves for the onslaught. Tea came at a steady rate, and as the hours passed, they became more mechanical, tiredness conquered by repetition.

The light began to fade, the clouds ripping over the endless sky and Alec closed his eyes. His bones were tired, his shoulders ached, but he could only be grateful of the advances – that the winch saved so much back-breaking work, even though the work was no less dangerous or arduous.

Puggy stood up and spat over the side. The Old Man cast a steady eye over proceedings from the bridge, his hand steady on the wheel.

The rhythm of the work kept them going and if they could talk, they would, but mostly they kept their heads down and their backs bent, their thoughts drifting. What time was it? How many kits had they caught so far?

The deck almost clear, the net was hauled again. They stood knee-deep in writhing fish. Alec missed Letty, dreamt of her soft skin. He'd promised her so much, and he would make sure that she'd have it. The thought gave him energy and he set to again. He adjusted his feet, leaned back to ease the ache of his body. Once the holds were full, they would turn for home, and they wouldn't be reliant on a puff of wind.

They should've come to Grimsby sooner. His father didn't take risk enough and Robbie took too many. Instead of using a fish box to lean over the rail, his brother had leaped up onto it. The rail was slippery with water and as the *Stella Maris* had met the waves, he had lost his balance and went overboard. Alec would never forget the long journey home, nor the look on his mother's face when he gave her the news. He tried to block it out. It was his fault. He had promised his mother he would take care of Robbie, and he had not.

Beside him, Ben staggered, fell forward and Alec put out an arm and pulled him back. The boy was grey with exhaustion. His eyes were dead, his lids heavy and Alec mimed for him to go below for food. The boy shook his head, gave a sly glance to the wheelhouse. Alec gave him a nod of encouragement, an acknowledgement. They kept at it until the deck was clear and only then did Ben slip away.

Cookie came up with a fistful of mugs. Alec took two, walking down towards the foc'stle, the bow end of the ship, where he had seen the lad disappear. He found him with his back to the door, sobbing heavily. Ben drew his hand across his eyes and screwed his mouth. His eyes were sore and red from tears, as well as tiredness. Alec leaned next to him. 'Get this down ya throat.'

Ben reached out, his hands bloodied and raw with burst blisters and broken skin.

Alec recalled the pain of his first time handling the ropes, the gutting. He nodded towards his hands and leaned close. 'Piss on 'em, lad. It'll 'elp.'

The lad's chin wobbled and he tried to laugh it off, but snot fell from his nose and he wiped it away on his sleeve.

Alec patted him on the back. 'I can't say it gets any easier, but you gets used to it.' He showed his own hands, rough and scarred, reddened and weeping.

The boy nodded but tears threatened again, and he dipped his head, stuck his chin into his chest. His shoulders heaved, and Alec realised it wasn't the same. What did it matter if his own hands were rough and scarred as long as Letty didn't mind holding them. The lad wouldn't be sketching no more on this trip.

12

Towards the end of her first week, Letty had brought order to the shelves and rails of Parkers and turned her attention to the outside. She'd run her ideas past Norah and between them they'd worked out a way to implement the changes without Percy blowing a gasket.

Letty went out front with the tall stepladders. It was eight o'clock and the streets had long been busy with people going about their work. Ships landed their catch day and night and the lumpers – the local name for the dock workers – unloaded the fish after midnight. It was carted to the pontoon and the fish merchants gathered at six to bid for it. The market was almost ended and the sound of trains and wagons as the fish moved to all points of the country began to gather momentum. Setting the ladders in front of the window Letty pushed at them to test their stability, then went back inside for the dustpan and brush.

Norah followed her out. 'Do you need me to hold them steady for you, lass?'

Letty shook her head and began ascending the stepladder, the small brush in her hand. 'I'll be fine, they seem sturdy enough.' She put one hand along the ledge to steady herself as she reached up. 'Mind your head, there's plenty of muck up here.'

Norah went inside, twisting herself to peer through the glass door as months, if not years, of moss and guano dropped from the sill above the front of the shop.

Letty moved along, up and down the ladder until the shopfront was free of dirt, then swept the pavement, brushing the mess into a small heap which she scooped in a pail.

Gilbert Crowe, the owner of the tobacconists to the left of Parkers, came out of his shop, placed his bowler hat on top of his greasy black hair and looked up at the shop, then at her.

'Don't go doing too good a job.'

She emptied the last shovelful of dirt in the pail and stood upright. He leered at her, showing yellowed teeth beneath his black moustache.

'Why wouldn't I want to do that?'

'They'll be wanting more money when they come to sell.' He lifted his hat and walked past her, and she watched as he strutted down towards Gorton Street, her enthusiasm deflated. The Parkers hadn't mentioned anything about selling up. Letty stared at the pail. Was all this effort worth it?

She went inside for hot water and rags. Percy was leaning on the counter, chewing on a pencil, removing it only to add to the list on the sheet in front of him. He moved to one side as she came towards him but didn't look up. 'There'll be another day's daylight when you've cleaned that winder.'

'I'll take that as a compliment, shall I?'

'Now, now, don't go taking advantage of me good nature.'

She laughed. 'As if I could.' She noticed a smile play on his lips, but still he kept his head down as she went through the back to get rid of the dirt and fill her bucket with hot water. He had softened this past week, she hoped it was partly because he liked her but knew it was because takings were up. And it wasn't just the money, it was the people – new customers whose curiosity had got the better of them.

Norah was busy at the small table tallying the accounts ledgers and she looked up as Letty came in, her finger marking the line she was working on.

'Everything all right?'

'Don't let me disturb you, Norah. I'll be in and out for hot water. Would you rather I go round the back way?'

Norah shook her head. 'It'll take you all day if you do that. It'll probably take you all day as it is.'

'Would you rather I be in the shop?'

Norah wafted her free hand. 'Lord, no, Percy can manage, and he'll soon call me if he can't.'

The pan of water Letty had set to heat was hot and she took a cloth at the handles and poured it into a clean metal pail, added a handful of soda, refilled the pan and set it on the range to heat. Norah had already assembled an assortment of rags and she picked up a couple, tucking them into the waistband of her skirt and taking the pail through the shop. Up the ladder she went again, the pail in one hand. It was balanced on the top step and she began rubbing away at the signage. The dirt came away easily enough, but the water soon dirtied. It was as she had first thought – the paintwork wasn't in too poor a condition and the gold lettering of *Percy Parker – Ship's Outfitters* was intact. There was blistering and flaking around the edges of the board, but she had seen black paint in the back store and it would be easy enough to touch up. That was a job for another day. Today was preparation – of which cleaning the window was only the beginning.

People called up to her as she worked and she told them to go inside and see for themselves what changes were afoot at Parkers. Some did, much to her satisfaction. She noticed that all slowed their pace and looked to the shop, noticing it at last, and when her legs ached and her arms tired, she reminded herself of it. As she worked, she thought of Alec and briefly closed her eyes, imagining his kisses.

'Asleep on the job, Mrs Hardy?'

She snapped her eyes open, looked down. Anita was standing in front of her.

Letty came down the ladder, emptied the bucket into the gutter. Filthy water puddled among the cobbles.

'Where's Alfie?'

'I left him with Sally. Her lad's keeping an eye on him. They were making a cart. The lad found a couple of pram wheels, I had a bit o' rope. Y'know what kids are like.'

Letty nodded. She was about to ask Anita where she was going but thought better of it.

There was an awkward silence until Anita said, 'My Dan used to get his gear here. Bet old man Percy remembers him.'

'Why don't you go in and ask?'

Anita gave a small laugh, pulled her shawl about her shoulders. 'Another time.'

The door opened and Norah came out. She scowled at Anita. 'Off you go, can't you see the lass is working.'

'She was emptying her bucket.'

'Norah,' Letty's voice was sharp and Norah twisted to her. She hadn't meant it to be so but was shocked by Norah's attitude. She stepped beside Anita. 'This is my next-door neighbour, Anita.' There was another awkward silence.

Anita stepped onto the road, her feet muddied by the dirty water. 'I'll be on me way, anyways.' She gave Norah a tight smile and made her way towards the dock.

Norah watched her. 'No need to ask where she's going. And she's your neighbour?'

'She is.' Norah raised her eyebrows. 'Her husband was lost at sea.'

'Well, for that I'm very sorry,' Norah said, her voice softer now. 'But we don't want girls like her standing outside.'

Norah went back inside the shop and Letty sat on the bottom sill of the shopfront, her energy drained like the dirty water that was finding its way along the gutter. People passed by, but she didn't look up, her thoughts drifting to her mother, scrubbing the stone floors of the farmhouse on her hands and knees, children about her feet, Susie in the highchair with a crust in her chubby hands and golden yolk about her face. Father would be in the yard with the cows or out in the fields with the lads. Letty closed her eyes, trying to conjure up images of the golden sunshine and the way the wheat shimmered in the breeze. Her mother had sent a letter by return, keeping her up to date with news on the farm and in the village. Her eldest sister was expecting again, her younger brother walking out with a girl Letty went to school with. It was all so very far away, and she longed for it now, more than she longed for Alec's embrace. A hooter screamed out, another called in answer and she got to her feet just as Norah came out with another bucket refreshed with clean water, and placed it by Letty's feet. She was uneasy, screwing up her mouth, searching for the right words.

'I'm sorry if I upset you.' Letty shook her head, but Norah held up the flat of her hand. 'I know I did. I could tell by your face that I had.' Letty sighed, her mother said her face would always get her into trouble. 'You're a kind lass, and you're honest. I wouldn't want you to be taken advantage of. I hope you don't think that about me and Percy.'

Letty was aghast. 'I would *never* think that. You've been kindness itself.' Letty took a rag from her belt. 'And I did rather force myself upon you.'

Norah laughed. 'That you did, I can't deny it.' She put her hand on Letty's arm. 'I'm very glad you did.' She waited, then said. 'I'm sorry I was rude about your neighbour.'

'She's a nice girl. She has a little boy, Alfie, and she loves him dearly,' Letty explained, picking up the pail. 'Life played her a bad hand.'

Norah nodded, and went back into the shop.

Copious amounts of hot water later, Letty took a clean chamois leather and began to buff the window. Her muscles were tired now, but she gained energy from the way the light bounced off the glass. It was a shame it only showed more clearly the jumble that was the present display. That was her next job.

Letty stood on the pavement opposite *Percy Parker – Ship's Outfitters* and waited. The door to the shop opened and Norah half pushed Percy out of it and with a flick of her hand directed him across the road to where Letty stood, her hands clasped in front of her. Percy begrudgingly came beside her.

'What am I supposed to be looking at?'

'The window.'

He gave it a cursory glance. 'Looks clean.'

He made to go back over the road, but she caught hold of his arm and gently but firmly pulled him back.

'Is that all?'

He sighed. 'Lass, you've worked hard, no doubt about that – for which you've been paid. But it's a winder. A clean winder, thanks to you, but the same winder as been there since the day we bought it.'

'And the same stock too, I shouldn't wonder.'

'You cheeky mare.'

'Look again,' she insisted.

People walked past them. A chap touched his cap "Ow do, Percy.'

Percy acknowledged the greeting, distracted for a moment, looked back at the window, scratched his head. He rubbed at his bristly chin, lifted his glasses to the top of his head then put them back on the bridge of his nose. He threw up his hands. 'Tell an old man what he's meant to be looking at.'

'It's not so much the window as the people, Percy. Look again.' He looked at her, then back to the street. 'Lots of people pass by but they don't stop,' she said. 'They know what's in that window so they don't bother to look, why would they?'

'Saves 'em time then, don't it.'

Letty shook her head. 'But we want them to stop, Percy. We want them to want to come in and buy. When we had the market stall, we had to get people to buy from us and not from anyone else.'

'Aye, well, folks know what I sell. I've sold the same stuff for years.' He puffed out his chest.

'But you're not catching any new fish, and the old fish are swimming by. I want to hook them and reel them in to you, not Wiltshire's or the Coal, Salt and Tanning Company.'

'I can't compete with them, lass.'

This wasn't going as she had planned. The road cleared and he stepped out to cross it. Letty hurried in front of him, walking backwards.

'I can do so much more. If you'll let me.'

He had one hand on the door.

'I'm going to cover the window with newspaper,' she blurted out.

He turned and frowned at her. "Ang on. So, you spent all day cleaning the winder, and very nice it looks too, granted. And now you want to cover it with newspaper?'

'To build interest. We want to make people stop, then tempt them inside.'

'By blacking out me ruddy winders?' His voice was loud and people turned to see if there was going to be trouble. Percy scowled at them and they moved on.

Letty smiled. 'That was perfect, Percy. I couldn't have demonstrated it better myself. People are nosey – if they think something is going on, they'll want to find out what it is.' She thought of how the crowd had surged forward when they thought there was going to be a fight at Hammonds' office. She was due there later this afternoon so she needed to get Percy's agreement as quickly as she could. She stood in front of the door, barring his way. 'It's a fine-looking widow, Percy. It must have been a proud day when you saw your name written over it.'

'Aye, it were.' He pursed his lips. 'You're a crafty lass and no mistake.'

'But my intentions are good.'

He sighed. 'I know that. But it will be the thing that finishes us off. People will think we're shut for good.'

Gosh, he was a tough nut to crack, but she wouldn't give in so easily. 'Please. Give me a chance. It'll take me an hour and if you don't like it, I'll take it down. Immediately.'

He folded his arms across his chest, the buttons straining at his belly. He made shapes with his mouth, mulling it over. She waited, hopeful.

Norah opened the door and Percy almost fell inside.

'Well?' she asked.

Percy frowned, muttering under his breath. 'I might o' guessed you two was in cahoots.'

Norah raised her eyebrows, looked to Letty, then to Percy and back again. Behind her, a man leaned on the counter, tapping a coin. Percy lifted his head to him.

'An hour,' he said, 'then we'll see.'

Letty stood on tiptoe and kissed his cheek.

He rubbed at it and said, 'Gerrorf,' seeking refuge with his customer.

Norah handed her a pot of paste and pointed to the pile of old newspapers by the door. Letty stood on the small platform that constituted the window area and set to work quickly in case Percy changed his mind.

When she was finished, she went outside. Percy followed her out.

She had taken some black paint and lining paper and written COMING SOON and OPEN AS USUAL and plastered them in the centre of the window, the rest was blocked with pages from the local paper, apart from a small gap on one side. Percy pointed to it. 'You've missed a bit.'

'No, I haven't.'

He put his fists to his hips. 'Have ya gone blind as well as daft?' He pointed to the gap.

She took his hand and once the street was clear took him over the road. They stood where they had stood only an hour before.

'Watch,' she instructed.

A man with a bag across his shoulders, slowed as he passed the window, stopped, read the signs, his head moving from left to right, looked up at the name across the window, then down again. He leaned on the glass at the gap between the newspapers, a hand across his brow, peering into the shop. He looked up again and walked on. A few seconds later, a couple did the same, the man releasing his arm from the woman's shoulder while she stood on tiptoes to peer in the gap. She stood back so the man could get a look.

'Well, I'll be a monkey's uncle,' Percy muttered.

Letty laughed. 'The paper can stay?'

He nodded, then shook his head gently from side to side, his bewilderment clear.

'I need to collect my man's pay, but I'll be back early tomorrow morning and give them something to look at when the paper comes off.'

They walked back across the road and this time Percy held open the door and stood back to let her pass and Letty stepped into the shop feeling like the Queen of Sheba.

13

The queue at Hammonds snaked downstairs and onto the street and Letty leaned against the wall as she waited her turn. The sun was on her face and she chatted to people either side of her to while away the time. The queue moved quickly, and she soon found herself in front of Perkins. He glared at her, but she smiled back.

'Hello, Mr Perkins,' she said, not waiting for him to answer. 'Hardy, the *Black Prince*.'

He didn't run his finger down the columns as he had done the week before but placed his hands on the desk either side of the ledger, then said in a loud voice, 'Are you trying to swindle the firm, Mrs Hardy?'

She felt the heat rise in her cheeks and a cold shiver snaked the length of her spine. Had something happened to Alec?

'Is something wrong?' She gripped the counter, her legs suddenly weak.

He drummed his fingers on the ledger growing impatient. The man next to him looked away from her.

'The money has been taken.' Perkins scrutinised her over his spectacles. 'There's a queue. Now move along.'

Letty couldn't find her tongue, unable to make sense of things. 'There's been some sort of mistake. I... I,' she stammered.

People were muttering, growing restless, and the man behind her leaned over her shoulder. She felt the weight of him as he pressed against her.

'What's going on, Perkins? Give the lass her money.'

Perkins cleared his throat. 'The money has been taken. Mrs Hardy came to collect it herself.'

'Mrs Hardy?' she said through gritted teeth.

Perkins nodded. 'Mrs Hardy. Senior.' He ran his finger quickly down the ledger, swivelled it to show the signature.

Letty nodded, moved away. Dorcas. Dorcas who had said she wouldn't come onto to the docks until her son could bring her himself. Dorcas who hadn't said a word about it before she'd left that morning.

Letty marched down the stairs, her legs shaking with effort. On the street, everything seemed too loud and too fast; wagons hurtled past, bicycles charged like horses down towards the railway line, trains sounding like rumbles of thunder. She hurried along Fish Dock Road, head down, slipping her shoulders this way and that as people passed, her fists clenched at her sides. The old bitch. The sly old bitch. She had wasted her time, just as she was wasting her time with the Parkers' window if they were going to sell up. What a fool she was.

She didn't look up, couldn't bear to see her surroundings, the grey, the filth and the smell. She hurried on, blinded by fury, fighting back the tears, her cheeks burning with shame. Without lifting her head, she stepped out onto the road, then felt herself suddenly dragged back. Someone had caught hold of her collar. She stumbled, losing her footing, and lashed out with her arms, only to have a horse miss her by inches. Whoever it was gripped her by the arms and held her firmly until she had gained her stability. Sensing she had, the hands relaxed their hold and she turned to discover the new port missioner Colin Wilson, his face tight with concern.

'I'm sorry if I hurt you. You didn't seem to be looking where you were going.' He let her go, stepping back, and she brushed her hands down her sleeves, embarrassed at her own stupidity. Her fury had lessened only because of the fear of what might have happened if he hadn't been there. She was trembling violently. She tried to speak, but although she opened her mouth words didn't come. He took her by the elbow and gently guided her away from the people who were rushing past to make the junction before the railway crossing gates were swung into place.

'My mind was elsewhere. It was stupid of me.' Letty placed her hand to her chest to calm herself, her breath coming in short bursts. People were crowding about her now and he put out a hand.

'Give her some space.' He turned to her, and said kindly, 'Come to the mission. You can sit down, gather yourself.'

She nodded, grateful, and he guided her towards the building that took up the entire corner of Riby Square and Orwell Street, pushing open the dark doors with his free hand, using the other to steady her. It felt odd, another man's hand on her. She wanted him to release it but felt it impolite to ask him to let go.

He led her to a bentwood chair in the reception hall and she sat down. There was a bench the other side of the door where two men were waiting: one old, the worse for drink, the other a fresh-faced boy with pink cheeks who couldn't have been more than twelve. It was cool inside, the chequered floor tiles patched with light that spilled in through the large windows on either side of the entrance door. She had seen the mission building only in passing, the flag flying high on the rooftop, men traipsing in and out no matter the time of day.

'Wait there,' the missioner said. 'I'll get you some sweet tea.'

A man leaned at the reception desk, clasping his elbows, talking to the man in uniform. He moved aside to let the missioner pass. Mr Wilson said something to the man, patted his shoulder, exchanged pleasantries, then disappeared.

Letty was suddenly tired.

The doors to the right of the reception desk opened and two women bustled out. Letty stared down at the floor. Two navy blue shoes appeared in her eyeline.

'Mrs Hardy.'

She looked up. It was the young woman from the Bethel last Sunday, Alice Wiltshire's niece.

'Miss Evans.' She got to her feet.

Ruth Evans was with an older woman, her beady green eyes like the glass alleys she had seen the boys play with. She was dressed in an expensive coat and the fur collar about her face softened her sharp features.

'How lovely to see you, but such a pity. You're too late.'

Letty was confused.

Ruth tilted her head. 'You came for our meeting?'

Embarrassed, Letty was about to explain, when the missioner came to her rescue again, this time carrying a small tray. He placed it on the reception counter.

'Ladies.' He smiled at them, then gave his attention to Letty. 'How are you feeling, Mrs Hardy?'

The two women looked to her again and she felt her cheeks redden with heat. 'I'm afraid I was rather silly and almost walked out in front of a horse and cart. Would've done if Mr Wilson had not pulled me back.'

Ruth's blue eyes shone with admiration for the missioner.

The older woman insisted that Letty take a seat. 'What a dreadful shock. But lucky for you Mr Wilson was to hand. Quite the hero.' There was a twinkle in her eye as she spoke, revealing her observation of Ruth's adoration. If the missioner noticed, he didn't show it and handed Letty the tea, the sturdy white cup rattling on the saucer as she took hold of it with shaking hands. She took a sip, embarrassed that they were watching her.

'Better?' he asked.

Letty nodded, sipped again, the sweetness reviving her somewhat.

Ruth gave the missioner a sweet smile. 'I had hoped Mrs Hardy had come to join us.'

Letty paled.

The missioner shook his head. 'Poor Mrs Hardy, I brought her here for refuge and she'll think I'm looking for recruits.'

'Well, aren't you?' The older woman sat down next to Letty and put out her gloved hand. 'Mrs Frampton.' Letty's hands were red and sore from cleaning and ashamed, she held out her right hand. The woman's grip was firm. 'We could do with a few bright young things among our ranks.'

Letty sat up, feeling somewhat revived by Mrs Frampton's assessment of her.

'Mrs Hardy is only just arrived in town, Aunt Helen.'

Helen Frampton nodded, assessing Letty with piercing intensity.

Ruth continued. 'Aunt Alice introduced us on Sunday at the Bethel. I believe you're working at Parkers on Henderson Street?'

Letty nodded, amazed that a woman of Miss Evans' standing would remember her.

'Is that so?' Mrs Frampton got to her feet. 'All the more reason for you to join us. There is much work to be done among the fishing community. You seem to me to be exactly the kind of woman we need.'

'You must forgive my aunt.' Ruth glared piercingly at Mrs Frampton, who simply shrugged her shoulders. 'Mrs Hardy has had a shock, Aunt Helen.'

'And now she's recovered.' She held Letty with a determined gaze. 'We all need to help each other, isn't that right, Mrs...'

Amused, Letty got to her feet. This woman recognised her inner steel even if she had forgotten it momentarily. 'Hardy. It's Letty Hardy.' She handed the cup and saucer to Colin, who replaced it on the tray and turned back to the ladies. 'Unless it coincides with my husband being home, I'll come along.'

Helen Frampton smiled with satisfaction and turned to leave. The two women said their goodbyes and made their way to the door. One of the female staff held it open for them, bobbed a small curtsey as they left. She stared over at Letty. Letty smiled. The woman gave a slight nod of acknowledgement and disappeared through the door that led further into the mission. Letty looked about for her bag, slipped it over her arm. The missioner came beside her.

'Do you feel sufficiently recovered?'

She replied that she did. 'You've been so kind. The ladies too.' They watched through the window as Ruth Evans and her aunt got into a car outside the building. Their chauffeur closed the door behind them and walked round to the driver's side. 'Although I have no idea why they should be interested in me.'

The missioner gave a half-smile. 'Perhaps like recognises like. They are wealthy but not the landed gentry, Mrs Hardy. Mr Frampton made his money in newspapers and advertising. Her brother, Ruth's father, was, and is, a farmer. He invested in fish, then moved into shipping. Self-made men. Miss Evans lost her mother when she was a small child and so takes on the good work her mother would do were she alive. They obviously see something in you that's familiar to them.' The car moved off and they turned away from the window. 'Are you sure you are quite recovered?' he asked again, as people came and went. The woman who had earlier held open the door came past and called goodbye to the men on the reception desk. She slowed by the missioner. 'Thank you, for your work today, Molly.' She nodded to Letty. Did she know her? Letty couldn't place her face.

Molly opened the door, fiddled with something in her basket.

'I could walk you home,' he offered, and Letty blushed, embarrassed by his attention.

'I've already taken up far too much of your time.' Flustered, she waved a hand. 'I'll be perfectly fine.'

He walked with her to the door and Molly moved quickly and disappeared out into the street. Letty followed her soon after, taking her time, careful as she crossed roads, calmer now, her anger blunted.

When she opened the door to the house, the nets had been collected and small fibres, the only residue, danced in the light. Letty went through to the kitchen. The back door was open and Dorcas came back holding an enamel bowl. She didn't look at Letty and it was clear she was bracing herself for an argument. She would be disappointed.

Letty poured herself a cup of water and said pleasantly, 'I wish you'd told me you were going onto the docks today. For Alec's pay.'

Dorcas placed the bowl on the side.

'Did I need to? I didn't think you'd be able to leave your position at the shop.' Dorcas put a plate on the table covered with another plate. 'I've had mine.'

Letty removed the lid. Gammon hock and potatoes. A peace offering? She couldn't be sure.

'I waited in line when I had no need.'

Dorcas frantically scrubbed at a pan.

Letty picked up her knife and fork. 'Shall I take it that you will collect it each week?'

'Might as well,' Dorcas said, flatly.

Letty let out a long sigh, stabbed at a piece of meat. She must choose her battles wisely. This, she decided, was not one of them.

14

It had taken three days to prepare the window. Last Friday, Letty had borrowed a mannequin from Alice at Wiltshire's and carried it naked under her arm. That had caught attention, as was intended, and she'd endured the good-natured quips as she went the long way round to Parkers. Now it was Thursday and her third week working at Parkers. Percy and Norah waited on the narrow pavement in the cool morning air while Letty removed the newspaper and rubbed at the window to clear away the glue. When she finished, she came out and stood beside them. The sun had not yet reached over the rooftops to shed its light on the window but all the better. Letty had painted the backboard navy blue and the platform the same colour. On the right-hand side, she'd painted the points of the compass in white, four small arrowheads of gold at north, south, east and west. The mannequin was set to the left and had been dressed in thick pants, a heavy cream sweater and rubber boots, a muffler at his neck, a flat cap on his head. Hooks had been secured to the ceiling, from which was suspended a ship's wheel, borrowed from Pattersons' shipwrights. The mannequin's hands were adjusted to give the impression he was in the wheelhouse. Displayed about the rest of the window were ropes and pails, knives and lines so that as well as exhibiting the wares of *Percy Parker – Ship's Outfitters*, it also told a story.

Norah and Percy were silent, and Letty felt a flash of disappointment.

She sighed. 'It won't take me long to put it back to how it was.'

Norah shook her head. Letty could see her swallow hard, her mouth open, close. Percy took a crumpled handkerchief from his pocket, rubbed at his face, then his glasses, and put them back on again.

'Where did you get that ruddy wheel from? 'Ow come I didn't see you bring that in?'

'You were through the back. I borrowed it from Pattersons. They were glad to help, it's free advertising for them. Mr Patterson sends his regards.'

Percy stared at her, then looked at his feet. Norah still hadn't spoken.

Two men cycling abreast of each other stopped outside the window, their feet to the ground, blocking their view.

'You don't like it, do you?' Letty asked.

Norah squeezed her arm. 'Oh, lass. You've done us proud, you really have. I could never've imagined...'

More people slowed their pace and looked in the window, waiting and chatting. It was already causing a stir. Norah gave Percy a nudge.

'It can stay as it is,' he said, and walked back into the shop.

Two of the men gathered outside followed him in.

Norah turned to Letty. 'He's overcome. As am I.' She took Letty's hand and tucked it under her arm. 'All our dreams were wrapped in that shop. Percy had given up on it long ago and we were just tumbling along from day to day. And then you came along with all your ideas – and your energy. It's all a little too much for him. I rather think it is for me.'

They waited a little while longer and watched people come and go, nodding their heads, talking, pointing, and for the whole time, Norah didn't let go of Letty's hand. It humbled her to feel she had helped in some small way, and yet she felt they'd given her so much. They'd trusted her for a start, and they had faith in her, which was more than Dorcas had.

Inside the shop, Percy was holding forth and the two men lifted their caps as Norah and Letty came in and headed through to the back. Percy was describing how he had come up with the idea for the window and Norah stopped, was just about to correct him, but Letty shook her head.

'Don't. It's good to see him so bright and cheery.'

They watched him, his chest puffed out, holding court in his kingdom, and left him to enjoy it.

Gratifyingly, the shop was busier than it had been for years according to Norah, and even if some folk came in and spent pennies to disguise their curiosity, word was getting around.

Letty was in the middle of serving when a customer came into the shop and shouted across to her, '*Black Prince* is in dock, lass. Thought you'd want to know.'

For a moment, she forgot where she was, her thoughts immediately turning to Alec. The aching loneliness that clung to her dissipated and she thought only of being held by him.

The man she was serving gave a little cough and she quickly turned to the till, rang in the sum and gave him his change.

Percy was at the end of the counter yarning to the postman, who had called in after delivering a parcel across the street. He brought his conversation to an abrupt stop.

'You'll be wanting to be off, lass.'

She twisted to look at the clock.

Percy shook his head. 'Never mind that.'

She undid her apron and kissed his cheek. He became flustered and batted her away with his hand.

'Now, don't go thinking I'm going all soft.'

She called through to Norah that she was leaving and collected her coat and hat, barely able to fasten her hatpin such was her excitement.

Norah caught hold of her hand. 'Enjoy your time, lass. I bless the day you walked into our shop, bold as you like, and took Percy in hand. I've not seen him so happy in years.'

'Percy said he would take over serving,' she said as Norah followed her back into the shop to find two customers waiting. 'Although he's not in much of a rush.'

Norah gave a little laugh. 'He never was. It's the talking he's good at, but that's what people like.' She placed her palm on Letty's back and held it there. 'He's more like his old self and for that I can never thank you enough. Now, go, find your man.'

15

Letty tore down the street, the wind at her heels, and hurried along the dockside, looking up at the bows, searching for the *Black Prince*. Men streamed towards her, their kitbags across their shoulders, and she weaved through them, searching for Alec.

When she found the ship, she craned her neck; men were moving about on the deck and she stepped back a little, stood on her tiptoes, searching, waiting. She called out.

A man with dark curly hair leaned over the rail, gave her a quick glance, disappeared. Three faces peered down at her and one of them broke into a broad smile, a smile she'd yearned for. He pointed to the other side of the bow, then vanished from view. Within seconds, he reappeared, his kitbag across his back, and shinned down the ladder, his feet barely touching the rungs. Once he was on solid ground, she went to him. He dropped his bag, caught hold of her, gripping her arms, kissing her hard on the mouth. She ignored the ribald remarks, the nudges, the whistles, she didn't care. She felt him stretch out one arm as if to bat away the coarse comments. He pulled away a little, rested his forehead on hers, stared into her eyes.

'What a sight for sore eyes you are.'

A man punched him on the shoulder. 'Wait till yer get 'er 'ome.'

Alec simply smiled and it was as if the sun had come out from behind the cloud. He looked over her shoulder. 'Is Mother with yer?'

Letty shook her head. For one sweet moment she had forgotten Dorcas.

Alec took hold of her hand. His skin was rough, but it was a gentle hand that wrapped itself around her waist and held her close. 'Have you been all right, you and her.'

'I've been fine.' She didn't want to mar the precious hours with what was past. She and Dorcas would work it out eventually. Dorcas's animosity had subdued somewhat since the episode about collecting Alec's pay. Not that things were much better – but it hadn't got any worse. 'I got a job.'

They began to walk down towards Gorton Street. It was late afternoon and the dock was quietening down ready for the early hours when the fish would be landed.

'Mother teaching you to braid?'

'No.' Letty grinned, guiding him down Henderson Street. 'In Percy Parker's. It's a ship's outfitters. Been here years.' She told him of Percy and Norah, that she had organised the shop. The plans she had.

'You've been the new broom then.'

'More than that.' She made him stop outside the shop.

'Looks grand,' he said, giving it a quick glimpse and made to walk on. She tugged him back.

'I did that; the window.'

He gave a cursory glance. 'It looks marvellous.' He wasn't really paying attention, he was too busy looking at her hair, her eyes, her face and she grinned.

'You're not interested, are you?'

He nodded, shook his head almost immediately. 'Only in you. Why would I want to look at a window?'

She reached up and touched his face. 'Come and say hello?'

He clutched at her hand. 'Not today, Letty. Let's go home. It's what I've longed for.'

* * *

Dorcas was sitting in the kitchen braiding when they got back to the house. As soon as the door opened, his mother secured the needle in the net and went to greet him. He dropped his bag in the doorway and bent down and wrapped his arms about her, kissing her cheek.

'A good trip, lad?'

He shrugged. 'Skipper thinks we might have hit the market right, but who knows.'

Letty slipped behind them, glad she and Alec had shared precious time as they walked home. She prepared the meal, allowing mother and son to discuss his first trip on the *Black Prince*. The most part of it was gobbledy-gook, but she paid close attention, working out what each unfamiliar fishing term might mean. These things would be learned eventually, but as it was, she could only listen, the outsider.

Dorcas and Alec were talking about his settling money. The share fishermen were paid a wage by the owners, an allotment given each week to the wives and mothers. Settling money was what was left of the profit once all costs were taken out. If the ship landed its catch when fish was in short supply, the price would be high – a glut and it would fall. Many was the time men could end up owing the owners money. She knew that much from chatting to customers when they came into Parkers.

Alec's canvas kitbag was taken to the yard and emptied, ready to be washed come the morning, and after their meal, all three settled by the fire. Dorcas picked up her knitting and Letty sat on Alec's knee, his arm about her. Talk of the shop was of no interest to either mother or son; Dorcas talked of the neighbours, he of the crew. He told them of young Ben, the skipper's lad, and his talent for drawing, of the other men, the ship and how it handled, and Letty listened as best she could, longing for the moment they could go to bed. She felt time was leaking away. Alec would be ashore only forty-eight hours, a few more if she was lucky. They might only have two nights together. She longed to feel his skin, feel his arms about her, to be alone, just the two of them.

As soon as was polite, they went upstairs. They undressed and she laid in his arms scarcely daring to breathe, anxious of the noise they would make. The bed squeaked and they tensed, and then he didn't care – and neither did she.

* * *

In the morning, she untangled herself from his arms and left him sleeping. Dorcas was already downstairs, water heating on the stove, and she took a cloth to the handle and went outside into the yard. Letty followed her. The tub was full and Alec's clothing lay in a heap on the ground. His trousers were crusted with slime and guts, his sweater and obb socks likewise and the stench made her retch even though they were outside. Dorcas dropped them into the water and began agitating them with the dolly. Letty picked up the empty pan ready to refill it.

'I should be doing this,' she said, feeling she'd begun the day wrong-footed.

'I thought I'd make a start.' Dorcas looked up at the sky, which was thick with cloud. 'It'll be dry enough and the wind will help.'

'Thank you.'

The older woman nodded, and Letty began to feel that perhaps they could indeed resolve their differences. Working together with Alec as their focus had made Dorcas more amenable.

Letty took the large pan. 'I'll get water for the rinsing.'

Out in the yard, she found Bet at the pump. 'Dorcas's lad's back then?'

Letty nodded. 'Dorcas's lad', not 'your husband'.

Bet got her water and stood back, watching Letty work the pump.

'I hear yer was with missioner, t'other day.' Her tone was accusing.

Letty ignored her, filled the pan. Bet waited for an answer.

Letty stopped pumping, looked Bet in the eye. 'I was *at* the mission,' she corrected, then picked up the pan and returned to the house.

Back in the kitchen, she placed the kettle to boil and went to join Dorcas. The two of them scrubbed at Alec's clothing, Letty going back and forth for fresh water. By the time Alec came to join them, it had been through the mangle and was pegged out on the line that ran from the wall to the coal store.

Letty cooked bacon and eggs and the three of them sat down to eat. When they'd finished, Letty made a fresh pot of tea.

'I fancy I'll be in for a fair bit with me settling money,' Alec said, pushing away from the table. 'I thought we'd go to the theatre tonight or the picture house.' He glanced across to Letty, and she knew from his look what he was going to say next. 'All three of us.' It was only fair, and she had to remember that Dorcas loved him too.

'That would be grand,' Letty answered. 'There's the picture palace on Kent Street and the Tivoli on Duncombe Street. I noticed they had a variety bill.'

'You choose, Mother.'

Dorcas smiled; it was the first time Letty had seen her happy since they'd left Lowestoft. 'The Tivoli would be a real treat.'

'Tivoli it is then. Although I have a fancy that Let might have wanted to get a peek at Rudolph Valentino.' He tore a tea towel from the side and wrapped it around his head. Letty laughed and he reached out and pulled her to him, kissed her.

'That's all make-believe,' Dorcas said, getting to her feet, her hands pressing on the table. 'Now then, what would you like for your tea before we go out tonight? Suet pudding?'

Letty moved away from him, taking hold of his mug, his plate, and Alec stretched out his legs.

'I've been dreaming about your suet pudding for three weeks, Mother.'

Dorcas huffed. 'Aye, and other things.' She glanced to Letty.

He grinned at her. 'You know me far too well, Mother.' He got up. 'I'll go down and get me settlin', have a quick pint with the lads. While I'm there, I'll see how I go about sitting for me skipper's ticket. I might have to be away to Hull for it.'

'Then you'll need to put some of your settlin' money by while you take it. You'll not be earning for a week or two while you do that, and the landlord will still want his rent. I'll not have you use what we get from the sale of the *Stella Maris*.'

He put his hand on her shoulder. 'I won't. Shan't need to. I've done well getting with Skipper o' the *Black Prince* and wi' you and Letty here bringing money in, we'll do all right.' He grinned at her. 'Have you seen Parkers' window, Mother, what Letty did?'

Dorcas put her hand to her hip. 'I've not had time.' Letty caught a hint of something in her expression, a softening. Was it regret? 'I'll perhaps go down later.'

'Aye, we'll all go. You can take a look at the *Black Prince* afore she sails.'

He winked at Letty, and she smiled at him, but it only brought home how brief his time ashore was.

He turned back to his mother. 'Speaking of the *Stella*, have you heard anything from Uncle Eric, or the solicitor? He had someone interested before we left Lowestoft. It 'ud be nice to have the cash out of her.'

His mother opened the back door and checked the sky. Over her shoulder, Letty could see Alec's sweater dripping water, puddles on the dusty ground below it. 'Nothing yet.' Dorcas bent down and stuck the wedge under the bottom of the door. 'Let's hope we get word soon.'

Alec picked up his cap and Letty walked with him to the door. Alfie was sat on his doorstep.

'Hullo, lad.'

The boy looked up, grinned.

'All right, Alfie?' Letty said, touching Alec's neckerchief for the need of touching him as much as she could.

Laughter drifted out from the upstairs window and Alec tilted his head.

'Don't ask,' Letty said quietly. She'd had little time to talk of neighbours and Dorcas's telling would not be the same as hers.

Alec pulled a face. 'We won't be here long, lass. Better things ahead of us.'

* * *

The rest of the day revolved around Alec: his clothes, his food, his drink. Letty filled a jug with beer from the alehouse and bought meat and suet from the butchers on Freeman Street. Dorcas made the pudding and the afternoon passed quietly. When Alec's sea gear was dry, it was pressed and folded, ready for his departure, and Letty sat in the chair filling needles, watching the clock and waiting for Alec. Dorcas asked about her work at Parkers and Letty began to wonder that they couldn't find a way to exist happily together after all.

16

The queue for the settling was short and Alec pushed the notes and coins into his pocket. He shook hands with Skipper Harris.

'You'll sailing with us ag'in? Badger's leg i'nt healed and he'll be more of a hindrance than help if he makes this trip.'

Alec pushed up his cap. 'That'd suit me fine, Skipper. Although I feel for Badger. He'll not be earning.'

'He'll manage. If his missus has looked after what he's earned these past months.'

Alec was only too thankful that Letty was good with money; many a marriage had fallen apart for lack of it. On his way to Hammonds' office, he'd stopped to admire the window display at Parkers. It was eye-catching, like Letty. He'd been walking through the market when he had first laid eyes on Letty Palmer. A crowd had gathered, and he'd stopped, his attention caught by banter and good-hearted laughter. He'd pushed his way through to the front and watched her give as good as she got, all the time urging people to buy. The lass was fearless and had countered any remarks with her quick wit. She had spirit, and he'd needed a lass with spirit to make the move to Grimsby.

'You'll come an' 'ave a jar with us, Alec?' Skipper Harris slapped him on the back, jolting him from his thoughts.

'Aye, I will.'

They walked down to the Albion and had a pint, then moved to the Lincoln Arms. It was good to sup with company, the ground not moving, the view from the window fixed. The talk was easy and the room grew warmer as men came in from other ships, joking and jostling and trying to outdo each other with who'd had the best – or worst – trip. Tosh joined them and, shortly after, in rolled Puggy and Mouse. After another pint or two, they left and moved on to the Red Lion, closer to home. A ruddy-faced man staggered towards their table.

'Good trip, Michael?' Skipper asked as the man swayed unsteadily.

'Ruddy awful.'

Skipper shouted across to the barmaid. 'Stick a pint in for Michael, Mary.'

The woman raised her hand in answer, her large bosom fighting to escape from the tight blouse she wore. Her lips and cheeks were red with rouge as well as from the heat. The noise grew as the men drank. Alec drained his glass.

'Let me get you a pint in, Skipper.' Alec got up, somewhat unsteady, and ordered a round over the bar. As they were pulled, he passed them across to the lads at the table, scanning the room as he did so. He recognised the woman who was sat at the table in the corner as his next-door neighbour. She was leaning close, her lips almost touching her companion's ear, and, from the movement of her arm, grappling with his tackle under the table. He wondered where the boy was. Poor little beggar. Probably still sitting on that ruddy doorstep.

Mary placed the last pint down in front of him. The gold charms on her bracelet jangled to catch his attention and he drew coins from his pocket and handed them over. He supped the pint, wiped the cream from his lip with the back of his hand and went back to his seat.

The doors swung open and back as men came and went. Mouse got up abruptly, mumbled a goodbye and left them to it. Alec took his place next to Tosh.

'He'll be braver for a jar or two.'

'Whadda yer reckon on his missus being there?' Alec asked.

'Oh, she'll be there all right. She'll take the money off him no problem. Poor bastard.'

Alec drank back his pint. 'And I'll be back to mine. I'm teking the lass and me mother to the Tivoli.'

Puggy put his hand on his shoulder and pushed him back in his seat. 'Not yet, you're not. Get that down yer neck.' He placed another pint in front of him.

Alec licked his lips. He'd already stayed longer than intended. He took a sup. Tosh smacked him between the shoulders and he spluttered, the beer sloshing over the glass and down his hand. Someone reached across and opened the window. The smoke lay in a cloud above his head, rising up to the nicotine-tinted ceiling, and he pulled off his cap, loosened his neckerchief and leaned back against the seat. One more wouldn't hurt.

* * *

Letty paced about the small front room, peeking out of the curtain whenever she heard movement. Dorcas had said not to fuss, that Alec would be home shortly – but shortly had come and gone. She was done with adding water to the steamer. The suet would be ruined. She took the pan off the stove and Dorcas got the plates from the warmer.

'We might as well have ours.' Dorcas started ladling the food on three plates. When she was done, she placed another plate on top of Alec's and put it in the warmer. As she did so, Letty heard voices in the courtyard. She got up, glancing at the clock. They wouldn't make the first house, they would have to wait for the second. Irritation flashed and she pushed it down again.

Letty opened the door and saw Anita and a man the worse for drink staggering unsteadily towards her. Anita pushed the man through the door to her house. She was red-cheeked and Letty caught a waft of ale and cigarette smoke.

'Have you seen Alec on your way home?' Letty asked.

'In the Red Lion,' Anita answered. 'Still there, I shouldn't wonder.'

The man reached out and pulled her inside and the door banged shut.

Letty remained on the doorstep, trying to hold back the rage that was coming up from her stomach and into her mouth. Alec hadn't given her a thought. His empty promise of the theatre had been drowned in beer. She pictured him in the pub, laughing and joking with his crew mates, and she closed the door, leaned her back against it, trying to tame her anger.

Dorcas called out, 'Food's on the table.'

In the kitchen, Dorcas had started without her. Letty sat down, stared at her food. Dorcas's jaw clicked as she chewed and slurped and it irritated. Letty picked up her fork, stabbed at a chunk of meat, tried to eat, couldn't, let her fork drop.

Dorcas stared at her. 'What's got into you?'

'Alec's still in the pub.'

It didn't seem to bother her mother-in-law. 'He'll be back when he's ready.' She carried on eating, mopped her gravy with a chunk of bread, cleared her plate.

Letty felt her anger build. Alec had been with his men for three weeks. Hadn't he had enough of them? Was she not worth coming home to? She thought of Becky, beautiful Becky, heard Dorcas's words again, that Becky knew the ways and Letty did not. Would Alec have rushed home for her? Letty's anger built. He'd brought home his dirty fishing gear, had taken what he wanted from her body and now it didn't matter. He had money and he had beer. She got to her feet, went to the stove, picked up a cloth and removed Alec's meal from the warming oven, took a fork and spoon from the drawer.

Dorcas pushed her empty plate away from her. 'What are you doing?'

Letty stared at Alec's plate, the cutlery in her hand, wanting to fling it against the wall. But no, she wouldn't do that, she wouldn't waste good food, lovingly prepared by his mother, for both of them, who had prayed for his safe homecoming, waited for him. And now they were waiting again, and her fury flared stronger still. She moved to the door. 'I'm taking it to Alec.'

Dorcas sighed. 'Don't be daft. He'll come back by and by. You know what it's like when they have a drink.'

Her throat was tight. 'No, I don't know. But I know he promised to take us to the theatre.' Letty began to tremble with rage, the plates rattled in her hand.

'Put it back.' Dorcas stood up, her chair falling back onto the floor. 'Don't make a fool of yourself.'

Letty drew back her shoulders. 'Oh, I'll not make a fool of myself. Don't you worry about that.' She turned on her heel and walked out the back door, banging it behind her, marched down the alley into the courtyard.

Dorcas was at the front door and she came out and stood before Letty. 'He'll not forgive you if you show him up in front of his crew.'

Letty looked past her, sidestepped, and carried on walking.

Dorcas shouted, 'Letty!'

Letty stopped but didn't turn.

Dorcas's voice was menacing. 'If you don't stop now, girl, *I'll* never forgive you.'

Letty inhaled deeply, tilted her jaw upwards. What difference would it make, Dorcas didn't like her anyway, she wasn't Becky, she could never be what she wanted her to be. More than that, she knew she didn't want to.

She carried on walking, not caring when people looked at her; fury drove her forward and she was blind to them. When she came to the Red Lion, she opened the door by turning her back and pushing it with her shoulder. It banged shut as she stepped inside, conversation fading as customers stopped drinking and stared at her. The air was thick with cigarette smoke and it caught in her throat, her nostrils. Her feet felt the stickiness of slopped ale as she walked towards the bar.

A blousy blonde behind it watched her, one hand on the pump, her gold charm bracelet catching the light. 'Can I help?'

Her heart was hammering in her chest, but it was too late to turn back. Letty cleared her throat. 'I'm looking for Alec Hardy.'

Men parted, the woman gave a nod of her head to her left, moved her arm, the bracelet jangled. Alec was sitting at a table, his cheeks red, as were those of his companions. He grinned stupidly when he saw her. One of them could barely raise his head, another slumped to the side. How much had Alec wasted? She'd thought she couldn't get any angrier, but blood raced through her veins, making her legs shake and she pushed herself forward, set the plate down, the knife and fork either side. He smiled, showing his teeth, pointing at her, nudging the man next to him to pay attention. He reached out to grab her and she slapped him away.

'Don't be like that, lass.' He frowned, hurt. He looked like a big, sense-less child and she longed to slap his stupid face. Tears threatened, but she was dammed if she would shed any in here. The pub fell silent, save for rumbles of soft sound in the snug beyond. All eyes were upon her. She removed the top plate, fought to steady herself, her voice.

'Get your tea down you, Alec. Your mother made it especially.'

He stared at it, his body swaying forward and back. He looked up at her, glassy-eyed, his bewilderment clear, and for a split second she wondered at what she'd done. Oh, she didn't regret bringing the meal, but she regretted falling in love with a man who didn't care about her.

Head held high, she turned on her heels and marched out of the room.

Tears fell as she made her way down Freeman Street, arms wrapped about her chest, fists clenched, past the line of people waiting outside the Prince of Wales theatre, couples with excited faces, their arms about each other, smart in their suits and hats. She blinked the tears away, furious at herself, with Alec. It didn't matter one jot that Dorcas wouldn't forgive her, but she'd thought Alec would keep his word, that she mattered more than drink, more than men he'd spent the last three weeks with. Had he missed her at all?

She turned into Duncombe Street, saw the canopy of the Tivoli Theatre, the queue filtering in through the open doors. She went to the other side, leaned against the wall and watched them while she caught her breath, wiped her face with the cloth and twisted it in her hands. She should have gone to the theatre by herself, not waited for Alec. She would never wait for him again. A hard lesson had been learned today.

17

Alec had staggered into the house sometime later and she heard him lumbering about downstairs before he fell into a chair. Dorcas had waited for him, but Letty couldn't bear to be in the same room and, after walking the streets to calm her temper, had come in the house and gone upstairs. She could feel Dorcas's disapproval seeping up through the floorboards and had sat up in bed, her arms folded tight across her chest, watching shadows play across the thin curtains. She heard Anita evicting a man from her house and they talked loudly, oblivious of the hour, and Letty wondered where Alfie was. The grimness of her surroundings suddenly seemed more so, as if only now had the reality of the poverty revealed itself to her. Why hadn't she understood what her mother was trying to tell her in her gentle way, not wanting to interfere, only to guide? Letty pulled her quilt to her chin, the quilt her mother and sisters had made as a wedding gift, and inhaled the cloth, trying to find some residue of the familiar smells of home. She'd been blinded by Alec's dreams; she'd thought they were her own, but they were not, and the realisation dragged at her heart.

Sleep was patchy, interrupted by Dorcas's tread on the stairs in the early hours, Alec's snoring from below, but most of all from anger and self-pity. By morning, she was more cross with herself than with Alec. What a blind fool she was.

He was still in the chair when she went downstairs and she moved about the kitchen clattering pans, banging cupboards, but he did not stir and when Dorcas came down and wordlessly moved around her, Letty had had enough. She took her coat and hat and, not waiting to put them on, went outside.

Kids were running up the yard with a hoop and stick. A neighbour was pegging sheets on the line that spanned one side of the courtyard to the other. A tall blond man waited to one side and when she was finished with one chore, she disappeared inside, came out and handed over his clean clothes in exchange for a handful of coins. The woman was insubstantial, like a small breath of air could blow her away. She managed, if one could call it managing, by taking in the washing of foreign fisherman who needed it back within the twenty-four hours before they sailed. It was back-breaking work, but it was work. Her husband had been killed on the dock railway.

Almost everyone who lived in the streets nearby were connected with the dock in some way, trapped by the poverty like fish in a net, but it was not for Letty. This was temporary. She pulled on her coat, removing her hair from beneath her collar, and made her way to Market Street. She walked over the bridge, stopped halfway, watching the trains and wagons push up and down, to and from the docks. In the distance, the dock tower stood like a lighthouse, guiding them all home. But it wasn't a lighthouse at all, it was just a water pump dressed in its best clothes. To the right, she could see the dock offices, the Royal Hotel. To the left of her, the rope works, the flour mill, the paper mill. She turned full circle, taking in the dirt and the poverty but also the expansion, the growth. She wanted to be part of that growth. Alec did too. Had she overreacted? Was Dorcas right not to make a fuss?

Letty carried on walking. If only she could talk to her mother, she would know what to do. She would write again, asking for advice, but in a guarded way so that her mother didn't worry, didn't get a sense of her unhappiness. One thing she was sure of: if she let Alec get away with broken promises once, he would do it again. And again. She went to retrieve her plate.

* * *

Alec's head throbbed like the very devil and he sat in the chair wondering which eye to open first. Someone was at his feet, building a fire; he could hear the twisting of the newspaper, the snap of kindling, and knew it was his mother. There was no other sound and he wondered where Letty was. He remained with eyes shut, forcing himself to remember the night before – before the drink had numbed his senses. His settlement had been a good one, he remembered collecting it, going to the pub and then... He groaned, opened his eyes, leaned forward and rubbed his hands over his face. Every bone ached and he had given up a night in a good bed, a night with Letty in his arms, for what?

Dorcas got up, pressing a hand on her knee to steady herself and wiped her hands on her apron. 'I'll get you a glass of water.'

He got to his feet and tried to stretch out the aches, his fists almost touching the ceiling. It would soon be June, but the damp little house was cold.

Dorcas came back with the water and handed it to him.

'Thanks, Mother.' His mouth felt like the bottom of a bird cage. 'Where's Letty?'

'No idea. She's a will of her own that one.' Her voice was sharp, unkind. If he'd wondered how the two women had got on while he was at sea, his mother had given him the answer. He ran his hand around the back of his neck, leaned into it.

'Is she at the shop?' He supped again at the water. Letty had said she had an agreement with the Parkers, that she could be home when Alec was home.

'The shop, the mission, the pub. Who knows?' She hurried into the kitchen and he followed her.

'The pub?' He laughed, uneasy. 'Letty's not the girl to go to a pub.'

Dorcas took a pan from the shelf and set it on the stove, cracked an egg into it, and then another. 'We've no idea what kind of lass she is.' She picked up a spoon, basted the eggs with fat. Her movements were brisk and he knew she was angry, and that it was not directed at him. He leaned against the door jamb, watching her. It felt as if his brain rocked when he moved. 'Sit down, boy. It'll be ready soon enough.' She took down a plate, cut a thick slice of bread, then another.

Why would she say Letty was at the pub?

'I'm sorry about last night, Mother, letting you down like that.'

She reached up, touched his shoulder. 'You didn't let *me* down. Is a man not allowed to celebrate a good trip when he's ashore?' She went back to the pan and slid the eggs onto his plate, gave a nod of her head that told him to sit at the table. 'Lass had no right showing you up like that.' The pan was put back on the stove with a clatter. 'She needs a good slap.'

'Mother!'

'Well!' She sat opposite, tilted her chin at him, wanting him to eat. He started at the eggs, picked up the bread and broke the yolks. His mother resumed her ranting. He ate, he drank, trying to let the words go over his head. 'I can't imagine how that looked. Her walking in the pub. Throwing food at you.'

'She didn't throw it. She set it down in front of me and left me to it.' To be truthful, he had half expected her to throw it at him and had braced himself as much as the drink inside him would allow.

His mother got up, placed the teapot on the table, filled a mug for him, took one for herself and sat down.

'Doesn't know her place.' She was scowling now.

He'd wanted them to get along. He'd thought they would, like the men on a ship. All different but with a common purpose, pulling together. He let his mother prattle on, let off the steam inside her.

'All these high ideas of hers,' his mother continued. 'I've not seen the like.'

'Aren't you glad of her ambition, Mother. She wants what I want.'

'Are you sure about that, boy?'

What was his mother trying to say?

He moved the bread about his plate, taking up more yolk, drank more tea. Dorcas reached across to the pot, removed the lid and checked the contents, got up and added more hot water. He ran the back of his hand across his mouth.

'We went to the Bethel. Not that I wanted to. But it's a good job I did.' She sat down, stabbed at the table with her finger. 'That port missioner, making sheep's eyes at him she was, and mixing with those people. Trawler owners and the like. She was there the other day. Bet Chapman, next door.' His mother tilted her head in the direction of her neighbour. 'Her daughter, Molly, she's a cleaner there. She saw her.'

He pushed the last bit of bread in his mouth. So, it was like that was it? Perhaps his mother was right. Perhaps he didn't know Letty at all.

* * *

Letty called at the Red Lion. A woman with a fag clamped to her lips was wiping the tables with a rag, and the woman she had seen yesterday was behind the bar polishing the bottles that lined the back wall. She saw Letty reflected in the mirror and turned, her bracelet jangling.

'Come for your dishes?'

The cleaner looked up, made slower sweeps with her hand.

The woman reached under the counter and placed Letty's plate and cutlery on the bar. 'I have to say, I admire your spirit,' the woman remarked. 'Most of 'em get a pint over their head, but you've got class.'

Letty wasn't sure that was a compliment. 'I'm hoping I won't have to do it again.'

The woman shrugged. 'Who knows. Once yer start putting up with the rum stuff, yer meking a rod fer yer own back. Not that lasses like you are good for my business.' She winked at her. 'He's a nice-looking chap. Your hubby, is it?'

Letty nodded.

'Keep yer eye on 'im. Bit of a charmer that one.'

* * *

The woman's words jangled in Letty's head like the charms on her bracelet as she walked back to Mariners Row. Clutching the plate as a shield, she stepped into the house. The fire was lit and Alec was stood before it, leaning with his hands on the mantel and staring into the flames. He turned when she walked in, his face like thunder.

'Where the 'ell have you been?' He stood away from the fire and she put the plate on the small table, took the cutlery from her pocket and removed her coat.

'The Red Lion.' She picked up the plate, walked through to the kitchen just as Dorcas slunk into the yard.

Alec came in behind her and put his arm across the door frame, barring her way.

She ignored him. She checked the pitcher for water, filled a pan and set it on the stove and remained there, watching over it. Outside, Dorcas was tugging at dock leaves along by the wall of the outhouse that hadn't troubled her before.

'Aye, Mother said you liked to go to the pub.'

He let go of the door jamb, folded his arms.

'Did she now?' Letty looked again to the yard. Dorcas picked up a broom, began sweeping. Letty stepped in front of him, unafraid. 'I went to get the plate. I've not stepped foot in a pub other than last night. And that was down to you.' Now it was Letty who folded her arms. 'And what else did your mother tell you?' she raised her voice, turned to the open door.

Dorcas looked at her, then away. As well she might, thought Letty, with all her meddling.

She checked the pan; the water began to bubble.

'That you're hardly ever home.' Alec stood his ground, his legs wide, filling the door frame. 'That you're at the shop, or the mission, making eyes at the blokes.'

Letty looked at the soft lummox, standing there with his great strong arms folded across his chest, his square jaw set – at his daft head. She thought of the long hours, the relentless minutes, when she'd longed for him, waiting for the day he stepped ashore. It shouldn't be like this; they were wasting time. He could be gone again by the end of the day. She could feel the seconds ticking away in her head but she had to make a stand. 'What should I be doing, Alec, while you're away for weeks on end?'

He stared at her. 'At home. Braiding nets with Mam.'

Letty nodded. His head was full of his mother's words, his mother's thoughts, but somewhere inside were thoughts of his own. 'So she can keep her eye on me?'

He looked over her head and into the yard and she waited for his answer. Eventually, he gazed down at her and she could feel the flame of his anger fading.

'What about what *we* want?' she asked him.

'You shouldn't have taken me dinner into the pub.'

She shrugged. 'You shouldn't have made promises you didn't intend to keep.'

He stared into her eyes and right at that moment she wanted to pull his arms apart and wrap them about her, but she couldn't give in.

'Stop trying to make me in the wrong, Alec. It was your treat. I didn't ask for anything, I was only too pleased you were home safe.' She stepped away, took the water from the stove and moved it to one side, fetched the teapot that was upside down on the draining and poured water in to warm it, swilled it about, set it down again.

He came to her, put his hand over hers. 'Let me take you out. To make up for yesterday.' His regret was written on every weathered line of his face and he reached out and pulled her close to him.

Dorcas came into the kitchen, skirted round them, avoiding Letty's gaze, and went through to the other room. Letty heard her pull out her basket, the rattle of braiding needles.

Alec kissed her, hungrily, his lips hard on hers. His hands were on her back, her waist, then her hair and she wanted to melt into him so they were one, so that they would never be apart. She couldn't be mad at him for long, their time together too short to hold on to bitterness and regret.

'We'll go to Cleethorpes on the tram.'

She smiled; she didn't care what they did as long as they were together and away from Dorcas's nasty tongue.

He smoothed her hair away from her face. Kissed her again, briefly this time, took hold of her hands. 'All right if I ask Mother? I promised to take her to the theatre too.'

Letty nodded, forcing back the disappointment that hung like a sack inside her. She washed her hands and splashed her face with the water to freshen herself, dried it and followed him through to the sitting room. Dorcas was filling needles.

'How about a trip to the seaside, Mother? I'll get us all an ice cream. We can stroll along the promenade. It's a bit windy out, but it'll still be grand.'

Dorcas dropped another needle into the basket and began winding twine onto a new one. 'You don't want me dragging along. Besides, I promised Bet that I'd keep an eye on her grandson while she nipped to the market.' He hesitated, but she flapped at him with her hand. 'Off with you.'

Alec leaned over and kissed her cheek.

'I'll bring you back a shell or two; like I used to when I were a lad,' he said and his mother smiled, remembering, her face alight with pleasure.

Letty glanced at the photos on the mantel; all that Dorcas had left was her memories. And Alec. But that didn't excuse her meddling and petty accusations.

18

They stepped off the tram opposite the Empire Theatre in Cleethorpes and it was hard to believe that they were only a mile or two from Grimsby docks. Crowds thronged along the promenade and they could see down the sweeping route to the pier that stretched way out into sea. Here, Letty felt a sense that something different was in reach, not beyond their grasp, as it seemed to be in Mariners Row. Here, there was light and open space. People walked slower, smiling, relaxed, and she felt her shoulders sink in response.

Alec held out his hand and she clasped it tightly as they made their way down towards the beach and promenade. It didn't smell of fish and coal, it smelled of sweet things, of rock and sunshine and clean salty air. Somewhere, in the distance, she could hear music from a brass band, laughter and applause, and her heart skipped with excitement.

Alec turned to look down at her and she felt her face stretch with the widest of smiles. Oh, Lord, how she loved him, how could she bear to let him go again.

'Happy, lass?'

She nodded, not wanting to speak, not wanting to break the spell of it all.

They passed stalls selling trinkets and charms and he bought her an enamelled brooch in the shape of a forget-me-not and pinned it to her jacket. They bought a cone of cockles, doused them in vinegar and shared them as they strolled along the north promenade, watching people in the swingboats, the carousel with its galloping horses painted bright colours, music from a barrel organ drifting on the air.

They came to a café and he stopped to read the menu, then took her inside. Young girls dressed smartly in black, their white aprons and caps stiff with starch, slid around the gaps between customers. They were led to a table and Alec pulled out the chair for her, pushed it under so she was comfortable. He winked at the girl serving them and she blushed, handed them a menu. The words from the woman at the pub floated into her thoughts. A charmer. They chose sandwiches, scones and jam and the girl was back in no time with it all neatly arranged on china plates. They tucked in, enjoying the treat of it.

Alec looked about him. 'Mother would have liked this. Perhaps she'll come with us next time.'

'She might.' Letty poured the tea.

'You two not getting on?' He picked up the cup, his big hands fumbling with the delicate handle. Admitting defeat, he held it by the sides.

'She doesn't like me working at the shop.' She wanted to add, 'she doesn't like me at all,' but knew he would disagree. Or would he?

He put his elbow on the table, rested his chin on his hand. 'She worries. About me. About you.'

'Oh, I know she worries about me. She makes that quite plain. Like I'm some flighty piece that will be off with any chap that happens to pass my way.'

He gave a small laugh and it irritated her. 'It's not like that.' He fiddled with a teaspoon.

'Isn't it?'

'No, Letty. It isn't.' They were quiet for a time while they ate. Letty didn't want to mar their precious time talking about Dorcas but Alec seemed hell-bent on defending his mother.

The waitress came and took their empty plates and they stopped talking until she walked away.

His tone changed, sombre now. 'She's seen it all, over time. Women who go astray, women who are widowed and can't keep a roof over their head.' He looked at her. 'Women like Anita.'

Letty put down her cup. Through the windows, she could see people still promenading along, and as the door to the café opened and closed, it let in sounds of laughter, of lightness and happiness. She bit back her temper. Why ruin the day? 'I don't want to dwell on what might or might not happen, Alec.'

'It's not about dwelling. It's about being practical. It's about being able to take care of yourself, your family. *Our* family.'

She sat back in her chair. 'And how would I be doing that, Alec? It wouldn't be by braiding, would it?'

'I thought it might help, bring you together. Your working at the shop unsettles her.'

'Does it now.'

The waitress came and placed the bill on the table, Alec took it, read it, put his hand in his pocket.

Letty got up. His mother had spoiled her day again. She didn't wait for him to pay, just walked out of the café, away from him, glad to be outside, in the fresh air with the smell of chips and sweetness and the call of seagulls as they floated and turned on the breeze.

He caught up with her. Walked beside her.

'What's wrong, Let? What did I say?'

She kept moving forward, heading back towards the station. Through the railings, families were embarking, cases in hand, and she wished for all the world that she could get on a train and go back to the farm, but she was a married woman now. She had stood in the village church before her family, before Alec, before God, and made promises. She had made no such promise to Dorcas.

She stopped and people parted, moved around them. 'I feel like I'm having a conversation with your mother, not with you. She fills your head with thoughts, and you don't even sift through them for anything that might be true or real, you just take her word and repeat it to me.' Her voice trembled with anger and disappointment and she strode ahead of him.

He took her hand, and she didn't let go, she didn't want to. Her love for him was as strong as it ever was, she loved the very breath of him, but she had to make her feelings plain.

For some time, they didn't speak, kept walking, past the ornate fountain, the gilded shelters, the intricate patterns that decorated flower beds behind low railings. Eventually, the promenade petered out and they found themselves in open land that led to dunes thick with marram grass. Families and courting couples sat hidden in the valleys between them and Letty walked on until she found a clear space, swept her hand down the back of her skirt and sat down. Alec settled beside her, his heels in the sand, his hands between his knees, pulling at bits of grass and flinging them up into the wind. They stared out across the water. Kids were paddling, running and splashing in the ebb tide. She took his hand, traced the lines on it with her finger.

'When you come home, Alec, I can hear a clock in my head, ticking away the minutes. So, so fast. When you're away, every minute lasts an hour with longing for you.' She let go of his hand and he put it around her shoulder and she leaned on him. 'Our time together is too important to waste. I made a choice to be with you, for good and bad.'

'For richer or for poorer?' he asked.

She pulled herself away from him, twisted on the sand to face him. The wind caught the loose strands of her hair and whipped it across her face. He reached up and stroked them away, tucked them behind her ear, then leaned forward and kissed her, so, so gently, and she longed to kiss more and forget about everything. But she couldn't. They had to sort things out and there was little time to do so.

'Poorer we will be if you go throwing your money about on drink.'

He hung his head. 'I got carried away. You know how it is.'

She shook her head. 'No, I don't know how it is.' A child ran down towards the sea, its mother close behind, and Letty thought of their future. 'You said wanted your own ship,' she challenged. 'A fleet, you told me.'

He sat up straighter. 'Aye, and I'll have one. I had to have a jar or two with the crew. It's expected.'

'One or two, maybe. But there was no limit last night on how much you drank. Or spent!' She was exasperated. 'Dreams cost hard cash if you want them to become reality.'

He was quiet and she left time for her words to sink in.

'If we want a better life, we need to do better. That's why I'm working at the shop. I fill the needles of an evening. I'm still doing the work your mother needs me to do, but I can do so much more away from the house.'

'Mother's heart's in the right place.'

There'd been little evidence of Dorcas's heart as far as Letty was concerned.

She took hold of his hands, rough and calloused from hauling ropes and gutting fish. 'I don't want your mother's way of life, Alec. I want my own.' He nodded, but she knew from his face that it wasn't as simple as that. 'We're making a new way, the two of us. I'm working in a shop, but perhaps one day we'll have our own shop.'

He frowned. 'I thought you wanted land, with pigs and hens. I said I'd buy you land, and I will.'

She'd hurt his pride, but it wasn't about pride, it was about shaping a life to their fashion.

'I don't doubt it. But it'll be quicker if we're both working towards the same thing. Don't you see?'

He turned away, looked out to the sea. Trawlers moved along the horizon. He put his arms behind him and leaned back into them.

'The way I sees it, you and Mam are like a ship with two skippers. One of you has to be mate.'

Letty agreed. 'And your mother is skipper?'

He shook his head and when he turned to her, he looked so sad. 'No, she's not, Letty. She's adrift. Bobbing about in a great big ocean without Pop. She's trying to steer a course and she's lost in a storm.' He got up, brushed the sand from his trousers, held his hand out to her and she let him pull her to her feet. He put his hands about her waist. 'I can't tell you what to do, Let. I know better than to try.' He gave a small laugh. 'But I know you'll do what's right by us all.'

* * *

When they got back to the house, the ship's runner had been. The *Black Prince* would sail on the evening tide. They did not get a chance to spend the sweetness of night together and when he left, Letty wept for the wasted time. She sat in front of the fire, eyes red and sore, and Dorcas brought her a mug of hot milk. The unexpected kindness filled her throat so that, at first, she couldn't drink but hugged the mug, grateful to have something to hold on to. Dorcas settled herself in the chair opposite and took up her knitting needles. For a long time, the only sound between them was the crackle of the fire and the click of her needles.

Eventually, Letty uttered miserably, 'How can you bear it?'

Dorcas stilled her hands and stared first at her and then into the flames. 'Because we have to.'

19

They had one hell of a game getting Mouse aboard by means of the ladder, Alec pushing on his backside and the lads hauling him up from the deck. They had bundled him into his bunk to sober up and there he had remained, dead to the world, as the *Black Prince* made its way up the river and out into open seas. The crew pulled together to make up the slack and the nets were ready, the gear checked, by the time he roused himself a good fifteen hours later. He ignored their good-natured leg pulling and in the end they left him to his sore head and sore heart. Things had not gone well during his time ashore and rumour was that his missus had gone back to her mother.

A few days later, they were sitting at the mess table after their meal. Ben was settled in the middle, men either side. As usual, out came his sketch pad and pencil and he sat quietly absorbed in his work. Alec tilted his head to look at the drawing and saw himself. Ben stopped sketching and withdrew his hand so that Alec could get a better look.

'Is that me?'

Ben nodded.

Alec slapped the lad on the shoulder. 'You've even made me look handsome.' He furrowed his brow, grinned at him. 'I keep telling the missus how gorgeous I am an' you've proved it.'

Tosh craned his neck, as did Puggy. Mouse kept his head bent over the paper. His mood had not improved as the days passed. They'd tried to lift his spirits but failed and, in the end, had left him to his bad humour; once they got to the fishing grounds, he wouldn't have time for brooding.

Ben placed his sketchbook on the table and carefully tore the page and handed it to Alec. 'You can have it if you like.'

'By, lad, that's terrific. I'll give that to the missus. I reckon she'll like that.' He ruffled the lad's hair and his cheeks reddened. He had the look of Robbie and a sharp pain stabbed at Alec's heart.

Puggy leaned back, resting his back against the bunk. 'Will you do one for my missus, young Ben?'

Alec grinned. 'He can't work magic, Tosh, you ugly old sod.'

Puggy laughed and Tosh punched Alec's arm playfully.

'Yer, think a lot of yerself, Hardy, don't yer?' Mouse said. 'Mebee yer missus is sick of yer face already and don't wanna look at it more than she has to.'

Puggy glanced to Alec. The man was itching for a fight, but they were pinned between the table and the bench and the most damage Mouse could do was spout off.

'Yes, ruddy misery,' Tosh said. 'Better when yer don't speak.'

'Din't say nowt you wouldn't have said.' Mouse snatched at his paper.

Alec got up to leave, giving a nod to Ben to come with him. Better away from Mouse's nark, a bad mood could be contagious.

* * *

Mid-afternoon, the skipper told them to cast the nets. Four hours later, they were dressed in their oilskins and knee-deep in fish. They worked, heads down, until the deck was almost clear. There would be a brief lull and the nets would be hauled again. The net was hauled three times and by the time they were halfway through the last of them, they were almost working in their sleep. Their movements were slower, clumsy. This was the time when hands were cut, mistakes were made. Alec shook himself, tried to keep focused, kept his eye on the men.

Ben tossed an entrail as a curtain of water washed over them. It caught Mouse in the face. Mouse went for him, his gutting knife in his hand.

'Why, yer little bugger. Yer did that on purpose. I'll teach yer to watch what yer doing with yer ruddy precious hands. Yer won't 'old a bastard pencil when I've finished with yer.'

Ben was transfixed. The ship rose and dipped with the swell, water washed over them again. Ben floundered. Alec leaped between man and boy. Fish were under his feet and he slipped and fell, regained his balance as Mouse took a swing at him. The ship rolled and he twisted his shoulder back. Mouse stumbled, his balance off, and Alec caught his arm, twisted it up his back and pushed forward. The knife dropped from his hand and Puggy bent and retrieved it. Mouse fell to the deck and Alec sat astride him. The man lashed out with his fists, flailing his arms, thrusting his head backwards, fighting to get Alec off. Alec stayed where he was until Mouse's temper was spent and the man began to cry like a child. Alec glanced up, Ben was before him, his terror clear.

'It was an accident.'

The mate called up the ladder and the skipper came down from the wheelhouse.

Alec slid off Mouse's back and Mouse struggled to his knees, breathing heavily. They caught another wave, were drenched, the ice-cold water running down their necks, their backs. Alec wiped his face with his hand. 'A misunderstanding, Skipper. Mouse slipped on a fish or two.' He pulled the man to his feet.

Mouse dragged his hand across his face.

Skipper glanced to his boy, then to Mouse. 'Tek him below.' He turned to the other men who had stopped. 'Get on with guttin', lads. The net's full and we'll be a man short.' He shot a quick glance to his lad and went back up the ladder to the wheelhouse, releasing the mate to his duties.

Alec took hold of Mouse's arm and moved him forward. There was no resistance and he allowed Alec to guide him down below to the mess. He shouted for Cookie to bring tea and they were no sooner settled than Cookie appeared with two mugs in one big hand. 'Skipper dropped a tot in it,' he said, pushing them onto the table and leaving them to it.

Mouse stared into his drink.

'Get it down yer. 'Twill do yer good.'

Mouse drank a big mouthful. Alec did the same; the rum hit the spot. He needed it as much as Mouse. It had taken all his strength to subdue him, for a man in a temper was no easy match and he was glad for his bulk and his strength. The boy wouldn't have stood a chance.

'Yer give the lad a fright.'

Mouse nodded. ''Tweren't his fault.'

'Aye, we all know that. Perhaps the lad don't tho'.'

Mouse dropped his head onto the table. 'What a ruddy mess.'

Alec pressed a hand to his shoulder. 'What's up?'

It was a while before he answered, and the ship rolled with the swell. The pair of them should've been up there gutting, but the lads would understand. They were all in this together and it was an unspoken rule that when a man was in trouble you took up the slack.

'Missus has gone. Took the kiddies.' He drew his hand under his nose, wiped it on his sleeve. 'Took me money when I landed, then she buggered off. I come back from pub and the house was cold. I fell asleep. Well, I was well oiled.' He made to cough to hide a sob. 'I woke up an' there was a note.'

'Where's she gone? D'ya know?'

Mouse sat back against the seat. The hum of the engine throbbed on their backs.

'Mother's in Shields. She always threatened.' He caught Alec's eye.

'It's tough for the lasses with us away so long.' He thought of Letty, of his mother. 'I'll help you sort it when we gets back in dock. Perhaps Skipper'll be able to get word. Send a wire.'

Mouse nodded, swallowed back his drink. Alec took the mugs and slid from the mess table.

'Let's get back on the fish. Take yer mind of it. That ugly bunch'll be needing a hand.'

Mouse was subdued, but the lads teased and sang and before too long, his outburst was forgotten. When Ben struggled with a dogfish, Mouse was the one who stepped forward and showed him how to handle it. They worked until the deck was clear, then went down for their grub and their beds.

Alec left them to it and went up on deck for a smoke. The skipper was up in the wheelhouse, the small light over his charts. Alec felt as miserable as Mouse did right now. Uncle Eric had sent a letter, along with the balance from the sale of the *Stella Maris*. The sum had been a bitter disappointment. When all debts were paid, the bank loan settled, his share had been forty guineas. His mother had raged into the night, calling Uncle Eric the very devil, but when she'd calmed, he had reasoned with her. Uncle Eric had been more than fair. The money would sit in the bank and hopefully more would be added to it. He was a long way off being able to invest in another ship, but someone might be ready to invest in him. A lifetime's work, of toil and risk; his father's lifetime. For forty guineas.

He was far from home, far from Letty. Had his Mam been right? Should he have married Becky? Should he have stayed in Lowestoft where Letty was near her family? Letty knew her own mind – which was what had attracted him; and what troubled him. He drew on the last bit of his fag and dropped the tab into the sea.

Cookie came and nudged him. 'Tek this up to Skipper.'

Alec rubbed at his hands, took the mug and went up the ladder. The skipper was looking at his book and he closed it when Alec came inside. Alec looked away. A man's charts were the key to his success. The years of watching, working out the channels, the places and the times of year, of the day when he had found the bounty. Skipper Harris was a good skipper. He'd been fortunate to sail with him.

Alec handed over the mug and turned to leave, but the skipper stopped him.

'Stay awhile, lad.' He whistled down the tube for Cookie to bring another brew. 'You handled Mouse well. My lad all right?'

'Seems to be. I'll keep an eye on him.'

'Well, although I've missed ole Badger, I'll be sad to lose you as crew.' He supped loudly. 'Can't think that we'll sail together again if you're set on going fer yer skipper's ticket. But if you ever need a ship, you know where to find me.'

'You'll be me first choice.'

Skipper leaned one arm on the ridge of the window frame and opened it. The air was cold and fresh on their faces. 'Being skipper is more than keeping the ship on course, it's keeping the men on course too, knowing when to act and when to let things take their own direction.' He put down his mug and took up his pipe, began to fill it, pushing the strands in with his thumb. Satisfied, he turned his back to the window, struck a match, held the flame to it and puffed until it was alight. Smoke was snatched out of the window. 'I'll put in a word for you with the gaffers at Hammonds. They're a good firm and always looking for good skippers.'

'I appreciate that.'

The man studied the skyline. 'What's the game with Mouse?'

He told him of Mouse's wife leaving him.

Skipper took his pipe from his mouth. 'It's a tough life if you don't weaken, eh, lad?'

Cookie rapped on the door and handed Alec a brew. It was thick and dark and sometimes he thought it was only the tea that got them through the bad days – and there were plenty of them.

The two men watched water lash over the bow, run down the deck and drain away, relentless. The sky was black, the stars clear and bright.

'Nowt like it when the going's good though.'

'No,' Alec agreed, feeling the sway of the boat as it cut through the waves.

The skipper tapped the wheel. 'Accepting the struggle is the key. Knowing when to risk and when to hold back.' He shut the window, pushed his pipe between his teeth, and looked straight at Alec. 'Always be in charge of your ship, and your destiny. The two are one and the same. Don't let anyone tell you otherwise.'

Alec nodded. His father had always guided him before. Now he was alone, steering by the stars, and hoping he kept clear of the rocks.

20

Dorcas did not mention the braiding again and Letty made sure she filled as many needles as she could in the evenings when she got back from Parkers. Each week, she took a little of her payment in needles so that Dorcas would have little reason to complain. They lived frugally, for there was always the fear of the bad trip, that Alec would come back to sixpence – or that he would not come back at all.

Letty's mother sent a parcel of honey and preserves and hoped she might be able to visit soon, though where she would stay, Letty had no idea. But it kept her spirits up, as she knew her mother had intended. Alec had remained with Skipper Harris as Badger, the man whose place he had filled had sailed with another Hammonds ship in need of an experienced third hand. Each trip, the *Black Prince* had returned in good profit. The Parkers had taken Letty on full time, Dorcas braided, and their days at Mariners Row settled to a steady rhythm. The shop was her escape and she'd grown fond of Percy and Norah. Her half-days and Sundays were spent at the mission, helping to raise funds, writing letters, supporting women whose husbands had been lost at sea. It was a reminder that stability was fragile, and they all depended on one another. When Alec's ship landed, she went with him to collect his settlement, relieving him of the majority of his money so that he couldn't spend it lining the publican's pockets. At least on that the two women were in agreement. It was perhaps the only thing.

Each day as she walked to work, Letty saw familiar faces and people called out in greeting. She passed the curers and filleters, the great hulks of men who emptied and loaded the ships, the carters and the lumpers. She knew the people in the offices and shops, from the fish pontoon and from the market. Mostly they were cheerful and somehow the lack of green and open space didn't matter as much as it had done when she'd first arrived.

Alec had sailed two days ago and as Letty made her way to Parkers that July morning, she'd begun to feel that she was as much a part of the dock as it was part of her. On Henderson Street, carts trundled past, laden with rope and fish, with rags and boxes. Gilbert Crowe was standing in his doorway next to Parkers, and he glanced at Letty, checked his watch and went inside. Letty stepped onto the tiled entrance of Parkers and pushed at the door. It wouldn't give. She tried again and, realising it was locked, put her hand to her brow and leaned against the glass. The shop was in darkness. She rapped on the glass, rapped again, harder, but there was no sign of either Percy or Norah and instinct told her something was wrong. Hurrying down the side alley, she unlatched the gate and ran up the path. She was about to hammer on the back door but thought better of it; if something was wrong, she didn't want to alarm the Parkers any more than was necessary. When she felt somewhat calmed, she banged on the back door.

Norah called out, 'Who is it?'

'Letty. It's Letty.'

The key was turned in the lock, the door opened a little. Norah's hair was escaping from its usually tidy bun and her face was pinched and grey.

'Letty, love.' She hesitated and Letty feared the worst as Norah considered whether to let her in or not. 'You'd better come in.' She put her finger to her lips and opened the door wider for Letty to step inside. It was warm and stuffy and she slipped off her gloves. Two chairs faced the fire and Percy occupied one, his back to her, a blanket across his shoulders. At the side of him was a stool and on it a bowl of thin porridge.

She whispered, 'Is Percy ill?'

Norah filled the kettle and set it on the stove. 'Took badly during the night. I've had to get the doctor to him.' She looked exhausted, her face more lined, her eyes dull, and Letty's heart ached with concern for the pair of them. Poor Percy, he would hate to be so helpless and poor Norah too, for Percy wouldn't be a good patient. 'Make a brew, will you, while I see to him.'

Letty watched Norah as she picked up the bowl and sat down on the stool. She raised the spoon to Percy's mouth. He tried to lift his arm and it flopped heavily back down again. Norah tried again, but Percy moaned loudly, and she dropped the spoon back in the bowl with a sigh. Letty made the tea and waited in the background. Percy was a proud man and wouldn't want Letty to see him so weakened, but how could she help otherwise? Norah came to the sink, placed the bowl on the side. Instinctively, Letty reached out and rubbed Norah's shoulders.

'Is there anything I can do?' Letty asked quietly.

Norah seemed to stand for a long time, staring out of the window at the brick wall of the yard that divided them from Gilbert Crowe, gripping the edge of the countertop. Her wedding ring was loose on her fingers and she rubbed at it.

'Can you open up? I'll be in shortly.'

Letty handed her the tea, made her drink some of it.

'You don't need to come in at all.' She looked across to Percy.

'It's a stroke. A bad one,' Norah said, dully. 'It's paralysed him down one side. He can't move his arm or leg much, and his face...' She put her hand up to her own cheek, gazing into the middle distance.

Letty rubbed at her shoulder again, picked up her own drink and one for Percy. The two women exchanged a look, Norah's heavy with a gentle warning.

Percy growled when he saw her, made noises, and Letty knew he would hate her seeing him so indisposed, but they couldn't pretend it hadn't happened. Even so, she was shocked when she saw him. He had aged twenty years overnight. His face had dropped on one side and saliva spilled from the corner of his mouth which he dabbed at with his good hand.

'Now then, Percy,' she said cheerfully. 'We'll have none of that. Here's your tea, you grumpy old thing.' She placed the mug on the stool and was about to kiss him on top of the head, then thought better of it. 'You know where I am if you need me.' She looked across at Norah, winked at her, then made her way into the shop, her heart breaking with the shock of seeing Percy so useless in his chair.

Behind the counter, Letty stopped for a moment, wiping away her tears with her sleeve and swallowing down the lump in her throat. She would be of no help to the Parkers if she gave in to pity and that would be the last thing Percy wanted.

She hurried to the front door and unlocked it, drew back the covers on the till and the counter. The sun filtered through the glass door, spilling a band of light across the floorboards. She thought of the first day she had called into Percy Parker's, marching in, as bold as brass. She recalled how happy Percy had been when she revealed the window display, how proud. Tears pricked again. The best thing she could do was make sure they had nothing to worry about.

* * *

Trade was steady and she wrote down each sale on a piece of paper so that Percy could read it when she finished at the end of the day. He would like that, but not as much as he would like to be standing at the counter. She kept herself busy and when there was a lull, she took out the tin of lavender polish and began to work on the counter. She was still buffing it up to a shine when Norah came through. She placed her hand at the spot where Percy always stood, and stared at it, as though she was touching him, then tapped it and looked up at Letty.

'He's sleeping.' She leaned back against the counter.

'Is it bad?'

Norah nodded. 'The doctor didn't seem to think he would get the use of his hand or leg back. Or his speech.' She stared out at the street, the shadows that passed by the shop. 'The times I've told him to stop moaning, Letty. I'd give anything for him to grumble at me right now.'

The bell above the door rang and a couple of young lads walked in together. The taller of the two headed across to the seaboots and peered into them, picked one up and handed it to his mate.

Norah slipped from behind the counter. 'Hello, gentleman. What can I do for you today?'

Letty watched her, smiling, helpful, making sure the boys got what they needed, guiding, reassuring. Thereafter, she popped in and out during the day, but more for the need of a break than to help Letty. No one was allowed to go into the back rooms as they once might have done. Percy wouldn't take kindly to people fussing over him, nor the fact that he was incapacitated so severely. If he couldn't talk—

* * *

Letty locked up at the end of the day and tallied the till, then took it through to the back room. Percy was awake, still in the chair. His glasses had slipped down his nose and he pushed at them with a tired hand. She put the till drawer on the table at the side of the room and handed him the sheet of sales.

'I marked everything down, Percy, so you can see how we're doing. Then when you're back behind the counter, you'll know I've not been diddling you.'

He tried to smile, and it almost broke her, but she was determined not to show pity, knowing the old man would hate it. He managed a small nod of the head.

She peered over into the coal bucket. 'Now I'll be filling that before I go.'

Norah was working at the table, the dark green chenille cloth covered with papers, and gave Letty a grateful smile as she went out to the coal hole. When she came back, she added a lump or two to the fire, wiping her hands with the cloth by the hearth.

'You might as well sit skiving all night as well as all day, Percy.'

He stared at the fire and she felt she'd been over jolly, but what else could she do? Percy would hate the fuss.

She went to Norah. 'Can I do anything else?'

Norah shook her head. 'There's nothing either of us can do now. It's a waiting game.'

Letty didn't have words for comfort, knowing there were none. 'I'll come early tomorrow, that way if you do need anything, I can do it before I open the shop.' She hated to leave them, but Norah insisted they would be fine.

As Letty made ready to leave Norah scooped broth into a bowl and went to sit by Percy, blowing on a spoonful to cool it. Letty paused at the door, watching the tenderness that passed between the couple. Would she and Alec grow old together? She closed her eyes and said a small prayer. God willing, they would.

She walked home, blind to the traffic and the comings and goings of the day's end. Her eyes were blurred with tears and she looked up only to safely cross the roads. Poor Percy, she loved the curmudgeonly old devil, and she couldn't bear that he would never grumble again.

Letty stopped at the mission and waited until someone was free. Word had quickly travelled about Percy's stroke, but here was one person in particular who Percy would allow to visit. Norah had given her permission for Letty to get word to him.

'Is Walter Stevens here?'

The receptionist looked down the ledger. 'He's due in tonight.'

'Could you give him a message.' The man picked up a pencil. 'Please tell him Percy Parker is unwell. Ask him to call in when he can.'

The man nodded.

Letty could see someone moving about in the back room and at the sound of her voice, Mr Wilson, the port missioner, came out.

'Is he all right?' He looked embarrassed. 'I couldn't help overhearing.'

Letty lowered her voice. 'He's had a stroke. He's lost movement down one side. Lost his speech.' Her voice broke on the words and he made to come round to her, but she held up her hand to stop him, aware someone might gossip, angry that she had to be on her guard, because of Dorcas, because of tittle-tattlers like Molly. She took a deep breath and composed herself. 'I'm quite all right. My concern is for Percy.'

Colin Wilson turned to the man beside him. 'I'll visit this evening, see if there's anything they need.'

She'd hoped for as much. A visit from the port missioner would not be untoward.

'Mrs Frampton and Miss Evans were asking after you. They'd heard that the *Black Prince* had sailed and were wondering whether you'd be at the meeting on Friday?'

She couldn't think that far ahead. Not with Percy the way he was.

'I don't know.' An image of Norah's face swam before her. The fear, the concern. The love. How she longed for Alec to be with her, to fold her in his arms and comfort her. Would she ever get used to these long absences? Of all the boys she'd met, why did she have to fall in love with him.

* * *

Letty was quiet when she got back to the house. Dorcas had been working in the kitchen and a half-finished cod end was suspended on the pole that had been fixed over the table, the basket of needles empty. She was busy at the stove and glanced up at Letty as she came in. Letty poured herself a mug of water and drank it back. Dorcas took two bowls down from the shelf and set them on the side and began ladling stew into them, then set them down at the table. 'You're very late.'

'I am.' Letty was in no mood for her criticisms.

'You've been at the shop all this time?'

'Percy had a stroke in the night.'

Dorcas sat down at the table and Letty did likewise. 'And is he all right?'

Letty shook her head, for she couldn't speak without her voice betraying her, and she didn't want to cry. She blew onto her spoon and was reminded of Norah spooning thin broth into Percy's mouth.

'Will he recover?'

Letty shrugged, cleared her throat. 'It's early days.'

Dorcas pulled at a piece of bread. 'You think a lot of them, don't you?'

It wasn't a criticism, and Letty didn't take it as such. Over the weeks she'd been there, she'd grown inordinately fond of them. The truth of it was that she felt closer to them than she did to Dorcas.

Letty talked about the day at Parkers and Dorcas listened – which was something she had rarely done before. Letty had ceded to Dorcas since her conversation with Alec about a ship having two skippers. Not that Letty wanted to take control of the house, it wasn't fair when she was in it so little and Dorcas was hardly ever out of it. Couldn't they find a way to be equal?

The two of them washed and cleared away, after which Letty took up a ball of twine and the basket of needles and began to fill them. For once, Dorcas set aside her knitting and worked alongside her. Letty was grateful for the small but significant gesture. She looked at the photos on the mantel and thought of Dorcas and Will, that perhaps she too had hoped they would grow old together, and for the first time Letty truly had a sense of the loneliness Dorcas must feel as old age stretched before her.

The needles full, Letty went out and filled the pitchers with water and got things ready for the following morning. She planned to be out early to do the washing for the Parkers and whatever else they needed. When she went back in the house, Dorcas was warming milk in a small saucepan. Two mugs were set upon the side and she poured it into them, then pushed one towards Letty.

'How will they manage, do you think, Mr and Mrs Parker?'

Letty leaned back against the sink. 'I suppose he'll be all night in the chair. I doubt whether Norah will be able to get him upstairs.'

Dorcas nodded. 'My father was the same. But I wasn't so much thinking of the night, more about the days to come.'

Letty shrugged. 'I'll help best I can. Only time will tell.'

Dorcas nodded but didn't say more and Letty didn't want to dwell on what might or might not be, she could only pray that Percy recovered.

21

The small room at the back of Parkers became the centre of the universe. Word about Percy's stroke spread quickly and a daily parade of friends popped by for a minute and stayed an hour or two. Percy still couldn't hold a conversation, but that didn't stop the likes of Dennis or Wolfie Turner. These were the older fisherman who no longer went to sea but took posts as nightwatchmen on the trawlers, adding a shovelful of coal every now and again to keep the boilers going while the ship was made ready for another trip. They called in on their way to work or after it. Those still sailing would drop by during their short time ashore. The teapot was constantly being topped up and, for all the world, Letty imagined this must be what it was like on a ship, the men together round the mess table.

Letty manned the counter the majority of the time, while Norah kept up with the paperwork and occasional trips out to fetch medicines or supplies. The doctor had not been called since that first night but stopped at the shop if passing to check on Percy. For this he did not charge and as such showed how much Percy was liked and respected in the area. But then he and Norah had been there a long time. How much longer would they remain? Letty tried to distract her thoughts by going out to clean the window.

She set the pail down on the pavement and no sooner had she done so than Gilbert Crowe came out from his tobacconist shop next door. He looked her up and down, and as she bent to get the cloth from her bucket, she muttered under her breath. He unsettled her, with his greasy black hair and waxed moustache.

'Now then, Letty. Norah behind counter?'

She wanted to be sarcastic. It would hardly be Percy, and with customers in and out they'd have to be serving themselves – but she merely nodded and began to rub down the paintwork.

Through the glass, she watched Gilbert walk up to Norah who was serving a customer. He waited at the entrance to the counter in the spot where Percy always stood, and Letty felt her hackles rise. She watched him, saw Norah shrug her shoulders, turn away from him, then back, busying herself with something. He was leaning over the counter and Letty just knew that Norah would be feeling as she did, that no one stood there except Percy. Gilbert looked about the shop, pointing to this and that and Letty got more irritated, rubbing and wringing out the cloth in temper. She emptied the dirty water in the gutter and went to refresh the pail.

When she walked into the shop, Gilbert leered at her. 'I'll get you to do my window next. It could do with a clean.'

She gave him a fake smile and caught Norah's eye.

He pressed himself along the wall for her to pass, but she waited until he came and stood at the customer side of the shop before slipping through the back way to fill her bucket.

Percy was in his chair. Wolfie was adding more hot water to the teapot. There was still water in the pan, and she used it for the bucket, topping it up with cold water.

'You and Norah ready for a brew?' Wolfie asked.

She shook her head. 'I'll finish the window first. Norah's talking to him from next door.'

'Oily Gilbert?'

Letty nodded. 'Oily on his head, and his manner.'

Percy grunted, shook his fist.

Letty pressed her hand to his shoulder. 'She can handle him, Percy. Don't you fret.'

She went back into the shop. Gilbert was just going out of the door.

Norah was faffing about, bending down for something and then looking elsewhere. Letty was concerned.

'Everything all right, Norah?'

Norah put her hand to her neck, peering about the shelves, distracted. She wouldn't look at Letty. Something had unsettled her.

Letty placed the pail on the shop floor. 'Did Gilbert upset you?'

Norah flapped her hands. 'Good Lord, no.' But she was upset, and Letty wasn't going to leave it. If Gilbert had said something, she would go next door and give him a piece of her mind.

'Wolfie's just brewed. Shall I get you a hot drink before I start on the glass?'

Norah shook her head and turned away from Letty.

'He did upset you! Why the creepy...'

Norah moved her hand to make her stop. When she'd composed herself, she turned about. 'He offered to buy the shop. Thought it might help us out.'

'Oh.' Letty didn't believe for a minute that Oily Gilbert was thinking of the Parkers, and she knew from her tone that Norah didn't believe it either.

'He's offered before. Percy sent him off with a flea in his ear, but...' She sighed heavily. 'Well, it's something to think about. Things are different now.' She gave Letty a bright smile. 'But it's only a thought. We've managed so far.' Norah was putting on a brave face, but the stress was taking its toll. She'd looked frazzled from the first day Letty had met her, but now she was depleted. Letty helped all she could, but it wasn't enough. Percy spent most of the day and evening in the chair and each night someone would come and help him up to bed. If not, he remained where he was as Norah didn't have the strength to get him upstairs. More often than not, the two of them spent the night in the chairs in front of the fire. Percy had many friends, people he'd helped over the years by putting stuff on the slate so they could get to sea and earn a living, and they'd all rallied round. Outwardly, he was a curmudgeonly old sod, but inside he was as soft as a downy feather bed.

'You can't manage forever, Norah,' Letty said kindly. 'I know I'm being selfish, but I could never work for that man.' She'd have to look for something else, eventually, but she wouldn't leave while they needed her.

'It won't come to that, Letty, and he'd have to offer a lot more than he did. We're not the dwindling business we once were – thanks to you.' She made scooping movements with her hands. 'Go to that window before the water is stone cold.'

Letty did as she was asked, glad to use her energy cleaning. How much longer could the Parkers manage if Percy deteriorated further?

* * *

Back behind the counter that afternoon, Letty tried not to think too much about the consequences of looking for another job, her disappointment and worry mingled with sadness for the Parkers. This shop had been their whole life, how could they bear to leave? Yet she knew it was only a matter of time. Norah was already exhausted, and Percy had made little progress. She was deep in thought when the bell rang over the shop door and a cheery face came towards her.

'All right, petal. What a delight it is to see your lovely smile.'

'Ah, Walter you old charmer. I could say the same for you.'

He came towards her, with his swaggering gait. You could always tell the men who went to sea by the way they walked, as if they were still on a rolling deck. Walter's swagger always seemed more pronounced, as if he was permanently coming through a storm and he had, in a way. Losing his wife and having his children taken away was not a storm Letty would want to face. He came to the counter and leaned on it. 'How's the ole bugger today then? Any better?'

She shook her head. 'Hard to tell.'

'By, it's a rum ole do. Not the same without him leaning on this 'ere counter. Thought he were glued to it and nowt but a bullet would shift 'im.'

'I don't think he did either.' To her horror, her voice cracked and she coughed and spluttered in a small attempt to disguise it, but Walter was not to be fooled.

'There, there, lass. 'Twill be all right. He's a stubborn old devil. He ha'nt found 'is fight yet, but he will.' He rubbed her back and gave her a hug. He smelled of tobacco and coal and for a moment she was with her father.

The bell over the door rang again and she sprang back, ready to serve the customer. Walter gave her arm a gentle squeeze and went through the door to Percy.

They were busy that day and she was glad. It meant her work here had not been in vain if the value of the shop had increased. She comforted herself with the thought that she had hopefully made life a little easier for Norah in her hour of need. Letty was getting to know many of the regular customers and they her, the name of the ships and the companies they were with. They chatted of their catch, if the market was paying a good price, what ships were due in, which ones were late. She had surprised herself of her knowledge when she'd had so little before, but it was from Norah she learnt her skills. It wasn't a question of knowing the stock and where it was located but what it was used for. A man could walk in and Norah would know the size of every item without being told. Slowly and surely, Letty was learning too.

In the late afternoon, Norah came with a brew and stood with her, leaving Percy in the company and care of his mates. From time to time, a wave of laughter erupted and the pair of them raised their eyebrows, wondering what the cause of such merriment had been; no doubt the tales were not for mixed company.

'We've good friends, Letty,' Norah said. 'We've a lot to be grateful for.'

Letty chewed on her lip, fighting to stem her tears. She must not weep again. Norah needed her to be strong. She almost snorted into her mug trying not to cry and the pair of them laughed.

'That's better, lass,' Norah said, her voice soft. 'It's not as bad as it seems, it never is.'

22

Letty was in the small back room at the Bethel Mission Hall with the other volunteers who gathered on the last Sunday in each month. Three tables had been drawn into the centre and the women were sorting the donations into piles. Letty was in charge of children's clothing. The Hewitt sisters, Rosa and Lucy, were on ladies clothing and occasionally tried on hats and jackets, not that they were in need; their father had passed away, leaving them a substantial sum. They were financially secure and had time on their hands. Instead of frittering it away, the two middle-aged spinsters supported many charitable causes with both money and time – which, in Letty's eyes, was a far clearer indication of their kind hearts. She found a little jumper that might fit Alfie and held it up to get an idea of the size. It looked too big, but he would grow into it and it would keep him warm when he was sat on the step.

'I'm going to take this for my neighbour's child,' she called out, folding it and placing it to one side. Mrs Barton, on men's clothing, peered over her gold rim spectacles. Letty took a penny from her purse and walked to the collection box at the side and dropped it in.

'You don't need to do that, Letty. If it's a child in need.' Ruth Evans was trying to sort an accumulation of socks, pairing those that were serviceable and putting others to one side that could be darned. A third pile would be unravelled, the wool reused, and those beyond rescue set aside to be sold to the rag and bone man.

Mrs Barton stopped sifting.

'I'd rather give a contribution, Ruth,' Letty replied. 'It all helps in one way or another.'

Mrs Barton nodded her silent approval. Letty's friendship with Ruth had been viewed with suspicion by the older women, but over the weeks, they had come to accept it as genuine. Ruth was not one for following the rules and Letty had an idea her strong-spirited aunts had something to do with that. Alice Wiltshire and Helen Frampton were a formidable combination and their influence was widely respected.

Mrs Barton, never Lydia, was the eldest of those gathered and permanently clothed in black. She'd lost her husband, brother and son when the *Sceptred Isle* was lost with all hands off the Scottish coast. She was not a tall woman but was sturdily built and had an indomitable spirit. Outwardly, she was terrifying, but Letty had glimpsed the tender side as she handed over clothes to young lads who turned up at the mission, parentless and alone. Funds were always needed, and Lydia Barton was not backward in coming forward when looking for donations.

When the piles were sorted, they were placed into baskets. These would be transported to the mission superintendent's house in Orwell Street. From there, they would be distributed among the families in need or offered to those who turned up at the mission with very little of their own.

The mission cart arrived, and the driver and his lad heaved the baskets onto the back of it. The caretaker came with his keys.

'All done, ladies?'

'Yes, thank you.' Ruth turned to the other ladies to get their agreement.

Mrs Barton slipped her bag over her arm. 'A good job done. Onward to the next.' Her face was stern, but there was a twinkle in her eye.

The Hewitt sisters helped each other on with their coats and gave each other looks of approval, that they were indeed presentable. They linked arms and the caretaker held the door open for them and Mrs Barton followed them out.

Ruth turned to Letty. 'Are you going straight home?'

Letty picked up her bag. 'No, with Alec away I'll go to the mission. I'll spend an hour or two writing letters for anyone who wants me to. Or reading to them.' Of all the things she contributed to help the mission, this was the thing she loved most. To send the brief missives home for boys and men who couldn't write. Even if their loved ones couldn't read, someone would be found who could. Many times, it was a simple message on a post-card. Her thoughts turned to Alfie again and she ran her hand over the jumper. At least Anita was making sure he could read and write. Whatever their circumstances now, his mother was trying to secure him a better future.

'I'll walk with you.'

Letty nodded. It was not unexpected, for Ruth would want a legitimate reason to respectably visit the mission and the chance of seeing Colin Wilson – although Letty wouldn't mention it and Ruth might deny it if she did.

They walked together, the distance taken up with easy conversation, of Alec's progress and of her work at the Parkers'. Their lives were poles apart now, but one day, if Alec achieved his dreams, they might yet be a trawler-owning family too.

The mission entrance was busy with men seeking accommodation, kitbags piled in one corner. Sunday was not a day of rest here. Ships would arrive any time of the day and night and the door was always open. As Ruth stepped into the lobby, Norman, at the reception desk, disappeared to the office. Letty waited with Ruth and, as expected, Colin Wilson came out to greet them. Ruth's eyes sparkled when she saw him, and Letty hid a small smile. She didn't mind being an excuse for Ruth to drop into the mission.

'Letty. Miss Evans.' He gave a little nod of his head in respect.

'Ruth, please,' she corrected him.

'Ruth.'

She smiled with delight. 'I thought I'd call in before I made my way home to Father. In case there were any messages. Or...'

'Nothing other than we're short staffed. We've lost one of our cleaning team.' He addressed Letty. 'Marie Turner.'

'Oh, Lord, poor Marie.' Letty was concerned. Marie was a widow with three children to support. A prolonged bout of illness would be disastrous for her. 'Is everything all right?'

'It is, thankfully. She's getting married.'

Letty let out a long breath in relief. 'That was a whirlwind romance. I never knew.'

'It was a bit rushed by all accounts, but then these things are. If a man has to go to sea, he has to go to sea.'

Letty nodded. At least Marie would have someone to care for her and the kiddies and Letty hoped it was a marriage of love and not convenience. Almost the entire female staff at the mission were widows of fishermen or their orphaned children. It was one of the many ways the mission helped those in need, and those too proud to take charity. It was a delicate balance for both parties.

Letty peeled off her coat. 'Can I be of help?'

Colin glanced over his shoulder, where new arrivals waited to be allocated a bed for the night. It was clear things were chaotic. The waiting men were getting restless. The smell of food drifted out every time the door opened, no doubt making hunger pangs more sharp.

'If you could strip the beds, that would be helpful. We'll pay you of course.'

Letty shook her head. 'I don't want payment. There's a woman somewhere who needs the money to keep her family afloat.'

'Well, if you know of anyone?'

Letty touched the jumper. 'I might.'

To their surprise, Ruth took off her expensive jacket. 'If Letty shows me what to do, I can help too.'

Colin was horrified. 'Oh, Miss Evans.' He corrected himself, 'Ruth. We can't expect you to.'

Letty doubted she knew one end of a pillowcase from another, but she was willing to step out and contribute; and whether it stemmed from her good heart or for the attention of the port missioner, what did it matter. A good deed was a good deed.

Ruth could not be dissuaded and so their jackets and bags were stored in the office and Colin led the way to the surprised supervisor, Mrs Crumb, who gave them aprons and showed them where to find the clean sheets and deposit the soiled ones. It soon transpired that Letty was right about the pillowcases, but although Ruth was not used to the work, she was willing to do it and soon they had picked up a fair pace together. The beds in the dormitory were stripped and Letty insisted on taking the sheets to the laundry, leaving Ruth to put on the pillowcases. When they were done, Letty led the way to the staffroom and Ruth flopped into a chair. Her face was red with effort, but she couldn't hide her smile.

'What on earth will your father think?' Letty passed her a mug of water.

'Outwardly he'll be cross. Secretly he'll be glad.'

'Are you sure?'

Ruth drank, nodded. 'He worked for his wealth, Letty. He's a farm boy at heart. He'll be out on the land right now, loves nothing better.' She eased back into the chair, but her back was perfectly straight. 'I've been given everything, as have my brothers, but we have also been told that it comes with great responsibility.' She smoothed at her skirt, her gaze on her hands. 'My mother was all for public service.' She paused, was quiet for a time, then looked up, smiled brightly. 'My father expects me to carry on her good works. As do my aunts. And I'm happy to do so.'

'But surely not menial work?'

'Why on earth not? A contribution is a contribution. Like your penny for the jumper. It all counts, doesn't it?' Her face clouded. 'My brothers are involved in the running of Hammonds. I am not allowed to be involved, though my brain is just as quick. I can have responsibility, but only as my father sees fit.'

'But your work and their work *is* of value. And perhaps they don't have a choice either,' Letty ventured. 'On the farm, my parents are equal. It couldn't run without Mother and Father working at their own jobs. It's hard to say who works the hardest. If Mother sat down, her hands were always busy – knitting, darning, feeding a pup who couldn't suckle. Every day was a workday, for the pigs and hens don't know any different.'

'You sound like my father. He never stops working.'

'Habit perhaps.'

'Perhaps. Or perhaps he's just lonely.' Ruth got up, took Letty's mug and rinsed it out. 'I went with Aunt Helen to hear Bertha Brewster speak at the Methodist Hall. The world is changing and we must change with it; to shape the world we want to live in. For ourselves and for our daughters. Don't you agree?' How could Letty not. Ruth continued, 'When I'm with Aunt Helen, I see how strong the women are. Their men are away at sea and they have to manage on very little money. I've seen the squalor, the poverty. When I was old enough, my mother took me around the village to give assistance to anyone who needed it. But it was nothing as to the things I have witnessed here.'

Letty was quiet. She lived among that squalor, but it was only temporary. Between them, Alec, Dorcas and herself would get something better and that day wasn't far off. She thought of Anita, trapped by circumstance, of the boys who could not read so were doomed to remain in low paid jobs. There was no doubt the world was changing, but was it changing fast enough?

* * *

Ruth's car had been called for and she had been driven home by her chauffeur. Letty's head had been full of their conversation as she made her way home. How much easier it was to embrace change when you had choice. Ruth was kind-hearted, but she had little idea of the reality of scraping by. Most of the women Letty knew were too exhausted by the daily grind to contemplate changing anything, and what little that could be put by was soon used up if anyone in the family fell ill.

Letty took the jumper she'd bought for Alfie and knocked on Anita's door, opened it and called out. Anita came from the back way, drying her hands on a cloth. Alfie was sitting at the small table, drawing on his slate.

'I found this little jumper. I thought it might fit, Alfie.'

Alfie turned round, watched his mother.

Anita held it out, assessing the size. 'That's a lovely bit of wool. Cheers, Letty. Look at this, Alfie, that'll keep you warm come the winter, won't it?' She leaned in the doorway. 'Had a good day?'

'I have. And I learned something that might be of help. There's work at the mission if you want it.'

Anita shook her head. 'Nah. But ta for thinking of me.'

Letty pressed her. 'But it would help get you out of this...'

Anita laughed. 'With that ruddy pious lot? Give off! Letty, they'd think I was after the fellas. I wouldn't stand a chance.' She grinned. 'Neither would they.'

'But...'

Anita's expression changed and she shrank back. Letty turned to see a copper. He wasn't the dock police, she'd have recognised him. He was large and thickset, with a mean face.

'Now then, Nita. A word?'

He barged past Letty and forced his way into the house.

Anita almost pushed Alfie off his chair and out into the yard. 'Doorstep.'

Letty held out her hand, shaken. 'Come on, Alfie, come with me, love. We'll see if there's some jam left.'

He slipped his small hand in hers and the door was banged shut. Letty shuddered. The copper clearly wasn't there on police business.

In her own home, Dorcas had dozed in the chair and moved sharply when Letty came in. She looked to Letty.

'It's not for long. Anita has a visitor.'

Dorcas looked down her nose at the boy and Letty felt Alfie's grip tighten. Letty didn't linger, took him through to the kitchen and cut a slice of bread, slathering it generously with jam and hoping Dorcas didn't come in with her tutting. She heard a clatter from next door. Something was banged hard against the dividing wall. Anita?

She smiled at Alfie whose eyes showed his fear, and she ran a hand over his head. 'What have you been doing today, Alfie? Been playing with the other kids?'

She squatted down before him and they chatted, trying to ignore the sounds coming through the thin walls. Her stomach churned. What could she do but stand by and listen, for it couldn't be ignored – and it couldn't be reported, for the police looked out for their own and women like Anita were asking for it, weren't they? Sally had put her right about that.

Letty sniffed the jug of milk to check it was not sour, poured Alfie a glass. Ruth was wrong. People like Anita were trapped.

Dorcas came bustling through the kitchen. 'What in heaven's name is going on next door? I've a good mind to call the police.'

'It is the police,' Letty snapped.

Dorcas looked at Alfie with pity and returned to her chair.

A short time later, they heard Anita's front door slam and a shadow pass across their window. A while after, the door opened and Anita stood back and called for Alfie. The two of them came out of the kitchen. Anita's hand covered her cheek and as Letty got closer, she could see the deep red marks about her neck, the dark patches where bruises were beginning to show. Anita tried to adjust her blouse to cover it and revealed the angry mark across her cheek.

'Oh, Anita.' Letty wanted to weep for the girl, but Anita held her head high. 'Can we do anything to help?'

She shook her head. 'I need to take my boy. Come on, Alfie love.'

He ran to his mother and tugged at her skirt. Anita kissed her hand, placed it on his head, then his shoulder, held her to him.

'Thanks,' she said, taking Alfie home.

Letty could only stand at her open door.

Across the yard, Sally Penny stood on her doorstep, shaking her head in pity. What had Ruth said about building a better world for their daughters? Change couldn't come fast enough.

23

At the end of August, Alec studied at the Institute for his skipper's ticket. He sat paper exams and oral and had to show proficiency in all manner of things. For the full two weeks he was home, Letty had sought the right time to talk to him about buying Parkers. The words had danced on her tongue and there they had remained, for she had not found the right moment – or the courage – to broach the subject. In her head, she had it all worked out, it seemed so logical; how could he say no? And yet something gnawed at her stomach. It wasn't so much his response she was afraid of, but his mother's. Would Dorcas agree to use the money from the sale of the *Stella Maris*? Letty made no mention of her idea to Norah because that's all it was at the moment, an idea, but one that could become reality if she could persuade Alec to invest. They couldn't rely on the whims of the fish market, she knew that much. For every ship that landed a record catch, there were many that didn't. The more knowledge she gained, the more she knew they needed to find security elsewhere.

Letty found a pair of size nine sea boots and handed them to the young lad who was sitting on the chair waiting for them. Fourteen and fresh-faced, he had walked in beside his father, who now stood in front of him, Norah at his side. The three of them watched as the lad adjusted his thick socks and pulled the boots on. He got to his feet and walked about the shop with a little more swagger than when he'd come in, and Letty smiled at the transformation. Would it last? For the tales she'd heard of seasickness, let alone the brutality of life aboard a deep-sea trawler, were obviously far from the lad's mind.

The father watched his lad. 'I got my first pair of sea boots from Parkers. As have your brothers. I'm hoping your chil'ren will be buying their boots 'ere one day.'

Norah picked up the boots and held them as the lad replaced his walking boots. They were repaired and worn but still serviceable and Letty thought that perhaps his sea boots would be the first pair of new boots the boy had ever had.

The sale made, Letty was writing out a receipt when Gilbert Crowe walked in. He nodded to the father and idled over to the racks of clothes. Letty seethed as he hovered about. Norah devoted her attention to father and son. They shook hands, the boy growing in stature as he did so, Norah offering a few words of encouragement as they left, walking with them to the door and closing it behind them. She glanced at the clock over the counter. 'Do you need anything, Gilbert? Only I need to get back to Percy, and Letty needs to be off on time as her husband's home.'

He placed his forefinger in the fob pocket of his waistcoat, studied the nails of his other hand. 'Then I'll be blunt.' He looked up at her. 'I wondered if you'd had chance to think over my offer. Times ticking on, and you and Percy could get something better suited now that he's...' He twisted his mouth, showing his yellow teeth. 'Not the man he was, shall we say.'

Norah's back stiffened. She had humoured the man, way beyond what Letty would have done, but he had overstepped the mark. As Letty watched him, she realised that had been his intention. Norah marched back to the door and opened it.

'I've not given it a thought, Gilbert.' Her words came out like gunshot. 'I've been far too busy. Now, if you'll leave us, we'd like to close *our* shop.'

He tapped his watch, the gold chain dangling between his fingers. 'Well, my offer won't stand forever – and it'll be a nice clean sale. My solicitor has the paperwork ready for you to sign.'

'That's rather presumptuous of you.' Norah pulled the door wider.

He strode past her and Norah shut the door behind him and leaned on it.

'I detest that man. Detest him.'

Letty pulled the covers over the glass cabinet that held the knives and compasses and took out the broom and began sweeping the floor.

Norah held out her hand. 'You get off to Alec. I'll finish this. I need to take my temper out on something. By, if I were a man, I'd have grabbed hold of him by his collar and thrown him out.'

'You should have said,' Letty replied, handing over the broom. 'I'd have been quite happy to do it for you.' The two of them shared a smile. Norah was exhausted. Letty longed to tell her of her plan, but she couldn't do that until she had spoken to Alec.

The bell rang out as the door opened and in he strode.

'Too late.' Norah began pushing the broom across the floor.

'What for?' Alec said, coming up and giving Letty a peck on her cheek. He took hold of her hand.

'I was coming to meet you.'

'Well good job you didn't. If them fellas get a look at you, they'll only feel miserable going home to their wives. I wouldn't want to do that to any of 'em.'

Norah laughed and Letty was glad that Alec had cheered her.

'Right, Letty. Get yourself off. I'll lock the door after you.'

Letty went through to the back to collect her belongings. Percy was by the fire, an empty look in his eyes. It made her heart ache to see him so frail and Gilbert Crowe's words bit sharply. She touched his hand, kissed his forehead and gave him her best smile. The passing weeks had not seen much improvement in him.

'I'll be back in the morning, Percy. Be good, no moaning at Norah.'

He grunted and she patted his hand again and went back into the shop for Alec.

As soon as they were outside, he slipped his arm about her waist, kissed her cheek. Gilbert was drawing his bolts across his own door and she looked away, drew close to Alec.

'A good day?' she asked him.

'Not bad. 'Twer easy enough, stuff I already knew, what me father taught me. But I've got to have that certificate. I won't get me insurance otherwise and I won't get a ship.' He put his hand up in greeting to an old boy who came towards them. The man touched his cap to Letty as they passed. 'I saw Sam Harris again. He's put a word in for me with Mr Hammond. I'll have my ticket, but it might be a while afore I get me own ship.'

'So you've passed then?'

He grinned. 'Not yet. But I will. Father was a good teacher, the best. And the *Stella* was a lovely old boat.' His voice became wistful and she stopped at the end of the road.

'Let's not go straight home, Alec. Let's walk a little.'

He released her, made an extravagant bow, sweeping his hand towards the floor. 'Where to, m'lady?' When he stood up, she punched him playfully, laughing, and he put his arm about her again.

They turned right and headed down towards the dock tower. Wagons rolled down the street, trains rattled past in the distance. She had grown used to it now, the noises and the smells. She pointed out different parts of the docks, the roads that led down to this and that. Who cured the best fish, where the different shops and offices were. She knew the tide times and market prices, what ships were due and when.

He grinned. 'Well, for a farmer's daughter, you've certainly got a good grasp of the fishing.'

She released his arm from her shoulder and took his hand as they walked along. 'It's my business to know. *Our* business.'

He nodded, squeezed her hand. 'I'm real proud of you, Letty. What you've learned, what you've done for the Parkers. For us. We're on our way now, that's for sure. Me ticket's almost under me belt and afore long I'll have me own ship – then we'll be looking to move out Mariners Row and get something better. More befitting a skipper's wife.' He released her hand, put his arm about her shoulder and pulled her close again.

They walked towards the lock gate, found a wooden rail and sat down on it. Seagulls screamed and soared high in the air. In the distance, they could see the factories and warehouses, the carriers laden with cargo to travel far and wide. Alec put his foot up on a capstan.

'Nothing ever stops, does it? Ships coming and going on the tides. You think they can't possibly get any more ships in the dock, and they do.'

'Aye. We made the right decision coming here,' he agreed.

'We did.' She had to say something, had to ask. 'Alec. I...'

'Spit it out, Let. What is it?' He frowned. 'Sommat bad happened?' She shook her head. 'Sommat good?'

Oh, she was being ridiculous. If she wanted to run a business and deal with the likes of Gilbert Crowe she needed to toughen up.

'I want to buy Parkers,' she blurted.

He nodded his head. 'Are they sellin'?'

'Not yet. And not to Gilbert Crowe... But Norah can't carry on forever, not if Percy doesn't improve.' She summoned her courage, she had to make him understand. It was about building their future. Security. 'It's a good little business.' He smiled and she was encouraged. 'I've helped turn it around and I know I can do more.' She told him of her plans, of what she could do, that they could live above the shop and save on the rent, ploughing the profits back into the business. 'The books are good, I've seen them. It's showing a good solid profit and it's got so much potential.'

He put his hand to her cheek. 'Where's my girl gone? The girl who wanted her land and her hens?'

She shrugged. That was far away, a dream, but reality was the here and now.

He bent forward flicked at a stone and tossed it into the water. 'How much do they want? And how are we going to buy it?'

She took a breath. Surely he knew?

'I thought we might borrow from what was put by from the sale of the *Stella*.'

He sat more upright. It made her nervous.

'It would be a loan and I'd be able to pay it back quickly. We could get your first trawler without borrowing too much from the bank.' Owning a trawler was way out of reach, years away, costing thousands, three or four at least. His dreams would take years, but this was something within reach. She knew it was a lot to ask. It wasn't just money. Wrapped in every penny was his father, his brother and so much more.

Eventually he said, 'Let me think on it. It's not just down to me. It's Mother's money too. I'll have to talk it over with her.' He gave her a small smile of encouragement, but at the mention of his mother, Letty's heart sank. Dorcas would never agree. He got up from the rail and held out his hand to her. 'Let's go home. I told Mother I'd pick up some fish and chips for tea.'

24

After they'd eaten, Letty cleared away, leaving Alec to chat with his mother. When she went to join them, he was filling needles.

'That's my work,' she said, teasing.

He shrugged. 'It's mine too. I have to mend the nets when we're at sea. Why don't you have a go? Mother'll learn ya, won't yer?'

Dorcas took a knife and sliced at the twine. 'Didn't think the lass wanted to.'

'I didn't, not to begin with,' Letty said truthfully. 'But I can see how useful it could be to learn. It would help me in the shop, if I had a better understanding.'

Alec nodded, gave her a small encouraging smile. Dorcas seemed reluctant.

'And when babies come along,' Letty added.

Alec winked at her. Dorcas picked up another piece of twine and began wrapping it about the needle.

'Yes, well. That's what I said *weeks* ago. You could be a good speed now if you'd started then.'

Oh, she was going to make her suffer wasn't she, and if Alec hadn't been there, Letty would have told her not to bother. But she sensed Alec trying to bring them together and if she had to meet her halfway, then so be it.

Dorcas kept winding the twine over and through the eye, over and through. She finished, cut the line, dropped the needle in the basket.

'Get the pole, Alec. We'll put it on the hooks on yon wall.'

Alec sprang to his feet.

'Bring that basket of needles over here, move that chair.'

Alec fixed the broom handle on the hooks that were either side of the wall and went back to filling needles. Dorcas moved the ball of twine to her left, the basket of needles to her right. Deftly tying the twine with practised hands, she made loops, tied a knot on the left side of the pole.

'First we make a series of clove hitches,' she said to Letty, making sure she was paying attention. She placed the back of her hand across the pole, palm open, and used it as a measure, drew the twine over it and pushed the needle through the back and over, moving her left hand again so that a series of loops, all a hand's width, were created along the top. 'Did you get that?'

Letty nodded.

Dorcas got up and made Letty take her place. 'Your turn.'

Letty sat down, took the twine and the needle. She made a loop, tied the first clove hitch, placed her hand against the pole and slowly made her way along it. It took much longer, her hands awkward, Dorcas watching her intently.

The first row finished, Dorcas pulled the rope off and made her do it again. When she was satisfied Letty could manage the first row, she began to work the second row. She looped the needle through the last loop on the pole and began making her way back along the first row, creating another series of loops. Letty began to see the net take shape. Dorcas was a good teacher for Letty had watched her often, her hands moving at ten times the speed she was now. She got up and stood to the side, indicating for Letty to take her place on the chair. Letty sat down and began to make the row, Dorcas nodding with approval. She finished the first row, Dorcas checked it.

'Now, same thing again, but coming back t'other way.'

Letty moved, slow and careful, trying to make the diamond shapes even.

Dorcas checked it, pulling it taut. 'Not bad, but you'll have to get your speed up if you're to make any money.'

She flicked her hand in the air for Letty to move and sat back down, moved rapidly across the net, a quick rhythmical movement that was quite hypnotic. Letty picked at the sisal fibres that had stuck in her hands.

'Aye, that's another thing. We should've put a few rags on your hands to stop that. You'll get used to it.' Letty didn't want to get used to it. It was good to learn another skill, but she had no intention of ever having to use it. Dorcas got up, made Letty sit down again. 'Keep practising. It's the only way you'll pick up speed. You did well.'

Letty could hardly believe her ears. It was the first nice thing Dorcas had said for weeks. She saw Alec grinning to himself as he filled the needles and she smiled at him when he caught her eye. Crafty devil.

* * *

Alec passed his exams and got his ticket. He called briefly in at the shop to share his good news in a week when it was badly needed. Percy had suffered another small stroke that had set him back. Despite great care and much cajoling from his visitors, he hadn't yet found his fight as Walter had been so sure he would.

'I'll be back late, Let,' Alec told her. 'Don't wait up. Me and the lads are going to take on the town.'

'Has the town been warned?' Norah said, a twinkle in her eye.

Alec pushed his cap back on his head. 'Nah, we plan on taking her by surprise.' He kissed Letty and went back out into the street where a couple of fellas were waiting for him. The two women walked to the window and watched as they slapped him on the back and set off in the direction of Freeman Street. No doubt they would call in at every pub along the route.

'You're always a happy lass, but by, he puts the colour in your cheeks.'

'Maybe he won't so much tonight, but he deserves to celebrate. They all do.' He would be drunk as a lord and stink of ale, the house would rattle with his snores and she didn't care one bit. He was home for now, but come the morning, he would be after a ship – and he still hadn't talked to Dorcas about the shop.

* * *

Despite Alec's saying not to wait up, Letty did, as did Dorcas, the two of them winding twine by lamplight. Letty braided on the pole, Dorcas overseeing her work, and she had begun to build up a little speed. Dorcas had been impressed and, as a consequence, more bearable. If she'd known the difference it would make, Letty might have learned sooner.

After midnight, they heard Alec stumble through the courtyard and Letty got up and went outside. The moon was bright, and she could see him steadying himself against the wall, muttering as he did so. He took a deep breath, forced himself away from the wall and staggered forward. He startled a little when he saw her in the shadows, then, recognising her, gave her a daft grin. 'Letty, oh light of my life, dear Letty. What a beautiful sight you are.' He stumbled again, gathering speed, and she rushed to him, caught hold of his arm and walked beside him, guiding him towards the front door. Dorcas was in the open doorway, the light casting her into silhouette, and she stepped out and caught the other side of him, the two of them pushing and pulling him into the warmth of the house and the safety of the chair. He gave them another daft grin. 'Oh, Mother. What a time I've had.'

'Aye, I can see.' Dorcas half smiled, looked at Letty, and in that instant the three of them were united. Something had changed and Letty liked it. They both loved him. Both of them.

'Passed me ticket, I did.' He tapped his breast pocket. 'Got it here, next to me heart. And you and Letty are next to me heart, Mother.' He belched loudly.

Dorcas tutted and Letty bit her lip to suppress her laughter.

'I'll get him a glass of water.'

When Letty brought it to him, his hand was unsteady, and so she held it with him as he drank back.

'Ta, Let. I've got hell of a thirst on.'

'And you've not managed to quench it all evening?' his mother said.

'Not beer enough in Grimsby to quench me thirst.' He drank more water, pushed Letty away. 'Me own ship next, Mother. By, Father would be proud, wouldn't he? And our Robbie.' He hung his head. Was he going to be maudlin now that he was sobering a little?

Dorcas poked at the fire, stirred the coals and flames burst up and licked around them. Her face took on a reddish tone. She looked up at the photographs on the mantel, touched the frame of the one with Robbie.

Alec thrust himself back in the chair and it creaked under his weight. He held out his finger, wiggled it towards Letty. 'Hardys are going up in the world, Let.' Another grin, another belch. He scratched his chin, frowned, smiled as if only just seeing her. 'What a team we make, eh. You with your shop and me with me ship.'

Dorcas turned from the fire, her hand resting by the photograph of her son. The mantel was full of Hardys, but there was not one of Letty's family. Dorcas had not left space. The flames took hold, spat out a spark of wood. Letty watched as it glowed then cooled on the hearth.

Alec started again. 'Oh, yes. We'll buy Parkers first. Then a ship, a fine ship.' He got to his feet, put his hands on his hips, swayed. 'Everyone will know the name Hardy. The whole ruddy world.' He swung out his arms, stumbled. Letty sprang forward, caught his arm.

Dorcas was watching her, digesting his words, rolling them around in her head, trying to make them fit, frowning, her grey eyes glittering in the light. Letty's heart began to thump against her ribs.

'Let's get you to bed, my lad.' Letty gripped his arm, his muscles hard, trying to bear his weight, keep him upright. She made for the stairs, Alec grasped the rail, put a foot on the lower step.

'What does he mean – buy Parkers?'

Letty paused, turned to look at Dorcas, still holding on to Alec, who swayed unsteadily. He lolled forward, a hand on the stair to steady himself.

'He's drunk.' Her voice betrayed her, and she knew it; her whole body betrayed her.

'I've seen him worse.' Dorcas's words were like the sparks that spat in the grate.

Letty must keep going up the stairs. Alec moved his leg to the next step,

Letty kept close, holding on, her hand to his back – not that she could have stopped the weight of him if he fell.

She heard Dorcas sit down in the chair. 'No doubt he'll tell me in the morning. Goodnight, Letty.'

There was no affection in her final words.

Letty pushed Alec the remainder of the way and he flopped onto the bed. She managed to remove his boots and belt, loosen his shirt and pushed him over to make room for herself, balancing precariously on the edge of the mattress. She didn't undress, simply laid next to her husband, who snored like one of her father's old sows. She dug him in the ribs with her elbow and he grunted, snuffled. He stopped for a while, then started again, thunderous this time. Propping herself up on the pillows, she watched the light break, the sounds of the day begin, wondering what it would bring. 'No doubt,' as her mother would say, 'it would all come out in the wash.'

25

Dorcas didn't mention the shop the following morning and Letty knew it wasn't because she'd forgotten, for her face was set hard, with no trace of the softness Alec restored to her. Letty left for Parkers dreading what she would come back to. Alec would be out, looking for getting a ship, but Dorcas wouldn't have let him leave the house without an explanation. Letty wondered what had been said. He should have talked to his mother sooner, avoided his drunken ramblings, but perhaps he didn't have the courage – and for that she couldn't blame him, for hadn't it taken long enough to broach the subject herself?

Letty was distracted, jittery all morning. She had handed over the wrong change, which was soon rectified, and when the customer left, Norah said, 'What's the matter, child?'

Letty sought to reassure her. 'I'm tired, that's all. Alec went out celebrating, he was late – and very drunk. I couldn't sleep for his snoring.'

'But that's not all it is.' She held Letty's gaze and Letty couldn't lie. Norah had been so kind, a mother to her in the absence of her own. She pulled at a stray thread on her sleeve; she must mend it tonight or it would surely unravel. She tucked it under her cuff.

'In time...' she began.

Norah tilted her head to one side, giving her her full attention. A man came in the shop and went over to the jackets, pulled at a few. Letty made to move and Norah stayed her with her hand. 'In time?'

Letty took a deep breath. She glanced to the man who had taken a jacket and pulled off his own. She should serve him.

'He can wait,' Norah said, gently.

Letty made her voice a whisper. 'I know it won't be for years yet, but... If you did decide to sell, would you consider selling to me, and Alec.' The words were out, and she felt ashamed. Wasn't she as bad as Gilbert Crowe? Her cheeks burnt with embarrassment, but Norah only smiled.

'Oh, Letty. When the time comes, for come it will, it will gladden my heart to leave it in your capable hands.'

Letty felt the tension she had held on to since last night ebb away.

'It was only an idea. Alec has to talk it over with his mother first.'

Norah raised an eyebrow. 'Oh, I'd like to be a fly on the wall for that conversation.' Norah knew all about Dorcas's opposition to Letty working in the shop. 'Now, go and serve that young man and I'll pop back and check that Wolfie hasn't chewed Percy's ear off.'

* * *

At the end of the day, Alec appeared at the shop. He was cheerful enough to Norah, but Letty could tell by his face that things hadn't gone well.

'I hear congratulations are in order, Alec.' Norah came from behind the counter and shook his hand. 'You'll be well on your way now you have your skipper's ticket. I expect it won't be too long before we're reading of your record catches in the *Grimsby Telegraph*.'

He laughed. 'It'll be a while yet afore I get a ship of me own, there's nothing in the offing – but thanks for your confidence.'

'Not at all misplaced. You're a young man with ambition. Much like your lovely wife here.'

Letty caught her breath, hoping that Norah wouldn't say anything, but she chatted only of the trawlers that had landed that day.

Out on the street, Alec was quiet until Letty asked, 'Did you get another ship?'

He thrust his hands in his pockets. 'Aye. The *Falberg*. As mate. It sails tomorrow afternoon.'

'Oh,' she couldn't hide her disappointment. She'd grown used to him being home at night, drunk or sober.

'I can't afford to spend more time ashore,' he said, pragmatically. 'I need to be earning to make up for what I didn't earn to sit me ticket.' He pulled out his baccy and papers, stood against the wall to roll one, folding the paper, making a line of tobacco, licking the edge and rolling it closed. He pulled out a match and struck it on the wall, turned his back to the wind, cupped his hand, puffed out the smoke. He didn't take hold of her hand as he usually did, and so she threaded her arm through his as they walked down the road towards the railway crossing. The safety gates were over, and they waited among the crowd for the fish wagons to rattle down the track.

'How's your head?'

He shrugged. 'Oh, Let. It's not my head, it's my mouth you should be asking about.' He drew on his ciggie and blew out as the train rattled past, on and on, wagon after wagon, and he stopped talking as the noise grew too loud for them to hear each other. When the last one cleared, the gates were swung back and people surged forward.

'You talked to your mother about the shop?'

He nodded.

'And?'

He took one last draw on his cigarette and tossed it into the gutter.

'She weren't too happy. I said you'd be better explaining it. Aw, Let, I'm all right with 'owt to do with a ship – the wind, the stars, the movement of the moon and the tides – but I can't explain your idea properly. You're going to have to do that.' He took hold of her hand and she felt its warmth, its strength. 'We'll do it together.' He gave her a small smile, but she didn't feel encouraged.

* * *

Dorcas was making pastry when they got back to the house, her hands in the earthenware bowl, rubbing fat into flour. She looked up only briefly when they joined her, but long enough for Letty to see the blaze in her eyes. The braiding pole was fixed to the wall, a half-woven net on it, the basket beneath.

'So, you want to buy the shop, do you?'

'Eee, Mother. Lass's just got in the door. Give her chance.'

Dorcas continued with the rubbing, flour and fat falling through the air and into the bowl.

Letty took off her coat and hung it up; it felt heavy in her hands, the hook too high.

Dorcas picked up a small jug, splashed water into the bowl and thrust it at Alec. 'Get more water, lad. Make a brew.'

Letty reached out to take it from him. 'I'll get it.'

Dorcas snapped her head up. 'No, you won't. My *son* will get it.' She glared at him.

Alec went out to the pump.

Letty touched at her neck, her throat restricted; she couldn't quite get enough air. She wanted to open the door but held back, feeling sure it would give Dorcas more to criticise. The tea caddy was on the shelf next to the savings tins and she reached up for it. She had saved quite a sum these last months, and Dorcas must have saved too; there were now enough needles filled of an evening to keep Dorcas busy all day. They were all working together, helping each other, for something better, something bigger than all of them. She should have spoken to Dorcas herself. Now she'd had all day to stew over it. She clasped the tin, drew it down.

'Didn't take you long to make your move. By, you're a fast worker, I'll give you that. A fast worker.'

Letty turned. Dorcas was gathering the pastry, rolling it about the bowl, scooping up stray pieces and pushing them in place. She scattered flour over the table and slapped the lump of pastry down on it. Every movement was sharp, hard. Angry. Dorcas fixed her gaze on the pastry, picked up the rolling pin.

'It wasn't...'

Dorcas put the pin on the pastry and rolled it forward, her hands fast, her arms thick. 'Something else you want to rush into without thinking it through the pair of you. Just like when you got wed. I shouldn't think that poor woman knows what's hit her. First her husband, poor soul, and then you... You.' She shook her head. 'Didn't take you long to get your feet under the table there; forcing yourself on 'em, making 'em grateful with all your *good deeds*. Washing their sheets and fetching their coal in.' She looked up, narrowed her eyes. 'Oh aye, nowt gets past me. People like to gossip.' She heard the door.

Alec came into the kitchen, set the pitchers on side by the window. He looked at his mother, then to Letty. Her cheeks felt like they were on fire. The rolling pin went up and down, the slap of the pastry on the table as Dorcas moved it.

Alec touched the braiding pole. 'Shall I put this through the other room?'

'No.' Dorcas looked up. Paused. 'And that's another thing. Sneaky that was.'

'What was?' Alec frowned, but Letty had an idea what was coming next. He pulled at a piece of pastry and Dorcas slapped his hand. He laughed but his mother did not.

'That one, getting me to teach her to braid. Now she wants sommat, she's happy to sit there of a night pretending she wants to learn!'

'I told her. I thought it might bring you two... to a...' Letty held her breath. '...A better understanding.'

'Don't make excuses, lad.' Again, Dorcas pressed at the pastry and Letty thought it would be as hard as the knockers of hell by the time she was finished. She wanted to laugh. It was all so ridiculous. This misplaced rage. She was trying to help. She must speak out. Dorcas was like the bull in the field, beating at the ground. She needed to calm her, not run away.

'Dorcas, you've got it all wrong, you really have.'

Dorcas stood back, her hand to her hip. 'Well, didn't you just know it, boy. *I've* got it all wrong. I might have known it'd be my fault.'

Alec reached out, put a hand on his mother's shoulder. 'Let her speak. Give the lass a chance.'

Dorcas wrested her shoulder, and he moved his hands, splayed them by his side and urged Letty to step in.

'I was thinking of the future, of all our futures.' She looked to Alec, and he moved his head, urging her to go on.

Letty stepped forward, pulled out a chair and sat down. Dorcas picked up a plate, flipped the pastry on the rolling pin it and slid it onto it.

'It was an idea. I had no intention of buying the shop. It didn't even cross my mind until Gilbert Crowe came in. He owns the shop next door.' Dorcas picked up a jar of jam. Her mother's jam; they'd made it together, when the fruits were plump and full of flavour. Dorcas spooned it into the centre of the pastry, spreading it out to the edges with quick movements. 'Norah doesn't like him, Percy loathes him.' Dorcas looked at her, her mouth a thin line. 'He keeps coming in the shop, offering to buy it. Norah doesn't want to sell to him. But she might have to, if Percy...' The words caught in her throat. She must not think of the worst. 'It got me thinking. We could buy the shop and live above it. I'm sure we could run it between us.'

Dorcas lifted the bone-handled knife, picked up the plate and balanced it on her other hand. She spun the plate slowly, taking off the excess pastry with a knife; it dangled, longer, and longer then fell on the table.

'Between us, eh?' She set the plate on the table, brushed her floury hands down her apron.

'In time.' Letty looked down at her hands. They were sore from braiding. One of the sisal fibres had gone deep into her hand and she rubbed at it, hard and rigid beneath her skin. 'It would give us a choice.'

'Choice?' Dorcas dropped the knife in the bowl and set it in the sink.

Letty swallowed, looked at Alec. He was frowning. She would have to explain herself. To both of them.

'So that Alec wouldn't have to go to sea, if he didn't want to. And our children, if we should have them. We can keep them safe.' Alec stared at her, confused. 'I thought to save you sorrow. You've already suffered so much loss.'

Dorcas's back was to her. She pressed her hands on the sideboard, her head up, then down.

Alec stepped forward. 'Letty, you've...'

Dorcas glared at him and he was quiet. She turned to Letty.

'Look at him,' she said, moving her chin towards where Alec stood. Dorcas leaned her back against the sink. 'Can you see the lad behind a counter, selling boots and sea gear.' She sneered at Letty. 'You think having a shop will stop him going to sea! It's in his blood. You might as well tell him to stop breathing.'

She snatched the tart from the table and went to put it in the range. Heat flooded out as she opened the door, then banged it shut.

Letty looked to Alec, but he turned his back to her. She got up and went to him, turned him to face her, looked into his eyes – and she knew she'd got it all wrong.

Dorcas barged past them. 'Tell her, lad. Don't let her get any more daft ideas about you not going to sea.'

He let out a long sigh and Letty knew she wasn't going to like what he had to say. 'Mother's right. It's not about choice. It's the hunt for the catch, the challenge, man against the sea. The adventure.'

Dorcas nudged him away from the sink with her elbow. 'How can you expect her to understand? A farmer's daughter. She's for the land, not the sea. Not like us. I told you...' She stopped, but Letty could guess at what would come next. That he should have married Becky.

There was silence then, a huge looming silence that filled every scrap of that small room, and suddenly there wasn't enough air for them all to breathe, and Letty pulled open the kitchen door and stepped into the yard. It was barren and grey, the walls thick with smuts of smoke, and the air smelled of coal and fish and filth. She yearned for the smell of cut grass and blossom, to watch the cabbage whites and red admirals dance among the meadow, to hear the lark and the thrush sing so sweetly instead of the wild screams of trains and ship's horns. Her grey future stretched before her. Dorcas was right and she hated her for it.

26

Letty closed her eyes, put her hands to her face, to block out her surroundings, to try to think, to try to see something better, light and colour, but she couldn't, and she wanted to weep for all she had left behind, for the beauty, but mostly for her family, for a sense of belonging that she did not feel here, and doubted she ever would.

Alec came out to her. 'Come inside, love.'

She shook her head. She didn't want to go back, not yet. 'I need to walk.'

She made to move. He stepped forward.

'I'll come with you.'

She shrugged, not caring, and stepped into the alley, made her way onto the street. The air was chilled, she should have gone back for her coat, but too late now. She didn't want to turn back, so she tugged at her cardigan, pulled it about her.

'Don't be mad, Letty.'

'I'm not mad.' He put his hand out to her, she pushed it away. 'I am *not* mad.' She sounded ridiculous.

He let his arm fall, pushed his hands into his pockets and walked beside her. Her eyes smarted with tears of humiliation and she brushed at them with her hands.

'Letty,' he said softly.

'Don't,' she managed to say, 'please don't.'

They walked towards the railway line; he kept pace with her, silent until she sat down on a wall, tired, cold, her temper spent. He reached out again, gently rested his arm across her shoulder, and she let him. Encouraged, he pulled her close.

Eventually, she said, bitterly, 'Your mother is right.'

She wanted him to disagree with her, but he didn't, and loneliness washed over her like a great wave.

'She's older. Wiser.'

Letty stiffened, shrank away from his hold. 'And so we can't ever choose to make something different of our lives? Just follow a pattern, a clove hitch and a sheet bend, patching up the holes as we go through life.'

'I never wanted another life, Let, only this. I can't explain to you what it's like when you go to sea and leave all this behind.'

'Leave me behind.'

'No, Let, that's the hardest part. The best part is coming home to you. But I can't give it up.'

'I would never understand?'

He shrugged, sighed. 'I don't know. You knew what I did when we met.'

She nodded. 'Knowing is one thing, understanding is another. There wasn't time.' She felt sick, Dorcas's words ringing truer the more they talked. 'I don't want your mother's life, Alec. I don't want her sorrows.'

She got to her feet, started walking again, not wanting to let the fear take hold. He caught up with her.

'Don't you have faith in me? I'll be a grand skipper, like my father.'

Like his father who was no longer here. She wanted to scream at him. What did faith have to do with it. She bit at the inside of her cheeks, the skin broke and the metallic taste of blood filled her mouth.

He grabbed hold of her arm. 'One day you'll have your land, Letty. I made a promise and I intend to keep it.'

She thought again of home, of the fields. If she closed her eyes, she could see the wheat as it shimmered in the sunshine, could feel the warmth of the sun. She opened them again. She could see the love in his eyes, but it didn't comfort her.

His face was set, determined. 'Soon I'll have my own ship, I'll be in charge of my own destiny.'

'Your destiny,' Letty corrected.

'Aye.' He touched her face and she wanted so much to forget about all this, all these stupid, stupid words, but she couldn't.

'And the shop?'

He dropped his hand. 'Aw, Let. Forget about the shop. The Parkers aren't selling and by the time they do, you won't want it. You'll have kiddies to look out for, and your land. You'll be busy with our boys.'

'Who'll go to sea? Like their father?'

He nodded, expectant pride in his eyes, and she felt her heart break beneath her ribs. It was a hard physical pain and tears fell now, a dam broken, and she turned away from him, away from the docks and the ship that would carry her love away.

'I wish we'd never come here.' Her voice cracked with sobs and she began to run down the street. He ran after her, caught her. She looked up at him, her eyes sore from tears. She must look so ugly, and she was so stupid. How could he love her?

He smoothed his hand over her face, pushed her hair back and kissed her, and she knew she loved him, would always love him, but she couldn't make it right in her head. Something didn't fit, but she couldn't work out what it was, and she was too tired now to think.

'Don't let's argue. Not tonight. I'll be gone tomorrow.'

They walked back in silence, her hand tight in his.

That night, she gave herself to him, but her mind was elsewhere, and her heart was not full of love as it should be. Tears fell down her cheeks and into her ears, her neck, her hair. And when he had finished, he lay beside her, his hand to her belly and he slept. At least one of them was content.

27

By morning, Letty had made up her mind. She *would* buy the Parkers' business. Alone if she had to. She and Alec had plenty of time to argue over their future – and their children's future, should they be so blessed. She thought of Norah and Percy. A life without children and only Dorcas for company would be unbearable.

Alec and his mother were in the kitchen when Letty went downstairs. Dorcas was quieter, civil even. Letty had laid in bed, listening to them, their voices low, Alec's firm, and she had a sense that he was telling his mother of their conversation. But what had the two of them talked about really, only of her fears? He'd expected her to behave like his mother, to fall into a set pattern. He was mistaken.

'I thought you might like a lie-in,' he said, tentatively. 'You were tired.'

Dorcas cracked eggs into a frying pan. The fat sizzled and spat. 'Sit yerself down. There's fresh bread in the crock.' She was almost pleasant.

Letty lifted the lid, took out the bread. Alec handed over the knife. Letty cut a slice, scraped it with butter. Dorcas put a plate in front of her with two fried eggs that seemed to stare back at her.

'Thank you. I was tired. I laid awake all night thinking on what you'd said.' She took her bread and broke the yolk, ate the golden sunshine. Not as good as eggs from home. 'You were right, Dorcas,' she said, tucking into her food, hungry now. 'I know so little of the fishing life.'

Dorcas gave her a satisfied smile. 'I knew you'd see sense in the end.'

Letty nodded. 'The thing is,' she continued, finding her voice, her confidence. 'We came here for something better. Didn't we, Alec?' She stared at her husband. 'You said things were different here, that we would get left behind if we stayed in Lowestoft, that they were stuck in the past with their sail drifters.'

'I did.' He shifted awkwardly, looked to his mother.

Dorcas took a cloth, dipped it in the washing-up water, wrung it out, wiped the cloth around where Alec had been eating earlier.

'Did we do the right thing?' Letty looked to them both, serious, questioning. She placed her fork on the plate. 'I thought we did at the time. You made it all sound so exciting, so possible, Alec.' They were watching her, curious. She ran her bread around the plate, soaked up the egg.

When she'd finished, she got up, went to the sink and put her plate in the bowl. It sank in the greasy water. She looked out of the window. The yard was as grey and bleak as it had been yesterday, but in between the bricks, where the mortar had worn away, there were small splashes of green, speedwell and dandelions thriving among the muck and grime. She would thrive too.

'I didn't think things through, did I, Dorcas? I fell in love with your son, and I forgot about everything else.' But she hadn't forgotten about her family. She twisted, lay the cloth on the side, turned to Dorcas. 'I had no idea what lay ahead for me, for us. I only knew I loved Alec. I thought that was enough. But it isn't, is it?' Alec opened his mouth to speak, but she stopped him. 'You said yesterday that your mother was wise. She is. I should have listened, but I didn't.' Her own mother had asked her if she knew what the life entailed, but she had been so full of love for Alec, for want and need of him. They could surmount all the obstacles, she'd been so sure of it. Only she'd had no idea how lonely she'd be, without him, without her family. 'I'm not going to rush into anything. Not like I did when we married. I need to build something more solid.'

Alec was watching her and she looked steadily into his beautiful blue eyes. She loved him so much, remembered clearly the day he took her along the quay and asked her to marry him. He'd kissed her and the whole world had faded away. There was nothing else. Not her family, the farm, the wide-open sky and the trees. Just him. And she loved him still – but it was not enough.

'I will buy Parkers, or another business. Eventually. I truly believed we came here to build something better. Together. But that's not the way it is, is it, Dorcas? It's you and Alec. Your family. Then there's me. On the outside.'

Alec got to his feet, pushed the chair back. 'Now, come on, Letty, that's not fair. We've always included you.'

'Have you?' She turned to Dorcas, whose face was black as the smut-covered walls outside. 'It's your family, your ways – and your money. *Your* destiny, Alec, you said that only last night. Not *our. Your.*'

'But we're all in this together.' Alec was coming towards her, but she held him back. He stood next to his po-faced mother. Alec was not yet his own man; no matter what he talked of his destiny, or tried to make it theirs, it was his dreams for the future, the way he saw it – and his mother.

'I thought we were too. But your mother thinks I'm only after your money. *Your* money, *family* money. I'm no part of it.'

'That's right, you're not,' Dorcas pitched in. 'That money *is* family money, for my sons. The *Stella Maris* was there long afore you came along.'

Alec didn't contradict her.

Letty felt suddenly cold, deflated. She knew it was what they thought, but hearing it said out loud hurt her heart.

'Mam's right, Letty. It was always meant to go for another ship. It's Father's legacy. And Robbie's.'

She swallowed away the bitter taste that came in her mouth.

'And when our sons come along? What then?'

Dorcas took the pole from the wall and her basket of needles. She rested them on her hip. 'That's years away.'

Alec walked towards her, reached out to touch her arm, but she shrugged him away.

'It seems you can only see your mother's point of view. You've not considered mine.'

'I could say the same for you.'

She stared at him. She had been swept off her feet by this charmer, this man who was full of life and fun. Her mother had tried to warn her. Dorcas had tried to warn her, and she hadn't listened. Now their words were clear and sharp – and she couldn't bear to be in the house one minute longer. She turned away from him and hurried out into the courtyard, away from the house, as far away as she could. And this time Alec didn't try to stop her.

She remembered Norah telling her about a park and she walked until she found it, glad to be among the green of oak and ash that reminded her of home. Prams and dogs paraded past her, but she couldn't see them, couldn't hear the sound of birdsong, only the words of her husband, her mother-in-law, sharp like needles. She walked on the grass, ignoring the signs not to, leaned against a lime tree, felt the bark beneath her fingers. The splinter in her hand caught and she picked at it with her nail until it bled as the fibre came forth. On the path, she saw two women, pushing a pram, one holding a toddler's hand, and felt a stab of regret, knowing she would never do that with her own mother – and she could never imagine doing so with Dorcas.

She walked further. There was a bandstand, the Salvation Army band in their navy uniforms preparing to play. She paid for a deckchair and sat down, let the music wash over her. She'd forgotten it was Saturday, the days blending into one another, for ships came and went every day. It was much like the farm in that respect. Except Alec wasn't in bed at the end of the long day as the men were at home. Her father, her brothers. She missed them. Her mind worked out how many days a year he would be home, of the Christmases they would not spend together.

The band played a medley, slipping from one tune to another, and she remembered dancing with Alec at their wedding, being close, the smell of his hair, his skin, the sweetness of his kisses. They were young, they would work it out. She was suddenly overwhelmed with love for him. Why was she wasting time, on sailing day. Oh, Lord, it was sailing day. She sprang out of the deckchair, pushed past the other people sitting there and hurried away from the park.

* * *

When Letty returned, the house was empty. The back door was open, and Dorcas was in the yard. She looked in the room for Alec's bag, but it was gone. She went to the step.

'Where's Alec?'

Dorcas twisted, looked at her. 'Gone.'

Letty froze. 'When.'

'A half-hour since. He waited, thought you'd come back.'

A seagull swooped down and sat on the outhouse roof. Dorcas shooed it away.

'He can't leave. Not like this. I need to tell him...' Letty turned on her heel. 'What if something happens?'

'You should have thought of that earlier.' Dorcas came back into the kitchen, closed the door, blocking out the light.

'But I have to see him.' Letty glanced up to the clock. 'There's plenty of time before his ship sails. Couldn't he have waited?'

'He shouldn't have to wait.' Dorcas spat through gritted teeth. She pulled out a chair and sat down at the table and put her hands to her face, rubbed them up and down. When she withdrew them, Letty could see how tired she looked, and for a moment she felt for her. How could she bear to let her son go back to sea when she had already lost her husband, her Robbie. Letty would never understand, never. Dorcas sat back in her chair, placed her hands on her lap. She stared down at them, hands made rough from years of braiding, the skin thick, the nails short. 'Oh, lass, you have so much to learn.'

Letty couldn't move, she wanted to talk, she wanted Dorcas to explain, she truly wanted to understand. She loved Alec, loved him. 'If anything should happen...'

Dorcas looked up at her. She didn't say anything, she didn't have to.

Letty snatched at her jacket.

Dorcas got to her feet. 'What do you think you're doing?'

Letty froze. The clock ticked loudly behind her, ticking away the minutes. Too fast, it was ticking too fast. The blood was pounding in her ears. She had to say goodbye. 'I have to see him...'

'It's too late, I said.' Dorcas raised her voice, came towards Letty, so close that Letty could see the sadness in her eyes. 'He's gone. You can't go to the docks and see him off. It's bad luck.' Dorcas grabbed hold of her wrist, began to shake her. 'Don't you understand anything at all, you silly, silly girl?'

Letty wrested her hand free. It couldn't be too late. It was only too late when... She had to see him. 'Oh, be damned with your stupid superstitions.'

'Stupid they might be, but what else do we have to hold on to. If anything happens and word gets round...'

Letty wasn't listening. She tore out of the house, Dorcas calling out to her.

'On your head be it.'

She flew down the street. She had a good hour or so yet. Even if the *Falberg* was first out the lock, she would have time to give him one last kiss. Just one. She would be happy with one. She ran over the railway bridge, down the other side and stopped at Riby Square just as the crossing gates came across and blocked her way.

The last carriage went by and the gates were pushed open. People walked past, eager to make their way. Men with their gear over their shoulders walked on, throwing the change from their pockets to kids who scrabbled about for them. Men came towards her, some with arms wrapped about their sweethearts, children at their heels, glad to be home. Safely home. That was what counted, wasn't it? That they were safe.

Dorcas's words came to her. If the catch was poor, if the nets were lost, if anyone was lost overboard, if... They would blame her. She daren't even go and see the Parkers in case anyone saw her and reported back to Dorcas. She couldn't move.

A woman stopped in front of her. 'Are you all right, lovey?'

Letty nodded, shook herself into action. Too late now. Too late. She turned away from the docks and made her way home.

28

The overwhelming nausea that had washed over Letty as she turned away from the crossing that day hadn't left her. It was worse in the mornings when she woke up in the empty bed, longing for Alec to be there beside her, and she couldn't bear to eat, couldn't bear to look at Dorcas. In three weeks, they'd barely exchanged a handful of words. Letty no longer filled the needles for Dorcas in the evenings. Instead, she helped at the mission – anything that kept her out of the house. Mostly, she wrote letters for the men or read to them. One or two of them she was teaching to read and write for themselves. It made her feel useful, made her forget her fears, for she couldn't think of her own troubles while she was helping someone else.

Norah had known something was wrong from the moment she walked into the shop on the Monday morning after the *Falberg* sailed and Letty had wept and told her some, but not all, of what had happened, angry with herself for being weak, for being afraid. Norah had been a comfort whereas Dorcas had not. There would be no comfort until Alec was safely home.

One evening, Letty was sitting at her table in the corner when Walter came over and slid into the chair opposite. The room at the mission was almost empty. A couple of young lads were playing cards, another, older, had nodded off to sleep by the fire. Molly was making her way around the room with a broom, her movements languid. Letty had just finished a letter to her mother, thanking her for the parcel of jams and preserves she'd sent to help them through the coming winter. Instead of cheering her as it once would, it only made Letty more miserable.

Walter took a seat opposite her. 'How you doing, lass?' He reached across and tapped her hand. She was tired, but she found a smile for him. 'Not long now and your man'll be home.' She hadn't said anything, but Walter had sensed her sadness. Perhaps having shared enough of his own, he was quicker to see it in others. He moved his hand, rested it on the paper beside her. 'I wondered whether you'd write me a letter.'

'Of course.' She stopped her daydreaming and picked up her pencil, pulled a sheet of paper towards her. 'Who do I address it to, Walter?'

'The Hull Orphanage. I believe that's where my three boys were sent when the missus died.'

She leaned forward, clasped his hand in hers, and it felt so wonderful just to touch someone, but only made the pain and longing for Alec stronger than it had ever been. 'Oh, Walter. How did you find out?'

Molly pushed her broom under the table, and they moved their legs out of the way. Letty smiled at her. She returned her attention to Walter, let go of his hand.

'I did a bit of asking about. Young missioner helped. Said they'd have records.' He sat back, his hands resting on his stomach. 'Found my daughter too. She's in Louth.' His voice was heavy with pride.

'She's apprenticed to a milliner, getting proper training, and her lodgings.' He took out his pipe and baccy pouch and began to fill the bowl, packing it down with his thumb. He chewed on the stem without lighting up and Letty could see his eyes shine with tears – tears of happiness, but perhaps of sadness too. 'She were taken in by a lady who took her from the orphanage. No one told me where they'd gorn. And for a long time, well, I was in no fit state to care. The drink.' His voice broke.

'That doesn't matter now, Walter. What matters is you've found one of your children.'

He chewed again on his pipe. 'She thought I were dead. And she knew I couldn't read nor write.'

'So how did you find her?'

'Dolly Pope. She moved with her lass to Louth when she married. She lost her man, Pat, off the Western Isles.' He nodded again, thoughtful, gave a small laugh. 'Went to buy an hat, Dolly did. An hat, I ask yer! She saw our Betsy. Just knew it wer' our Betsy. Spit of her mam, she is.'

'You've seen her? Oh. That's wonderful, Walter.'

He waved his hand at her. 'Not yet, but that's how Dolly knew it was our Betsy. "Spit of your Maisy," she said – that's the missus. She was a fine looker was my Maisy.' He cast his gaze downwards, remembering, then looked up to Letty. 'Dolly's lad got word to me.' He rubbed a hand over his forehead. 'I haven't had time this trip, but now I know where she is, I can go next time I'm ashore.' He nodded to himself, his mind busy with plans.

Letty didn't rush him, only waited until he was ready to speak. She watched Molly move about the large dining hall. A sullen girl, Letty didn't think she'd ever seen her smile. Other women here had suffered loss, but they still found a cheerful word no matter their circumstances, but not Molly.

'I've got hope now, Letty. Summats I niver had before.' She turned back to him. 'My lads might have thought I was gorn too. Like their mother, God rest her soul. They've no record of them at the orphanage here, but missioner thought they might have gorn to Hull. So, if they has, I want to know.' He sucked on his pipe and she heard the air pass through it. 'I want them boys to know I 'ant forgot 'em.'

Letty nodded, moved by his words, his restraint. How hard it must have been for him. To come home to find his wife dead and buried, his children gone, and to have to go straight back to sea.

'No time to waste then, Walter. Let's get this letter written. Tell me their names.'

'Aye I will. Will you look out fer the letters? While I'm gorn. So they write back to you?'

She smiled. 'Of course, Walter. I'll be glad to.'

It didn't take long to compose the letter and she read what she had written back to him before placing it in an envelope. It already bore a stamp and as soon as she gave it to him, Walter got up.

'Thank ya, my darling.' He kissed the envelope, kissed her cheek. 'I'm gorna pop out and post it right now.'

She watched him as he threaded his way through the other tables, not stopping to chat as he would normally do.

Molly was by the window. It had taken her an age to do a simple job. She leaned on her broom, gawping out the window, then moved her way to the door.

Letty gathered her writing materials and placed them in the cardboard wallet that was kept in the front office, suddenly more cheerful. Walter had hope. It was a wonderful thing to have. His good news had put a spring in his step. Good news, it was so precious. When Alec came home, she could give him hers. For she had twice missed her monthly bleed and she'd soon realised that the terrible sickness was not only down to their parting.

She placed her hand to her belly. Life beginning. There was hope for them all.

29

Alec had been desolate when the *Falberg* made its way out of the fish docks and into the Humber three weeks since. He'd stood in the wheelhouse with the skipper, knowing Letty would not come, but hoping to see her dear face one last time before they went through the lock. He'd closed his eyes and tried to picture her there, as he did so many times. He wanted to give her the world. He *would* give her the world, only he wasn't sure what she wanted any more. She had talked of a farm, a world he knew nothing of, but it was only fair, for didn't he spend the majority of life on the sea. She would be lonely, like his mam was lonely, without Father, without Robbie, their old life lost to them now. Never had he been so full of doubt. It was not a good thing, for to go in search of fish, a man needed to be an optimist, the odds were stacked against them.

It was with an even heavier heart that he sailed back into Grimsby. It wasn't that it was a bad ship, and the skipper was fair enough, but it had been one ruddy thing after another. They'd moved from fishing ground to fishing ground only to find other trawlers had beaten them to it. One night they'd met with a squall that knocked the deckie learner off his feet as they battled to get the net aboard; the third hand had almost gone over the side. The fish hold had not been full as they had turned for home, and the quality poor.

Now, as they waited in the estuary for the lock to open, trawlers to the front, side and back of them, he made one last tour of the deck, then went up to the bridge.

The skipper eyed the accumulation of ships, their place in the queue. 'Looks like we'll be making poverty corner by the look of this lot.'

Alec agreed, they were definitely at the end of the line.

'It's not what I hoped for when we set out, but old feathery legs has been on our backs since we sailed out.'

Alec nodded; the devil had been on his back way before they left port.

He slapped Alec on his shoulder. 'I'll make it up to you next trip, lad, if you're back with me as mate.'

'Aye.' Alec nodded. 'Hardly likely that I'll get a ship of me own yet.' Trawlers were in short supply. The admiralty had requisitioned a number of them, trialling them as minesweepers. It was an uncertain world they were living in.

The skipper leaned out of the open window and shouted down to someone. 'How's deckie learner?'

Alec didn't hear the reply, the answer muffled by the wind.

The skipper leaned back in the wheelhouse. 'He'll be home with his feet tucked under the table tonight. His mother fussing about him. He'll soon forget.'

The lad had been lucky. If Robbie had moved quicker, Alec might perhaps have saved him. He'd heard tales of how men had been washed overboard with one wave and washed back again by another. Chance, that's what it was. Chance.

Skipper looked at his watch, blew down to the chief. 'Moving upriver now.' He took the wheel. 'By, lad, it'll be good to be home this time. Missus'll have the fire in the grate and food on the table. Keeping your bed warm.'

'Sommat like that.'

He nudged him with his elbow. 'Lusty lad like you.'

Alec laughed. They listened to the men calling out across the dark water.

'Wife wasn't too happy when I left.'

'Ah, she'll have forgotten all about it. Women are contrary like the fish. The chase is part of the excitement.'

Alec was not elated as he shimmied down the ladder to dry land. In his gut, he knew they would barely cover the costs when the catch went to market. The crew would be paid, but there would be no bonus share for them. They might have made a bit from the cod livers, but when the loss of the gear and repairs were taken out, there would be no point coming for pay tomorrow. He wanted to get back to Letty and be loved, as much as he wanted to get back to his ship and make a good catch, change his luck. More than three miserable weeks and no money.

He'd had plenty of time to think about Letty's idea for Parkers but couldn't bring himself to use his father's money for it. It had to be set aside for a ship. It was his heritage, his and Robbie's – and his mother's. He understood Letty's fears, for they were his too, but he'd learned to put them aside, as his father had and his father before him. Fishing was more than a way to earn a living, it was in his blood – and he was the last remaining Hardy to carry it forward. He hoped Letty would understand that.

* * *

The sight of the fire when he opened the door lifted him, but not as much as seeing Letty. His mother had dozed off, but Letty turned at the first click of the door and went to him. He dropped his bag, suddenly less weary, less sad, and they held on to each other, two people tossed about in a storm. Her lips were warm on his.

Dorcas stirred, leaned forward and raked at the coals.

He let Letty go and he went to her, kissed her cheek. 'You look tired, Mother. Have you slept all night in the chair?'

'We got word you were due in. Had to welcome you home with warmth, boy.' She got to her feet and said, 'I'll be after getting you something to eat,' and disappeared into the kitchen.

Letty kissed him again and he longed to take her upstairs, but that would have to wait. His mother would want to know the ins and outs of the trip, and now he was home he had a hunger that he hadn't had in days, for food – and for Letty.

He sat down by the fire and Letty removed his boots, his socks, eased his shoulders, and they went through to the kitchen. His mother put a plate of food in front of him and took the seat opposite. Letty leaned against the sink, her back to the window.

Alec told them of the trip, how the skipper was fair but they'd met with obstacles at every turn. 'I'll not make a bean and I don't want to have to dip into the pot, but...'

Dorcas tapped the table. 'Well, you've your lass to thank for that. She went after you the day you sailed.'

Letty glared at Dorcas. Why the evil old sod. 'I wanted to see you before you sailed,' she said quickly. 'I made my way down Freeman Street and the crossing was over. I thought better of it and came back. I knew not to.'

Alec nodded.

'You didn't tell me that?' Dorcas snapped.

'You didn't ask.'

'You wouldn't have told me if I had.'

She didn't answer her.

Alec cut into his bacon, stared down at his plate. 'No need to ask how you two have been getting along.'

Letty turned her back. She would not allow Dorcas to spoil their time together. Not this time.

Dorcas topped up Alec's mug. 'She's never here. Always out somewhere.'

Letty laughed. 'I'm at the shop or at the mission.'

Alec glanced at her, she smiled, shook her head. It seemed to irritate Dorcas, who got to her feet.

'I have no idea what you get up to away from his house. All the time at the mission. Around the men. Walter Stevens kissed her the other day. In full view.'

Letty snapped. 'He kissed my cheek. That's all. As a thank you. And who told you that? Bet's daughter? Molly? That lazy little so-and-so.'

Dorcas folded her arms, faced her, goading. 'Widowed, she is, working to feed her kiddies and you taking work from a woman that has no man to take care of her.'

'What I do at the mission I do for free.'

Dorcas raised an eyebrow. It incensed Letty, but she wasn't going to let her get away with it.

'I was writing a letter, as I always do, for the men. To their mothers and wives, those they have left behind – as we have left those we love behind.' Her father would be in the fields now, her mother stirring the porridge before she fed the hens.

She looked to Alec, who had not interrupted, had let them have their words. He looked so tired, so disappointed. And she knew that was not just with the catch. She and Dorcas were like two flints rubbing at each other. She'd longed for him to be home, but Dorcas was always there to spoil things, and always would be.

'When I write those letters, I think of Alec, and oh, yes, Dorcas, I think of you. Of how precious those words are to a mother. To a wife.'

Alec finished his food and Dorcas took his plate, put it on the draining board.

Letty moved away from her, closer to Alec. 'Walter had good news. He's found his daughter; he might yet find his sons.'

Dorcas snorted. 'What do we care. Alec's the most important thing in life – or he should be. He is in mine.'

Letty would not be distracted. She was close to Alec now; she could smell the salt and the fish on his skin. She took his hand in hers. 'He had good news and I have good news of my own to share. I was waiting for you.' She placed his hand on her belly. It should have been such a happy moment, one she wanted to share with him alone. But there wasn't time, there was never enough time. Things had to be said. She'd played it over in her head. How she would tell him – just the two of them. 'You're going to be a father.'

He stared at her, the words sinking in, and as they did, his face broke into the loveliest smile that filled his blue eyes with such a sparkle. He got up, pushing the chair away, put his arms about her and lifted her off the ground.

'Oh, Let. Oh, my darling lass. When?'

'March.'

He kissed her, over and over. 'A son, Mother! I'm going to have a son!'

Letty laughed, happiness bubbling up inside her. 'It might be a girl.'

He kissed her again, clasped her hand. 'No, it's a son. I know it. Oh, Letty.' He lifted her again, and his arms were strong and she felt as light as the air about them. He put her down, pushed his cap back on his head. He looked to his mother. 'Another Hardy, Mother. Isn't it grand?'

Dorcas nodded, contrite.

His trip was bad, the next one would be better. He would soon get his own ship. He would be master of his own destiny and Letty had already worked out a way to be mistress of hers.

30

Over the coming weeks, the sickness left her and Letty felt strong and hearty. Norah was delighted and even Percy managed a lopsided smile.

'You'll be leaving us when the child comes.'

'I will not,' Letty was adamant.

'But Alec...?' Norah was cautious. 'He'll want you at home.'

'With my mother-in-law. I don't think so.' She folded a pile of long johns that had been pulled about that morning. 'As long as you don't mind, and as long as you need me, I'll be here for you both.'

Norah clasped her hand. 'You're a good lass, but you might think differently when the baby comes.' Norah paused before speaking again. 'A child is a precious thing. Your man is doing well. You won't need to work afore long. He has the ways. I've seen it before. Built for success.'

These were the words Letty turned over in her mind as she made her way home. Was Norah trying to let her down gently? There had been little talk of selling the shop, nor of Letty buying it, and she wondered if Norah would think of selling to Gilbert Crowe now that there was news of her child. Alec had had a run of better trips, but it was October; winter was coming and who knew what lay ahead.

Letty called in at the mission to see if there was news for Walter, or if anyone was in want of her letter writing, but as there was not, she made her way home.

Dorcas looked up from the basket of needles she was threading, surprised to see her. 'You're early.'

Letty nodded. 'No one needed any letters.' She went through to the kitchen.

Dorcas called to her. 'I left you some tea on a plate. A bit of stew.'

Dorcas had softened towards her now that she was carrying Alec's child and she was only too glad to sit down to a hot meal instead of cold boiled meat and bread.

Letty lifted the plate that covered the pan and served herself. Her hunger had returned once the sickness had passed.

She stuck her head around the door. 'Thank you, Dorcas. That's very welcome.'

Dorcas nodded – and was that the beginnings of a small smile? Letty ran her hand over her slightly swollen belly. Perhaps they could come together yet.

She ate alone, hearing the needles clatter into the basket as they were filled. When she'd finished, she cleared away and went to sit in the chair opposite the fire. She took up a needle, feeling a little more inclined to meet Dorcas halfway.

After a while, Dorcas said, 'You've a good colour to your cheeks these past few days.'

Her voice was soft, and Letty responded accordingly. 'I feel much better. I don't feel sick of a morning.'

'That's a good sign.' Dorcas stared up to the mantelpiece, the photos of her boys. 'I had bad sickness with Alec. Not so much with Robbie.' She looked down at her needle, cut the twine with her knife and dropped it into the basket, took up another. 'A long way to go yet.'

'Yes.' Letty wasn't even halfway there. Sometimes it seemed so far away, at others so near. She fiddled with a knot in the twine, picking at it with her nails. 'My mother suffered sickness so badly with my little brother she had to take to her bed. We girls had to feed the hens and keep the house going.'

Dorcas tilted her head to one side, listening, and it made Letty want to weep. How had they remained as strangers all this time? When they loved the same man?

'I was afraid that might happen to me.'

Dorcas kept winding the twine, watching Letty as she talked. 'Some women suffer. It's the same with labour. Some are lucky, some not.'

They were disturbed by someone rattling the front door handle and the two exchanged glances. It was an odd sound, with no force to it, but an urgency nonetheless. Letty let the twine fall and went to answer it.

Alfie was shivering on the doorstep, his arms wrapped about him, white-faced, his lips blue.

'Alfie, whatever's wrong. Where's your mam?'

The boy reached out for her hand and tugged her forward. Letty glanced back at Dorcas. 'I'll be back in a minute.'

Dorcas nodded, carried on with her winding.

Alfie's hand was like ice and once inside the house, Letty knew why. There was no fire, the house in darkness, and as he led her towards the stair, she stopped and lit the lamp before following him. The sound of dull moaning came from above and as she ascended the stairs, the unmistakeable stench of stale blood and urine made her gasp.

Anita was lying in the bed, her face like marble, her dark hair damp about her face, the sheets wet around her head. Letty set the lamp on the upturned crate by the bed, took hold of Anita's hand and with the other touched her forehead. It was hot and wet.

Anita opened her eyes.

'Letty.' Her voice was a whisper. The smell was overwhelming.

Under the bed, the pot was a strange mixture of urine and blood. Behind her, Alfie fidgeted. She turned to the scrap of a boy. How long had his mother been like this? She couldn't recall the last time she'd seen Anita – she'd been at the shop, the mission, meetings with Ruth and her aunts, too busy avoiding Dorcas.

Letty turned to Alfie and squatted down before him, taking his hands in hers, hoping to reassure him, trying to hide her own fear. Did a four-year-old have any notion of what was happening? His cheeks were sunken, his eyes dark, and she could only wonder how long he'd sat alongside his mother in this cold house. She smiled for him. 'Go back and get Mrs Hardy, Alfie, can you do that?'

He didn't need asking twice and Letty heard him tread carefully downs the stairs in the darkness.

Shortly afterwards, Dorcas clattered up them, muttering about the smell, the inconvenience, stopped when she walked into the bedroom. 'What in heaven's name...'

Letty twisted, shushed her. 'Get Sally. And take Alfie? I don't think he's eaten in a while.'

'Or washed,' Dorcas said. She put a hand on his shoulder. 'Come on, boy Alfie, let's get you sorted.'

He shook his head, ran to his mother's side.

Dorcas tugged at him, but she was gentle. 'You can come back. We need to get Sally from over the way. Come help me.'

He looked to Letty, his pointed chin wobbling, eyes brimming with tears.

She went to him. 'Go with Mrs Hardy. I think she has some biscuits in her tin.'

Dorcas was thin-lipped but Letty knew it wasn't in anger at Anita, more at the circumstances. Letty felt the same.

Anita stirred herself, struggled to raise her head from the filthy pillow. Her voice was scratchy and thin. 'Go, Alfie. Good boy.'

Dorcas held out her hand and the boy took it. Only when she heard the door close did Letty speak.

'Oh, Anita. What on earth?' She lifted the sheets. They were soaked in blood, old stains and new, her thin nightdress more red than grey. The smell made Letty want to heave. She let it drop.

'Baby. Tried to get rid.' She coughed into a rag and Letty saw the blood in her sputum. Were they too late?

She was relieved when Sally hauled herself upstairs. There was no need for words when she entered the room, the two of them exchanging silent glances.

'I'll get some hot water on. Get the range going,' Letty suggested.

Sally peered across at Anita, shook her head. 'Aye, lass, that'll be the thing to do.'

Letty hurried downstairs, found another lamp and lit it, opened the range. The ashes were cold, and there was no telling how long Anita had laid up there. She found kindling and coals, struck a match and got it going. It would be quicker to get water heated next door and she grabbed a couple of pans from the kitchen and went out to the pump, back down the alley and into her own kitchen. Alfie was settled at the table with a plate of biscuits and a mug of milky tea. In the light, they could see how filthy he was.

'It'll be quicker to heat water here. Fire's out next door,' Letty explained.

Dorcas nodded towards the range. 'Take what I've got. I'll get another pan on.'

She didn't linger, grateful for the speed, filled a pail with the hot water, found some washcloths. Dorcas handed her a towel.

Alfie looked up at her and she smiled and felt her heart tear. 'We're just going to wash your mam.'

Dorcas was grim-faced.

Letty hurried back with the water. Sally had opened the window and the room was icy cold, but Anita still burned with heat.

'She's gone again. Keeps drifting in and out,' Sally said, softly. 'I found an old blanket and sheets. We can clean her up a bit.'

Letty struggled to hold back the tears.

Sally nodded towards Letty's belly. 'Are you all right with this, lass. Did you want to stop with the boy and send Dorcas in?'

Letty shook her head. 'No, I'd rather be here. Anita is my friend.'

Sally gave her a warm smile. 'Well, I doubt she's had many. Poor lass.'

Between them, they gently cleaned her, rolling her on her side and propping her up with rags while they washed her back, removed the sheets; the mattress would have to be burned, but for the time being, they laid newspaper on it and covered it with an old sheet. When they were done, Letty took the bloodied sheets and dropped them outside in the yard. It was still dark, but there was light enough from the moon to see. She put her hand on the line to steady herself, feeling faint, pressed her other hand to her belly.

Dorcas came out. She handed Letty her woollen shawl. 'It'll be cold in that room, more so when you're tired. How's things upstairs?'

Letty could only shrug. 'Alfie?'

'By the fire. I gave him a good wash.'

Letty nodded. Dorcas was kind when she wanted to be, it just didn't seem to happen very often.

Back in the house, Letty searched about Anita's kitchen. There was a mouldy heel of bread, a few potatoes that had shrivelled and sprouted, a packet of oats mixed with mouse droppings and not much else. Sally called down to her and she went back upstairs.

'Can you sit with her?' Sally had brought up the small chair from downstairs and put it by the side of the bed, the grey nets fluttered with the breeze from the open window. 'I'll send for my lass for old Mrs Wilkinson.' She leaned close to Letty as she went with her to the bedroom door and whispered, 'I think we're too late for the doctor and Mrs Wilkinson will know what's best for the lass.'

Letty settled herself at Anita's side, pulled the shawl about her shoulders and took hold of her hand.

Anita opened her eyes. 'Alfie?'

Letty leaned forward. 'He's next door.'

Anita closed her eyes. 'Box on side.' She lifted her finger to point.

Letty got up, searched about, found a tin, lifted the lid. It contained papers, a ribbon, a couple of shells, a cheap brooch. A card from her wedding day with guidance on how to be a good wife, a good husband. Only the simplest of treasures but treasures all the same and it caught at her heart to think that Anita had so very little happiness in her life. She bit back tears that threatened to overwhelm her. Anita had started her married life with such hope... When she turned she found a smile from somewhere within her and placed the tin next to Anita.

'My family.' Her eyes were pleading. 'Don't take Alfie to the poor house.' She moved her head. 'Not like Dan. No.' She gripped Letty's hand. 'Promise.'

Letty nodded, swallowing down the lump that had lodged in her throat and managed to say, 'I promise.'

She laid her hand on Anita's brow, hoping that Sally had got word to

Mrs Wilkinson. She was used to death on the farm, used to the beginnings and endings of creatures, but she'd never been alone. Anita was too young. Alfie needed her. The desperateness of the situation weighed heavy on her and she sank down onto the chair and took hold of Anita's hand. Her friend didn't open her eyes again and her breath become so shallow that Letty had to lean close to her chest to discern any movement. Despite their efforts to clean her, the smell was dreadful. Letty sat with her until the first fingers of light played through the window, showing the desperateness of the room. There was nothing of comfort, nothing at all.

Anita stirred, mumbling. 'Alfie? My Alfie.'

Letty shot across to the window, pushed aside the net and leaned out. A woman who she guessed was Mrs Wilkinson had arrived and Sally was talking to her.

Letty shouted down to them. 'Get Dorcas.'

Below her, the door opened and Dorcas looked up at her.

'Alfie. She wants Alfie.'

Dorcas disappeared, pushed the boy out of the door and Letty heard him climb up the stairs, one step, then another. He slipped between Letty and his mother.

Anita opened her eyes, smiled at her boy. She reached out for his hand. 'Be good, boy. For Letty.'

He nodded and she closed her eyes. Letty pulled him to her, and he sat on her knee. The breeze picked up, blowing the nets further into the room, and rain began to spatter the windows. It wouldn't be long now.

Sally came in, followed by Mrs Wilkinson. She took off her bonnet, her snow-white hair thick and plentiful beneath it, and smoothed it into place.

Letty got up and stepped away from the bed, taking Alfie with her. He stood in front of her and she rested her hands over his shoulders. They watched the old woman as she checked Anita's pulse, shaking her head. She pulled at her eyelids to check the pupils.

'She's gone.'

Letty choked back a sob and squeezed Alfie's shoulder. He hadn't made a sound the whole time he'd been there. Letty took him from the room, somehow made her way downstairs and back next door and collapsed into the chair by the fire. Alfie stood beside her and she pulled him to her. She must not weep, she had to be brave for the boy.

She composed herself, spoke gently to him. 'Your mam has gone to the angels with your dad. Do you understand?'

He stared at her. Did he?

Dorcas went into the kitchen. Letty heard her shoes click across the tiled floor, the clock ticking away the minutes, the fire crackle and spit. She wanted to close her eyes and open them and know that it was all a bad, bad dream. What happened to Anita could so easily happen to her. If she didn't have Alec, how would she manage? She could go back home. But what of Dorcas? She had no one but Alec. They were all trapped, weren't they?

Dorcas sat down in her chair, bent into her basket, took up an empty needle. 'Bring yonder stool and sit by me, boy. You can help.' She glanced to Letty. 'Best keep busy.'

Letty agreed. Alfie did as Dorcas had asked; Letty got to her feet.

'I'll pop back next door.'

Sally was downstairs talking with Mrs Wilkinson. 'Burton will be here presently with his cart. He'll take her to the mortuary.' Anita's tin box was open on the small table. 'Can't find no funeral insurance. It'll be pauper's grave. Poor lass.' The woman was matter-of-fact and somehow it stilled Letty's panic. How many times had she faced death? She nodded towards Letty. 'When's your time, lass?'

'March.' She felt strangely adrift. Like things weren't really happening, that Anita would come downstairs any minute and tell them to 'clear off.' Alfie's slate and chalks were on the table. He was working on the letter P and Anita had drawn a pig with a curly tail. She picked it up. 'Alfie's letters.'

Sally picked up her cardigan. 'I've paid Mrs Wilkinson, there was money in the lass's purse.' She looked about her. 'Not a lot to sort out when all's said and done. She didn't have much. Sold most of what she had when her husband was lost.'

Mrs Wilkinson shrugged. 'Nothing new under the sun, my dear.' She smiled kindly to Letty. 'Call me if you need me. Sally knows where to find me. Anyone round here knows where to find me.' She stepped out of the house and into the yard and Sally followed her.

Letty pressed the lid down on Anita's tin box. Not much for a life; a few papers, a shell.

Sally came back. 'You might as well go home, Letty. We'll hear Burton when he arrives with his cart.'

'I don't want to leave her alone.' Her voice broke and she swallowed back her tears. Sally wrapped her in her arms and she sobbed, feeling the comfort of Sally's hands as they rubbed at her back.

'Nothing else you can do for her now, lovey. Nothing at all.'

31

The doctor came to certify the death and, soon after, the cart came with the plain open coffin on the back. Shortly before seven, Anita's body, wrapped in a plain coarse blanket, was taken away. Alfie had fallen asleep, his head on Letty's lap, and she had gone through her own tiredness and out the other side. Her body had been weary, but her mind agile. Dorcas had started early on the nets, neither of them taking to their beds and they had sat in quiet companionship. Letty ran a hand over Alfie's head. He weighed next to nothing, but it was painful sitting for so long, and she adjusted her position to ease her discomfort. He stirred slightly but did not wake. Dorcas peered over at her.

'What's to become of her boy?' Her hands were quick, knotting and looping the twine, the net growing row by row. Small fibres danced in the air about her. The room would be thick with them by the end of the day.

'She has family.' Letty glanced over to the tin on the small table. 'There are birth certificates. Marriage. Although I know her husband had no family. He was from an orphanage.'

'Doesn't mean he doesn't have family.'

'No.'

Alfie stirred again and once more Letty adjusted herself in the chair.

The clock chimed the half-hour. 'I need to go to Parkers.' Gently, she lifted Alfie away from her, pulled at his chin. 'Alfie, love. Wake up, there's a good boy.'

He opened his eyes, closed them again. She gently jiggled his shoulder and he sat up, blinking, checking his surroundings. He looked bewildered, as well he might, she thought. She placed him on the floor and got to her feet, put her hands to her back and stretched.

'What are you going to do with him?'

Letty leaned on the mantelpiece and stretched again. Her bladder was full, and she needed the privy, more so now Alfie had moved.

Alfie watched her. She smiled, hoping to reassure him.

'He'll come with me.'

Dorcas gave a small laugh. 'You can't do that. What will the Parkers say? The woman's got enough on her plate.'

She touched his shoulder, his ear. Alfie looked up at her, his eyes big in so small a face. 'He could stay here.'

Dorcas shook her head. 'Oh no, don't drag me into your do-gooding.' The needle went into another loop, another knot, faster and faster, and Letty knew she was getting a temper on her. 'You can leave him with your friend the missioner on the way. Wasn't his father a fisherman?'

Letty frowned. 'He's not a bag of washing.' She didn't want to talk like this in front of the boy, and she desperately needed the privy. She made a dash for the door. He followed her, holding on to her skirt. 'Wait here, Alfie. I'll be back in a minute.'

* * *

The boy stood by the door waiting for Letty's return. Dorcas watched him, still as a statue. He had been no trouble at all last night, his hunger evident from the way he attacked his food. Poor little mite. She'd given him bread and cheese. He'd been polite, had only spoken when spoken to. His manners were perfect. He was loved, of that there was no doubt, but there was no joy in the boy, no light in him. She'd watched him as he ate, remembering her boys at that age, of their energy and mischief. She'd never seen that in the boy in all the time they'd lived at Mariners Row.

She left her braiding, got up and went to the window, moved the net.

Letty was talking with a neighbour. They were looking towards Anita's house, up at the window, turning back again. No doubt they would want all the gory details, but Letty didn't strike her as being inclined to give them.

Dorcas touched Alfie on his shoulder. 'Come to the kitchen.' He followed her.

She put the porridge to warm through and poured him some water. He stood in the doorway, watching, his eyes round.

'Cat got your tongue, Alfie?'

He shook his head, took the mug. 'Ta, missus.'

She nodded, ran her hands down her apron. 'Get yourself on that chair.' She went to the range, stirred the pot, opened the back door. It was a bright morning, the air fresh and crisp. It made her feel less tired, for her bones ached and the day would be long. All the days were long now. She closed the door and set a bowl of porridge in front of the boy, stirred the pot again as Letty came in, the long night showing in her face. Dorcas put the bowl on the table. 'You'd better eat.'

Letty sat down and started on her porridge. Dorcas spooned tea into the pot.

'I was thinking,' she said carefully. 'Leave the lad here.'

The boy stopped eating, placed his spoon in his bowl. He looked to Letty and she smiled at him, carried on with her own food.

'I'm sure Norah won't mind, not for one day. Until we can find his family.'

Dorcas drew in a breath. 'That's just it, Letty. One day will turn into two and before you know it...'

'The difference being?'

Dorcas put the pot on the table, pulled the cosy over it. She moved closer. 'You don't want him to get used to something he can't have.'

Letty's brow furrowed, then she nodded, understanding what Dorcas was trying to say. She began eating again. Dorcas watched her. She didn't say anything more and Dorcas was relieved. She'd expected a battle. This was no time to be sentimental about the boy, she'd have her own child soon enough. She picked up the pot, poured the tea. Letty drank it back, got to her feet.

'Come on, Alfie. Time to go.' She went to the peg, got her own coat, took down Alfie's threadbare, oversized coat she had brought from next door.

Dorcas began to clear the table. 'I said to leave him with me.'

Letty held out Alfie's coat and made for him to put his arms in the sleeves. The lass glared at her, speaking between gritted teeth. 'I heard what you said.' She took Alfie's hand and the boy stared at her.

Dorcas looked away, she didn't want to look too long, for his eyes were the deepest of blue, like her boy's, her Robbie's.

'Letty, it won't do to get too attached.'

The lass's eyes were blazing, her anger spiked. If she could just make her see that it would be harder to let him go.

Letty shook her head. 'Last night, I thought we had come to some sort of...' She sought for the words, couldn't find them. 'I promised Anita that I would take care of him.'

Dorcas stacked the bowls, glanced to Letty's swollen belly. 'You have your own child to think of. Another mouth to feed, another body to clothe.'

Letty placed a hand on Alfie's head. 'I am well aware of that. But I don't want to come back and find you've taken him... somewhere. That was the last thing Anita wanted.'

Dorcas sighed. 'It's all well and good, having these airy-fairy ideas, but he's not your responsibility.'

'I promised.'

She began to walk off. Dorcas hurried after her, touched her shoulder. If she could only make her see how difficult it would be.

Letty twisted, shrugged off her hand. 'To think that I would have come home and...' Her voice trembled with fury and she turned away. Alfie's slate and chalks were by the door and she snatched them up.

Dorcas sank down in the chair. What was the damn girl thinking of? Couldn't she see it would only make the parting worse; for loving was easy, it was the losing that was hard to bear.

* * *

Letty's confidence began to falter the closer she came to Parkers. She chattered to Alfie as they walked, but as they approached the shop, her only thought was how Norah would react.

They went in through the back door, Letty clasping Alfie's hands firmly in hers. Norah was sat in front of Percy, a soap-laden shaving brush in her hand, a towel over her lap. She was leaning forward, lathering Percy's chin and didn't look up when Letty came in, merely called out her greeting. Letty placed a gentle hand on Alfie's back and guided him forward. Norah caught sight of him as she sat back.

'Oh,' she said in surprise. 'And what have we here?' Her face erupted with the widest of smiles and Letty relaxed a little. It was such a lot to ask, even for one day, and she remembered Dorcas's words, that she'd forced herself on the couple – and here she was again, doing the same thing. But what to do for the best? She hadn't wanted to let them down and she couldn't leave Alfie with Dorcas, not now. Norah placed the brush on the table to her side, picked up the cut-throat razor and snapped it open. Alfie clutched at Letty's skirts.

Percy grunted, 'Wha?' and Norah pressed her hand on his knee.

'We have a visitor.' She beckoned to Alfie.

Letty looked to the razor and Norah, understanding, closed it, put it down. She gave Alfie another gentle nudge and Norah stood up and walked towards them. Letty leaned down to Alfie and said, quietly, 'This is Mrs Parker. Say hello, Alfie.'

'Hello, Mrs Parker.' His voice was so quiet that Norah had to lean in to hear.

There was a commotion from Percy as he fought to be included. Norah took Alfie by the hand and brought him in front of her husband. Letty came to stand so that Percy could see her and began to giggle, because there was grumpy old Percy with soap around his chin.

'Wha? Wha?' Percy grunted at her.

Letty bent down picked up the mirror at Norah's table and showed him his reflection. 'You look like Father Christmas, Percy. I knew I'd seen you somewhere before.' He pulled a face, but she could tell he was amused.

Norah laughed too, then placed a hand to her throat, briefly turned away. She looked to Letty, then to Alfie. 'I'd better get Father Christmas cleaned up, hadn't I, Alfie? Make some tea, Letty, if you please. Then we can all chat together, can't we, Percy?' Her voice cracked when she spoke, but she smiled and Letty realised that it might not be as bad as she'd thought.

Norah sat Alfie in her armchair opposite Percy, and he watched as Norah shaved him, wiping his face with the damp towel. Then she gathered the things and took them to the sink to stand with Letty.

'He's a quiet little thing.'

Letty turned and leaned against the draining board, Norah beside her. Alfie sat in the chair looking at Percy, who must have been pulling faces for Alfie was entranced.

'Oh, Norah. I am so sorry for bringing him with me, but I didn't know what else to do.' She told Norah of his sorry circumstances. 'I didn't trust to leave him with Dorcas. I don't think he'd have been there when I got back. I promised his mother that he wouldn't end up in the poor house. It's just until I can have a word with the port missioner.'

Norah shook her head in sorrow. 'So much sadness in the world.' She pressed Letty's arm. 'You did a kind thing, lass. And by the look of it, he'll keep Percy entertained for an hour or two.'

Letty took up his slate. 'I brought this with me. I'm sure he'll be no trouble.'

'Don't worry. Anything we can do to help, we're here for you. I hope you know that by now.'

Tiredness and Norah's kindness overwhelmed her, and a sob caught in Letty's throat. Her eyes pooled with tears and, to her embarrassment, one dropped onto her blouse. She rubbed another away from her cheek and Norah took her hand, turned and pulled her close. Letty could not hold back, and ashamed, she cried, not for herself, but for Anita and for Alfie, and the pathetic waste of a life.

She withdrew from Norah's embrace, apologising. 'I'm so sorry. As if you don't have enough of your own worries.'

'Bah,' Norah batted her hand in the air. 'I've already survived worse than this. You'll know, when you get to my age. You learn that you get over things, and you survive. And these things don't hurt as much as they do when you're young.' She indicated towards Alfie. 'Look at that little chap there. His solemn little face. He has no idea of things, of the life ahead of him. But he has people about him, good people, and that's what counts.' She squeezed Letty's hand. 'Come on, lass. Dry your tears. We've a shop to open.'

* * *

How Letty managed to get through a full day at the shop she had no idea. She remained sharp when writing the invoices and checked and double-checked the change, not wanting to make any mistake that would cause Norah problems. She was so tired, her emotions exhausted, no energy to think of what to do about Alfie. She'd popped through to the back room throughout the day, but Alfie had been content – and it seemed to have lifted Percy. As his pals came in, they all had something to say to the boy and Letty had found Wolfie teaching him to tie knots with a length of old rope. Dennis had taken up Alfie's slate and drew a pan, as he explained, 'To replace the P-I-G. Can't have the boy say that if he's to go to sea. It's a grunter from now on.' He made Alfie repeat it. 'Grunter, like ole Percy 'ere.' He'd roared with laughter, Percy too – after a fashion. Alfie had smiled.

'Ah ha,' Dennis had said, pressing his fist towards Alfie in play and pinching at his cheek. 'I knew there was a smile in there somewhere. Did you see that, Percy, ole pal?' Percy had looked to Letty and there seemed to be a sparkle in his eye. Or was it just a reflection from the fire? They had to snatch at happiness where they could.

At the end of the day, she brought in the items that were displayed outside the shop, locked the front door and drew the bolts across, pressed her head to the glass. She longed for home, dreading it at the same time. Muttering a small prayer to herself, she went to tot up the till, then take it through to Norah. Alfie was asleep in the chair, and Norah had covered him with her shawl. Percy had nodded off too.

'Sleeping beauties,' Norah said as she came in. 'Well, one of them.'

Percy opened one eye and Letty grinned at him.

'Gud.' He moved his head to Alfie, nodded, pointed. Letty almost dropped the till in surprise.

Norah's face was aglow. She took the drawer from Letty. 'I know. Small wonders, eh.' Letty nodded mutely. 'It looks like having the little chap here has been company for Percy. Not too demanding, not like trying to keep up with his pals.'

Letty ran her hand over her face, pushed back her hair.

'Bring him tomorrow, Letty, can you do that? It's what Percy wants.'

Percy nodded to her.

A huge lump came from her chest and up into her throat.

'Until you get something sorted.' She reached out and gave Alfie a little shake until he opened his eyes. 'Time to go home, Alfie dear.'

The child wriggled himself awake, slipped from the chair and picked up the length of rope, looked to Percy.

Percy nodded and Alfie stuffed it into his pocket, walked over to Letty and slipped his hand in hers. She galvanised herself to move, wanting more than anything to stay, got Alfie in his coat, put on her own. Norah came with her to the door.

'Oh. Letty, what would it have been if you'd come into our lives earlier? The difference it would have made.'

Letty was overwhelmed, her emotions all a tumble, but managed to utter a simple 'Thank you.'

Norah touched her shoulder. 'Try to get some sleep. Everything seems better after a night's rest.'

Letty doubted it would, but somehow, as the two of them walked back to Mariners Row, she felt a little more certain of what her next steps would be.

32

To Letty's surprise, Dorcas had made them food – a meat pie with potatoes and carrots with gravy left over from yesterday's stew. She'd prepared herself for another confrontation, but Dorcas was civil. It had wrong-footed Letty. Was there a catch or was Dorcas finally learning that Letty would stand her ground, no matter what?

When all was cleared away, Letty settled Alfie in her chair before the fire. Dorcas took up her knitting. Only last night they had been getting on and Dorcas had seemed to reach out to her. Would they patch it up and make it right again? It had taken only four and twenty hours to turn a life topsy-turvy.

Alfie took the rope from his pocket and began to tie knots, looping the string this way and that, over and under, over and under. He made a reef knot, pulled it apart and started again.

Letty took Anita's tin and began reading through the papers. She'd never known Anita's surname, but her marriage certificate showed that she was a Fletcher and before that a Lewis. She read her birth certificate. 'Well, I never.'

Dorcas looked at her. Letty held the certificate out, but Dorcas shook her head. 'What does it say?'

'Anita's parents. Her father owned a draper's store in Boston. Might still own it.'

'Hardly likely. What would she be doing here? Living like...' she paused.

Letty folded the certificate and placed it to one side. Letty was from a good family too, but if she was widowed with a child... She instinctively touched her belly.

'I've no idea, but it's helpful. They would be known in the town. Someone might still know of them.'

'If they're still living.'

'Why wouldn't they be?'

Dorcas concentrated on her knitting, the wool tugged and wrapped, over the needle and through. 'I'd have thought she'd be in better circumstances than she was.'

Letty continued to go through the contents of the tin. There was an envelope, inside it a letter and another envelope. She took it out. It had a Boston address, the name of the Lewises. She opened the letter and began to read. It was Anita telling her parents of her husband's death and asking for help. Letty went back to the first letter, one from Anita's mother telling her in no uncertain terms that she had made her bed and she must lie in it. She had chosen Daniel against their wishes and must bear the consequences. Letty stared into the fire.

'How could anyone be so heartless?' She was unaware that she'd spoken aloud.

'Heartless?'

She passed the letter over, but Dorcas lifted her needles to indicate her industry.

Letty told her the contents of the letters.

'Well, you'll not get any help from that quarter, so at least it will save you the price of a stamp.'

Letty disagreed. 'They might have a change of heart. When they know they have a grandchild.'

'They might have other grandchildren. Ones that have good mothers.'

'Anita was a good mother.'

Dorcas raised an eyebrow in disapproval and Letty was about to challenge her when the door opened and Sally came in from the yard. Letty was glad of the interruption.

Sally had her shawl about her shoulders. 'I came to say to take what the boy needs from next door, and yourself for your trouble. No doubt the landlord will take what's left and get it let again.'

Letty thought back to the months when they had arrived, to the squalor of Mariners Row. She hadn't discovered anything of the family who lived in the house before them and tomorrow all traces of Anita and Alfie would be wiped from next door. She got to her feet, gestured for Sally to sit down.

'All right, Alfie?' Sally said, taking a seat and ruffling him quickly on his head. She looked to Dorcas, to Letty. 'What about the lad?'

'He's staying with u—' She caught Dorcas glowering. 'Me, for the time being.' Dorcas put down her knitting, was about to speak, but Letty spoke across her. She indicated the tin, closed the lid. 'He has family. I will write to them.'

Dorcas let out a long, noisy sigh. 'I told her to save herself the bother.'

Letty looked to Sally, hoping for support.

'That's a kind thing to do. You can but try.'

She was glad Sally was here, not simply because of her support, but that she feared Dorcas would take Alfie as soon as her back was turned. She lit another lamp. 'I'll go and see what I can bring.'

Alfie got up to follow her, but Sally touched his shoulder.

'You'll be all right with me and Mrs Hardy awhile, Alfie. Letty will be back soon.'

He looked to Letty.

She reassured him with a smile. 'I won't be long.'

She took the key from the shelf and went next door, glad she had the forethought to take a lamp. It was black as pitch. She placed the lamp in the window. If a house could take on the misery of its owner, then number four was proof if it were needed. The pitiful rooms were heavy with sorrow, or was Letty being fanciful? She smiled. It was not something her mother would have said of her, perhaps her younger sister, but never Letty. She longed for her mother to be at her side. Dorcas was no substitute. She'd hoped that they would grow closer, two strangers in a strange town.

She found another lamp, containing a mere drop of oil and lit it. It would last long enough for her task if she kept the wick low. There was little downstairs, nothing much in the kitchen except for a few utensils. She picked up a small cup that she knew Alfie used, a bowl. She gathered them on the table, took the cushion from Anita's chair, the small stool that Alfie used when sat by his mother. There was a Bible on the small table by the fire, and she opened it. It was inscribed to Anita from her parents, and Letty recognised the same heavy precise hand as in the letters she'd found in the tin. She placed it with the other things. Alfie might want it.

She made her way upstairs, sadness washing over her, recalling the events of the night before. The back room was empty except for a narrow bed and Letty removed the sheets and folded them, rolled up the mattress. There was the small sweater she'd rescued from the mission and she made a pile of Alfie's few things: a flannelette nightshirt, a pair of short trousers. The floorboards sighed and creaked beneath her feet as she moved about, and she paused at the doorway of what had been Anita's room and took a deep breath. The window had been left open, but the stench of blood and death lingered. What a terrible waste it all was.

She held up the lamp and shone it around, throwing dim light into every corner, and made her way over to the trunk she'd noticed the previous night. She knelt before it, placed the lamp on the floor and lifted the lid. Inside were sheets, good ones too, and Letty ran her hand over them, surprised at the quality. She saw the logo of the Royal Hotel. Had they been in payment, like the fish they had shared, or had Anita worked there at some point? She would never know.

A noise from below made her stop and she called out, 'Up here.'

There was no answer, and Letty dismissed the sound, thinking she'd imagined it, or that it came from outside. She got off her knees and onto her feet, closed the trunk and turned, startled to see at a figure in the doorway.

'Now, then, Nita.'

Letty stammered, overcome with fear. 'I'm not Anita.'

'Where is she?' Letty squinted in the darkness, her heart pounding. 'Helping her out are ya, while your man's away, poor bastard.'

She reached down for the lamp, trying to dodge him as he rushed towards her, but she wasn't quick enough. He took hold of her arm and thrust her down onto the bed, his breathe stinking of strong spirit. She scratched at his face and he cried out.

'Why you dirty little whore.' His rage ignited and he twisted her over with one quick movement, shoving her face into the mattress. She retched at the smell, thrusting her body, flailing her arms and legs to get free. He punched her between the shoulders and the pain ripped through her and took the breath from her. He removed one hand keeping her pressed down, his palm in the middle of her back. She could hear him undoing his belt and she screamed until he shoved her face back into the mattress with such violence that she thought she would suffocate. He bent forward, his arm pressed across her and began to push up her skirts.

She thrust herself about with all the energy she had, but she was so tired, and she cried out, the sound muffled by the mattress, 'My baby, my baby.'

And then it all stopped. He fell on top of her, a dead weight. She could feel him being dragged at and she pushed and shoved at him with what energy she had left. The man slumped and fell on the floor.

As she turned herself, gasping for air, she could make out that it was Sally, a rolling pin in her hand. The tears came then, and the shaking and the fury.

Sally took her hand and pulled her to her feet. 'Let's get you back home. He'll wake soon enough and we don't want to be here.'

Letty looked down at him, shaking uncontrollably. Rage engulfed her and she lashed out with her foot, kicking into his side, his legs, over and over, until Sally dragged her away, the pair of them half stumbling down the staircase.

'I doubt we'll see him again,' Sally said as they went out into the cold night air.

Letty bit on her lip, knowing that she would.

Back at the house, Dorcas was all for calling the police, but Letty wouldn't hear of it.

'Nothing happened.'

'Close to!' Dorcas fumed. 'You might have lost the babe. If it hadn't been for Sally's quick thinking, who knows what might have...' She shot a look to Alfie.

Letty tried to think kindly of her, hoping it wasn't just her unborn child she was concerned about.

Sally agreed with Letty. 'They might blame me. I did hit him good and hard.'

They sat quiet, listening for sounds next door, hoping that Sally had only knocked him senseless.

Some time later, they heard him stumbling about, then thumping down the stairs, banging about on the wall as he descended. A shadow passed across the window and they waited a for a fair few minutes before Sally went next door.

Letty got up to go with her.

'What do you want to do that for?' Dorcas said, in exasperation. 'Haven't you had enough of a fright for one night.'

'There are things I set to one side. Alfie's nightshirt and such. There's a trunk upstairs with some good sheets.'

Dorcas got up and stood beside Sally. 'Then we'll get them, you stay here with the boy.'

Sally nodded for her to obey and Letty sank down beside the fire and stared into the flames.

Gilbert Crowe. Had he known it was her? The lamp had been on the floor, had her face been in shadow? Surely, he would have spoken her name if he'd recognised her. Her back ached, her shoulders too, where he had thumped her. Would he have harmed the baby? She touched her stomach. She needed to wash her face, her hands. All she could smell was the blood from the mattress and the sour stench of whisky.

Alfie reached up and took her hand and she squeezed his in reassurance, not knowing whether it was for him or for herself. She laid back in the chair and closed her eyes.

33

Alec had been called into Hammonds' office when the *Falberg* landed its catch. On his way there, he'd met Skipper Harris coming down Fish Dock Road, a grin as wide as the mouth of the Humber, his son Ben at his side.

'Yer, lookin' please with yerself,' Alec said. 'A good trip?'

Harris slapped him on the back. 'Bit better than that. I'll be off to fetch me new command with me laddo here, straight off the blocks from the shipyard in Newcastle. A beauty she is.'

For all the months at sea since they'd met, Ben seemed no more comfortable with the life and Alec guessed that although he was pleased for his father, the news of a new ship didn't excite him as it did the two older men.

'I'm on me way there meself. Gaffer wants to see me.'

'Aye,' Harris said. 'I'll be hanging about a bit. Our Ben's gonna run a few errands for me. How about we meet in Solly's café for a bite and a yarn?'

'I'll look forward to it.'

* * *

Harris was sat by the half-curtained window, the café noisy with conversation, the smell of bacon and eggs fighting with the stench of fish and sweat. He lifted a hand and Alec walked over to him, pulled off his cap and put it on the table.

Harris sat back grinning. 'They gave you the *Black Prince*?'

Alec slid into the seat opposite Harris. 'They did. And I have you to thank.'

'I might have put a word or two in the right ear, but it's well deserved.'

Alec reached across the table and the two of them shook hands. It had been good of Harris to mention his name. Not every man was willing to help another. There was much competition, and rightly so.

It was a grand day, one he'd like to have celebrated with his father.

He shouted up to the counter for a brew.

'You're in charge now. How does that feel?'

'Heavy.' Although he was thrilled and excited, a part of him was afraid.

Harris caught his eye. 'Aye, no one to blame if it all goes wrong.'

So much could go wrong. Not hauling enough fish was the smallest of worries. He had to keep the gaffers happy or he would soon find himself without a ship. He wasn't only at the whim of the weather or the sea, the owners would want him to come back in profit – and that was dependent on many things out of his control. And he had to keep his men safe as well as himself. It was a challenge that many would not take on.

The waitress stuck a mug of tea in front of him. Harris handed her his own for a top-up.

'Everybody has an opinion, lad.' He leaned back against the wall. 'They'll tell you the sun shines out of your arse one day and that you're the most useless bastard that ever took to the seas another. Ignore it. Bit like Kipling. *If you can keep your head* and all that. Do you know who you've got as mate?'

'Tommy Stocker.'

Harris took out his pipe from his deep pockets and tapped it into the tin ashtray, poked around the bowl with a matchstick. 'A good man. He'll be good fer yer.'

The waitress returned with his mug.

'Careful who you surround yerself with. When do you sail?'

'Tomorrow. It's due a refit, but they want to squeeze a couple more trips out of her instead of having her idle.' It would mean a few days more with Letty when they did.

'Aye, don't like 'em to be idle.'

'Or us.'

Harris gave him a wry smile. 'I've no doubt you'll do well. You know how to handle the men, that's key.'

Alec's thoughts immediately jumped to his time with Harris. 'How's Mouse?'

'Doing all right. Him and the missus seemed to have patched things up.' He raised his eyebrows. 'You'll be wanting to tell yer own missus of yer news. You've got a gud 'un there, from what I hear. She's certainly put a bob or two in the Parkers' pockets.'

It could be their pockets if she bought the shop. But Alec didn't want her working, not now he was skipper. It was a matter of pride. She hadn't mentioned the shop again and he thought perhaps she'd given up on the idea, now that they had a kiddie on the way.

Ben tapped on the widow and his father gave him a nod and got to his feet. 'I'm here any time you need a word.'

Alec drained his mug, slapped coins on the table. 'If I need anything, you'll be the first person I'll ask.'

He left Harris outside the café. He'd wanted to hurry home, but word had got round and he was stopped every few yards by men who wanted to wish him well.

Later than intended, he was glad at last to turn into Mariners Row. They wouldn't be here much longer. His mother and Letty deserved better than this. He tapped on the window with a coin, a simple tune that Letty would recognise. The door was flung open and she ran into his arms, getting as close to him as her extended belly would allow. She looked bonny, her skin aglow, her cheeks rosy. He ran his hand over her hair and rested it on her cheek. 'By, Letty, how I've missed you. Where's Mother?'

'Inside, at her nets. Where else would she be.'

He kissed her again, wanting to take her upstairs and lie together, but he wanted his mother to hear the good news too. The lad from next door stood in their doorway. 'Hello, Alfie. Yer mother busy?' He looked to the upstairs window and Letty tugged at his arm, glared at him so that he knew to stop talking.

She bent to Alfie. 'Go tell Mrs Hardy that her son is home.'

As he walked into the house, Letty told him briefly of Anita's death and stopped when his mother came hurrying in from the yard and into Alec's embrace.

'We expected you sooner,' his mother said, pulling away from him.

'I was detained.' He tried to suppress a grin and be serious, cleared his throat, leaned on the mantel and stared at the frozen images of his father, of Robbie, and then turned away from them. 'Sit down, Letty, Mother.'

They did as he asked. The boy stood by Letty's side. He hadn't had time to ask why the lad was here.

'I met with Sam Harris. It was him who put word in for me.'

'A word?' Letty said, picking up on his barely suppressed excitement.

'Mother, Letty. Alfie,' he said, including the boy. 'You are now looking at the skipper of the *Black Prince*.'

Letty leaped to her feet and rushed to him and the pair of them were laughing with excitement as they embraced. When he released her, his mother returned to her chair. She was holding the photograph of his father stood beside the *Stella Maris*.

'Your father would have been so proud.'

Letty made for him to sit down but he pressed her shoulder and made her sit.

'We need to get another chair,' she said.

'We need to get another house.' He stood in front of the range and told them of his meeting with old Mr Hammond. His tale was interrupted by a knock on the door. One of Sally's lads was calling for Alfie and Letty sent the boy out to play. Finishing his own story, Alec asked for more detail of Anita's. Letty told him. 'Poor lass. No one deserves to have that end. And Alfie?'

Dorcas opened her mouth to speak, but Letty was swift to jump in.

'I kept him with me.' He noticed she didn't say 'us'.

Dorcas tutted. Alec put up a hand to stop her interrupting.

Letty said, 'It was dreadful, and he was alone with her for God knows how long.' Her voice trembled. 'Anita's husband was in an orphanage. She didn't want the same to happen to her boy. I promised to help.'

'It's not our business,' Dorcas snapped.

Alec was quick to correct her. 'But it is, Mother. We've got to look out for each other. Who else is there to look out for him?' He thought of Sam Harris's kindness, that the man would be there for him, if he needed advice. It was everything, being there for someone. Yes, his father would have been proud, but he wasn't here. Alec had to make his own decisions, and no matter what his mother thought, he was the head of the family. 'How is the boy, in himself?' he asked of Letty.

'Very quiet. I've written to Anita's parents,' she said. 'I'm waiting to hear from them.'

Dorcas interrupted her. 'You should have let the authorities take him.'

'He's a little lad, Mother. Letty did right.'

'He's a tie,' Dorcas nagged. 'And to think you was ready to take on a shop – and a baby coming.'

'I will have a shop one day.' Letty looked to Alec. 'My mother coped perfectly well every day of her life running a farm and bringing up six children.'

Dorcas was not convinced. 'That's different. Alfie is not your child.'

'Aye, and it's not hurting, is it? Giving the lad a bit of comfort in his time of need.'

Alec was getting tired of the sniping; it was meant to be a good day. 'If Letty doesn't mind the extra, for a time.'

'I can cope. The Parkers love having him. He sits with Percy. It's helped him.' She told him of how Percy had taken to the child, Norah too.

'Aye, word's got round what you've done for the Parkers. Sam Harris was saying you've transformed the place.'

His mother huffed and got to her feet.

'You'll be at the pub to celebrate with your pals, I suppose?'

'Not yet. I thought we'd all go out together.' He wasn't going to make that mistake again. It was hard cramming all your living on a short time ashore. There was never enough of it, but Letty and their family would come first, his mother too. 'We'll get the tram into Cleethorpes. Get the boy, Letty. Let's mark the day.'

She got up and went to the door to call him and her smile was the best reward. He thought of lads he'd worked with, with no family to go home to, leaving one institution for another, and he was glad he had a family, depleted such as it was. He interrupted his own maudlin thoughts. He'd have his own son soon enough.

'You're getting as daft as she is.' His mother took her irritation out on her cuff.

He got up, put his hand either side of her shoulders. 'Mother, you'd have done the same yourself if Letty hadn't beat you to it.'

*　*　*

They had a fine time in Cleethorpes and Alec was kindness itself to Alfie. They strolled along the promenade and through the gardens, ate fish and chips from the paper, sitting with their backs to the wall to protect them from the wind. He bought Alfie a bar of chocolate and they smiled indulgently as he enjoyed every bite, chocolate smeared about his cheeks. Dorcas took out her handkerchief and wiped at his hands, his face, muttering about the mess. Alec and Letty grinned at each other, knowing she was enjoying every minute of her fussing despite her words. When Alfie's pace slowed and his eyes grew heavy, Alec picked him up and carried him in his arms and they caught the tram home. He laid him on a blanket when they got back and talked with Dorcas, while Letty dressed the lad in his nightshirt and readied him for bed.

Alec picked him up once more and turned to Letty. 'Where does he go?'

'He's been sleeping with me.'

Dorcas cleared her throat. 'You'll not want him with you tonight. Put him in my bed.'

Letty caught her eye and she looked away.

Alec went upstairs and laid him on the bed, pulled the blankets over him. One day it would be his own son he would be watching over; he hoped he had a better life than Alfie's.

That night, while they lay in each other's arms, Letty didn't want to sleep, wanting to be awake for every minute of their time together.

'It was good of your mother to let Alfie sleep with her. I know she didn't think much of Anita, but I found her a good sort. After everything that happened, I didn't have the heart to send him off to the orphanage. You hear such terrible things.'

'It won't hurt for a few days. He'll have a little bit of happiness to remember.' He turned her towards him. 'You're not to go getting too attached though, Let.'

She couldn't look at him and when she did, he knew what she was thinking. It was already too late.

34

Anita was buried in an unmarked grave in a neglected corner of Grimsby cemetery. Letty fashioned a small cross from two pieces of wood and marked her name on it. On a cold and brittle November day, she and Alfie fixed it in the ground and said a small prayer for his mother. That she rest in peace. Alfie did not cry, but looked to Letty, his hand tight in hers, and she promised that she would not let him go.

A letter came to the mission two days after Alec left on the *Black Prince*, this time as skipper. She didn't tell Dorcas, only said that she hadn't had a reply and would write again, that the letter must have gone astray. In truth, she couldn't bear to tell her that she was right, that the Lewises wanted nothing to do with Alfie. She'd been disgusted but she would not give up so lightly. Alfie was their grandson. Another letter was sent and she waited, and in that time, Alec came back from his first successful trip. He was surprised that Alfie was still with them but told her he had faith she would sort it out, that she would do what was right for Alfie. She'd thought she couldn't love him any more than she did, but she was wrong. It comforted her more than she could ever tell.

They celebrated Christmas in January, delaying the celebrations until Alec was home. It was the way things were. For a good month, it was Christmas in at least one household about the town. Dorcas was vocal about the lack of communication from Alfie's grandparents, but Letty told her she would keep trying. Most of the time, she kept out of her way, making sure Alfie was always at her side, for she wouldn't put it past Dorcas to take him to the orphanage at the first opportunity. Her attitude to the boy couldn't have been more different to the Parkers, who were besotted with the child and had spoiled him with little gifts at Christmas – as had Letty, eager to bring a little joy and happiness his way. Alfie and Percy had struck up a rare friendship and by degrees Alfie emerged from his shell like a hermit crab, understanding where he was safe and where he was not. Gilbert Crowe had kept his distance for which Letty had been grateful. She had told no one of that night and had asked Sally and Dorcas to do the same, wanting to put the whole sordid episode out of her mind.

On the first day of February, Letty called in at Coopers, the greengrocers, and bought supplies – potatoes and apples – and Mrs Cooper gave her two large oranges, 'for the baby'.

It was with a weary step that Letty called into the mission to write letters after she had finished her half-day at Parkers.

There was a ragtag of men in the reception and she caught Walter's eye, raised her hand in small greeting. He ended his conversation and came over to them, winked at Letty, then focused his attention on Alfie.

'Nah, then, Alfie. Are ya looking after Mrs Hardy?'

Alfie nodded. 'I am, Mr Walter, sir.'

Walter laughed, put his hand in his trouser pocket, produced a silver sixpence and held it out to him. 'That's for you, boy. You're doing a fine job. We need to look after Mrs Hardy, don't we, as she looks after us.'

There was more nodding as Alfie took the sixpence and wrapped his hand about it.

Walter smiled at her. 'And how are you keeping, Letty?'

'I can't complain, Walter. But I'll be glad to see my feet again.'

He smiled at her. 'My missus allus was glad when the babies came.' He tugged at his cap. 'Well, I'll be off to the *Albion*.' He gave a toss of his head towards the other men grouped about him. 'There's a pint waiting on the bar for me, and I don't want some other beggar to beat me to it.'

He left, as did a couple of other men, and Letty went to check at reception desk to see if there were any letters. Norman handed her two; one in the heavy hand she recognised and another she didn't. She opened the one from Mrs Lewis, hoping there had been a change of heart. There had not. It was abrupt, a reinforcement of what had been written before, and this time a cheque for ten pounds to cover any costs at the orphanage. It ended with instructions never to write to them again. *No further communication will be entered into.* Letty was appalled. That they thought money could absolve them of all ties, all responsibilities. She stuffed it into her pocket with force.

Alfie was opening and closing his hand over the sixpence, over and over, to check it was still there. She smiled at him, at Walter's generosity.

More men came into the reception and she took Alfie over to one side, out of the way. By the window, she opened the second envelope, read it, and read it again. At last. Good news. She grabbed Alfie's hand, waved the letter across the room to Norman at the reception desk.

'News of Walter's boys. I'll be back soon enough.'

It more than made up for the Lewises' rejection. If they could turn their back on their own child, what hope did Alfie have? It had been foolish of her to expect anything more. There were wicked people in the world, but there were good ones too. Walter was one of them.

She picked up her basket and hurried out of the mission and round Riby Square towards the *Albion*. The streets were busy, and it was noisy with the sound of carts and horses and trolley buses. She tugged Alfie close to hurry him along. Her joy at being able to give Walter news gave her energy she had lost. Letty saw him further ahead of her, talking to a couple of pals, and she waved her hand to catch his attention. A pal nudged him, and he looked up, saw her, smiled. She waved the letter, still hurrying forward, her stomach heavy, her basket cumbersome, and all the time holding on to Alfie. Walter began to walk towards her, and she called out to him.

'Good news. Your boys.'

He hurried towards her and she let go of Alfie's hand to adjust her basket. As she did, he dropped his sixpence and it rolled away from him. He dashed forward to stop it and Letty saw the cart coming towards him. Alfie ran into the road, stopped, bent down to pick up the sixpence. The cart kept coming, someone shouted, it startled the horse and as the driver pulled on the reins, it reared up. Letty dropped her basket. Apples and potatoes rolled about her feet as she cried out. The oranges.

Walter dashed forward and grasped Alfie, threw him out of the way. There was a loud, heavy thud as the horse's hooves caught Walter's head and Letty screamed, running towards him, but strong arms gripped her and held her back. The horse came down on Walter's chest. Alfie scrambled to his feet and stared at the scene until someone pulled him away. A crowd gathered, and in between the gaps, Letty glimpsed Walter laid on the road, blood pooling about his head. Her legs went limp, and she was glad she was being held for she was shaking violently.

The driver of the cart leaped down onto the road, pulled a blanket from the back of his cart, passed it to a man in a suit and a bowler hat, who immediately pulled off his jacket, rolled up his sleeves. From somewhere behind her, a policeman blew a whistle. Cyclists stopped. The road became cluttered with people and bicycles and somewhere on the road was Walter.

The crowds parted as men carried Walter from the road on the blanket and the thought of him lying on the cold, hard pavement galvanised her. She managed to say, 'The mission. Please take him to the mission.' It was eerily quiet around her, but the sounds of life going on was clear in the distance.

She searched for Alfie. She called his name and a man who had picked him up and held him in his arms placed him at her feet. He was crying and his face was dirty with smeared tears. She pulled him to her, grasped his hand in hers. Why had she let him go? Why?

They followed the men who had gently lifted Walter and were carrying him ahead. A woman and her daughter had picked up her basket and restored as much as they could to it, and they too followed, handing the basket to one of the men as they stepped into the cold reception of the mission building. Word of the accident had travelled fast and the entrance space was thick with people who parted like a wave for the men carrying Walter. Letty could hear murmurings, snatches of words that didn't make sense. She could hear Colin Wilson's voice, giving instructions, and Letty, dazed and unthinking, followed the crowd.

They laid Walter on a bed in a side room and the men departed, leaving Letty with Colin and Norman. Someone had bundled a cloth about the wound on Walter's head. His chest was sunken and he hadn't moved or opened his eyes. She closed her own eyes. The last thing she could see was the surprise on his face. Happiness. His boys. She put her hand to her mouth to stifle a sob, leaned against the wall while Norman adjusted the sheets, the pillow, and made Walter comfortable.

The doctor appeared within minutes and Norman took Letty out of the room. Men were walking down the corridors, they glanced at her with sympathy, tipped their hats as they passed. She stared at the wall, at the pictures of trawlers, wishing Alec was with her, and—

'Where's, Alfie?' She pressed her hands to her face. 'Oh, no, where's Alfie.' She twisted this way and that searching. 'I let him go.' She began to sob, huge racking sobs. 'It's all my fault.'

Norman pressed his hands on her shoulders. 'He's all right, Letty. He's with the men in the dining room. They've got him a drink and bite to eat. He's playing dominoes with Stan and Hector. They'll look after him.' He caught her by the elbow. 'Let me get you a hot sweet tea.'

She shook her head. 'No, I want to see what the doctor says. I can wait.'

He remained with her and shortly afterwards the doctor came out, grave-faced, followed by the port missioner. She knew from the look in his eyes that it was hopeless.

'Can I sit with him?'

Colin gave a small nod, looked to Norman.

'Stay with Letty while I see the doctor out.'

Norman opened the door for her, and she stepped inside the room, quiet save for the sound of Walter's laboured breath. He took a chair and pulled it next to the bed, pressed her into it. Norman said gently, 'I'll go and get you that tea.' He left the room, pulling the door close to. She could hear footsteps as people came and went along the corridor.

Letty leaned forward, kissed Walter's head, and tears fell onto her face, onto his, and she gently wiped them away. His dear face was distorted on one side, the mark where the horse's hoof had connected with his head swollen heavily and already darkly bruised, but the other side was unmarked and it was at this side she sat, taking his hand in hers. She reached in her pocket for her handkerchief and touched the paper, remembered the letter, opened it to read to him, only to find that it was the letter from the Lewises. She threw it on the floor, went to her basket and found the letter that the official from the orphanage had sent and began to read it to him.

'They found your boys, Walter. They're in Hull. Well, two of them are, George and Albert. Young Walter, your eldest, he's at sea. A trawlerman. Following in your footsteps.' Her voice cracked and, no longer able to trust herself to speak, she was quiet.

Norman came and placed the tea on the small bedside cabinet at her side and waited.

'I'm all right, Norman. I know you have duties.'

He went back to the door. 'I'll come back shortly. Don't worry about Alfie. We'll take care of him.'

She knew they would, each and every one of them would reach out to him, when his own flesh and blood were willing to pay not to have the inconvenience.

* * *

She had no idea how long she stayed with Walter, people came and went, were kind. Molly came and took the empty cup and saucer, fussed about behind her, until, irritated, Letty told her to leave. Norman brought Alfie to the door.

'He wanted to know you were still here.'

Letty kissed him, told him to be a good boy and off he went. Silent. She knew he was safe. That was all she'd ever wanted to be, safe.

'Oh, Alec. Alec,' she whispered to herself, holding her arms about her. 'Why can't you be here.'

She went back to Walter's side and remained there. Colin came with a blanket and put it about her shoulders. As the night deepened, Walter's breath ebbed away, until, with a final sigh from his poor crushed chest, he left this world. Letty hung her head with misery and exhaustion, her tears silent. There was nothing left inside her.

Colin took the sheet, ready to pull it over Walter's face, but Letty touched his arm to stop him and bent down and kissed Walter one last time. Then she left the room and went in search of Alfie.

Colin insisted she eat, but she didn't have the stomach for it. She glanced at the clock. It was three in the morning. 'It will soon be time for breakfast. I'll eat then.'

In the dining room, Alfie was asleep by what remained of the fire and Norman was in the armchair opposite smoking on his pipe. He made to get up so Letty could take his seat, but she held him back with her hand.

'If I sit down in front of that lovely fire, I'll not want to leave.' She moved to wake Alfie, who stirred a little but fell back to sleep again.

'I'll carry him,' Colin said, peeling him from the chair and taking him in his arms. Letty tried to protest, but Colin was already walking towards the door. 'Not in your condition, Letty.'

Letty picked up her basket and followed him out into the streets. At the corner, she glanced down at darkened road, seeing only the horse rearing up on its hind legs, and she looked away. They crossed the road and Letty led the way, wishing the day had never happened.

35

There was no sleep. Letty lay in bed, one hand on Alfie's back, feeling his ribs through his shirt. She hadn't bothered to undress him and he laid in his outdoor clothes, as did she, too tired, too numb to care.

When the light began to appear and the birds to sing, she went downstairs, raked the range and checked the pot for water. It was empty, so she went out to the pump and filled both pitchers. There was little movement in the yard. A dog barked inside number five. Lamps were lit in Sally's house and the curtains pulled back. A young couple had moved into Anita's old house. He worked on the carts, his wife at Tickler's jam factory.

Back in the house, there was movement in the kitchen and Letty went through with the jugs, filled the pot and placed them on them on the side. Her throat was like sandpaper, her eyes sore and itchy and she was glad for the gloom of the room. Dorcas had her back to her and was staring out of the window.

'You were late back.' Dorcas was curt, her voice clipped, but Letty thought it was because she was tired. Things had improved since Alec had gained his own ship. Dorcas had mellowed at his success, she supposed; or was it because Alec had been more of his own man, not so easily swayed by his mother's words?

'There was an accident.'

'I heard.' She rapped at the window and two pigeons fluttered up. Letty sank down at the table.

'It was our friend, Walter.' Letty rubbed her hands over her face, trying to rub away the images that kept flashing into her head. 'He saved Alfie's life.'

Dorcas twisted. 'Ah, yes. Alfie.' She put her hands in her apron, drew out a letter and placed it on the table, pushed it in front of Letty. 'When were you going to tell me. Or Alec?'

Letty blinked, picked up the envelope, recognising Mrs Lewis's hand. She placed it back on the table.

'Where did you get this?'

Dorcas folded her arms, stared at the letter. 'You haven't answered my question.'

'You had no right to read it. It was—'

Dorcas huffed. 'I'm not taking lessons in what's right from a liar. You deceived me and, more than that, you deceived my son.' Spittle flew from her mouth. 'Pulling the wool over his eyes. What would he want with someone else's child – and a whore's child at that.'

Letty held the letter. How had it got here? She tried to think, to rewind the day. She had read it, put it into her pocket, so angry... in the room, looking for Walter's letter. Dear Walter. She closed her eyes. She had thrown it on the floor in disgust. But? She forced herself to think, not looking at Dorcas, seeing only her arms stretched out before her, her fists clenched. And then she remembered. Molly. It could only have been Molly.

'The letter was not addressed to you,' she said, not wanting to talk, nor to defend herself. Her head was too full of other thoughts, other images, there wasn't space for anything else. She wanted to quench her thirst. She got up, poured herself cold water from the jug, drank it back. It hurt as she swallowed. The pot boiled, the lid began to rattle, she moved it away. When she turned back, Dorcas had moved from the table.

'It might not be addressed to me, but it concerns me, and my house, my family. My son.'

Letty sighed. 'I am your family, Dorcas. I left my own behind to become part of yours, and Alec's. I'm going to have his child. Your grandchild.'

'So you say.'

Letty snapped her head up. 'What do you mean by that?'

Dorcas picked up a cloth, wiped her hands.

'With you at that mission all the time. It might not be my boy's child. What am I to think. What will folk think? Well, 'appen I know what they're thinking—'

Letty instinctively pressed her hand to her abdomen. She was achingly tired, and sorrow lodged in her stomach like a great boulder. Now she felt an added sickness. 'I don't want this. Not today.'

'No.' Dorcas took down a small pan, threw in a handful of oats. 'Now that you've been found out.' She gave a small laugh. 'I was right, wasn't I? They don't want him, do they, the Lewises. You should have done what I said all along and took him to the orphanage on Victor Street. It would have saved all this...'

The hairs bristled on the back of Letty's neck. 'All this what?'

Dorcas turned from her.

'Go on,' Letty said. 'Don't stop now. You've been holding all this back since we came here, so why not get it all over and done with.' Her stomach hurt, the skin stretching across her belly and down to her groin tingled. 'Go on, get it all off your chest instead of your petty sniping.'

Dorcas glared at her. 'You're too wilful by half, madam.'

Letty nodded. 'My own mother says the same.'

'Well, there you are then,' Dorcas said, triumphant. 'I'm not saying anything your own mother wouldn't say.'

Letty's body was rigid. 'There's one difference, Dorcas. My mother loves me.'

'As I love my son.'

'My husband.'

Dorcas turned to stir the porridge. 'It's different. As you'll find out. With your own child, not someone else's. If you had...'

'Had what?'

Dorcas spun round, the spoon in her hand, porridge sagged and began to drop on the stone floor. Letty stared at it, a cream blob on the red tiles. Dorcas waved the spoon about, punctuating her words. 'If you'd have taken him off in the beginning, he wouldn't have been there yesterday, would he, the child. He wouldn't have been there to run into the road and—'

Letty gasped and the two of them stared at each other. There were no more words, none that would make any difference. Hadn't Dorcas simply spoken all the thoughts that had been running through her own head, thoughts that had kept her from sleep?

Dorcas lowered the spoon. Slowly, Letty got to her feet. Outside, she could hear doors opening and banging as people moved about to begin their day. She gripped the table, as if she was hanging on for dear life, for that's what it was. Life. And she didn't want to live it here, with this woman. And a spiteful one at that. She willed herself to leave the room and went upstairs, took a sheet and dropped her clothes into it, put Alfie's on top. She gathered the ends and tied a knot, then woke Alfie, his face still stained with dirty tears. He opened his eyes, opened his fist. In his hand was the sixpence. Tears pooled in her eyes. How could she have chosen anything else? She had been trying to do the right thing, to be kind.

'Come on, Alfie. We need to get up. Be lively, there's a good boy.'

He wriggled along to the side of the bed and she pushed on his boots, tied the laces and he followed her downstairs. She laid the bundle down by the door, told Alfie to wait and went to fetch their coats.

Dorcas glanced to the hall, to the bundle on the floor. 'What do you think you're doing?'

Letty couldn't bear to look at her.

'I'm doing what you always wanted me to do. I'm leaving. It's up to Alec what he chooses to do when he comes home.'

Dorcas caught her arm. 'Don't be stupid. You can't leave.'

Letty pulled herself free, gave a small, sad laugh. 'I can't put back the clock, Dorcas. No matter how much I wish I could. Believe me, my heart aches with all I've done wrong.'

She went to the kitchen, took the tin with her egg money, put it into her basket and slipped it over her arm, went back and picked up the bundle, opened the door, guided Alfie through it.

'You were right about Anita, about taking on Alfie, about what people would say and think. I might have listened if you'd said it with the tiniest bit of kindness instead of the disdain you clearly felt for me.' She stopped, smiled at Dorcas. 'I understand now, why I was drawn to Walter, and to Anita. They were kind – and they were on the outside, like me.' She followed Alfie into the courtyard.

Dorcas called after her. 'But what about Alec?'

Letty stopped, turned back to look at her. She looked distraught; well that made two of them.

'He'll have to decide for himself.'

She was shaking as she walked out of the courtyard. She had no idea where to go, but anywhere was better than living with Dorcas Hardy.

36

Letty struggled down the street, not wanting to let go of Alfie's hand, pushing back thoughts of the accident as carts clattered by, startling her. It all sounded louder, the pavement closer, and she tried to keep away from the edge of it, hugging the shopfronts and buildings, the basket and bundle heavy in her other hand and arm. The baby turned inside her, its feet and fists pressing forward, and she felt as if she was being battered on the inside as well as the out.

It was a relief to wait at the crossing as the morning trains trundled past, wagons taking the fish to London. She longed to be on a train, making her way back home to her family. Maybe soon she would be, and she would take Alfie with her. She looked down at the boy and as if sensing her gaze, he looked up at her and she knew she could never leave him behind.

The blind was down at the shop and she went around the back, letting herself in. Norah took one look at her and dashed forward, took the bundle from her and then the basket and placed them in a corner. Percy peered from round the chair and pulled himself to his feet, using his hands to grip the furniture, the mantelpiece. Letty gasped, and then the tears came.

Norah pressed her into a chair. 'Oh, my dear child. What on earth.'

Letty fumbled in her pocket for a handkerchief, couldn't find one. Percy pulled one from his pocket, shook it for Alfie, who fetched it and gave it to Letty.

Percy said, 'Better. Better.'

Letty nodded, laughing and crying at the same time, overwhelmed. Coming here had always felt like a place of safety. 'Oh, Percy. Look at you.'

Norah smiled as Letty rubbed at her nose. 'He's doing well, isn't he? Been practising when his pals are about to help. He's determined to get back behind that counter.'

He grunted, gave a lopsided smile.

'He thinks we're running riot in there, Letty.'

'We are.'

He nodded, slipped into the chair beside her, landing with a thump.

'Now, then,' Norah said. 'Enough of Percy and his escapades. What's happened to you?'

Letty took Alfie's slate from her basket and gave it to him. He settled by Percy and began to fashion his letters.

'Me and Dorcas had words.' She coughed to clear her throat, stop her tears. 'After what happened to poor Walter. It was too much.'

Norah reached up and took her hand in hers, rubbed at her shoulder with the other. 'Wolfie came to tell us last night on his way to his watch. Poor Walter.'

It made the tears run again. 'It was all my fault.'

'It was an accident.'

She looked to Alfie, who was settled on the rag rug in front of the fire. 'If I hadn't kept Alfie with me. If I hadn't let go of his hand.' She saw the flashback again, of Alfie chasing his sixpence, the horse, the sound of—A sob caught and Norah instantly drew her to her. It was uncomfortable, her belly too big, too awkward, but she didn't want to leave Norah's embrace.

'Don't talk daft, you silly girl. He was so happy for Alfie, for what you'd done. He said so often.'

'Did he?'

Percy touched her arm and she looked at him through swollen eyelids. 'Did. Did.'

'He wished someone had been able to do the same for him, when his wife died,' Norah soothed.

Being here with Norah, not having to be careful of what she said was such a relief. It would be easy to let go and give in to more tears, but that wouldn't solve anything.

'His boys. I had news. That's what I was going to tell him. I had a letter.' She withdrew it from her pocket and handed it to Norah. 'He'd found Betsy, his daughter. I had news of his sons. Now they've lost him again. Twice over is too much for any child. I wish I'd never written that letter at all.'

Norah's answer was brisk. 'You can't blame yourself for what happened. It's as daft as blaming Walter for giving the lad sixpence.'

If only it was so simple. Letty pressed her lips together, tipped her head to hold back the tears.

'You can't go on like this, Letty. You're exhausted. Why don't you go upstairs and lie down, I can manage in the shop and Alfie's good company for Percy.'

Letty blew her nose, shook her head. 'I'd rather work in the shop. Take my mind off things. I wouldn't sleep anyway.'

Norah nodded, understanding, and Letty got to her feet. She splashed her face with cold water, tidied her hair and went to open up, glad to keep herself busy, her mind and hands occupied.

* * *

Norah came in mid-morning with a drink and a sandwich and made her sit down.

'Feeling better.'

Letty nodded, her mouth full of food that was hard to swallow.

Norah shook her head. 'It's not good for you or the baby all this upset.'

'I'll be fine. The baby's fine.' She held her stomach. 'Think he's going to play for the Mariners at this rate. He's a right little wriggler.'

'Do you hope for a boy, Letty?'

Letty pushed her empty plate onto the counter and got to her feet. She felt better for having something inside her. 'I hope for a healthy child.' She patted her belly protectively.

Norah rubbed her hand over her mouth. 'Letty, I...' She paused, considering her words and Letty was suddenly nauseous. If the words were difficult for Norah to utter, then it could only be bad news. She felt ashamed. How could she have been so stupid. They didn't want her any more did they, not in her state, lumbering about like a whale. They could easily get someone else to help in the shop, someone that was less trouble.

'It's all right, Norah. I understand.'

Norah furrowed her brow. 'Understand what?'

'You have enough to deal with, without me bringing my troubles to your door.'

Norah batted her hand in front of her. 'The very idea!' She clasped her hands together and Letty waited for her to speak. 'I don't want to interfere; or come between you and your mother-in-law.' She rubbed at her chin. 'I'm sure you'll work it out in time but... well, you can stay here as long as you need to. You and Alfie.'

Letty protested. 'I wouldn't dream of such a thing. You and Percy have been so very kind to me. I can't take advantage any more than I have already, forcing myself on you...'

Norah put her hands on her hips. 'Forcing yourself? Whoever put that idea into your head?' She didn't reply and Norah, guessing, said, 'Oh. Well, it doesn't matter. You stay here tonight. You'll perhaps feel different in the morning.'

Letty was too tired to argue and even if she had, she knew Norah would have none of it. The only thing she could think of to say was, 'Thank you.' It seemed so little, but it was all she had.

* * *

By the end of the day, Letty was exhausted, and glad to be so. Hopefully, sleep would come to her and then she would be able to think. Kind and generous as the Parkers were, she couldn't stay here indefinitely. What would Alec make of it all? She rubbed at her temple, her head tight. She would think about it tomorrow, it would be easier then.

She went outside and began taking in the things that hung outside in the display, the oilskins, the boots that dangled from the chains fixed to the window frames.

Gilbert Crowe came out of his door and stood on the street, looked one way and then the other. He walked over to her.

'Got your feet under the table good and proper here, haven't you?' He leaned closer, his breath foul, and she stepped away, feeling the fear of him again. He followed her. 'Likely you'll work for me when I buy this place. I'll be in need of a good woman.' He came towards her and she clutched the oilskins to her, wanting to turn away from his sickening face.

She put out a hand. 'One step closer and I'll tell your wife where you got that scratch on your face and that lump on your head the other month.'

He stood back, and she watched his expression change as he tried to work out how she knew. She wasn't going to enlighten him, not unless she had to.

She picked up the boots and went inside.

Norah had cooked a stew and she made Letty sit down at the table with them. Alfie and Percy had been playing Snakes and Ladders, the board still set out on the footstool for another game. It was cosy and warm, it felt like a home – the first time she'd felt anything like it since coming to Grimsby.

Norah stood at the end of the table slicing bread and Percy took a slice and began to take up a knife. He buttered it with great awkwardness and handed it to Alfie, held onto it until Alfie, understanding, said, 'Thank you, Mr Percy.' Percy gave him his lopsided smile and patted him on the head, his movements laboured – but he was getting there. Norah had been watching, Letty too, and she was grateful that some good at least had come from keeping Alfie with her.

37

Dorcas slipped into the back pew at the Bethel Mission Hall. She was lucky to get a place for every seat was full and men stood along the sides, pressing themselves further towards the front as the congregation swelled. She had never met Walter Stevens, had only ever heard Letty speak of him. Of coming home and finding his wife dead and his children gone. What did that do to a man? The walls were studded here and there with plaques to beloved sons, husbands and brothers. Was any of it of comfort? Did anyone notice other than those who it didn't hurt to read them? She knew she belonged with the people gathered in this chapel; who sat and knitted and worried when the wind howled down the chimney and rattled through gaps in doors and windows, who tried not to look at the newspaper headlines calling of ships lost and yet read them anyway, hoping against hope it wasn't their man, their son, feeling guilty because you hoped it had happened to someone else. And yet it hadn't happened to someone else? She was that wife, that mother.

The service was short; she stood to sing 'Eternal Father, Strong to Save' and 'Abide with Me', she sat and listened to the sermon, she repeated the Lord's Prayer, and although she was within a crowd, she felt more truly alone than she'd ever done. If only she could have reached out and taken the kindly hand Letty had offered.

As the congregation rose and the coffin was taken up, she caught a glimpse of Letty, who was comforting a girl that could only be Walter's child. Dorcas burned with shame. How cruel she had been.

She caught the shadow of surprise in Letty's face as she passed, and the lass gave her a nod of acknowledgement that she was there. It was brief, but it was not hostile. Behind her walked an elderly couple who she took to be the Parkers. She was an upright woman with steel grey hair, her husband taller and somewhat stooped, his right leg dragging, his hand clawlike at his side. Holding his hand was Alfie, who looked at her, his eyes wide, unblinking, so like Robbie's, and something inside her cracked wide open. Her legs became boneless and she clutched at the ledge in front of her.

The man at her side, caught her arm, whispered, 'Are you all right, missus?'

She nodded, turned to him and managed a small smile. She was rewarded with one much warmer and the hollowness inside her widened. She sat down, aware of the congregation as it filtered past, staring ahead at the altar. Was there a God? Was there anything to believe in at all?

* * *

It was bright outside, the low winter sun doing its best to break through the clouds as they moved slowly across the sky. A train trundled past on the line that ran along the end of the street, the sea to the other side. Letty stood with Betsy, speaking to people who stopped to pay their respects. Some of the women remembered her as a child, recalled her mother as well as her father, and Letty felt glad that Betsy had found a connection to her past. Threads that she could hold on to when she went back to Louth. Letty hoped that she had good friends. She was a sweet girl, possessing the same generous countenance as her father, her sandy hair an array of thick unruly curls that escaped from her small dark hat as Walter's had fought from his cap.

Letty stepped back to stand with Norah, glad the service was over.

'He was a popular man,' Norah said, looking about her as people drifted off and down the street while others clustered in small groups and spoke in whispers. 'They'll be off to toast his life down at the *Albion*.' Norah indicated to a group of old sea dogs rolling down the road with the distinctive trawlerman's gait.

'Walter would approve,' Letty said. It made her smile.

Norah caught her eye. 'It's good to smile, Letty. Remember Walter with happiness and not sorrow. He wouldn't want that.'

'I know.' She felt the tears well up, remembering his smile, his kindness, and blinked them back. 'I know the hurt will soften eventually, but just now it feels very heavy.' She wiped away a stray tear with the back of her hand, forced herself to smile as Betsy turned and walked over to them.

'I'll be after getting my train,' she said quietly. 'Thank you for being here for me, Letty.'

Letty struggled to speak. She took a breath. 'It was the very least I could do. Your father was so very kind to me. To everyone.'

The girl nodded and her eyes glittered with tears. 'He was a hero, wasn't he?' She looked to Alfie who was at Percy's side.

'He was, all that and more,' Norah said kindly. 'Would you like to come back with us for a bite to eat before you leave, child?'

'That's very kind of you, Mrs Parker, but I'd like to get the earlier train. It's a fair walk when I get back and I'd rather do it when it's not so dark.'

'I'll walk with you to the station,' Letty said, looking back at the Bethel. She had been waiting for Dorcas to leave, to say something, although she knew not what. She must have left already. No matter, there was time yet. Sitting in the church, she had been able to think, the stillness and peace comforting. Life was too short to dwell on things, on poisonous words stirred by gossip and hatred. She'd thought of Walter coming home from sea to find his wife and children gone, how it must have torn at his heart. She linked her arm through Betsy's and turned to Norah. 'Would you take care of Alfie until I get back?'

Norah raised her eyebrows in amusement. 'As if I could tear him and Percy apart.' They watched as Percy was helped into the carriage they had waiting. Wolfie lifted Alfie to sit beside him. He held his hand out to assist Norah, who settled herself opposite them. Letty and Betsy waved their goodbyes and made their way to the small station at New Clee.

It had been a solemn day, a day of thought and reflection, and the walk home to Parkers had helped her order her thoughts. Betsy had asked her to keep in touch and wanted to have news of her brothers. They were young now, but one day they would have families of their own and Betsy wanted to be part of that. When all was said and done they still had each other and Letty was able to take some comfort in being able to bring them together. She would not forget. There were many things she would not forget, but she could find it in her heart to forgive.

* * *

Norah had not been surprised when Letty told her she would be going back to Mariners Row. 'I had hoped you might, Letty. Much as we've loved having you here, it's not where you belong. In time, your mother-in-law will see that too.'

Letty folded her clothes and laid them in the sheet once more. Norah was sitting on the end of the bed holding Alfie's blue sweater, picking at small threads, brushing her hand gently over it as if it were the boy himself. The two of them looked at each other.

'I'll be back in the morning,' Letty said, trying to make light of it, though her heart was breaking. 'You can't get shut of us, you know.'

Norah got to her feet, placed the sweater on top of the pile of clothes. 'I hope not.' She squeezed Letty's hand. 'You're doing the right thing. It will all come right, it always does.'

She led the way and Letty followed her down the stairs and back into the sitting room. Alfie was settled on Percy's knee and the old man was stroking his hair. He looked up, glassy-eyed, when Letty came in, and gave her his crooked smile.

'Come on, Alfie,' she said softly. 'Mrs Hardy needs us. Say goodnight to Mr Percy and Mrs Norah.'

He reached up and planted a kiss on Percy's cheek, taking the old man by surprise. It was swiftly returned. Alfie slipped off his knee and onto the floor. 'Can we come and play in the morning?' He looked to Letty.

Percy said, 'Yes! Yes!' and Alfie's face lit with pleasure. He slipped his hand into Letty's and Norah walked with them to the door.

'Be safe, lass.'

Letty nodded, looked ahead into the darkness of the yard at the back of the shop. Out in the river, she could hear the hoot of a tug, men shouting across the docks, the clatter of chain and wood as life went on.

'I'll be back in the morning. We both will.'

* * *

Norah closed the door on them and went back to sit in the chair opposite Percy. Just the two of them, as it had always been. For a time, she stared down at her lap and, when she looked up, caught Percy dabbing at his eyes with a crumpled handkerchief.

'Sad,' he said. 'Like dor-ter.'

She reached out and clasped his hand. 'She is.'

He nodded and they settled back in their chairs, their thoughts their own. For one wonderful week, they had been a family and it had been precious beyond any words.

* * *

Letty was weary when she reached the door to number three. Alfie opened it for her. Dorcas was in her chair knitting and Letty noticed that it wasn't the thick oiled wool of sweaters and socks but soft and white, the tiny sleeve of a matinee jacket taking shape. She set down her load, told Alfie to go through to the kitchen and get some water. She laid down her basket, unfastened her coat.

'I didn't want Alec to come home and find us gone.'

Dorcas paused, looked as if she was about to say something, stopped. The two of them stared at each other. Then Dorcas carried on with her knitting and Letty felt the chasm between them shrink a little.

38

Luck was on their side as the *Black Prince* came into port. Mr Hammond was on the dockside – Alec could see his good coat and his shiny shoes from the deck.

Alec shinned down the ladder and the man was waiting at the bottom with his hand outstretched. There was a sharp wind and his hands were cold, his grip firm.

'Another good trip, Hardy. Keep going like this and you'll be my top skipper before long.'

'That's what I'm aiming for, Mr Hammond.'

'Enough of the Mr Hammond. It's John.'

Alec let go of his hand. How soon things improved when all was going well. He'd a couple of good trips under his belt, but the winter weather was a challenge so far north.

'I'll see you in the office in the morning for settling. My sons will be with me. It will be good for them to get to know you. Jonathon is back from America, and Laurence finished his schooling – now for the hard part of life, eh, Alec. That'll be a shock to their system.'

'It will.' Although how much of a shock was down to circumstances, wasn't it? To have a father to set you up so well was half the battle. Alec thought of his own father. His legacy had been a part share in the *Stella*

Maris. The money from the sale was safe in the bank. Would it be wise to invest in the part share of a trawler or was he wiser to invest in something else? Or someone. He'd had plenty of time to think in the long hours on the bridge, just him and miles of ocean when the ship was steaming home. Home. That was what it was all for.

They chatted a short while and Hammond took his leave to meet another of his skippers. Alec knew he was one of many. It was a timely reminder, as if he needed one.

Alec's bag was where he had left it on the quay and Jimmy Whittle, another Hammond skipper, whistled to get his attention as he walked up to him.

'Had a good trip?'

'Over two thousand kits. Plenty of good cod and a fair share of haddocks. The lads'll make a bob or two on the cod livers.' It was a good haul, but he would do better next time. 'How about you?'

'Fair to middlin'. I can't complain.'

'But you will.'

He threw back his head and laughed as Alec slung his bag and rested it on his shoulder. 'Word gets round about the grumpy bastards.'

They began to walk from the dockside, Jimmy keeping step.

'Time for a brew in the *Albion*?'

Alec shook his head. 'Any other trip. Not this one. I want to get home, see Letty.' Another delay was the last thing on his mind. 'Not long till the baby's due.'

'No need to go home,' Jimmy said. 'She's at Parkers.'

Alec checked his watch. 'Not now she won't be. Way too early.'

Jimmy thrust his hands in his pockets. 'She was living there, last I heard.'

Alec dropped his bag. 'My Letty?'

Jimmy's mouth twisted. 'Aye. Oh hell, lad. I thought you might have heard. You must've sailed a day or two after it happened.' He told him of Walter's accident and that soon after he'd heard Letty was living at the shop. 'I expect she's needed with old Percy getting bad with his stroke, like. Must have hit him hard. They were great pals.'

Alec didn't think that had anything to do with it at all, and from his edgy manner he didn't think Jimmy did either. He picked up his bag, slung it across his back. 'Best go and see for myself.'

He tried the front door of the shop, but it was too early for open doors and he went round the back. He already felt on the back foot with Jimmy's news and had gone over in his mind what might have happened that Letty would leave. Perhaps he'd jumped to conclusions, and wrong ones at that. He rapped on the door and waited, heard the bolt slide across at the top and bottom of the large black door, the key turn in the lock.

Norah smiled at him, pulling the door wide. 'Oh, Alec. I thought it might be Letty.'

'She's not here?'

Norah was guarded. 'You heard otherwise?' He nodded. 'Then you'd better come in.'

Half an hour and a good strong mug of tea later, Alec arrived at Mariners Row. Someone was already awake for he was greeted by the smell of baking bread. He dropped his bag on the floor beside his mother's latest nets and kicked them to one side. She wouldn't be doing that much longer, wouldn't need to.

His mother came to the doorway, looking older than her years, but her face brightened when she saw him. Wiping her hands on her apron, she came towards him and he put his arms about her, kissed her cheek.

'How are you, Mother? You look tired.'

She tapped at his chest. 'I'll be good for years yet, me lad. Don't you worry.'

He heard movement upstairs, two voices, and looked up to the ceiling. 'The lad's still here then.'

Dorcas pursed her lips. 'He is.'

There hadn't been any need to ask, Norah had told him as much, but he wanted to check his mother's reaction. There was a lot to say and never much time to say it.

Letty soon came downstairs, followed by Alfie, and Alec felt his heart swell when he saw her. She was big at the front now, and as she came closer, he could see how pale and drawn she was. He walked to her, held out his hand for her to take hold of and when she did, he pulled her towards him and kissed her, placed his arms gently about her. He wanted to protect her, but Letty was not a lass that needed protection. She was her own woman, always would be.

He held her hands, stood back, and her face glowed with her smile, but she couldn't hide the sadness in her eyes. 'I heard about Walter Stevens. A sad do.'

'It was. Too sad.'

He bent down on one knee and called Alfie to him. 'All right, Alfie. Have you been a good lad for my Letty?'

The lad nodded, stuck close to Letty. Alec smiled and the boy tentatively smiled back. Who knew what godawful things he'd already seen in his short life? He went to his bag, brought out a tin train he had picked up at the stores on the way home. He crouched down to Alfie's level and handed it over. The boy reached out and took hold of it, but Alec held tight.

'Can we be friends?'

Alfie nodded. 'Yes, Mr Alec.'

'That's the ticket.' He let go of the train, got up. Letty was smiling, but his mother's expression was unreadable. He didn't pass comment, simply said, 'Did you say you had a brew on, Mother?'

He put his arm around his wife and they went through to the kitchen. He made Letty sit down at the table.

'You're looking bonny, lass.' She squeezed his hand. They could hear Alfie playing with the train on the floor in the room. 'He's still very quiet.'

'Better than he was.'

His mother put tea in front of them, took the bread from the oven and turned it out of the tin. She put some bacon on to fry. The tension between the two women was obvious. There had to be a way to bring them together. He couldn't be worrying about them while he needed to keep his mind on the ship and the catch.

'You two have been all right then? While I've been away?'

His mother slid a plate of bacon in front of him.

He looked to her, to Letty, sliced through the meat and pushed it into his mouth. Letty spoke first.

'It's all been fine.'

Alec swallowed. 'That why you went to stay with the Parkers?'

His mother looked to Letty, then turned back to the sink. Letty looked done in and he didn't want to drag it out of her.

'When was you going to tell me? Or were you going to tell me?' He drank some of his tea. 'Thing is, I'm a skipper now, and I'm getting a good name for meself. When people are talking about me, I want it to be about the good catches I'm landing, not what me wife and mother are up to.'

'It was my fault,' Letty said quickly. 'I left in a temper. I shouldn't have, but Walter had—'

He'd known Letty would take the blame. 'Is that right, Mother?'

Dorcas shifted uneasily. 'It's all done and dusted now. Folk just gossiping.' He caught her looking to Letty.

'Has to be more to it than that.'

The clock ticked behind them. Letty put some jam on a slice of bread and got up with some effort and took it through to Alfie. He heard her telling him to eat and get dressed ready for work.

'What did Letty lose her temper over, Mother?'

She sucked at her lips. 'That boy. She wrote to his family. They don't want him. I knew they wouldn't. She kept it from me.' Letty came in, took a seat. 'Someone else took great pleasure in telling me.'

'A gossip,' Alec said. 'With nowt better to do than cause trouble. As if there isn't enough of that in the world.'

His mother still didn't look at Letty. 'It wasn't gossip though. It was the truth.'

Letty interrupted. 'I was going to tell you?'

'When?' Dorcas snapped. 'You left it too late.'

Letty was too tired to fight. 'I didn't want to give up on him.' She got to her feet. 'I'm sorry, Alec, I have to go to work. Just for the morning.'

He stood with her. 'I'll walk with you.' He helped her on with her coat, then turned to his mother. 'We'll talk later.' He planted a kiss on her cheek.

She was on the defensive, as well she might be, but Letty was the one who needed caring for now and he had to make sure that he sorted a semblance of peace before he went back to his ship.

He put out his hand and Alfie took it and for a while they walked with the lad between them, then Alec stopped, swung him up on his shoulders. 'You'll get a better view up there, Alfie boy.' Alfie clung to his shoulders and they continued walking. 'There,' he said to Letty. 'That leaves you with your hand free to put in mine.' She did and people called out to Alfie, riding on his shoulders, and he waved at them. It made him wobble, but Alec put a hand on his leg. 'I won't let you fall, boy. Don't you worry about that.' He turned to Letty. 'And I won't let you fall either. So best you tell me what's been going on.'

They talked until the very last minute and he was well aware that she was watchful of every word, not wanting to put any blame at his mother's feet. They stopped at the front door of Parkers and he took Alfie down and placed him on the ground.

'I promised Anita that I wouldn't let him go to Victor Street, to the orphanage. I have to keep trying.'

He put his hand to her cheek. 'You don't have to try any more, Let. The lad stays with us.'

'But your mother...'

'I'll talk to her.' He sighed. 'She's not the woman she was. Robbie... well, losing him that did for her. It's like she's forgotten how to be soft. Perhaps when the baby comes.' He put a hand to her belly, felt the babe kick. They shared a smile. He looked up at the shopfront. 'You know you don't have to keep working here any more. I'm doing well, better than I thought. I want to look for moving to another house.'

'It's not just work though, Alec. Norah and Percy are like family to me.'

'Aye, and you to them by all accounts.' She looked at him, he shrugged. He chucked Alfie under the chin. 'Better get to Mr Percy, Alfie. Put a smile on his face like you do my Letty's.'

The lad reached up and pressed the latch on the door and went inside, leaving it ajar.

'What time will you finish?'

'Twelve. We've taken a young girl on to help. Business is good.'

He didn't doubt it; hadn't she made it so, with her quick mind and her kind heart. 'I'll be back for you at twelve, Cinderella.' He put a hand to her hair, kissed her forehead, her nose, her lips. 'Doubt I'll have a carriage, but I'll be waiting for you.'

* * *

His mother was at her net when he returned home. As a child, he had been mesmerised by the speed of her hands as they flew across the pole, the way she used the length of her hand as a measure to build the squares. How quickly with a deft flick of the wrist she produced the knots that kept it all in place, the work and skill that went into it that was rewarded with coppers. It had kept them all afloat when their father died. She'd done whatever she could to keep her boys with her.

Alec sat down beside her, picked up an empty needle and began filling it.

'You did that as a child,' she said, not looking at him. 'Shouldn't think you do that any more.'

'No, Mother. I have the crew to do that for me.' She concentrated on her work, building the mesh that would snare the unwary fish. 'I've moved on now. As we all must. I have to concentrate on the men, the ship, keeping the gaffers happy.'

'A big responsibility.'

He reached out and stilled her hand with his own. 'About the boy.' She stared at the net in front of her. Did she know what he was about to say? He didn't want to hurt her, not for the world – but he didn't agree with her, not on this. 'We all have to look out for each other, Mother. The crew and me, well, we're a family. All fishermen are a family, you know that. When we hear that Mayday call, we don't stop to judge. Any competition between us flies out the window and we haul our nets and go to help.' She began braiding again, slower this time. 'Alfie needed help, Mother, and Letty heard his call. She upset you, she knows that, but she did the right thing, the only thing.'

She stopped her work. 'He's not your child. He's not your responsibility.'

He understood her fear but wouldn't play into it, not as he once would have done. He took the needle from her hand and pulled her to her feet. 'Get your coat on, Mother,' he said, his voice bright. 'We're going out.'

'I have the nets.'

'You do that out of habit, for something to do, to take your mind off...' he hesitated, '...things. Now, go and get your coat and we'll have a bit of time together, just you and me. Just like it used to be.'

* * *

They strolled down Freeman Street and called in at the Co-operative store. He bought her a coat. Thick and warm for the winter. In all her years, she had never had such a fine coat, but the pleasure he had in getting it for her and the pride she felt in him was immense.

'You look bonny, Mother. Does it fit well? Is it warm?' He tugged at the shoulders and she ran her hands down the front of the fine wool, felt the softness of the fur collar. When the assistant asked if he wanted it put on account, he took great pride in telling her he would be paying cash in full. She felt like a queen as they walked out of the shop and back into the busy streets, her old coat a parcel under his arm. 'You can give this old thing to the mission. Someone will be glad of it.'

'I'll keep it. You never know what's around the corner.'

He stopped and she did too. People weaved past them.

'No more holding on to old things, Mother. We're looking to the future now.'

She linked her arm in his. People stopped and chatted to him and he introduced her, his mother, Mrs Hardy, and she realised how much she had kept herself shut away at her nets. Alec was right. It was habit. It made her feel safe. It was what she'd done to keep her boys fed, a roof over her head.

In the café, he ordered coffee and cake, amused and delighted when she gasped at the extravagance.

'It's high time we got used to other ways of doing things.' He took hold of her hand. 'We need to talk about the future, Mother. The Hardys future – and that includes Letty, and Alfie.' She tried to withdraw her hand, but he wouldn't let her. 'It's not a tug of war,' he said, gently. 'We're all pulling at the same end of the rope.'

39

The *Black Prince* steamed north. Foghorns piped eerily in the distance and Alec listened hard, leaned out of the window of the wheelhouse, casting his eyes about for a shape that might mean disaster. It had been hard going, the seas fierce. The chief was keeping stock of the coal stores. Enough to get them out there, enough to catch the fish and enough to get them safely home. Big Mick was third hand. The two of them got along fine. The man was father of six. Another good man sent his way by Sam Harris. He had a lot to thank the man for. It was a lonely life and he was beginning to realise that being skipper was lonelier still. A few of the men had stayed on from the last trip, but a couple of the deckhands had signed on elsewhere. If they didn't like hard work, he didn't want them. The fog became patchy and he made out the *Carlisle* to his port side.

Mate, Tommy Stocker, came into the wheelhouse. 'No better on deck. Sight is only a few feet, but it looks like it might clear up. There's a wind coming from the east and, with a bit o' luck, it should blow this some other bugger's way.'

Alec picked up the speaking tube and shouted down to the chief to steady the engines while they cast the nets over. Tommy went down on deck to rouse the crew. Dark shadows appeared below him as his men gathered in the gloom and started pushing the nets over the side. It was eerie, quiet, low visibility. All they could do was carry on and hope that when they lifted the nets, they were full. There was a swish of water as the engines slowed. To a man, they would keep watch for the hidden dangers that might catch out the unwary.

* * *

It had been a week since Alec had left, an awkward week, but things were gradually improving. Letty spent more time at the house and slowly the two women were beginning to find a way forward. Dorcas had to remember that Letty was Alec's choice and not her own.

Shame pricked at her. The pain when she lost Robbie was raw and savage. Alec had reassured her of the happiness to come. When he landed, the next generation would have arrived to greet him. The thought sustained her. There was still time to make things right.

She pulled the fur collar of her new coat about her face; the wind nipped at her cheeks. A woman hurried past, pushing a perambulator. Dorcas peered at the child. She would be a grandmother soon. She thought of her words to Letty that painful night when she had left. How could she have been so cruel. She could have ripped out her own tongue. But she had been hurt too, that Letty had lied. She'd gone over this in her head as she sat at her nets, weaving row after row. Alec was right, she did it out of habit, for money had been coming in steadily. They were each of them doing well, but they had all been doing it separately. She'd finished her last net that morning; when they were collected on Friday, that would be the end of it. She prayed to God that she would never have to do them again, that He would keep her boy safe.

Letty had been cleaning the house when she left, nesting no doubt. The baby's arrival was imminent. She was a size, her ankles and legs swollen from standing too much. Alec had asked her to give up the shop, but she wouldn't, she liked it, loved being with the Parkers. Dorcas took that to mean it was better than being with her. She'd taken umbrage all too often. Hopefully, now she would go some way to making amends.

Inside Parkers, she waited while Norah served a woman and her son. She looked at the goods for sale, how neat it was, how organised, feeling ashamed. The Parkers must have blessed the day Letty walked in the door. If only she had been so gracious.

The couple called out as they left with their goods and Norah came towards her, a frown of recognition on her face.

Dorcas put out her hand. 'Mrs Hardy. Letty's mother-in-law.'

Norah smiled warmly, shook her hand, gripping it tightly. 'Of course. I recognise you from Walter's funeral.' She pressed her hand, suddenly concerned. 'Is Letty all right?'

'As well as can be expected. I think she's very near her time. I left her cleaning the house like a demon.' She looked about the shop. 'I wondered if I could have a word?' What she had to say needed to be said in private.

Norah must have sensed her discomfort. She said something to the young girl behind the counter and took Dorcas through to the back of the shop. Percy was asleep in an armchair in front of the fire and Norah rattled at it with the poker. He stirred a little but did not wake.

Dorcas removed her gloves, placed them in her bag. Norah pulled a chair away from the table and they both sat down.

'I know what Letty will have told you...' Dorcas began.

Norah put up a hand. 'Let me stop you there, Mrs Hardy.'

'Dorcas, please.'

'Dorcas.' She paused. 'Letty might have said you'd had words, but she didn't say what those words were. So any tittle-tattle has not come from Letty's lips.' Norah's tone was kindly but, even so, Dorcas felt her cheeks flush. Behind her, Percy snorted. A quick glance showed his eyes were closed.

'I misjudged the girl.'

Norah smiled. 'We all make mistakes, misjudge, it's so easily done. Whatever mistakes Letty makes, she makes with a kind heart.'

Dorcas looked down at her hands, at the purple veins that ran across them. Kindness. It was important to Letty. 'I've been such a fool. Letty gave my boy the courage to start anew, and I resented her for it, dragging us here, away from all we knew.'

'I doubt it was her idea.'

'No,' Dorcas agreed. 'But he knew he could make the move with her. There was another girl...'

'There always is.'

Dorcas nodded. 'I thought she was better suited. I was wrong.'

Norah said, 'Letty's ambitious. They're a good match, don't you think?'

Dorcas agreed. 'It frightened me – her determination. Made me feel adrift, like I couldn't find solid ground to stand on. She reached out to me, but I pushed her away.'

'It felt safer?'

Dorcas nodded. 'When I saw them both together, the excitement they had for the future, it reminded me of what I'd lost. My husband. My son.' She was quiet. 'We all start out with our hopes and dreams.'

Norah looked across to Percy and her face glowed with the warmth of her smile. 'We do. We might not get everything we want, but we have to make the best of what we do get.'

Dorcas felt a lump form in her throat. If only Will were still here, that she could sit in old age with him by the fire. She ached with longing and loneliness for him.

'That's what I came to talk to you about. The shop.' She sat up, tried to be more businesslike. She hadn't come here to pour her heart out, but talking to Norah had helped. She could see why Letty liked being here. 'Letty had mentioned that when you retired, she'd like to buy the premises. I want you to know that when you are ready, the money is there, waiting. We have cash, savings from the sale of my...' She corrected herself, remembering Alec's words. 'Family money. Mine. Letty's. And Alec's.'

Norah was awkward and Dorcas watched her, unsure. Had she overstepped the mark? She had said, when they were ready.

'I'm sorry if I've offended you. I don't want to be hectoring. I simply wanted for you to bear it in mind.'

Norah clasped her hands in her lap, stared down at them for a moment or two.

Dorcas became anxious. 'I'm trying to make amends.'

'I know you are.' Norah sighed. 'It puts me in an awkward position.'

'Oh.' Dorcas got to her feet. 'It was silly of me to hope.'

Norah made her sit down again. 'I wasn't to say anything...'

Dorcas stared down at her hands, her wedding ring.

'I'm sorry. It was rude of me to put you in this position. I wanted to surprise Letty.'

Norah sighed, leaned to the right to look to Percy. 'I gave my word to your son. Alec called in before he sailed. He asked me the very same thing.' Dorcas sank back in her chair and Norah said quickly, 'I got the impression he'd only just thought of the idea. I'm quite sure he would have talked it over with you before he did anything. It was simply... well, he wanted to stake a claim, for Letty.'

Dorcas clasped her bag on her lap, pressed her lips together. 'I'm glad.' She paused. 'He loves her.'

'As she loves him.'

Dorcas agreed.

Norah sat back in her chair. 'As I told Alec, it would have to be agreed with our shareholder.' Another grunt from Percy, a snore. Norah shot him a look, but the man was still asleep. 'I can't see there being any problem.'

Dorcas was only too grateful that they would even consider it, sorry she'd left it so late. 'Thank you.'

Norah shrugged. 'I haven't done anything.'

Dorcas glanced about the room, the mantel with its clock and clutter of ornaments, the pile of newspapers by the hearth, a Snakes and Ladders board on a small footstool she knew must be for Alfie. 'You welcomed them, both of them.'

Norah gave her the warmest of smiles. 'Your family grows, Dorcas, you're a fortunate woman.'

'I am. I didn't appreciate it.'

'Plenty of time to catch up,' Norah said encouragingly.

Dorcas found a smile. 'I hope so.'

40

Letty had woken that same morning with a burst of energy she hadn't felt in weeks. The loss of Anita and then Walter had weighed heavy, the deceit over Alfie more so. And still there was more. She should have told Alec and Dorcas that instead of taking more money from the Parkers for her extra work, she'd asked them for a small share, to be increased accordingly as business blossomed. She should have told them, but there hadn't been time. There was never enough time. Her thoughts had been tangled and knotted, but as the days progressed, she'd gradually felt them unravel. She grieved for the loss of her friends, how angry it had made her, and it came some way to helping her understand Dorcas's grief. Her mother-in-law had not only lost her love, her husband, she had lost a part of her, her own flesh and blood. Worse, she had lost hope. She went upstairs with a pail of hot water and a cloth and set them down on the floorboards, went to the window and pushed it open. A blast of cold air hit her face and blew at her hair. Some of the kids from the courtyard were running around. Alfie looked up. 'All right, Alfie?' she called down to him.

He stood to wave and Stanley, Sally's boy, ran up and tagged him. 'You're it, Alfie, You're it.'

He laughed and ran after them. He laughed a lot these days, they all had more to smile about. He had warm clothes, and Alec had bought him new boots. Dorcas had a new coat. He had wanted to treat Letty, but she'd said to wait until the baby was born. Undeterred, he'd indulged her in a new hat.

The baby moved and she touched her belly. She lowered herself to her knees and started scrubbing at the floor. The dust from the twine got everywhere and she was glad that those that waited downstairs for collection in the morning would be the last. Alec had insisted that his mother give them up and, to Letty's surprise, she'd agreed.

She scrubbed hard between the gaps, her arms stretched, her belly almost touching the floor. She scrubbed to the sound of laughter and gleeful shouts floating in through the window. The steady movements soothed her. Back and forth, back and forth. When Alec next came home, he would be a father, they would be a family. They had been looking for a new house. Would they agree on that? It would all come out in the wash, just as her mother always said.

When she was satisfied the floor was clean, she picked up the pail and made her way downstairs, ready to start on the room below. She kicked at the nets as she passed. They should be in the yard, she would move them. She heard a shout from outside, more laughter, heard Alfie calling out, his voice sharp – was it in pain. Had he fallen? She turned, rushed forward, stumbled. Her foot caught in the net, she tried to free herself, tried to let go of the pail but too late and she fell forward, the pail clattering and splashing about her. There was a loud crack and then only darkness.

* * *

Alec checked the clock. The net had been over the side for three hours. He checked the waves; the weather was on the turn. He leaned out of the window and the cold blast hit his face. He ran a hand over it, flicked away the water. The clouds were thick, the moon obscured, and he waited for the wind to blow them across until there were patches of light.

He called down to the mate, 'Haulo,' and the men set to, operating the winch. The duckboards came up, the warps reeling in. They'd just cleared the fish pounds and stowed and there would be another load if they were lucky. It had been a poor catch so far. He needed to haul two hundred kit a day and he'd been lucky to make half that.

The ship rocked as it cut through the waves, the water crashing over the bow, crashing down onto the deck and running over the sides, the rail. She was a good solid ship and he talked to her like he would talk to Letty. With love.

The lass had loved her new hat, and by, she'd looked bonny in it. He would buy her whatever she wanted once this ship landed its catch. He was glad he'd not been too late for the Parkers – word was about that Gilbert Crowe was after it. There wasn't much went on that half the docks didn't know about. He could trust Norah to keep his confidence. She'd promised to discuss it with their shareholder. He wanted to tell Letty and his mother together. As a family. It was what his mother needed. She couldn't push Letty away any longer.

He watched the net and the men set too, hauling it over the rail, the trawl doors opened, the warps tightened, the net was over, then swinging above like a pendulum as the ship chopped through the waves. Big Mick ran a hand under the cod end, caught hold of the rope and pulled. At last, it looked like they'd made a good haul.

The men set to work, water lashing over them, knee-deep in blood and guts. Seagulls swarmed from nowhere as they always did, helping themselves. The mate shouted up, a good fifty baskets.

'Drop the dan buoy over. Mark the spot.' Alec took the pencil from behind his ear, made a note in his log. He would stay here while the fishing was good and the weather held.

* * *

Dorcas was thoughtful as she headed home, grateful that Norah had told her, glad that Alec had supported his wife. If she'd not been such a stubborn old woman, she would've supported Letty too. She waited while the carts and cycles passed by, crossed the road with care, turning over Norah's words as she walked down Freeman Street. She stopped outside the Co-operative, admiring the window display, feeling the fur of her collar. The woman was right. She had a lot to be grateful for. The pain would never go, but she had to learn to live again, she had a lot to live for. Things would change. She would change.

The children were in the yard when she got back, their faces red, their eyes bright. She looked for Alfie, saw him sitting on the doorstep, and for a split second it caught her off guard. But it was their doorstep, not his mother's. As she got closer, she saw his face was wet with dirt and tears and he had bloodied his knee. She hurried towards him.

'What's the matter, Alfie?'

'I felled over.' He clutched his knee, raised it to show her.

She bent forward, checked it. 'We'll give it a clean.' She pulled at his shoulder to get him to his feet. 'Why are you sitting on the doorstep?'

'Mrs Letty won't let me in.'

'She's cleaning. She'll let you in if she knows you're hurt.'

He shook his head. 'She won't.'

Dorcas laughed, tried the door, but it wouldn't open. She pressed the handle, pushed hard. There was something in the way. Another push, harder this time. It gave a little and she looked down, caught a glimpse of Letty's hair, her head. Dorcas shoved her shoulder to the door, screamed out, 'Letty! Letty!'

Alfie began to cry and the children stopped their game.

She shouted over her shoulder, 'Stanley, get your mother.'

There was no need. Hearing the commotion, Sally was already running across the yard.

'It's Letty,' Dorcas gasped. 'She's collapsed.'

Stanley stood by his mother, waiting for instruction, and when she said, 'Go fetch Mrs Wilkinson,' he ran from the courtyard.

The two women hurried down the alleyway and through the back door to number three. Letty was as still as stone, her foot tangled in a net, lying in a pool of dirty water.

Dorcas fell to her knees, gently shook her, tried to wake her. Sally stepped across her.

'Get her away from the door, out of the draught.'

Dorcas took the tangled rope from Letty's foot and together they moved her as gently as they could, away from the water. Her hair stuck about her face and an angry red lump was swelling on her temple.

Sally looked about, took a cushion and put it under her head, quickly checked her over. 'There's no blood. And she's breathing.'

Dorcas felt the energy drain from her. 'If anything should happen to her... the child.' She looked to the nets.

'Nothing's going to happen to her. Likely she's knocked herself out, that's all. She'll be all right when she comes to.' Sally's voice was steady, meant to give comfort, but it did not.

'Will she?' Dorcas took Letty's hand in hers and as they waited for help, she began to pray.

* * *

At best, the day was a grey twilight and then it was black for more than eighteen hours. Other ships were gathering in the distance and Alec kept an eye out for Sam Harris and other skippers, communicating with Morse code, the weather being foul. The net was not full. Should they move or stay where they were? He would try one more haul.

The gale was whipping up and he held back making the decision for the second net to go over the side. He blew down the speaking tube to the engine room for an update on the coal reserves. The nets went over again. The gale gathered energy, the seas rough, a solid wall before them. Hard rain and spray lashed over them. The men stood their ground, cursing the weather, each other, cursing him. The weather was filthy, but he pushed them onwards. This would be the last catch, then they would head for home.

He ached like the very devil, but he forced himself to stay alert. His eyes stung with lack of sleep. If he lost concentration for a second, it could be the end of them all. He scanned the seas, the skies. One more haul would fill the pounds. It would be touch-and-go; trawl for two hours, then hope for the best.

* * *

Letty could hear voices, recognised Dorcas's voice and another. Was it her mother? No, Sally, it was Sally. Her head hurt and she didn't want to open her eyes, not yet. The darkness was soothing. Someone held her hand, it was warm, she felt safe. She wanted to lie there a little longer, but she smelled something funny under her nose, raised her hand, pushed it away, coughed and opened her eyes.

'Thank, God,' Dorcas said. 'Thank God.'

41

Letty's waters broke soon after. Sally had said it was the shock, but it was Letty's time, she knew that. They'd got her up on her feet, kept her walking about the room. Dorcas had been told not to let her sleep, to keep talking – and talk she did. It puzzled Letty, this sudden eagerness to know about her family, the farm, but urged on by Dorcas, she spoke of her parents, her siblings, what it was to swim in the stream on the land, to climb the trees, the freedom, the taste of fresh laid eggs, the sunlight as it rose over the barns and lit the yard a warm amber.

About them, Sally instructed her kids to make the fire and bring in the coal. Water was plentiful and sat ready on the range. Mrs Wilkinson scrubbed the bowls, the table; fresh towels and plenty of newspaper were taken upstairs to the bedroom. Letty and Dorcas followed soon after. Letty walked about, holding on to the furniture, the walls, but she was so tired. A wave of a pain came with the contraction, tightening her belly, and she puffed and panted her way through it. She was hot, the window open, the net billowing like a sail and she wanted Alec so badly.

Dorcas remained close, wrapped in her cardigan, her shawl over the top. Talking, talking. Sweat poured from Letty's head and she felt dizzy. She squinted, blinked, tried to see properly, but it all felt odd, like the room was twisting and buckling around her.

'Lie down, Letty. Save your energy,' Mrs Wilkinson said, her voice soothing. 'It's going to be a long night.'

She did as she was told, and Dorcas ventured a smile.

'That has to be a first.' Dorcas held her hand as she lowered herself onto the bed, then propped her up on the pillows.

'Where's Alfie?'

'With Sally. She's taken him home to feed him with her lot. Don't worry about Alfie, we need to concentrate on you. And the baby.'

Letty closed her eyes, wanting it all to be over. Wanting the baby out and in her arms, wanting Alec. Another wave of pain began and she bent forward and cried out.

Mrs Wilkinson got up from the chair that had been brought from downstairs, examined her. 'You've a way to go yet, lass. Don't waste what energy you have on calling out.'

Letty sank back onto the pillows exhausted. Her nightdress was already damp, and she began to shiver, though sweat ran between her breasts.

Dorcas pulled the chair beside the bed, took her hand in hers. 'You can do this, Letty. Squeeze into my hand when the pain comes. I'm stronger than you think.'

* * *

The winds increased and Alec shook his fist and cursed out of the window. 'Bugger off, old feathery. Be damned with ya.'

'Haulo! Haulo!'

Tommy came up the ladder, water drenching him from every quarter. He pulled the door to the wheelhouse and almost fell inside, the door swinging on its hinges. He reached out and pulled it shut. Water ran off his clothes like a river.

'The net's caught on sommats,' he gasped, waiting for Alec to give him his orders. The weather was against them; there wasn't time to think of what it would cost, what would be deducted from the profit. It was all about getting back home.

'Cut the bloody thing away,' he shouted, the wind howling about them.

Tommy went back down the ladder faster than he had come up it.

Alec kept an eye on the sea, the compass, took the wheel, briefly glimpsing the men as they chopped at the nets with axes. He scanned his crew as they worked. He would rather go home a net lost than a man. He checked his charts again, his compass, took his bearings. Down on the deck, Big Mick waved his arm; the net was clear away. There was a fjord twenty miles north-north-east. He hoped he hadn't left it too late.

* * *

Dorcas sat all night in the chair, moving only when Mrs Wilkinson needed to get close to Letty.

She sucked her cheeks, looked at Dorcas, frowned. It unsettled her. Mrs Wilkinson beckoned her over to the window.

'I don't like the look of her,' she whispered. 'The doctor needs to be called for.'

Dorcas gasped. 'I'll get someone else to go. I don't want to leave her.'

Mrs Wilkinson went to find Sally. Dorcas felt sick with waiting.

The doctor came, undid his bag, rubbed his hands to warm them and quickly examined Letty.

'We have to get the child out. We don't want to lose the mother or baby if we can help it.' He turned to Dorcas. 'Do you give your say-so?'

Dorcas nodded.

Sally put an arm about her shoulder. 'Leave Mrs Wilkinson to assist. We'll only be in the way.' She led her gently down the stairs, settled her in a chair. Sally had kept the fire going and she brought the lamp closer, raised the wick. 'Let me get you a drink, a bite to eat.'

'I couldn't face anything.' Her stomach was hollow, nothing could fill it.

As the minutes passed, she heard them walk about the room, Letty's grunts and groans. She didn't know whether to run upstairs to help or out into the street. She got up, put more coal on the fire, got more water. She tried to knit, focusing on one stitch at a time, under and over, under and over. She went outside for air, unable to breathe. The wind was up and paper flew about, a pail rattled around in the yard and she picked it up and put it inside the outhouse. In the shadows, she saw her braided nets.

Sally's lad had moved them. If only she'd moved them sooner. Would the fall have harmed the child? She twisted her hands together, looked up to the heavens. Clouds scudded across the sky. 'Let them live, dear God, let them live.'

* * *

It was quiet when Dorcas went back into the house, just the sound of footsteps on the floorboards above. She pulled her shawl about her and sat again by the fire. She heard a brief cry, then nothing.

Mrs Wilkinson came down, a bundle of soiled sheets and newspaper in her arms. Dorcas got up, stared at her, not daring to ask.

'It's a girl,' said Mrs Wilkinson.

'And they're well?'

'The child is well enough. Her mother is... exhausted.'

Dorcas moved past her and up the stairs. The doctor was washing his hands in the bowl set on the chest of drawers, the water pink. Letty lay pale and ashen, eyes closed, her hair wet about her head. On the floor, Mrs Wilkinson had pulled out a drawer and the child lay in it, swaddled and asleep. Dorcas looked to Letty, to the doctor.

'How is she?'

'Her labour was complicated. I had to cut her. She's lost a lot of blood.' He picked up a towel, dried his hands, rolled down his sleeves. 'I'll call again tomorrow.' He began putting instruments into his bag. Dorcas picked up his jacket, held it out for him to slip into. He peered at her over the rim of his silver spectacles. 'I think she has the fight in her.'

Dorcas did not see him out. She left that to Mrs Wilkinson. Their voices came up through the open window as they stood on the doorstep. She felt Letty's cheek, took hold of her hand, spoke softly. 'Are you awake, Letty?'

There was a flicker of eyelids.

'Baby.'

'Do you want me to get her?'

Letty moved her head, such a small movement, and Dorcas bent down and picked up the child. It had dark hair, like her mother, thick already, with a peak to the front. Its face was pinched, its tiny fist at its side. A wave of love surged within her for the little scrap, part of Letty, part of her boy. She laid the child beside its mother.

Letty opened her eyes, looked down on her babe and smiled.

'A daughter,' Dorcas said, softly.

'Stella,' Letty whispered. 'Her name is Stella.'

42

The *Black Prince* had been sitting out the storm for three days. Alec, Tommy and the chief engineer sat at the table in the mess room. The chief gave him an assessment of coal supplies. They needed enough to get back home. It couldn't be squandered, and though they were safe in the fjord, sitting idle was still burning coal. The pressures were building like the steam. Alec felt the weight of each minute. Go or stay. Another twelve hours and the fish would be rotten and go to manure. He would give it another hour.

* * *

Letty slipped in and out of consciousness. She had no idea of the passing of time, only of shadows, light and dark, as day moved to night. At times, she heard voices, sensed movement about her. A man came; he smelled of disinfectant. His big cold hands checked her tummy, her pulse, her chest. Then a small hand in hers, a quiet voice. Alfie. It made her smile. It made her happy. She heard the cart come for the nets, church bells. She didn't hear a baby cry, not any more. There had been a baby in the beginning, but now there was not. Mostly she felt the same hand in hers, a woman's hand. Warm and strong, and the voice whispered, 'Hold on.'

* * *

Dorcas went downstairs to check on the child. Sally had swept them all along in her big full arms. People came and went, some Dorcas knew, some she did not. Ruth Evans and her aunts sent a basket of fruit; the port missioner arrived with a blanket that the men from the mission had collected for. Norah came every evening.

'You've been such a good friend to Letty, to me—'

'Family,' Norah corrected her. 'We're all family.'

That was when Dorcas sobbed, sobs that she muffled with her hand over her mouth. Her body shook, but she didn't want Letty to hear, didn't want to disturb her. Alfie came to her side, rubbed her back.

'That's a good boy, Alfie,' Norah said. 'That will make Granny Dorcas better.'

Sally's daughter came in with Stella. The children took turns to feed her, hold her. The wind gusted and the door slammed, it startled the baby and she began to wail.

Upstairs, Letty opened her eyes.

* * *

Wreckage of the *Carlisle* had been found off the Skerries, but there was no news of the *Black Prince*. It had been expected home three days since. Dorcas didn't want to tell Letty. No one was to speak of it until she had gained more strength. Dorcas kept the world at bay, though her own heart ached that it might be happening again. That she had lost them all.

* * *

Letty felt like she had slept forever. Dorcas came and went. Stella slept, and cried and cried, but Letty didn't mind. She'd been so frightened by the silence. Her milk came in and she fed the child, but now she was hungry herself. How long had she lain in bed? She'd lost count of the days.

She threw the blankets off and tried to stand. Her legs were weak, but she willed herself upright, clutching the bed frame.

Dorcas came in, chaffing. 'You're not to be up.'

'I can't stay there forever. Alec will be back. He'll think he's married an invalid.'

Though she fought to hide it, Dorcas's expression changed. Letty sank back onto the mattress.

'What day is it, Dorcas?'

Dorcas folded a sheet, checked on Stella, her back to Letty. 'Wednesday.'

'And Alec's not landed?'

'The weather is bad. Quite often they land late in winter and early spring, the trips are longer.'

'But not this long.'

Dorcas took Stella from the drawer, cradled her, rocked her from side to side. 'She looks like you today; some days, I believe she looks like Alec. She has your chin though.'

Letty got up again. Moved to the chair. She had laid too long, been out of step with the world too long. 'Dorcas?'

Slowly her mother-in-law turned. It seemed an age before she spoke.

'You're a strong lass, Letty. We need to be strong together. Alec should have landed three days ago. They found wreckage of another ship, the *Carlisle*. They'd been fishing alongside.'

It felt as if her heart had stopped beating. 'Nothing of the *Prince*?'

Dorcas shook her head. 'We must hope and pray, that's all we have left.'

'And each other,' Letty said, quietly. 'We have each other.'

* * *

It was good to be dressed, to be downstairs. Dorcas slept now, in her chair by the fire, and Letty got up and covered her with a shawl. At last, they had found a way to care for each other. She was only sad it had taken so long. Alfie was playing with his toy soldiers, Stella whimpered, sucked at her fist.

Letty went into the kitchen. Rain hammered on the window and she leaned against the sink, watching droplets run like rivers. She poured herself a glass of water, drank it and went back into the room, settled herself in the chair. It was cold, but the range was warm.

She sat with her head in her hands, her fingers pressing onto her sockets, tired and exhausted, not wanting to accept the emptiness of a life without Alec. The fire crackled and a log sank to ash. She closed her eyes, listened to the sound of the clock, its steady pace soothing. After a time, the rhythm was disturbed: another sound, a coin tapping on the window. A familiar tune. Alfie stopped his game; he'd heard it too, she was not imagining it.

She felt that her feet were leaving the ground as she made her way to the door, her fingers trembling as she pulled back the latch and turned the key. It was dark, the silhouette of a man on the doorstep, his cap pulled over his face, and for a moment she shuddered, thinking it to be Gilbert Crowe. But only for a moment. He took her hand, pulled her towards him and she nestled her face in his neck. He smelled of the sea, of salt and sweat, and she knew that it was him. 'Alec! Oh, my Alec.'

He held her close and for the longest time they stood on the doorstep, the door wide open and no one complaining about the draught until Dorcas came to them and said, 'You'd better come inside. Think of Stella.'

He put his hand to Letty's face. 'Stella?'

'Your daughter, our daughter.' She took his hand, pulled him inside, and in the light of the room, she could see how haggard he was.

Dorcas bent down to take the child from her crib and laid her in her son's arms. His face was alight with the broadest of smiles as he looked down on her.

'Stella. Eh, what a beauty you are; just like your mother.' He saw Alfie in the shadows, bent down on his knee and called the lad to him. 'Alfie lad, what do you think of your little sister? Isn't she the prettiest lass you've ever seen?' He put his arm out and wrapped the lad to him and together they gazed at Stella.

Letty felt her heart would burst. She closed her eyes, thankful that he was home, that they were all together, a family at last.

Dorcas came to her, pressed her down into the chair by the fire, guided Alec to sit in the other.

'You had us worried, my lad.'

He looked up, grinned. 'I had to sit the storm out, Mother. I thought it better to come home in debt than not come home at all.'

She patted his shoulder and Letty saw her swallow back her fear.

Alec eased back into the chair, looked to his babe, the fire, then Letty.

'I hope you kept your job, Letty. We'll be needing a bob or two until I can make up the loss.'

She laughed, they all did, and then Letty felt her cheeks wet with tears. Alfie dashed to her and she swept him into her arms, onto her knee. His small hand touched her cheek.

'Don't be sad, Mrs Letty. Mr Alec is home now.'

'He is,' she said. 'So he is.'

* * *

Dorcas opened the door and stood on the step, looked up to the stars and took in a great gulp of air. Along the estuary, ships would be heading out to the North Sea, men pursuing the catch, the women waiting, as they had always done. Not so long ago, she had waited alone, but now she had family, and she had Letty to thank for that. It was a future she had never envisaged for herself, but it was infinitely better than what she'd had before. She took another breath and muttered a silent prayer to the sky, to her Will for watching over their boy, then closed the door and went inside.

ACKNOWLEDGMENTS

How many of us, as we get older, say, 'I wish I'd asked my mum/dad/grandad/nan about their youth? About the war?' I've had this said to me so many times over the years.

When I was a child I was always asking my Nanny Lettie, my mother's mother, to tell me stories of her life. She was a woman who brooked no nonsense but had strong arms and a kind heart. She was there for everybody who needed help and a share of her inner strength. The eldest girl in a family of eight, she was second eldest after her brother, Alf Jnr, who was lost at sea in 1938 when his ship sank off the Old Man of Hoy in the Orkneys. She told me it was the first big shock of her life. The second was when she as widowed in 1941, left with two small children to care for. 'After that,' she said, 'all the other bad things didn't hurt so much.' Those words have stayed with me – as have her stories. 'Someone should write them down or they will be lost forever and no one will know what life was like back then.'

I promised I would write them down. It has taken me years, mostly because I didn't know where to start. Until now.

This is not my nanny's story but the world of Fisher's Wharf is created around and inspired by those first stories. I hope that her spirit and strength shines through in various characters that came to life as I wrote.

So, my first thanks are to my Nanny Lettie for the stories and for her love.

As always, any mistakes are my own.

To the fabulous Boldwood team, each and every one of them are diamonds. To Caroline Ridding, editor extraordinaire, Amanda, Nia,

Claire, Jenna, Shirley, Jade and the rest of the team who work so incredibly hard on my behalf. Thank you! Thank you!

To Vivien Green who urged me to begin – my forever thanks. To Gaia Banks – here's to a great future. Margaret Graham – the best teacher, the kindest of friends. Helen Baggott, my Monday mate who keeps me on track. What a journey! What fun!

To the bloggers and reviewers who shout about books – what would we do without you.

To all the skippers and wives who gave me stories over the years – John Meadows, Jim Evans, Ray & Janet Evans, John Evans, Alfreda Evans.

Carole Heidschuster and Dr Stella Jackson of the Cleethorpes & Grimsby Heritage Action Zones. Tracey Townsend and Adrian Wilkinson at Grimsby Archives and Lincs Inspire. David Ornsby of the Grimsby Fishing Heritage Centre

Angie Burnett, Chair of the Grimsby Central Hall Trust for info on the Bethel Mission Hall and the Fishermen's Chapel

Tony Jewitt and George E Gilmour for information and personal experience of their work with The Fishermen's Mission

Members of various Facebook groups who so freely gave of their knowledge and experience. Grimsby Memories, Cleethorpes Memories, Great Grimsby Fishing History, Great Grimsby Retired Fishermen, Grimsby Fish Docks Past & Present most especially: Tom Smith, Michael Sparkes, Steve Farrow, Mike Smith, Dave Smith, Trevor Ekins, Paul Fenwick, Peter Neve, Louise Hugill, Kathy Nicholls, Peter H. Pool.

To fishermen everywhere, past and present. The more I researched the more I admired them.

To their wives and children who waited for their safe return.

And to my family – last but never least. What a lucky woman I am.

MORE FROM TRACY BAINES

We hope you enjoyed reading *The Women of Fisher's Wharf*. If you did, please leave a review.

If you'd like to gift a copy, this book is also available as an ebook, digital audio download and audiobook CD.

Sign up to Tracy Baines's mailing list for news, competitions and updates on future books.

https://bit.ly/TracyBainesNews

ABOUT THE AUTHOR

Tracy Baines is the bestselling saga writer of *The Variety Girls* series, originally published by Ebury, which Boldwood will continue with. She was born and brought up in Cleethorpes and spent her early years in the theatre world which inspired her writing. Her new saga series for Boldwood is set amongst the fisherfolk of Grimsby.

Follow Tracy on social media:

twitter.com/tracyfbaines

facebook.com/tracybainesauthor

instagram.com/tracyfbaines

Sixpence Stories

Introducing Sixpence Stories!

Discover page-turning historical novels from your favourite authors, meet new friends and be transported back in time.

Join our book club Facebook group

https://bit.ly/SixpenceGroup

Sign up to our newsletter

https://bit.ly/SixpenceNews

Boldwood

Boldwood Books is an award-winning fiction publishing company seeking out the best stories from around the world.

Find out more at www.boldwoodbooks.com

Join our reader community for brilliant books, competitions and offers!

Follow us
@BoldwoodBooks
@BookandTonic

Sign up to our weekly deals newsletter

https://bit.ly/BoldwoodBNewsletter

9 781804 265215